Phil Hogan writes a weekly column for the *Observer* and is author of *Hitting the Groove* and *The Freedom Thing*, both of which are available in Abacus paperback.

Praise for *All This Will Be Yours*

'A sensitive, honest account of a family as tightly knit as the carpets they sell'

Observer

'To Hogan's measured, sensitive writing, the stock clichés of this genre – businessman, hippy, housewife – are given life, tragedy and meaning. The end result is a moving tale of trust and understanding. Every major character – and there are many, all well-realised – gets an education of some sort, mostly in the important lessons of humanity, ageing and communication. These are eternal, quite obvious teachings, but Hogan's examples are sufficiently sympathetic that they're remade anew. There's also an acute observational streak running throughout the text, lending freshness to its everyday settings and making *All This Will Be Yours* almost a tactile pleasure to read. In a word: a treat'

Irish Examiner

'Hogan resembles John Updike or Richard Yates, figures from that classical seam of American fiction so rich in detail, domesticity and murderous compromise'

Sunday Herald

'Hogan's tale weaves throug[...]
of the family unit and is a s[...]

D1331714

Also by this author

HITTING THE GROOVE

THE FREEDOM THING

All This Will Be Yours

PHIL HOGAN

ABACUS

First published in Great Britain in 2005 by Little, Brown
This paperback edition published in 2006 by Abacus

A CIP catalogue record for this book
is available from the British Library.

ISBN-13: 978-0-349-11764-5
ISBN-10: 0-349-11764-0

Typeset in Ehrhardt by M Rules
Printed and bound in Great Britain by
Clays Ltd, St Ives plc

Abacus
An imprint of
Little, Brown Book Group
Brettenham House
Lancaster Place
London WC2E 7EN

A member of the Hachette Livre Group of Companies

www.littlebrown.co.uk

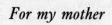

For my mother

Acknowledgements

Many thanks to Sara Menguc, Narinder Burchill and Jon Linstead.

All This
Will Be
Yours

Chapter 1

The house is the only one in the street with a turret. That was a deciding factor. That and the date, 1878, chased into the ribbed stone of the chimney stack. An Englishman's chessboard castle with four to five bedrooms and three receptions rising from its own quarter-acre in High Firs. If you stand on the little crenellated balcony at the back you can see into the football ground across town, looking under the floodlights like the greenest lawn. How could you not celebrate that? And it wouldn't just be a housewarming, Stuart said, but an occasion to mark his early semi-retirement and Rachel's elevation to the seat of greatness, a real party with family and friends. Already there had been a get-together with the staff, three weeks ago at the Beehive, a short walk from the warehouse. 'It's like *Dynasty*,' the visiting rep from Bryce's joked as Stuart and Rachel performed a ceremony of the keys for the photographer from the *Gazette*. Everyone laughed, even Josh the trainee, who has only just gone seventeen and has never heard of the old American TV show, but actually, that's how it is, Stuart thinks. Whatever you have you pass down, father to son, son to daughter. Everything's an inheritance. You pass it down like wisdom or a good heart or the colour of your eyes.

He sees Diane now emerge from the kitchen with a tray of luxury canapés from Wilson's, notices the pink of her cheeks and wonders if it's the heat from the oven, or the wine she's not used to in the daytime, or – if this isn't one of those myths you read about – the sign of a woman entering her later years. Certainly, sometimes these days she seems in a fluster for no reason at all. She throws him a sunny smile as she makes her way through with the little asparagus wraps and doughy bacon puffs and stuffed shrimp balls, as if he's a guest too, and he feels his own smile flare in fleeting response like sugar caught in a flame. She finds a vacant surface for the tray, her smile refusing to betray the anxiety that it's not her own work, her discomfort about paying all that money for caterers, shooing them off again practically the minute they delivered this morning. 'Penny, let me get you another drink,' she is saying, pushing a sprig of hair back behind her ear, the two of them with their heads together for a second, Diane in that long wispy dress she's had for years, hardly any make-up, her wild hair tamed by pins and a huge beetle brooch at the back. No personal vanity, unlike Penny, who can't pass a mirror without getting her toolkit out, that instinct for constant retouching, like the Forth Bridge. Penny covers her glass with her hand. 'I said I'd drop Emma at the station at six. She has to get back to London. Tony promised me on his *life* he wasn't going to drink, but guess what?'

'That sounds like Tony,' Stuart hears himself interrupt,

chuckling above the chatter and flutey classical music chosen by Diane and lifting his own glass in a toast towards the two women, their eyes still twinkling at each other, as if they were sisters almost, or at least real friends. Stuart nods his head to the music and feels his smile evaporate as he moves away. He has known Tony Ennick since their days in Woodhampton Road, days of nationalised industry and sideburns and pre-decimalisation, he with his father in the lock-up and Tony apprenticed to a tiler at Burwell's. Even then, Tony was more a sparring partner than someone you might be the best of friends with, though quicker than Stuart on his feet and always one step ahead somehow with the fatness of his weekly wage packet and the way he was with girls and the latest indecent joke, his eye more alert to novelty and opportunity, a tall man looking down at him. Today, they are substantial men of the town, with their names above commercial premises, the language of their rivalry seasoned by the intervening years to produce this easy ready-mix of badinage they have, this sales talk and gossip from the pages of the *Gazette* that feeds the social needs of trade, golf, Rotarian dinners or, as today, an occasion where their unfinished personal history draws them into the realms of pretended intimacy. A friendship of convenience, Diane once called it, but how many in a man's life are much more than that when you think about it?

He pours himself another drink and watches Tony, an imposing figure even seated, perched facing out on the short side of their new L-shape sofa in the drawing room, knees jutting in weekend slacks, deck shoes, his feet apart, tossing jumbo cashews into his mouth and interrogating the people from number eight. That's Sam, a solicitor with an office near the Town Hall, and his wife, also a solicitor, whose name has slipped Stuart's mind. Tony is gesturing towards the big picture window and the mature, solid neighbourhood beyond in the weak April sunlight, perhaps admiring the towering monkey puzzle out front – *also* the only one in the street, the agent made sure to tell Stuart. Tony is sounding them out, Sam and his wife, about *values*, as he likes to call house prices, in High Firs. Give him five minutes and he'll be selling them an Edwardian bathroom. Flutter of satisfaction, though, seeing him probing, wheedling – a man's choice of neighbour saying as much about him as the health of his business or the year and model of his car, or how his kids are doing in their lives, or how his wife keeps her figure. It's gratifying to see Tony here, sniffing greedily at the expense, where it sits on the scale of things, a vanity of sorts to have your neighbours scrutinised and found to be solicitors. This is the way we covet and admire, adjust our estimation of people. And didn't Tony admire Stuart's wife so much he married her himself?

Maybe at some point Tony Ennick will find himself explaining to one of these friendly High Firs strangers his connection with the Duttings, mentioning that, yes, his wife Penny was married to Stuart long ago, adding (or perhaps, actually, not) that his daughter Emma – with her fast-moving career in London and her neat bullet of a sports car parked outside her flat a stone's throw from Tower Bridge – is, strictly speaking, only his stepdaughter and that the person she calls Dad is Stuart, regardless of who insists on taking the credit for her successes and schooling and numerous accomplishments, understandable as that might be in the light of Tony having produced no natural offspring of his own. And if that is an unworthy thought, thinks Stuart – which it is, and so what? – maybe Tony should have married someone else's wife.

This is not a day for complaints, though, but

thanksgiving. After all, he has Diane, a full eight years his junior, and their children – Rachel, enough ambition in the girl to take over at Duttings, and young Luke, very promising in the sciences and IT, probably in his room by now, plugged into one of those games that inhibits blinking, exams next year. And, yes, there remains the complication of Oscar – forever the one-man travelling flea circus (or whatever on earth he gets up to), at the age of thirty-two going his own way, you dare to hope, but coming back again twice a year with his hair fastened up in knots like that, this time with a dog, some sort of whippet – but there is much to be satisfied with. And thinking about Oscar reminds Stuart that Diane was an ex-wife too when he met her, took her in, married her and brought up a child as his own, just as Tony did. Not uncommon these days, the whole nuclear family idea turned on its head with odd bits all over the place. You can't pick and choose. Oscar sees Stuart as his dad too, and of course he *is* his dad, in all the ways that matter, and he has always said so.

But last week's news – Oscar's letter coming as it did – makes this ring false now, and he has a taste in his mouth about Oscar that isn't the usual one of disappointment or impatience, but something less easy to declare – the tang of regret for things he has said without thinking (or thought without saying) down the years, shame even, because he knows the impulse behind every uncharitable notion he has harboured about Oscar has conveniently served to make the course of Emma's bright star seem more his own doing than Tony's – that it's the blood and not the bringing up that most counts.

'How *dare* you say that,' Diane once snapped, reddening suddenly and throwing down the potato masher, one Sunday it was, years ago, the week Oscar got the A-level results he deserved – two Cs – and Emma got the As that took her to Cambridge. 'A Dutting to her bones . . .' was all he said. But he knew what it was he'd really said – a prideful ricochet that hit Oscar and Diane like an insult. She vanished for the rest of the afternoon, leaving him to finish making lunch. That same week they found out she was pregnant again. They were both thrilled, but Diane walking out that afternoon was like a clumsy spill, something dark, seeping slowly across the months that followed, obliging Stuart to be watchful in his enthusiasm as the baby grew inside her, as though she might look into his thoughts and catch him hoping for a boy that was really and truly his.

More neighbours arrive, a small transfusion of newness. Stuart finds drinks for them, asks jokingly if they found the place OK. They laugh. Dave and Hilary. It turns out they have a boy in Luke's year at school. As he listens, Stuart feels the sprung twist of new carpet beneath his feet: English unpatterned wool textured loop, tufted; Diane's choice (for these rooms he would personally have opted for a classic deep ruby Axminster with a small diamond). At eye level, a carpet is like a vast ocean, he has always thought, whatever the colour or design or weave. He could have called one of the fitters in to do it but changed his mind, surprising Diane when she got back from Open Day at the Community College. 'New house, new beginning,' he said, putting his arm round her, feeling Diane's doubts resurfacing in the stiffness of her shoulders, the cost of it all, the questionable sense of it, with his stepping back – semi-retiring – from the business and only Luke to fill the other bedrooms. 'There's Oscar too, don't forget,' he said.

'You don't want Oscar here. You've said as much. You've made *me* say it.'

'Diane. Precious. He's thirty-two. Anyway, don't we deserve a little comfort after our hard work?' He was talking about the house but indicated with a sweep of his arm the expanse of carpet, like an old-fashioned TV presenter revealing the star prize. Cutting the carpet himself was symbolic. Like breaking champagne on a ship. And how long was it since he'd put work clothes on and got down on his hands and knees with a knife?

Rachel comes into the room. She drains her wine glass and starts collecting dirty plates and glasses. 'Hi, Dad.' He smells the drink on her breath as she comes near. She's a little tipsy. 'I thought you were going to make a speech,' she says. Is that a dab of something – egg mayonnaise, is it – on her blouse? He resists the urge to pick it off. You can't touch a woman's breast in public, not even your daughter's.

'I might say a few words. A bit later.'

She goes off to the kitchen with the plates. He watches her load the dishwasher and help herself to another glass of wine. She is saying something to someone, frowning, and a second later Emma comes out of the kitchen, an unlit cigarette in her hand. How different, the two girls, Emma being the more chic, you'd say, and if anything the younger of the two, though she's – what – two, three years older? He tries to read Emma's expression but she turns and exits via the other door to the path that leads down the steps to the back garden. Two daughters, half-sisters but not close. Regrettable. The classical music comes to an end, and is replaced by something modern and unfamiliar. Did Emma change the music? Maybe that was it, the wariness between them. It doesn't take much.

'Where *is* Oscar?' someone is saying. 'I hear he's had some good luck.'

Diane comes by, still smiling for Britain, and Stuart reaches to take a little heaped pastry from the tray she is carrying. He holds it for a moment between his thumb and

7

forefinger and nods while Dave says something about the traffic congestion somewhere in town, then pops it in his mouth in one go. Best way to avoid mess, but the stiff crusty pyramid with its whip of salmon and cheesy cream is bigger than it looks and he sees how his cheeks bulge in the mirror as he works at it with his tongue and jaws. He covers the unsightliness of this process from Dave and Hilary with a raised hand and turns to his right, his eyes resting momentarily on Penny across the room, blue dress, fifty-eight and poker-thin, a different person and yet the same woman he fucked nightly, sometimes twice, thirty-odd years ago, now more like a distant cousin or former neighbour. Hilary, nibbling too with one hand cupped beneath the other to catch the crumbs, says she is active in the PTA, and wonders mischievously whether Stuart will be able to help out at fundraising events now he has plenty of free time. Stuart laughs and asks Dave about the cellars in these houses, built sideways to the hill, as it were, giving an extra level at the rear. The previous owner went to all the trouble of getting planning permission for a basement swimming pool opening out on to the garden but never went ahead. Dave responds with astonishment. 'Now there's an idea,' he says.

Stuart washes down the gluey residue of canapé with the wine remaining in his glass, and wonders if he should say something now. Is everyone here? He looks around for Oscar. Maybe he's in the breakfast room. This isn't really his sort of thing and Diane wouldn't have minded if the boy wanted to duck out but Stuart made him promise to be here. It's either a family event or it's not. Stuart probes the fissure in an upper rear molar with his tongue and smiles at something he doesn't catch that Hilary is saying.

Oscar has gone quiet in the last couple of days. He and Diane both.

The 'good luck' is that Oscar's father has died – his real, biological father, that is – an almost forgotten character from Diane's history who ghosted into the present on Thursday while they were watching TV, Oscar appearing open-eyed at the door with the lawyer's letter he'd opened at last after a week thinking it was a speeding fine from Cornwall, though how he could speed anywhere in that old wreck of a van of his was anybody's guess. He had been dead nearly a year, according to the lawyer, and there was something for Oscar in the will. Diane didn't say anything when he read it out, even when Oscar reached the word 'beneficiary'. Just shook her head.

'So how did they get our address?' asked Stuart, not certain whether the news, on balance, was supposed to be bad, or at least sad, as well as good.

Oscar looked at Diane, as if struck by the same question. 'Mum?'

'His mother was in touch,' she said at last, taking a sip of tea. 'I don't know where she would have got the number from.'

'What – so you knew?' Oscar said.

'She rang while you were away, sometime in November. I didn't know where you were, and when you came home it seemed easier not to say. I suppose I should have told you. But it's not as if you ever knew him.'

'Well I won't now.'

She turned in the chair. 'Did you want to?'

Oscar shrugged and looked at the letter again. 'He was only fifty,' he said. 'I wonder what he died of.'

'A small legacy wouldn't go amiss,' Stuart ventured.

Diane looked at him as though he had said something indecent. 'Don't hold your breath,' she said.

Stuart is gripped by the need to pee, but Tony, he sees, has chosen this moment to head for the stairs leading to the

9

master bathroom, so he goes instead down to the little Swedish-style toilet and shower room in the basement, where the swimming pool would be if there was one. It's all pine-yellow shadows down here, underlit, with a ladder against the wall and a deflated basketball left by the previous owner. It reminds Stuart of an abandoned mini-gym. He unzips, waits for the flow to start, sighs with satisfaction as it drums on the polished steel of the bowl. The arrival of the letter about Diane's first husband, the way she knew about him dying but never mentioned it for some reason, brings to mind a story he read as a youth in one of those American *Tales of the Macabre* comics, about a stain that one day appeared through the wallpaper in a house and got bigger and bigger until something terrible that had happened in the past had been dealt with. He can't remember how the story ended. He knows nothing about Diane's first husband, other than he was the mistake that got her pregnant; that they hadn't been in contact since they broke up, apart from birthday cards for Oscar in the very early years when they were still in the two-bedroom terrace on Rawlington Road in the seventies.

Through the little window he sees Oscar's dog sniffing about under the trees near the shed. Maybe this is a good time. He zips up, flushes the toilet and turns to wash his hands, but there's air trapped in the pipe and the water shudders violently into the basin, splashing the front of his trousers. 'Damn,' he mutters. He tries to blot the damp patch with a towel and frowns. The trouble with light colours. He remembers making a full thirty-five-minute speech at the Willows once with a flap of white dress shirt protruding from his fly. No one said a word. Now he can't walk into a room without his hand going down there to check his proprieties. He dabs some more at the patch, then rinses his hands, feeling the warmth now in the smallness of

10

the space and seeing in the mirror his glistening scalp beneath his thinning hair, made naked by the bulbs in the ceiling, and the patches of sweat in the armpits of his blue shirt, the weight of his paunch overhanging his belt like a boulder you might shelter under in the old westerns. He takes a deep breath as he wipes his neck and forehead with the towel then drapes it over the rail. He switches off the light.

Back upstairs, he pours another drink and stands for a moment, then coughs and taps on his glass for silence with a teaspoon. Someone turns the music off. He sees Diane in the kitchen drying her hands on a cloth. 'I can't tell a lie,' she is saying to someone in her high, laughing, party voice, 'they're from Wilson's!'

Behind the shed, hidden by feathery evergreens from the house and the lawn and the bare, thorny rosebeds and ornamental birdbath with mermaid, Oscar lights the twisted end of a joint, takes a long pull and sits back on the garden bench, his feet resting on a wheelbarrow. Troy, his eyes and ears alerted briefly to the possibilities of fire and smoke (though he has seen it enough times before), settles with a mild air of thwarted expectation, his head between his paws. 'Good boy,' Oscar whispers. Away from home, travelling around out west, Somerset or down in Cornwall, he is accustomed to buying what he needs – his dope, occasionally ecstasy – in quantities suited for distribution at a small handling profit among passing friends and acquaintances, but back home he is obliged to Diggsy at the Green House, the late club where they both work on Green Street, near the markets. Oscar has two nights deejaying, Fridays and Sats, and gets extra money for writing the menu boards in a professional style he learnt out west. Diggsy runs the bar. Diggsy has offered him weekday bar shifts if he wants them but Oscar says he prefers the anonymity of the decks to the spotlight of fucking up customers' orders and giving them the wrong change. Diggsy laughs this off. Most of the customers wouldn't notice if you set them on fire, he says, and he should know with that blotchy skin of his, glowing at the pumps like Radioactive Man. And what's so anonymous about deejaying? he asks. The answer is, of course, that you're lost in yourself and part of the crowd at the same time. Diggsy knows this, but he asks anyway. Oscar and Diggsy dropped out of college together, travelled together for a bit, lost touch for a while, and then met up at a tree protest out west three or four years ago, trying to stop the bypass. Oscar saw the place again one night last summer on the way to Glastonbury, the trees now gone, replaced by a ribbon of glimmering white chalk curving into the distance through the landscape, dotted with yellow vehicles and equipment, men like ants under the brilliant lights. What stirred him, though, was not the expected sense of desecration and ruin, but the purity of this human enterprise, a vision of symmetry and beauty that suggested a force of nature in itself, almost as if the men *were* ants, driven to constructing from the raw earth and rock wondrous monuments to no god but themselves.

He can't bring himself to share this thought – this heresy – with Diggsy. But the truth is that nothing has been the same since – not the festival weekend, not the return to the village outside Taunton afterwards, to Edie's, with the others for the annual cheesemaking – all seems tainted with this omen of bad faith, as though Oscar's perennial odyssey, following the various caravans of eco-pranksters and neo-levellers and tunnellers, is grounded in nothing more than a wish to escape the scrutiny of his home town, to have fun, to get laid, to be uncomplicated, to have comrades in unwashed idleness. For all the days and weeks of his life spent chanting at barricades of tyres or chained to the gates of military compounds or gathered round community beach fires, he has never found himself outraged to the point of true excitability. If anything, home life as a Dutting, or at least as his mother's son, taught him serenity rather than rebellion. He has not been pushed into anything. He lacks authenticity. He is not like some of them. He's not like Bonner and Ralphie. Though Bonner – he knows this for certain – has slept with Edie too, and more than once. This they have in common. On the last trip, Bonner was already at Edie's when the rest of them arrived and was still there when he left. Bonner cannot imagine himself as second to anyone, and affects indifference to Edie's open preference for Oscar. She is always sorry to see Oscar leave.

'Why do you keep going back to your parents?' she once asked.

'Central heating,' he said.

What did she expect him to say? But Edie asking like that – as if choosing to go home occasionally was some deluded act of denial, some crazed offence against free-floating liberty and selfhood – seemed like a trap in itself, or at least something that demanded more of him than he could give.

'See you in the spring?'

'I wouldn't be surprised.'

Edie would have taken that as a free-floater's way of saying yes rather than a coward's way of saying no. But spring is now here in this whimsical new house in High Firs and so, still, is Oscar. Neither is his persistent presence lost on his father, who sees each day that passes without him driving off into the sunset as an opportunity to remind Oscar that he *is* thirty-two. Dad has not presented him with an ultimatum (Mum would never go along with that) but

13

has suggested that if Oscar plans to stick around he might be more comfortable in his own place. Given his current finances, a more comfortable place than his parents' home seems unlikely to Oscar. But moving up to High Firs, Dad is more sensitive than usual about Oscar's hand-painted green VW camper parked out front. He seems afraid that Oscar will alarm the Neighbourhood Watch. Dad's eyes follow Troy around, fearful that the poor dog will deposit a turd on his new carpet.

'Maybe after next week, you'll be in a position to think about it,' he said, meaning Oscar's visit to the solicitor's office in London. 'I could put some feelers out if you like. What do you say?'

'Feelers?' Oscar asked back, a question seeming a better stalling tactic than an answer.

Troy scrambles without warning to his feet now and dashes down the path and through the bushes. Oscar instinctively lets his hand drop to his side at the sound of footsteps on the gravel. Emma emerges with the dog circuiting closely, his whip of a tail flailing her legs.

'Surprise,' she says.

'Hey,' says Oscar, 'how are you doing?'

Emma sits beside him on the bench and crosses her legs. Jeans, casual top, red trainers. 'Fine. I can't stay long. I've got a train at six. What's that?'

'Not sure. Pretty good, though.' He hands her the joint. 'So. How's the filthy world of money?'

Emma inhales, holds and releases smoke. 'I was just telling Rachel if she needed some finance, I could probably help out. Genuine offer. There's a fair bit sloshing around at the moment at decent rates.'

'What did she say?'

Emma shakes her head. 'She probably thinks I'm trying to muscle in. As if.' She puts her feet up next to Oscar's.

14

Brown ankles. 'What do you think of her stepping into Dad's shoes?'

Oscar pauses, knowing what she means. 'Someone has to.'

'There's no reason she shouldn't make a go of it. She's smart enough. I hear she wants to take the business upmarket, take on more specialist lines, try and break into hotels and restaurants. Good luck to her. It can't be much fun number-crunching at the council your whole life.'

Oscar doesn't want to talk about carpets. He leans down to give Troy's ears some attention. 'Are you still going out with that bloke?'

'Vaughan? Yeah, I'm still seeing him. How about you? What have you been up to?'

'Bit of deejaying here in town. Just hanging out really.'

'What about this money Dad says you've come into?'

'Wishful thinking. He just wants me to move out.'

She nods, not asking more. 'What about your cheese girl – aren't you going back out west?'

He stares at his boots and smiles. Cheese girl. That's what Emma calls Edie in a gently teasing way. 'Might do, might not.'

'Lucky you,' Emma says, closing her eyes.

'Lucky how?'

'Oh, you know. All this drifting about, not knowing where you'll be this time next week. Riding with the dawn, travelling light, et cetera. I might take it up myself.'

'Yeah? Don't tell Dad.'

She laughs softly, her eyes still closed. In the shade her teeth look white against her spring brownness. He doesn't ask her where she's been and she wouldn't say, unasked, feeling the distance between them lifestyle-wise, financially. One of the things he likes about Emma is she is not a flaunter of herself and what she is. Maldives or somewhere,

15

she's probably been. Somewhere nice. Maybe he should go abroad again, he thinks, travelling. In '93, he made it all the way to Turkey, hitching, bar work, selling stuff up and down beaches. Following year, bus to Greece. He'd like, though, to go to California. Lie in the sun. She hands him back the joint and he tells her about the letter from the solicitor in London. 'Mum's freaked out by it all. She hasn't seen this guy for thirty years, then she gets this call out of the blue from his mother that he's died. She didn't want me to know. I don't know why. He means nothing to me.'

'I can understand. Why should you be burdened with the death of him when you didn't get the life?'

Oscar gives a squint, staring into the wheelbarrow at last year's leaves. 'I suppose,' he says.

'Funny how we're both in the same boat like that, having two dads.'

'Except you know your real dad and you can see him whenever you like.'

Emma goes quiet and smokes. They have had this conversation before. Perhaps she remembers, in the patch of garden at the old house in Rawlington Road when they were little, the mystery of how Oscar got to live with the dad they shared without even being his real kid. It was Emma who saw the pattern – the point being that, in common with all kids, they both lived with their mums. The rest of life arranged itself around that. This thing was about mums, not dads. Emma was analytical, the first among them to find the centre of things, where the rest radiated from.

'Did you never wonder about him?' she asks, turning, her hair falling back to reveal the tip of a cigarette behind her ear.

'Sometimes. But he was never talked about. I suppose it

16

occurred to me that wanting to know might seem unfair on Dad.'

'Did you ever think about tracking him down?'

'Back of my mind, maybe. Not seriously. But who knows? One day I might have. You hear about people doing that.'

'What was his name?'

'Michael, Michael Edwards. Last time Mum saw him he was working in a recording studio. Producing or engineering or something. He was just playing at it really, she said. Everybody was in those days. Old hippy type.'

'Not like Dad, then.'

'No, not like Dad.'

They both start chuckling. Drink talks, dope laughs, as Diggsy would say.

Shit. Rachel has nicked the top of her index finger on the blade of a kitchen knife hidden beneath the suds in the washing-up bowl. She makes a white fist and sucks at the slit of blood, feeling the heat of the water on her skin.

'You all right, love?' asks Mum. 'Why don't you use the gloves?'

But Rachel plunges her hands back into the water and scrubs at a baking tin. 'He might have just mentioned me at some point,' she says, shaking her head. 'It was all about him, and how he'll miss the *buzz*, and what he'll do with himself. And then all that guff about new neighbours. I mean, please.'

'Rachel, I don't know what you're talking about. He *did* mention you.'

'Barely. An afterthought. It didn't sound like a vote of confidence. Taking over the reins, him hovering in the background as a guiding hand. I bloody well hope not.'

It is gone six and most of the gathering has drifted out

17

into the garden, probably driven out by Robert, who arrived late – despite his promise to Rachel that he'd be here by three at the latest – and immediately began button-holing the other guests about housing issues. Rachel has only recently noticed Robert's habit of spitting bits of food at people when he gets talking in that irritating reasonable way about the creeping exploitation of the green belt or the underfunding of residential units and other acts of moral neglect perpetrated by the district council's planning committee.

Rachel turns to her mother. 'Tell me,' she says. 'What does he say to you? Because every time I have an idea, he shoots it down, says we can't afford it. I know he has centuries of experience, but he is so set in his ways. He runs the place like a 1960s pie shop. Nothing changes. We haven't even got our own website, for goodness' sake.'

'Rachel, you're the one he asked to take over.'

'Well, who else was he going to ask? Luke's seventeen, and can you imagine Oscar trying to close a deal with a senior buyer at the Dorchester or another five-star client? In fact, try and imagine Oscar even wearing proper shoes. Remember how he turned up for my wedding. Or your anniversary at the Balcombe. It might suit him to *think* the reason he was overlooked is something to do with Dad not being his real dad—' She stops herself.

'I'm sure he doesn't think any such thing,' Mum says. 'Oscar is fine.'

'Anyway. Obviously Dad had to choose me,' says Rachel. 'I just wish he'd be a bit more positive. I haven't even seen the accounts yet. Can you believe he's still sending them out to Walter? Who is now about seventy-eight and practically demented. Talk about new blood.'

She shakes her head again, slowly this time, and sighs. She is deflated with this talk about Luke and Oscar, which now makes her think about Emma. Of course, no one has actually ever suggested Emma as a candidate for the job. The idea is laughable. Even if Dad dared wish it out loud, there was no way, in his wildest, most secret dreams, that Emma would have given up a six-figure City salary to vegetate, as she would doubtless see it, in a market town in one of England's least populated counties. Nevertheless, contemplating this hypothetical scenario – in which winning the keys to the family business comes only at the price of Emma refusing them – has been a spur to Rachel, who in her mind has now begun to envisage Duttings (the Carpet People) as a force in the world, or at least force enough to provide her one day with her own open-top sports car, expensive sunglasses and life of Riley. But this afternoon the drink has turned things black and all she can see is Emma breezing into their lives whenever she wants, monopolising Dad and encouraging Oscar in his idleness, as though that wasn't Mum's job, Oscar having hardly shown his face all afternoon, out there with that dog and smoking that stuff as if the whole street can't smell it. Bad enough he turns up at the warehouse every five minutes, helping himself to tea and sitting around frightening the customers and keeping the staff from their jobs with his New Age idea of leisure. And the nerve of Emma, discussing the firm's finances when the Lloyds in town has served Duttings' interests perfectly well for fifty years or more. Let her stick to her management buyouts and dotcom startups. Does she think everything has to come from London? Born and bred here, too, but then sent to a private school, with all its advantages, so that's not surprising.

She can hear Robert outside now. He's coming up the garden steps, saying something is a disgrace. Odd that she used to find it attractive that Robert had the sort of voice that carried, first hearing it, she remembers, during an archaeology seminar when they were both at UEA, the boom of a mortar sending forth a question about chalk from the back row. That now seems a lifetime ago and whatever she learned about chalk that day has been forgotten. But there must have been a point, surely, when they thought they might really end up as archaeologists. It seems absurd now, though of course accountancy has some aspects of unearthing things, of leaving trails for others to follow. Everything is archaeology if you think about it. She feels a headache coming on. Her finger is still bleeding.

'I just think your father's finding it harder to let go than he thought he would,' says Mum.

'Well, he has to let go. If he wants me to do the job, he has to.'

Robert comes nosing into the kitchen. 'Any coffee going?'

Oscar is following, and reaches into the fridge for a beer. 'Sorry I missed Dad's big speech – you should have given me a shout.'

'Never mind,' Mum says. 'Have one of these, they're delicious.'

Oscar comes and puts his arm around Rachel. 'How's my favourite sister?'

'You only have one,' she says.

He kisses the top of her head. Stoned. He must be. 'Thanks for explaining my joke,' he says, moving off into the sitting room eating, the backside of his jeans hanging like a teenager's, ragged at the bottoms, those little bleached dreadlocks sticking out like bits of old rope. How old does he think he is?

'Well?' Mum says, as though Oscar is just being lovable.

'Well, what?'

The front door goes. Penny is back from the station. Mum turns and calls to her. 'Did she get off all right?'

20

'Yes, thanks, she had plenty of time.'

'Oh well, thank *goodness*,' mutters Rachel, running the cold tap hard.

Mum touches her shoulder, a gesture of restraint. 'Why don't you put a plaster on that,' she says.

Blood.

Chapter 2

It is Wednesday and Stuart is sitting alone in the break-fast room in his socks and dressing gown watching a DVD, *The Gardener's Year*, a step-by-step guide to gardening success, whatever the measure of your plot (large) or experience (small). The presenter, Hal Harold – a florid TV performer whom Stuart remembers once seeing assemble an elegant windbreak out of fallen tree branches – is explaining, with the aid of a mug of tea, what happens in April. 'When we talk about April, we're really talking about showers and sunshine,' the man says, glancing up at a scurrying sky.

'I think I knew that,' Stuart murmurs, taking the opportunity to investigate his scrotum, checking for unusual testicular shapes, as advised in an article he read recently in the paper. Both seem round enough, but peeing too has been on his mind, the recent nocturnal difficulties thereof.

'Many blooms will already be on their way,' Hal says.

'Right. Or bloody weeds,' Stuart says.

He frowns and adjusts his dressing gown. Is this what it comes to – playing with your bollocks and talking to yourself? It is only a month since the official handover but already the past feels like the proverbial Black Hole of Calcutta. How weird it was when it finally came upon him, his big day (as everyone kept calling it) being so ordinary and yet momentous too, the hours passing at the usual rate of knots but the shadowy mass of unknown territory getting nearer and bigger whenever he glanced up from the affairs of the moment, making his stomach churn. 'The last day of anything is like that,' Diane said, as they lay together in the dark that night, the sourness of wallpaper paste wafting in from the landing. 'It's the shock of change. It's like being pregnant for months and then suddenly having a baby to look after. That different world you have to get used to.'

'More like losing a baby,' he said.

'Stuart, that's horrible.'

'Well it's true.'

'Barbara seemed to have a few tears to shed,' she said, after a few moments. 'That was sweet. If slightly alarming.'

'One too many port and lemons, that's all.'

'End of an era,' Diane said.

'I suppose so.'

It hadn't seemed particularly like the end, though, when he'd arrived at the warehouse that morning in his best navy suit, rubbing his hands, sniffing the familar scent of tufted pile, singing a line of Sinatra. It seemed like every other day. *Fly me to the moon* . . .

Brian, his senior man, was there, tidying around with young Josh.

'Big day,' he said.

'Still work to be done,' said Stuart, tapping his watch. 'News on Bryce's?'

'They're on their way,' Josh said. 'Rachel said I had to ring them.'

'Good boy. But where are the fitters?' Stuart said, looking round.

'Out on a little job somewhere,' said Brian. 'I've got to go out too. Midbury.' He grinned, nodding at Stuart's suit. 'Looks like you and Josh will be unloading the truck.'

'You must be joking. We'll let Rachel and Barbara do it, eh, Josh?' he said, winking at the boy. Josh, still too new at this to try out his wit, smiled and went pink. 'In the meantime, let there be tea, if you wouldn't mind doing the honours, young man – milk, two sugars. And have one yourself.'

Josh skipped off to the kettle area in the dark den under the office. Stuart turned to Brian. 'Brian, give me a bell later, let me know how it pans out. And give my best to Keith. He's got two more apartments in that block.'

'Will do.'

'Oh, and Brian . . .'

'Boss?'

'Take the Avensis. It'll look better. Rachel can manage with the van.'

Fly me to the moon . . .

Rachel and Barbara were in the office, Rachel scowling at an invoice, Barbara behind her big *rat-a-tat* electric typewriter, glancing upwards. Eye make-up, wearing a dress for the occasion. What was she – mid-fifties? Not as old as him. Still a decent-looking woman.

'This office is ridiculously small,' Rachel said. 'I can't breathe without knocking something over.'

'It's always been big enough for me and Barbara,' Stuart said. 'How long have you been with Duttings now, Babs?'

Barbara hit carriage return. 'A hundred years?'

Rachel deepened her scowl. Stuart smiled.

24

When customers arrived, Stuart watched Rachel handle them without intervention, as promised, even on this, his last day. It was two years since she came into the business. She could pretty much do it all now. A little brusque on sales – cold even – but solid on detail. No umming or ahing.

He loved the colours down there under the strip lights. Half closing his eyes, it was like a painting he had done himself. All my own work.

In the evening there was champagne at the Beehive, and a big square cake Diane had baked that looked like a blue carpet with a cream-tramlined border, a little settee in one corner and a TV in the opposite one. Standing among the other staff, Barbara presented Stuart with binoculars and a package containing gardening and birdwatching books and DVDs. 'For when you get bored,' she said. All the suppliers' reps and trade acquaintances from across town had come to say their goodbyes. 'You don't get rid of me that easily,' Stuart quipped. 'I'll still be popping in to keep an eye on things from time to time. Isn't that right, Rachel?'

She gave him that thin smile of hers. 'Thanks for the warning.'

Was he doing the right thing? Doubt shadowed his mind even as he made his off-the-cuff speech, lightly seasoned with jokes at his own expense and full of thanks for everyone, including his late father, who had started the business from nothing but a handcart in the market from which he sold doormats and oilcloth. Alongside Rachel, he posed for the *Gazette*'s photographer, handing her the keys to the business. Everyone made a party of it. Diane danced with old Walter, who had come in for the accounts a day early. Barbara, touched by Stuart's remarks, in which he singled her out for her unswerving loyalty and support down the years, drank too much and became tearful. Stuart's speech and vision became blurred at the edges.

Tony Ennick arrived when the evening had reached the top of its arc and was winding down, some guests having left, others thinking about it. 'Long live the Carpet King!' he boomed from the door. Heads turned, glad voices rose in greeting. Everyone knew Tony, and those nursing the last of their drinks were persuaded to stay for more. 'Tony, what kept you?' Stuart said. 'Come on in.' Of course he was already in.

Was it merely timing that endowed Tony with the gift of drawing the fire of attention on himself? He called for more champagne and made a generous toast to Duttings, all the while trading wisecracks with these men of his own stripe, shaking this hand and then that, slowly becoming over the rest of the evening, in the resettling of this sluggish vortex of well-wishers, the new centre of things. Tall as a phone box and standing legs apart, he established court at the bar, scattering his corn amid the noisy laughter of chickens. Music played. He nodded his head in time and ate peanuts. Not many men could get away with that loud suit – a blue-grey squared check – in this town, but Tony could.

Barbara had Stuart pinned to the wall near the fruit machine. 'But it can't *possibly* be the same without you,' she was saying. 'Due respect to Rachel, but she can't do what you can.'

'We all have to move on, Barbara. *Plus ça change*, as the poet said.'

It was late when Tony's voice rang out. 'Hey, Stuart, what's this we hear that there's a link between carpets and young kiddies with asthma?'

Stuart refocused his vision and looked across at Tony's coiffure backlit by the bar lights. 'It's a myth,' he heard his slurring tongue loudly call. 'That asthma thingth a myth . . .'

'Thatasthmathingthamyth?' Tony mimicked, to the delight and hilarity of those around him. '*Thatasthmathingthamyth?*'

Stuart blinked smilingly against this uproar of mirth. Everyone was parroting it now. *Thatasthmathingthamyth? Thatasthmathingthamyth?* New versions of it rang around. *It-tha myth that asthma-thing. It-tha mythtery thith athma myth . . .*

He shook his head and turned to Barbara. 'Bloody fool,' he muttered, 'spouting rubbish like that. That's how damaging rumours get spread. It's been proved that dust mites can't survive in carpets. That's a fact. Or toxins. Your *wallpaper* gives out about ten times more poisonous gases than carpet. Did you know that?'

'I can believe it, Stuart.'

'That's the beauty of carpet – it *absorbs* pollutants.'

Sporadically guests came over to say good night and best of luck. When he looked for Diane, he saw that she too had been drawn into Tony's circle now, chortling with the others at some fresh mischief of his. Stuart couldn't shake it off. That night it returned in his dreams, its meaning remade as a nauseous presence in the growling upheaval of his stomach. *Thatasthmathingthamyth . . .*

He puts the gardening DVD on pause and heaves himself out to find a pen and a notebook. There are pens in the pot near the phone but the only paper he can find is the little pad Diane uses for scribbling messages. His plan is to make notes, then drive down to the garden centre on the peripheral and afterwards drop in at the warehouse to see everyone, perhaps even catch a spot of lunch with Brian or one of the reps who come and go in the week. He goes to the kitchen and pours another coffee. Diane left nearly a whole pot when she rushed out for her course this morning and it seems a pity to waste it. The point of this short starter course, she told him, is to bring her up to speed for summer school, which is the only way she can get the credits in time for September, when her Community College course begins. She explained all this while he was still half asleep, though she has told him a hundred times in any case, she said, as she dragged a brush through her tangle of hair in the mirror at her side of the bed. He's noticed she has started wearing it wild again, unpinned, as it was when he first met her, like an Afro, as they used to call it. 'What is it then, nuclear physics?' he mumbled. She didn't answer that, but said there was his Special K out on the table and some bacon going cold and coffee in the pot. Interior decorating is what she has her heart set on, he knows, but what sort of painting and wallpapering is so hard you need to go to college three times a week? He misses her already, hates the quiet of an empty house. Just when *he's* going to be around more, she decides to vanish. It's as though Diane is seizing some sort of chance before it's too late. Anyone would be unsettled by that.

He takes his coffee to his chair and reanimates the paused image of Hal Harold. 'Pests are becoming more active,' Hal is saying, his eyes protruding suddenly, as if this news is a revelation even to himself. He reveals a caterpillar in the palm of his hand and speaks of the need to watch for creeping thistles and shepherd's purse, or possibly curse, which can send its little seeds parachuting all over your garden even with the merest touch of an ill-controlled hoe. Stuart sighs. The prospect of avoiding a weed that will go to such lengths to spread its evil is faintly depressing. He fast-frames to tubers and dahlias, which Hal is saying can be procured from any good local nursery or garden centre. Brassicas too. Is that sprouts? Why are

28

they only ever eaten at Christmas? Stuart wonders. He has had enough of Hal. He switches him off and goes upstairs, takes a shower and gets dressed.

Knotting his favourite work tie in front of the mirror now, he feels better already, newly empowered, Superman pulling on the old tights and cape. It occurs to him that Oscar might still be in bed. He calls, then peeks into his room. The bed is a collapsed hill of duvet and looks long vacated. Stuart remembers that Oscar is going to London today. From the window, he sees that the VW camper has been moved on to the street, an eyesore in forty shades of green with those slogans on the side, but better that, he supposes, than having it blocking the drive every time you need to get somewhere in a hurry. He has a good feeling about Oscar's windfall, which must surely be enough at least to put a month's rent down on a modest bedsit across town somewhere.

Stuart backs the Lexus out of the drive. Unbeatable purr, fingertip handling. Nice touch of walnut. Plenty of room for a man of girth behind the wheel. He can't understand why Diane is so prickly about this whole Oscar thing, the father dying and all, and the letter. The way Stuart figures it, the man owes Oscar a little something. Where's the harm? He eases the car down the winding hill to the little crossroads, where he waits at the lights, thrumming his fingers on the wheel to County FM. Owner-manager at the Raj Kingdom giving it the admiring once-over, wishing he had one. Certificate of hygiene displayed in the window like a menu. Hearing Aid Center, next door: Deaf Awareness Week. Travel agents. Book with Confidence Here. Pedestrians. Look Both Ways.

The blue Avensis, formerly his, now Rachel's, is sitting on the forecourt when he arrives at the warehouse at midday.

He pulls in beside it and gets out, stands for a moment, squinting up at the sign. Duttings. Always gives him a turn-on, seeing his name up there. The bay doors are half closed to keep out the wind. No one is in sight, but then he sees the hunchback of Brian in the little office up the stairs on the 'mezzanine', as Rachel has started to call it. Two customers, he notices too now, as he passes down the aisles of carpet, inspecting a roll of sage hightwist. A couple, mid-twenties, with a child in a buggy and an older girl of about four. Brian hasn't spotted them yet. Stuart stops, feeling the old feeling, and walks up amiably, turning on the smile. 'Lovely product the Devonshire, madam. For a sitting room, is it? Lounge?'

'Yes, we were just looking, thank you . . .'

'Very hard-wearing. And easy to clean, which can be important with little ones in the house – am I right?' He winks at the little girl, who hides behind her father's leg but peers out grinning. 'What's your name?' he asks.

The girl is rocking back and forth, coyly looking up at Dad, finger in her mouth.

'You're right there,' the man says.

'The reason is, with the tufted twistpile, you get a couple of extra turns in the yarn, see? Look at that. Slightly rougher surface texture so it doesn't show the footprints. Wool with ten points each of acrylic and polyester.'

'Polyester . . .' The woman steps back to look at the price tag, then turns to her husband, doubt on her face.

'Eighty per cent wool, though, madam. You just need the manmade for the Meltbond system.' Stuart turns to the man. 'It's the low heat process that leaves a sort of web-like structure through the yarn. If you can imagine that, sir. Hence its hardwearing qualities.'

The man is nodding, as if, yes, he *can* imagine that. Stuart loves this.

'What dimensions are we talking about?' Stuart asks. 'The room?'

The man looks at his wife. 'Fourteen foot, is it?'

She is holding a piece of paper but has the figure in her head. 'Fourteen six by thirteen six,' she says, still frowning.

'Perfect,' Stuart says, pointing, 'because this is fifteen, which means it goes down in one go, so no seaming required. Let me just price that up for you. Fitting included, of course.'

The man is looking again at the roll of carpet, but his wife has started to move off down the aisle, leaving him with the buggy. The little girl runs to follow her. The man takes a breath and lets out a low whistle while he thinks for a moment. 'When would you be able to fit it?' he blurts.

'Whenever is convenient. Within a few days, certainly. Let me just check our schedule.' Stuart walks away. He hears the man summoning his wife back. Give them a minute together, he thinks. Do the bickering in private. He sniffs the air of this place, homely in a way that home isn't.

Brian is still up there in the office. Stuart can just see the side of his head. Drinking coffee. Catch him doing the crossword. He labours quietly up the little flight of stairs and opens the door a couple of inches. 'Gotcha!' he says, grinning, full of himself, where moments before he was empty.

Brian looks across, surprise on his face. 'Aye, aye, stranger,' he says, eyes widening.

'Haven't been out of it that long,' Stuart says. 'Got a bite on the Devonshire down there,' he adds. 'What's in the diary this week?' He takes a step into the office, and sees now that someone is in the other chair, coffee steaming on the desk beside him. The good biscuits are out.

'Gareth Newnam,' the man says, getting up and offering

31

his hand. Blond streaks in his hair, sharp charcoal suit, white cuffs bringing out his tan.

Brian is on his feet now. 'Gareth, this is Stuart, the . . .' Stuart sees him falter, perhaps not quite seeing the way to introduce Stuart now that he's not in charge, not officially. 'Stuart Dutting,' he says, 'Rachel's father. Recently retired.'

'More *semi*,' says Stuart. 'Still keeping an eye out.'

'Ah. Old habits, eh?' says Newnam. He flips a card out of his top pocket and hands it to Stuart. 'Rael Eastern,' he says. 'I'm just waiting for Miss Dutting. Brian has been telling me all about your operation here.'

Brian looks faintly alarmed. 'Just coffee and a chat,' he says, putting his pen behind his ear. 'No classified secrets.'

Stuart peers at the card as though it's in a foreign language. 'Rael Eastern. Not a familiar one with me. Are you on the manufacturing side?'

Newnam sits down, picks up his coffee and crosses his legs. He is drinking from the personalised Formula One mug Stuart got from Soames's junket to Silverstone last year. 'Importers,' he says as he sips. 'Turkish and Iranian, mainly, but some north African, Pakistani. Sumptuous quality. We've got some very nice contracts, and entirely exclusive to Rael. They have two of our carpets at the Japanese Embassy in New York.'

Stuart nods. He wonders when Duttings became the sort of firm that supplied Turkish and Iranian carpets to foreign embassies in New York or anywhere else. He wonders when Rachel stopped being Mrs Parsons and started being Miss Dutting again. 'Where is Rachel, anyway?' he says.

'She had an appointment,' Brian says.

'Her car's outside,' Stuart says.

'Yes, someone picked her up.'

Stuart nods. 'Anybody I know?'

'Know anyone who drives a red Corsa?'

Stuart ponders on that. 'I shouldn't think so.'

'She said she'd be back by twelve.' Brian checks his watch, as though he's in trouble, then out of the window. 'Ah, there she is now, in fact.'

Sure enough, Rachel is down there on the sales floor, speaking to the young couple with the baby and the little girl. She glances up to the office, impatience pinching her expression as she walks towards the steps. Stuart gets to his feet and comes down the stairs to meet her, Brian at his shoulder. 'Rachel,' Stuart says, 'we were just talking about you.'

She looks right past him. 'Brian, do you think it might be out of the question to help these customers? They're interested in the Wilton.'

'Actually I was just sorting them out myself . . .' Stuart begins.

'So I hear. Just give me a minute, Dad, if you don't mind.'

She disappears up the stairs and comes back down after a few moments and guides him to one side. 'Dad, you really cannot come in whenever you like now and start serving customers. You're not supposed to be here.'

'I was just passing. I had to go to the garden centre.'

'In your suit and tie?'

'I thought I might pop out to the Beehive with Brian for a spot of lunch.'

'Well he can't, he's busy.'

'Why, where's everyone else?'

'Josh has gone to watch Tom do some fitting, and Paul is doing an estimate out in Norfolk. Barbara has rung in sick again, so I've got all the paperwork to catch up on this afternoon, as well as seeing people.'

'I could give you a hand.'

'No. Thanks.'

Stuart's eyes wander up to the office, this Gareth Newnam standing at the window holding his mug. 'So Paul's out in Norfolk? That's a bit off the beaten track, isn't it?'

Rachel stands with her fists resting on her hips. She looks tight-lipped at the floor and then back at him. 'Would you mind not doing this, Dad?'

'Doing what?'

'You *know* what,' she hisses, trying to keep her temper. 'We agreed.'

Stuart holds up his hands in surrender. 'OK, calm down.' They walk to the door and out on to the forecourt. 'So, who's this fellow you've got upstairs in there?' he says.

'An opportunity to move into the twenty-first century, I hope,' she says.

'What – Iran? Turkey? They're still in the dark ages.'

'Actually, they're not. Though it's true they do believe in old-fashioned craftsmanship and quality. I thought we did too.'

'Word of warning, love. There's no margin in hand-knotted rugs. Not unless you specialise, and we can't afford to do that.'

'We can't afford to be stagnant either, Dad. We need niche markets as much as the bread-and-butter stuff. Anyway, this is just one avenue of interest,' she says. 'In fact, at the moment it's just lunch,' she adds, looking at her watch. 'Or it will be if I ever get out of here.'

'Well don't let me stop you.'

'I won't. I thought you had some gardening to do.'

'I have.'

'So,' she says. She pauses, retreating a step, relenting, as she has always done when she thinks she has won the argument. 'How's Mum?' she asks.

'Pretty busy. Busier than me.'

He watches Rachel go back into the warehouse, feels the hurt of her pushing him out like that. He climbs into his car. Across the road, a tall young man in a suit is trying awkwardly to unlock the door of a crappy little red Corsa in the roar of the traffic, a box from Pizza Hut wedged under one elbow. Stuart waits, then eases the Lexus out of the forecourt and follows the Corsa as it pulls away, its exhaust audibly coughing as they move along the peripheral and take the looping road towards the railway station and up into the town, burning oil by the look of it. It slows at the Corn Exchange on Eastgate and takes a left through a narrow opening that gives on to a yard behind all the shops. Stuart carries on a few yards further then stops on the yellow line outside Halfords and peers back down the street through the V formed by the polythene-wrapped handles of his new spade and fork. After a couple of minutes he sees the young man – he's practically a boy – emerge from the opening and disappear into one of the shops. Stuart can't tell which one from here. He carefully reverses, past the opening, and halts in front of the shop, colour photographs of offices and retail sheds in the window. Is that it? Mallicks Commercial. He can see him now, shovelling pizza into his mouth from the box hidden somewhere out of sight as he sits at his desk, rearranging papers, pulling files up on screen. He's starving, eating as though no one's watching, as though he's at home watching late-night rubbish on TV. What do they teach them these days, what dos and donts, sitting there in the window like a chimp in a cage.

Stuart waits in the car for a minute longer. He is imagining a later scene in which he will touch upon the subject with Diane, perhaps in bed, the moment when she closes her book, switches off her lamp, turns the bulk of her soft warmth away from him to lie in the dark, worrying (as he knows she sometimes does) about Luke going off to college next year, or whether she's up to the demands of this course of her own, and now, this past week, about Oscar. He imagines himself asking what she thinks of Rachel viewing new premises with an agent from Mallicks. He hears the weariness, now familiar in Diane's sigh, as she points out that Rachel quite possibly knows what she's doing, reminds him that Rachel has spent the past year impressing him without condition or qualification, so why the doubts now? You made your choice. Give her rein. Let her express herself, as Diane herself must do with paint and curtain swatches and wallpapers. Go to sleep, she'll say. So, yes, he'll leave the subject hanging there in his thoughts like an unworn suit in the wardrobe, his eyes wide in the sickly light of the radio alarm, not after all speaking the fear that makes his heart pound, pulling back instead, saying good night.

Chapter 3

Oscar surfaces from the tube at Kentish Town and crosses the railway line northward, following the route he has marked in his *A to Z* to an office above a dentist's surgery on Highgate Road. He is carrying a brown envelope containing his birth certificate and his passport, which he noticed (though not until he was on the train) expired last year. It is badly dog-eared, with stamps from Turkey and other countries in it, his twenty-two-year-old face looking younger than he remembered. He hopes the lawyer doesn't notice or says it doesn't matter.

The woman at the desk up the stairs takes his name and asks him to wait. She says Mr Hawkins is in with a client at present, and glances at Oscar once or twice – at the braids in his hair and the straggle of beard, at his relaxed notion of male grooming – and smiles faintly. He smiles back primly, hiding the gap between his teeth. He did give some thought as to how he might present himself today,

37

but then all his clothes look like this – low-slung combats and jeans, worn T-shirts, boots borrowed from Diggsy the previous summer and not returned. In any case, he guesses it doesn't matter how he looks here in London, where no one cares too much about anything. He could be a rock star or a conceptual artist. He imagines the woman at the desk knows he is neither of these things. She knows his story before he does. 'Can I offer you a tea or coffee?' she asks after a few minutes.

'I wouldn't mind some water,' he says.

She brings him some chilled from a cooler in the back somewhere. Standing, he gulps it down in one. 'Thanks,' he says, and gives her the paper cup back. She smiles but doesn't say anything else – like the police, Oscar thinks, when they won't tell you what's going on or precisely what law it is you're supposed to have broken. There's a map of London on the wall. Oscar has passed through the city a number of times on his way to various places but doesn't know it well. He knows Mum met Dad in Earls Court when he was too little to remember. He walks up to the map and finds Earls Court, touching the spot with his finger. There was a pub here where Mum was working when Dad was in town for a trade show. He ate in the pub and asked her out on Sunday. That was after she'd been married to Michael. He doesn't know what went wrong with that. It seems they were young and foolish and he, Oscar, was the unplanned fruit of those carefree, liberated days. At home in the box there are two or three photographs of Oscar as a one-year-old in Hyde Park, Mum in the flowing garb of the day and that mad hair being wooed by Stuart, an off-duty carpet salesman. There is one of Stuart – moustache, open-necked shirt, unfashionable slacks – rolling a ball for Oscar. He wasn't bad-looking, but would a girl like that go and live in a little town in the sticks for a man like that? When asked, Mum used to say with a smile that Dad came along and swept her off her feet. It's not hard to locate Hyde Park on the map, an oblong of pistachio ice-cream between wafers of yellow road.

Mr Hawkins calls Oscar in. 'Mr Dutting?' he says. 'Please, take a seat.' He shakes his hand and gestures him into the chair opposite his own. Oscar has been expecting someone older – as old as Dad, perhaps – but this is a guy his own age, maybe not even that, a man who eats a big dinner by the look of him, though, and probably enjoys it. It seems odd to call each other 'mister', but Oscar links the formality to the need to establish detachment, as if what follows somehow won't be legal without it. 'I'm sorry to keep you waiting,' Mr Hawkins says with a practised smile. He has a file in front of him with Oscar's name on it, and Michael's too. Michael Edwards.

'No problem,' says Oscar. 'I was just looking at your map.'

Mr Hawkins looks up. 'Oh. Did you find the place OK?'

'Sure. Straight across the railway line.'

Mr Hawkins nods. He puts on reading glasses and gets down to business, shuffling papers with this same ease of familiarity, asking Oscar to confirm that he is the son of Michael Charles Edwards and Diane Rachel Forest, despite having a different name. 'That's me all right,' Oscar says. Mr Hawkins glances at Oscar's documents and hands them back, telling him how, as outlined in his letter of the four-teenth, the late Mr Edwards, of an address in London that Oscar doesn't quite catch, has made provisions in his will, a copy of which will be made available, though Mr Hawkins reads from it anyway, or the parts that count. Oscar leans forward, tries to extract particular meaning from the gen-erality of what is being said, and sees that this too, this blur of words, must be endured before Mr Hawkins can give him the nub in English, because though Oscar has as good a vague understanding of 'executors' and 'testator' as the next man, in much the same way that we know – but don't need to know when what we're hungry for is the whole deal – that something is made of flour and eggs or whatever, long sentences are not his strong suit. Mr Hawkins knows this, of course, and seems to want to get through the preliminaries as much as Oscar wants him to. Oscar waits and listens. 'In essence,' Mr Hawkins says, at last, beaming, 'you can see that the bulk of your father's estate is left to Mrs Florence Edwards, the deceased's mother, with a cash amount for yourself held in a separate account with funds currently standing at four thousand, five hundred and sixty-two pounds and twenty-two pence. If you could just furnish us with your own bank details at some point, I'll have it transferred.'

Furnish? Oscar doesn't have any bank details as such, not having a bank account as such, and his mind has snagged on this 'your father' whom at first he thinks means Stuart but of course it's the other father, the Mr Edwards, Michael, the deceased, whose money it was, the figure itself – the moment he's been waiting for – almost slipping through unnoticed. 'Four thousand, five hundred?' Oscar repeats with surprise in his voice, but Mr Hawkins is now explaining about an unspecified amount of property forming the second and final part of this bequest, 'which, in short,' he says, 'comprises the contents of the deceased's business premises, a small office or workshop, I'm not sure, but the lease we understand is paid up until the end of this month. The address and the keys to the office are in this envelope. It's in Camden Town. I'm afraid you'll need to make your own arrangements to clear the place out, but if you could return the keys to us at your convenience. You can go and see it whenever you like. There's no great hurry – though obviously the sooner you can do it, the sooner we can wind things up at our end,' he adds. He smiles again. It's not too hard to imagine him at the weekend, some nephew's favourite uncle, swinging by in a big sweatshirt to take him to the zoo or McDonald's. Nice job too, Oscar thinks, telling people they've come into money without the downside of grief you usually get. Of course, bit unseemly it would be to come out and actually congratulate him on his windfall, just in case Oscar was feeling weird about it, which he is, though hardly on the point of tears.

'How did he die?' Oscar asks.

'Mr Edwards? A heart attack, I believe.'

'So when did he make this will?'

Mr Hawkins works out the dates from the documents in front of him. 'About three months prior. Just after Christmas.'

'So did he know it was going to happen?'

'I really couldn't say. Perhaps his mother would know,' he says, squaring the edges of the papers on his desk and sliding them into a plastic folder. He looks at Oscar. 'I realise the situation here. I gather from your . . . your grandmother that there was a long estrangement.'

'We've never met, if that's what you mean.'

'I had the idea she might like to. I think your father had it in mind too. I could put you in touch with her. If that's what you want.'

Oscar nods in a way that means he'll think about that one, and tells Mr Hawkins that, by the way, he doesn't have a bank account. 'I used to have one but it got closed down.'

'I'm sure that won't be a problem,' he says. 'Just give me a ring when you've sorted one out.' He organises all the things Oscar needs quickly and neatly and slots them into a Jiffy bag. 'Any further problems, please don't hesitate to contact us. He holds out his hand for Oscar to shake. This combination of legal decorum and friendly efficiency has made Mr Hawkins seem older and more substantial, while Oscar himself feels suddenly younger, and not in a healthy, vigorous way but in a stunted and unfledged way, as though the world has moved on in his absence, as though he has overslept and woken up in a different time, trapped inside the mind of the boy in his passport photograph, like the wrong sort of everlasting youth.

It oughtn't to be that difficult to find a use for four and a half grand. The van needs new tyres and a welding job on the sills. He could set himself up with some decent decks and try to get himself a summer residency at one of the clubs in Cornwall. Or go off somewhere for a couple of years, Thailand maybe, or even – and why not? – California, at last. Is there any place more laid-back than California? His geography is probably awry, but he still mixes California in his mind with the 'Big Rock Candy Mountains', a song he loved as a child, a land of milk and honey and soft-boiled eggs and cigarette trees, as Mum explained it, where there was nothing to do but hang out and drink free lemonade. 'Hotel California', too, was from those years, listening in the lounge with his mother and Rachel just a toddler, a song about desert highways and wind in your hair. You get the best weed, too, in California, or so everyone says.

He wonders now, though, at the poverty of these wishes. He has never been too concerned about his material circumstances, but this afternoon, biting into a doughy sandwich he has bought from an Italian café as he walks the mile or so southward to Camden Town, his 'legacy' (his birthright, perhaps you'd call it) is already beginning to seem like a burden. It is not that he is unaccustomed to free money – usually in the form of an express cash transfer from his mother if things got tight, which often they did. But this lucky bounty, falling from the sky as it has, seems too large a sum to squander, as if it's a specific challenge, like being given cryptic instructions to something, or a special sign, or tools to build an ark.

Oscar is not one to be troubled with a sense of purpose. For years, Dad's enthusiasm for lighting fires under him resulted only in Mum stamping them out again. 'For goodness' sake, give the boy a *break*, Stuart.' But what was she protecting him from? Perhaps it was understandable that Dad – uneducated beyond the age of fifteen – would pin his faith on academic success while Mum followed the metropolitan, free-thinking impulses of her own rudely interrupted youth, seemingly happy to allow Oscar to discover and nurture what latent talents he had, to harness his formal learning to his personal passions, whatever they might turn out to be. Eventually Dad gave up on the pushing – stopped asking if Oscar had done his homework, stopped taking him down to the warehouse on Saturday mornings, occasions when he genuinely seemed to expect a boy of twelve to derive satisfaction from putting names to the different sorts of carpets or from converting square feet into prices per square metre. It was a gradual change, eased further when Rachel started to shine at school.

He must have been fourteen and Rachel in her first year at the Girls' High when Dad went to a flooring show somewhere in Germany, and brought back, for reasons never to be explained, an American gift for Oscar – a leather catcher's mitt and baseball – and, for Rachel, a model, in kit form, with wires and polystyrene spheres, of the planetary system ('Technically, Rachel, it's called an *orrery*,' he said,

43

and made Rachel repeat this strange word from the top of the box). Obviously both gifts were equally baffling but you could see how his mind was turning. Oscar Dutting would be left to his vain idlings while Rachel was trusted with the workings of the universe. Of course, Dad also had Emma to be proud of, doing well at boarding school, and eventually – better late than never – Luke with his newborn promise. There was no blatant favouritism, as such, not even with Luke. If Dad ever consoled himself for Oscar's manifold disappointments with the fact that he wasn't actually the real deal – that he wasn't, strictly speaking, *his* son – his impatience never reached the level where he might risk expressing it in those terms. After all, he had done his best with him. But, with Dad, his attention – and whatever moments of affection or physical endearments might accompany it – tended to follow whoever was trying the hardest to attract it. And Oscar was too much at ease with himself by then to feel any compulsion to compete with babies and young scientists. At any rate, the pressure – such as it was – was off. And a boy couldn't complain about that.

His adolescence was spun out hanging out in town with friends, or lying on his bed with his headphones on listening to U2 and The Cure. He had a girlfriend for a while called Zoe, who loved his unusual name – unusual for this town, a brief source of amusement for boys at school – and used to take him to her room and allow him to play with her breasts. His mother kept him in money and ironed his T-shirts without making any unreasonable demands, except the usual ones about not staying out all night during term time. And even then it wasn't as if he did too badly at school. His pair of A levels were enough (to his father's surprise) to get him into North Essex, where he completed two semesters of a philosophy degree before taking himself off with Diggsy – whose glassy-eyed wonder in the face of abstract profundity so serendipitously mirrored his own – to a communal freeholding in Wales where they helped grow muddy vegetables and smoked dope and rode a horse without a saddle to the village and back.

A weariness overtakes him as he finds the street he is looking for. It's not just the walk that has turned his legs to lead, but something like the return of a familiar affliction, a sapping sense of foreboding that he dimly recognises as responsibility. He stops in front of a redbrick building that has the words 'Crown House' picked out in an arch above the entrance and looks at the vertical row of a dozen or so buzzers, each with a unit number and the name of a business inscribed in a panel beside it. The double doors, blue, and bound with metal strapping and barred at the windows, are open to the sunlight, and inside Oscar sees a stairway of dimpled, black iron steps spiralling up around the cage of a lift-shaft. The keys are in his hand as he mounts the stairs to the third floor, each one clanging gently beneath his tread, above his head the windows framing the grainy light in flat rectangles, like opaque lamps. It seems quiet, apart from the occasional door banging or the trill of a phone, but the offices – studios really, it seems to Oscar as he peeks in as he passes, some of them chic and minimalist beyond the yellowy, industrial brutality of the corridor – are busy with creative activity, artsy-looking types sitting at screens or drawing boards or engaged in some craft or other, coffee mugs on the desk beside them, or bottles of mineral water.

He moves down the corridor. Unit 44 is the last on the block. The larger of the two keys fits the full-length steel shutter. It rattles as he hauls it up on its roller, and he finds himself looking through the little window at the workspace beyond, its abandoned furniture and equipment lit by what light comes slanting in through the blind, which is lifted at one side, its pull cords hanging in a tangle at the other.

Gingerly he unlocks the door, pausing for a moment before entering. He walks around slowly, touching, peering, opening and closing drawers – a desk with a computer and other technical gadgets, a stationery cupboard with a tray and kettle and box of teabags on top, and a small fridge at the side that turns out to be empty and a sink with two inverted mugs on the draining board. Then there's a shelf of books – geology, genetics, a software manual – above a trestle table set with pots of paint, brushes standing stiffly in a small vase like wooden flowers, and, to one side, a box of pens and finer brushes, a number of flat packages wrapped in corrugated cardboard leaning in a stack against the wall under the calendar. The calendar is open at February last year, Oscar notices. He draws a face in the dust on the filing cabinet and gives it a smile.

It all has to be worth something. He feels the weariness return, the restraining quality of some duty, dragging at him like weeds in a pond. Will he have to call up one of those firms that advertise house clearances? Or should he get Diggsy to help? They could maybe hawk the stuff around town back home, get more money that way. Oscar doesn't know how much computers cost but this one looks pretty new. An Apple Mac in turquoise. He is about to pull a chair up when something else catches his eye in the corner of the room – a heap of something jutting under a dust sheet. He lifts an edge of the cloth and smiles. 'Wow . . .' He hauls the sheet off to reveal a full drum kit, all set up to go with cymbals, high-hat, chrome stands, cowbell, a bundle of sticks in a sheath laced on to the side drum like arrows in a quiver. 'Premier' is the name on the big bass drum at the front. Four drums in all. With that glittery red trim, they look like something you'd play years ago, in the days before digital beats, probably even before those first drum machines like the broken one they have gathering dust at the Green House in town. He sits astride the little stool, selects a pair of sticks and executes a clumsy but energetic roll on the tom-toms, ending with a mighty crash on the largest cymbal. 'Brilliant,' he says, breathing hard. He lays the sticks across the snare, quietly now, conscious of the disturbance he has made. He treads softly back to the desk and settles in front of the computer. He's no expert, though he has used the internet café in Taunton and has a current hotmail address. He touches the keyboard and the screen comes alive with an exclamatory *Parppp!* that takes him by surprise. Amazing that no one has bothered to switch it off in all this time.

An open email message materialises on the screen:

Michael!

I'm so excited about this, I tried to call earlier, but will try again. Great news on the two Bristol families. You really hit it there! Harold Way is thrilled with the results and now has plans to come over to 'the old country' and do some more 'digging' on his own, pending legalities, which I understand may take a few months. I wondered also if you'd made any progress on the Hackney Dawsons yet?

Best regards, Greville Wood

PS I gave your address to our sister organisation in Sydney, Australia, who have similar enquiries. Be in touch.

The email is dated 21 February. Was this the day he died? This is too weird, Oscar thinks. He imagines him – his father, Michael – popping out maybe at lunchtime and never returning, something happening to him in the meantime. Just leaving this message up on screen, thinking to himself that he won't be five minutes and then collapsing in the newsagent's or the chemist's. But who is he imagining? There are no pictures of Michael in his mother's album. Not one. He stares at the screen for a moment, then pulls up another email of the half-dozen sitting there in the in-box and starts to read:

Dear Mr Edwards,

I represent a small Australian charity . . .

There's a noise behind him and Oscar turns in his chair. A woman, girl, stands in the doorway, jeans and T-shirt with a pink sequin message on the front he can't make out, corkscrew hair that sticks out at the sides. 'What are you doing?' she says. 'How did you get in?' She's gesturing with a knife, though it doesn't seem to be a sharp one. She is no more than five foot tall.

Oscar stands up. 'I got the key from the solicitors,' he says. 'This is my stuff. I have to clear it out.'

'What do you mean, your stuff?'

'Well, my father's stuff. He died, so now it's mine.'

'Michael was your father?'

'Yes. Well, technically. Did you know him?'

'I have the unit next door. I'm Miriam,' she says. Her hands are muddy, he notices. 'Ceramics,' she says. 'I'm sorry about your dad.'

'I'm Oscar,' he says. He sees now that the knife is one of those you use for modelling, and nods towards it. 'You won't be needing that.'

She smiles. 'No, I'm sorry. We've had a few break-ins, people just walking in off the street. This is my dad's place. He owns the building.' She's still giving him the look, searching for a resemblance to Michael in his features maybe.

'I've got my birth certificate,' he says.

'That's OK, I believe you. You've got your dad's talent for the drums.'

'Was he that bad?'

She takes a moment to find the right word. 'Enthusiastic.' Oscar smiles.

'I didn't know he had a son,' she says.

'Neither did he,' Oscar replies. 'I suppose I shouldn't say that. He did remember me in his will.' He pauses. 'Do you know what happened? The solicitor says it was a heart attack.'

'I think so. The cleaner came in and found him one morning. It was awful.'

'What – it happened here?'

She nods. 'He worked late sometimes. Presumably there was no one else around. He was quite a loner,' she adds. 'Not in a weird way I don't mean. Just self-contained. Well organised. A pretty together sort of guy, he seemed. Such a shame.' Her eyes soften. 'If there's anything you need to know, you can ask my dad. He's on his way in. I'd better get back to my work, I suppose,' she says. She smiles, showing a gap between her teeth that matches his own. 'Come and have a coffee when you're done, if you like.'

'Thanks.'

Oscar doesn't know what to do now. He wonders whether it's OK to be going through a dead man's emails. Are they part of the property? They don't seem to be private anyway. More like business. He realises now that he hasn't asked Miriam what Michael did here. He picks up one of the packages stacked up on the table and turns it

49

over, weighing it in his hand. Maybe he was a drug traf-
ficker, he thinks, smiling to himself. He slits it open using
an artist's scalpel he finds in the sink drawer, rips the layer
of bubblewrap inside and pulls out a small shield made of
polished wood with a raised centre. It's the sort you might
use as a trophy for a cricket team, though without the
metal plate where the name of the team would be inscribed
and the year they won it. A little sticker on the back gives
the manufacturer's name and address.

He sits back down at the computer and spends twenty
minutes sifting through the rest of the emails, most of
which seem to be querying something or checking the
progress of an order, or – in the case of the one from the
small Australian charity – someone introducing himself
with reference to work Michael has done for someone else
and asking him to get in touch to discuss how they might
be of mutual benefit. Oscar goes back to the first email. It
occurs to him that there must be more mail just sitting in
the line waiting to be picked up. He tries to get a connection but there isn't one. He lifts the phone to his ear.
That's dead too. Ah, phone bill, he thinks. Of course.

There's a tap at the door and a man peers in, grey
cropped hair, in his fifties, bit of a belly under his Eagles
T-shirt, neat beard, earring. 'Ken Downey,' he says. 'I
gather you met Miriam.'

Oscar shakes his hand. 'I just came to see what was
here.'

'Yeah, a woman from the solicitors rang to say you'd
been in touch,' he says. 'Michael and me knew each other
from way back. Long before all this.' He gestures, meaning
the whole building, not this little room. 'Oscar, is it?' He
looks at him closely. 'I remember your mother,' he says.

Oscar nods. 'You know that I never knew him –
Michael, I mean.'

50

'That was one of his regrets. But your mother was against it, he said. He tried. I know for the first few years he sent a card and some money on your birthday, even after she took off with her new chap. Eventually, I suppose, he gave up. Water under the bridge, eh?' Ken seems keen to leave now, but Oscar has questions.

'So what kind of work did he do here?' he asks.

'Well, he had a stall down Camden Market, just along the road there. Fridays, Saturdays, Sundays. He did the shields. What do you call it? Family coats of arms, crests and so on. Customer comes along wanting to know about their family name, Michael looks it up in a big book, matches the name to some ancient heraldic design – three lions or whatever – and then makes up the shield for the punter to pick up the next week at the market, or sends it in the post. Pretty simple really. That's what all these paints are. He painted the crests on himself. Quite artistic, your old man. There was some skill there. And look at these books he had. All about tracing your family tree, which he'd started doing too, or helping people do their own, if they asked. That was about it.'

'Can you make a living doing this?'

'He loved it. It was as much a hobby as anything. But, yeah, I guess he made a living. He had his flat in Finsbury Park. I let him have this place cheap, but he always paid up front. You weren't thinking of carrying it on?'

'What?'

'This little business of his – the shields.'

Oscar smiles. 'You must be joking. I wouldn't know the first thing.'

'Well neither did he, to start with. He learnt from scratch. The books are all here. And he showed me some software he used to set up a family tree. It's all in there, in the computer.'

Oscar notices Ken has one of those little Chinese pigtails that used to be popular years ago. How time rushes away and leaves its remnants behind your back like that, he thinks. Older people don't mind. They're not afraid of staying in the era they feel comfortable in. He pulls a heavy book down from the shelf. It's genealogy, he sees now, not geology. 'Looks nice and complicated,' he says, leafing through. Old and leather-bound, colour plates. Maybe it's rare, he thinks. 'Nice book though,' he says. He looks at Ken. 'Had he been ill? Before his heart attack?'

'Oh no. Fit as a fiddle. Kept himself in decent shape. Gave up smoking years ago, occasional beer Friday night. But he did have a funny turn a little while ago, on his birthday, his fiftieth it was. We set up a bit of a surprise, just the people here who Michael knew – had a whip-round for a cake and a bottle of bubbly, bought him a little something. Nothing much, new pair of cufflinks. Loved cufflinks, Michael. Had loads of 'em. Anyway, walked through the door, looked at us all and just fainted away there on the spot. Fainted! He was OK, as it happens. I mean went down like a sack of spuds but came to his senses pretty much straight away and none of us thought any more of it. And then – what, eighteen months later – bang, he's gone. And in the exact same place, which is the amazing thing.' Ken's eyes are on stalks as he tells this. They stand and talk some more, or at least Ken does, recounting stories about Michael and the great times they had when Ken had a recording studio and Michael was the sound engineer, about the bands who came in – one of them actually going on to do quite well, though Oscar has never heard of the Windmills, who Ken in fact managed for a while before getting into property, hence this place and others like it in unfashionable parts of London when small businesses were springing up in the eighties and needed somewhere to start. 'Good old Maggie Thatcher,' says Ken. 'The country was the pits back then. She was the business.'

'Was she?' Oscar says. There's no point arguing about politics with older people. It's like explaining vegetarianism to a dog. Afterwards, when Ken has patted him on the shoulder and gone off, Oscar sits swivelling in the chair for a while smoking a roll-up. Then he takes the big old book with the glossy pages and a smaller one called *British Surnames*, and finds an empty rucksack hanging on a peg to carry them home in.

He thinks about taking up Miriam's offer of coffee, but when he looks in the little window she is eating a sandwich, holding it with both hands, as girls sometimes do, like squirrels. She's staring mesmerised at a little clay model on the workbench as she chews, an animal of some kind it looks like, hunched. Oscar stands and watches her for a moment, her eyes on this thing as her jaw moves steadily, as though the clay model is the centre of just everything and the rest of the room has been arranged around it, like in a painting. This is what Mum means when she talks about having a passion for something, something to love for its own sake, like Dad and his carpets. But where do they come from, passions like this? How do you know when you've found one? He hurries past before she sees him watching – sees in his eyes that she has something he wants.

Chapter 4

Rachel is aware of electric light, of the crackle and smell of cooking, and nearby movement. She raises her head slightly, uncertain of where she is for a few seconds, her uncomprehending eyes bringing the room into focus, waiting for its vague, circling familiarity to lock into place. At last she sits slowly upright on the sofa and, with some difficulty, removes a spit-glued strand of hair from the corner of her mouth, rubs her eyes and touches her cheek where the nap of the cushion has left its imprint. Robert is humming to himself in the kitchen while he clatters with knives and forks above the strain of radio news. He looks up cheerfully from the bubbling pan he is tending as she comes and stands in the doorway. 'I thought I'd let you sleep until dinner was ready,' he says. 'You must be exhausted. I didn't even know you were home till I saw you lying there like a little foetus. What happened to your car?'

She gazes at him, half asleep still, remembering. 'Oh,'

she says, tugging at the cuff of her jacket. 'It's at the warehouse. I had some business in Crowerton that kept me out all afternoon with one of the reps. It didn't seem worth going all the way back over there just to get back here. Can you drive me to the warehouse in the morning?'

He pulls out the grill and turns the pork chops with a fork as he answers. 'If you don't mind going in a bit early. I've got that interim with the greenfield working group. Do you remember me mentioning it?'

She remembers no such meeting, but nods. The smell and crackle of burning fat make her feel queasy here in the tiny overheated kitchen, with the news and sport droning, and Robert warming up, she can tell, to rehearse the fullness of his position on the greenfield interim with its multilateral policy factions that he gets so heated about and its special-interest jockeying and its cronyism, and that's just on the council's policy advisory group. Though it is years since he left the hopelessly poisonous council for the relatively fraternal comforts of a housing association, it is to these arenas of public combat that he so eagerly returns, as a member of this or that community pressure group.

'Hopkins is the unknown quantity, and of course it's his lot who might swing the balance when it comes down to the wire in June and it's thrown open to the general public,' Robert is saying, turning from the hob to reach into the cupboard above the sink for glasses. He puts them on to a tray alongside cutlery and the jar of mustard. 'And who cares what they think? Not Hopkins and his ilk. If we can't twist some arms ahead of that, I don't know what. We might as well say goodbye to any new social housing projects, with the exception of that handful of single- and double-occupancy units we managed to squeeze in on the docks.' He wipes his hands. 'Which was just a sop, the more I think about it. I mean, once public resources start being swallowed up and diverted – and you're talking fifteen hundred new homes on the Windhill site alone – infrastructure budgets will take up the entire—'

'Robert,' she pleads, raising a hand to shut him up. 'Just let me go to the toilet, for goodness' sake.'

'Better be quick then,' he says, frowning, his frenzy of policy issues having now dampened his initial ebullience as he tosses and scrapes the sizzling mess of mushrooms and tomatoes in the pan. 'This lot won't wait.'

She heads up the stairs to the bathroom, where she sits with her eyes closed and her bladder open. 'Mmm . . .' she murmurs, warm thoughts creeping back now of the afternoon's promise of future triumphs, conjured up with Gareth Newnam over a lunch that exceeded by far the hour and a half she had put aside for it, starting as they had with a couple of cold Campari sodas, followed by an expensive bottle of South African red that Gareth chose from the list to accompany their duck in a warm cherry and blackcurrant chutney ('Might as well push the boat out,' he chuckled, 'Rael can afford it') and ending up with not one but two ('Same again, Rachel?') fiery grappas once it became clear the day was already shot and business more than satisfactorily concluded. She was surprised to find herself emerging into the late afternoon sunlight so unsteady on her feet. A risk, now she thinks about it, Gareth having driven a car afterwards. A lot of sense talked, though. It was exhilarating to discuss ways forward in business in so civilised and constructive a fashion, in such convivial surroundings (a table at the Rumney, which Gareth said received a favourable notice from the *Telegraph*'s restaurant critic only last month) and with so cultured a companion. They could do a lot for each other, mutual benefits being mooted, unexploited opportunities in new markets. They raised their glasses as he wished her luck as the new head of Duttings, which he said sounded just the kind of forward-thinking enterprise Rael Eastern were looking to partner in their 'Most Favoured Distributor' scheme. Had she, for instance, thought about theatres or other consumers of luxury contract use? She had to admit she hadn't. It wasn't just designer hotels that were going in for traditional quality, Gareth said, as he sliced neatly through his layered parcel of sauced duck. Think of how many theatres there are in the country, including cinemas! Such a tidy eater for a man with large hands.

Robert is calling. She washes her face. By the time she gets downstairs, he has started without her. 'Sorry,' he says through a mouthful of food. 'Couldn't wait. Starving. You wouldn't believe the day I've had. Wine?'

'Actually, I won't, thanks,' she says, averting her eyes.

He returns to the iniquity of building a village of executive-style homes across the green belt north of Five Ponds Lane while Rachel slowly sets to work cutting her meat, transferring it from one side of her plate to the other in neat triangles. She's thinking about the power of advertising, which Gareth mentioned. Not just the *Gazette*, which Dad always used when they had a sale on ('Total Carpet Madness!'), but colour slots in the makeover magazines and the interiors pages of the Sunday supplements. Radio, too, might be utilised, not so much for its shouty, badly made commercials but for marketing purposes. '*Be* the news,' as Gareth said, smiling, leaning towards her and making an emphatic pinching gesture with his thumb and forefinger. Lovely clean nails for a man. And such a listener. It didn't seem odd that she found herself telling him how she felt Duttings had underperformed over the years, how Dad could have capitalised on current trends but had held back. Laminated flooring, for example, had risen but was now on the ebb. They'd missed that particular boat, but Rachel had been reading about developments in rubber and even leather. You had to keep abreast of the next thing. 'Indeed,' said Gareth gravely, agreeing with her even though it was hardly in his own interest, being a niche carpet and rug man.

'And I know it sounds as though I'm being disloyal to Dad—' she began.

'Absolutely not,' Gareth interrupted, laying down his knife. 'You have to grow the business as you think fit. Forgive me – and no disrespect to your father – but am I right in guessing that he hasn't had your advantages, education wise? Nor, if I may say, is he likely to have the vision required at this stage in his and the company's life to see past his own achievements. What I believe is, it's not simply your right but your *duty* to nurture the business, to make more of it than your father was able to, to take it to a higher level. Remember the parable of the talents in the Bible – the servants who each had to make something of their master's wealth? It's not just a gift, it's more like a stake, or, or ... like seeds that you plant and feed and water until one day the tree bears fruit. As they say in Africa, you can give a starving man a fish but how much better to give him a boat and a net that he might catch his own.'

It was her turn to lean forward, her eyes shining. 'Let me ask you something, Gareth. Is it out of the question to be thinking, down the years, not just about East Anglia but about national coverage with a hundred or whatever branches? Is that too crazy?'

'I don't think it's crazy at all,' Gareth replied, laughing at the very craziness of that notion. 'It's just your natural entrepreneurial spirit.' He paused, lifting his glass. 'And this is your moment.'

58

She could have hugged him. This *is* her moment. Isn't that why she has had the man from Mallicks out scouting for better premises – a showroom, not a warehouse, with properly designed displays, and in the town centre, not out on the peripheral among the oily tyre-fitters and plant-hire people? Of course they'll keep the warehouse, which is wholly owned anyway, though who by exactly – Dad or the business – she's not sure, all the company papers being with old Walter, which is another thing. The point is that modern consumers don't want to see the storage side of things. They don't want their shopping experience tainted by the sight of hairy-arsed carpet fitters sitting around playing cards and eating fried egg sandwiches. They want modern consultants, expertise, confidence, poise, creativity – a conduit for their dreams.

'Not eating?' says Robert.

'I've had enough, thanks,' she says. 'I wasn't really that hungry.'

His injured look appears. 'But you've hardly touched it. Come on, Rachel, I spend twenty minutes cooking you a nice dinner and you've eaten one mouthful. A little appreciation wouldn't go amiss.'

'Yes, yes, I know, I'm sorry. And thank you very much. But I didn't actually ask you to cook. I would have been happy with a yoghurt or something later.'

There's a silence in which they are made aware of the lowing sound of someone practising scales on one of the larger woodwind instruments next door, soft and deep and regular. Robert is staring at his plate now, his lips pressed together, gripping his knife and fork and breathing through his nose, as he does when he wants to give the impression that he is fighting with his emotions. 'To tell you the truth, Rachel, I'm not sure this is such a great idea,' he says at last. 'I mean, look at you – you're *exhausted*, you won't *eat*,

you're *irritable*, you don't have time to *do* anything.' He
enumerates each of these failings with a bulge of the eyes
and a small headbutting movement. 'When was the last
time we went out together?'

She blinks at him. 'You're not sure *what's* a good idea?'

He pauses. 'Well, this . . . this *carpet* fiasco you're getting
yourself into.'

Rachel gets up from the table. 'Thank you,' she mutters,
'thank you *so* much.'

There seems to be nowhere to go in this ridiculous tiny
house, so she stands facing the sitting room window with
her arms folded. Robert is behind her, surprised that his
opening gambit turned so quickly into this. 'Rachel, come
on. Don't take it the wrong way,' he whines. 'I'm just concerned for you. Well, for *us*. We never really discussed the
implications of this, this . . .'

'This fiasco. What do you mean, not discussed it? We
discussed it to death. We *agreed* it would be a good move
for me. You sat there at the table and agreed.'

'I know, but . . .'

'But what? What?'

'Well, other things,' he says, reasonably. 'You know, for
example, it doesn't seem that long since we were talking
about trying for a child. In fact, it doesn't seem that long
since Stuart was talking about grandchildren.'

'Well maybe he was talking about someone else having
them. Let Oscar have some. He's not busy at the moment.
Or bloody Emma.'

'The thing is, if . . . when we do decide, wouldn't it be
more sensible to stick to something you can do part time,
utilise the skills you have?'

'No it would not. I don't want to be a public finance
officer all my life. I want this chance. I want to broaden
what I am. I want something else.'

'OK, calm down, I know all that. I know.' He puts his hands on her shoulders. 'It's just that it seems to be taking you over. Don't you see?'

Rachel turns to face him but keeps her arms folded. 'Robert, I'm running a business. Of course it takes your time up. So does anything worthwhile. It's an investment in the future, isn't it?' she adds in a softer, pleading tone.

Robert seems mollified by this gentler talk of the future, and now looks as if he might be sorry he made such a fuss over the chops, though he probably thinks he has a point. Like many who work in the helping professions, Robert will go the extra mile to accommodate someone else's needs (whether they want him to or not), only to complain afterwards at their not being grateful enough. How often he seems to arrive home from the office in a mood of dark bewildered hurt, martyred with the arrows of his own unrequited thoughtfulness.

'Anyway, isn't it better to take advantage of my higher earnings now to start saving? We won't want to live in this rabbit hutch for ever,' she adds, feeling that this more than adequately touches upon Robert's anxiety regarding the remote possibility of children without her having either to share his enthusiasm or declare her invulnerability to maternal cravings. 'We could put our name down for one of those green-belt executive homes you were talking about.'

'Not funny, Rachel,' he says, but he smiles anyway, glad to have smoothed things over. Robert hates fights, preferring to teach others the error of their ways by persuasion and uninteresting statistics. He kisses her on the forehead. 'Come on, have some wine.'

They sit back down at the table. 'Having said that,' she frowns, watching him pour, 'I must speak to Dad. I'm not sure he should still be taking a salary out of the business.

It's supposed to be a retainer, for consultancy, but frankly I could do without it. His consultancy, I mean.'

'But you must have agreed to it.'

'Well, yes, naturally I did – I didn't have any choice, did I? But it does seem excessive. And that car – he's driving around in that huge Lexus while I've just got his old Avensis. That can't be right.'

The gulp of wine she takes to emphasise her point draws her headache into the next pain belt, adding an underlying hum to this unwanted conversation with Robert, whose silence on the question of her father's ambiguous 'steering' role at Duttings wearies and dispirits her further, speaking as it does not only of his pessimism regarding the enterprise and its effect on their marriage but now of her going back on promises made. Rachel raises a hand to her right temple. She needs to put her head down somewhere, to recapture, perhaps in a good night's sleep, those clean vistas dreamed up over lunch with Gareth, those endless miles of blue unshadowed by the rolling cumulus of life's naysayers and doubters.

'Maybe you have to be patient with Stuart,' Robert is saying. 'Look at it from his point of view—'

'Actually,' she interrupts, 'I think I might get an early night.'

He gives one of his rueful smiles, reaching across the table to take both of her hands in his. 'Why don't I run you a nice hot bath?' he murmurs. 'I could give you one of my special massages if you like. How does that sound?'

Robert is an enthusiastic believer in the mood-enhancing properties of massage, and though he is far from being even a competent practitioner he is inclined to call upon its rudimentary powers as a soother in all matters of marital disharmony and an all too transparent conduit to sexual foreplay. Rachel has neither encouraged nor objected to

62

this ploy, even when Robert announced plans to 'broaden' his range with lessons in Indian head massage at the Community College, an aspiration stymied in the end, she remembers, by a block of late meetings of some committee scheduled for the first six Wednesdays of the course. Impossible moments like this seem to stifle possibility itself, but it is not in Robert's nature to countenance inevitability. For all his bluster, public service has sharpened in him the art of compromise. He prides himself on being able to catch things before they break, to acquaint himself with the geography of likely disappointment. Here at home he identifies every emotional crevasse that opens up before him as a practical challenge, there being none so wide that it cannot be spanned by an act of kindness, every negative force offering the opportunity for a countervailing gesture of love. He has learnt to balance his tendency to irritate or bore people – colleagues, strangers, his wife – with rewards for putting up with him. He buys cake to share in the office; at weddings or other social gatherings he might be found advising someone on the best way to get to this or that remote tourist attraction; he brings flowers home for her. Sometimes, coming to bed late, she finds he has squeezed a loving slick of toothpaste on to her brush. For all his faults, Robert is not irredeemably *anything*. But while she is often fatigued by his tireless faith in simple remedies, here she is suddenly shamed by his attempt to retrieve something from the evening when she would have been as happy not to, and, absurdly, even finds herself overcome with feelings of charity for the chop he grilled for her while she slept, arranged now in pieces on the plate like a symbol of cold neglect. The wine, which might on another occasion have stoked her to bloody-mindedness, vividly illuminates this difference between them – this one-sided effort to halt the recent slippage in their marriage that

63

she has felt but failed to acknowledge – and brings grateful tears to her eyes. 'That would be nice,' she says.

So, yes, she allows Robert to prepare a hot bath and to gently manipulate her temples with his fingertips as she reclines, drowsy in the soapy water; and afterwards, perfumed and still faintly steaming in the bedroom, consents to making love doggy fashion, the intrusive farting notes of the mystery woodwind still filtering through the wall from next door, the chance of being spotted by other neighbours across the street – theoretically possible in this light through the net curtains – adding a charge of danger and bravado that seems to drive Robert beyond the compass of his usual endurance (already he is entering into the spirit of things as though there may be a prize for most considerate spouse) while paradoxically drawing Rachel into a parallel reverie in which for some reason she feels wickedly free to imagine these rearward thrustings and gruntings to be those of Gareth Newnam, a man she hardly knows at all.

Chapter 5

Three weeks or longer has passed since the housewarming at High Firs, and Stuart is out tasting the air at the Willows Golf Club, some four miles east of the town. Everyone is so busy. Diane he has left experimenting with paint colours in the upstairs lumber room, as she calls it, and Oscar sprawling in the lounge with the books he brought back from London and others that he borrowed from the library. They're to do with family trees, he says. Diane hates it that Oscar seems to be delving into the past (or her past, as she sees it), and yesterday, out of the blue, demanded to know who this Miriam girl was who had rung twice. ('He *is* thirty-two,' Stuart reminded her at breakfast. 'Who knows, maybe he'd like to settle down and get married.') Diane has become fanatically silent on the subject, preferring to fill what conversational interludes they share these days overpraising Rachel's ambitions to drag dull, antiquated Duttings into the present day. 'You need to just stand back for a while,' she said. 'Give the girl some room.'

'Room? The way she's going there'll be enough room to stage *Ben Hur*. What she needs is guidance. And not only on the technical side – there are right and wrong ways of doing things. I'm supposed to be consulted. I want to be consulted. That's what I'm there for. I can insist. I am still a director – and the major shareholder.'

'We are, you mean,' she said quietly. 'Between us. But what's the point in having new blood if they don't do something different? Isn't that why we gave her the thirty-four per cent?'

'We gave her the thirty-four because she held out for the thirty-four.'

'Even so, she's either running the show or she's not. You mustn't resent something just because you didn't think of it yourself.'

'What am I resenting now?'

'I don't know. Whatever it is you're so worried about. Thinking about new premises, looking at new suppliers. What you really seem to be worried about is Rachel not being an identical version of yourself. You can't stick labels on people, Stuart, especially your children. Marj at college says we should celebrate their capacity to surprise.'

'I don't see you celebrating Oscar's capacity to surprise,' Stuart found himself saying. 'What would Marj at college think about that?'

Diane stood up and stamped off to the kitchen, but then almost immediately came back. 'He's not being surprising, he's being secretive.'

Stuart looked up from his coffee. 'But Diane, my love, that's because you're being so uptight with him. And what's so secretive? He's got his four grand, he's inherited a load of junk that will no doubt end up in our garage and he's taking an interest in something for a change, even if it's only those family histories. What else is there?'

'Stuart . . .' She sat down and composed herself to speak, resting her palms on her legs. 'It's this whole other scene in London that I left behind years ago. I just don't want anything to do with it now. It was my decision to make a clean break with Michael, and there was a lot of ill feeling at the time. I don't want Oscar dragging it all up again, and I just feel he is somehow. It should be over. It *is* over. I just find it upsetting.'

'But look, it's not as if he's running off to find his real mother. If anyone should have a problem with it it's me, and I don't. Give the boy some room.' It was a mistake to throw that back at her, with Diane just starting to open up, with the opportunity approaching maybe to broach the question of Oscar's money, and how he might use it to find a little flat somewhere and get started with some gainful employment if his wandering days were as over as they seemed to be.

'Oh that's very clever. What I don't understand is – since when did you start standing up for Oscar? You're the one who's been on his back for years. You're just being awkward because of Rachel.'

'Let's not go back to Rachel.'

'Well, I don't want to talk about Oscar.'

'Fine, so let's not talk.'

He put it behind him, but with the completion of golf the feeling returns, this sense of his waning influence over things. It's not just Rachel, but Diane too, as though they're instinctively shifting away from him. They're like animals that can tell when your time is up. Leaving him to the wolves.

Fly me to the moon. Close behind him, that's Tony whistling *his* song. Stuart has been humming it all the way

67

round the course and now Tony has stolen it. Stuart adjusts his bag where it digs into his shoulder. It is late afternoon, and there is a fine gauze of drizzle in the air as Stuart's foursome approach the clubhouse with its red sloping roof and the long window of the restaurant extension looking like a pleasure boat, he always thinks, the way it faces the weather full-on, revealing the soft glow of white napery on the tables inside, empty at this time of day. Laughing now and ribbing Gordon Malloy over his six-inch putt at the seventeenth, they each heave their bags and waterproofs into the spacious boots of their respective expensive vehicles before breezing into the panelled lobby area, with its mahogany trophy cabinet and wall of photographs capturing past victories, pro-am press calls, the official opening of the extension by Jimmy Tarbuck, a visit by Prince Charles in Jubilee year. There's one, too, of Stuart himself wearing a chef's hat taken during last summer's charity barbecue.

'Come on, that was Pete's fault,' Gordon is still protesting in a high voice, 'putting me off with that whale joke.'

'Here we go,' says Stuart, feeling his spirits rise despite everything, with the warmth and promise of refreshed companionship. This can still be real and vibrant. The back door at the end of the corridor opens and Stuart raises his hand in greeting as Jos Raymond emerges carrying a bulk pack of paper towels. Jos is the clubhouse manager.

'Watch out, the reprobates are in,' he calls, presumably to Annie, who is out of sight in the store room next to the toilets. Stuart chuckles and ushers the others into the bar and calls for service. It's his habit to get the first round of drinks in ahead of Tony, to stand with his foot on the brass rail exchanging foolish pleasantries with young Chris behind the bar and picking from the dish of smoked almonds while he completes the order, laughing at his own raillery. 'Did you want rocks with that Scotch?' he shouts to Pete. Pete Tree – not his real name, Swedish parentage, apparently, or Danish, he can't recall – turns to answer, the baby of the group, barely forty but grey as a railway pigeon, balding fast too. Quite an odd sort of accent he has, a kind of upper-class English tinged with something else from having spent time with extended family in the fjords or wherever in his teens. He has that proper way of talking English you sometimes get from growing up with foreigners. Unusual in the roofing business, albeit one worth a million and growing by all accounts. Builders love him, those Scandinavian-style roofs across East Anglia, the timbers actually finished out there, then brought here. Traditional but with that cleanness they have, the Scandinavians.

Stuart yawns. The place is empty, though there's a couple of parties still out there in the drizzle, one of them half a mile down the hill now, knocking balls into the lake. He stares for a moment at the figures, one measuring up for a chip by the look of it, two others watching, one pointing, gloved hand resting on his club, no, *her* club. Tuesday is often golf for self-made men (or, of course, women now too) of the town who are free to leave their diaries empty for the occasional afternoon and take advantage of the cheaper rate, the half-deserted course and whatever sort of rain the season might bring. There's something sexy about a golfing woman. He glances at his friends – more like associates you might say – as he waits for the drinks, these familiar points of an irregular triangle in the fading light furthest from the window. They'll put the lamps on soon. It's a snug feeling, being in here with things getting squally out in the wild. Young Chris, hair swept up to a peak like praying hands, sets down the tray, thick-walled tumblers clinking satisfyingly with ice, white curl of the bill – twelve and a half quid – refracted there in the glass like a still life.

Stuart has been coming to the Willows since the club launched in the early seventies with its inaugural offer of eight hours' tuition with each full membership taken out. By the time Tony finally got wind and submitted his application, the bar staff were already familiar enough with Stuart's tipple to have it poured and ready by the time he'd crossed the threshold, and the chairman himself (old Len Wavesey, now dead and commemorated with a plaque and picture above reception) had had the downstairs rooms in his own substantial home at Ulstead entirely fitted out in Duttings' best deep English Deluxe burgundy velvet with Axminster borders at trade price, or very nearly. Of course, in truth there were only a few months between Stuart and Tony joining the Willows, and in view of this it seems a silly thing, especially given the years that have now passed, that it still pleases Stuart to think of Tony as the newcomer. But the fact is you can't catch up, no matter what. It's no different to being older than someone, or for that matter being the first to have slept with, and married, a particular woman.

Gordon is telling Tony, by no means for the first time, that the profits are being squeezed out of brown goods for smaller high-street independents, that his days are numbered, that he's glad his two boys have had the education at least and gone into solid selling careers in pharmaceuticals and insurance. Tony sits back with his legs apart, nodding as if he's giving it some serious thought, tossing nuts into his mouth. 'But what about digital?' he asks. 'And all these flat-screen plasma home-cinema set-ups we see going for six and seven grand?'

Can Tony really be interested? Though the same might be said of carpets. How often has Stuart found himself declaiming the merits of a Corinthian weave, or describing the majesty of a Wilton loom at full throttle – or even the humble working beauty of the 'tuft withdrawal tensometer', a machine he still has as a keepsake on the corner of his desk – to the glazed expressions of those around him?

('Have a guess what this does, Rachel . . .'

'No idea. Yoghurt-maker?')

It's only a trade, but you might as well be talking Hungarian to the girl. The way Rachel sees it, there's no value in persisting with Hungarian when you can get by without it. He sometimes wonders how she feels, crossing that historic Duttings threshold every morning. Has it hit her yet? Will it ever? He summons it to mind now, the mingling of old and new smells in the cold air, musty and chemical-fresh, before the heating goes on in the morning. Even the burr and click of the kettle paint an instant picture, steam on the window, Barbara officiating. Morning biscuits. The first phone call of the day. Ah.

'Makes no difference,' Gordon is saying, shaking his head. 'We're cut to the bone. And you can't add value in the way you could before, with expertise and taking the time to guide the customer through the features. There's no premium in the personal touch these days. It seems like a lifetime ago you could sell a television or tie someone into a long-term rental just on the strength of people liking you. Not to mention aftersales and so forth. No one's interested in the service end any more. The chains – and they're all out there on the peripheral and even further, where rents and rates are low and customers can drive right up to the door – they're cleaning up just selling boxes, and that's all the punter wants. Boomf, thank you very much, straight in the back of the four-by-four, more often than not with a wedge of extended warranty on top to make up your

71

margin. We can't compete. Typical profile of our customer is getting to be old people without cars who don't know how anything works. Might as well give it up tomorrow and join the early retired, like Stuart here. Spend all day playing golf.'

'Semi-retired,' says Stuart. 'Even I can't play golf every day.' He puts his glass to his lips and takes a sip, absorbing Gordon's faintly worrying tale.

'First step to an early grave,' says Tony, 'according to all the psychiatric research and so on. Men of our generation who give up the treadmill but then can't stop running. We're built for work. Once the old brain goes into decline, that's it. *Pooof.*'

'Oi, who you calling a poof?' grins Gordon, raising his glass.

'It's nature's way of accepting your three months' notice, old mate,' Tony says, ignoring Gordon. He scoops up the last of the nuts in the bowl and turns to ask Chris for a refill in that proprietorial way he has that irks Stuart. Still. It does seem like old times here, all of them dressed in their weekend gear on a Tuesday, only difference being that the other three got changed in the office and Stuart has his on every day. He gives another yawn and blinks.

'I hope we're not keeping you up, Stuart,' says Pete Tree, not a natural wit being Scandinavian, but still milking the success of his whale joke.

'Sorry,' Stuart says. 'Must be all the fresh air.' In fact, he realises, he *is* tired. Although he seems to do nothing but sleep these days, the truth is he's up twice a night to pee, which gives him something to think about until Diane's radio alarm goes off at seven-forty, by which time he is too exhausted to get up but too awake to go back to sleep, the county news and ads and pop songs forcing their messages into his muddle of a mind. Yesterday he dozed off for

72

twenty minutes just looking out at the starlings doing that walk they do on the back lawn.

'Stress can make you tired,' Tony announces.

'Stuart's stressful days are behind him,' says Pete. 'Lucky man.'

There's a silence while Tony makes a production out of lighting his cigar.

'How's Penny?' Stuart asks, as he is always careful to ask, after her womb problem way back when Emma was little.

'Fine. She's still on this HRT kick. Green tea too. All sorts of stuff. Diane?'

'Championship form, thanks. Emma?'

Tony gives a serious nod. '*Very* well. And young Rachel – how goes the empire?' He drains his drink and swirls the ice in the glass.

'I'd be the last to know.'

'I can't believe that,' says Tony, nevertheless edging forward in his seat to hear more.

Stuart contemplates his own drink. Tony revels in what he sees as the great folly of letting Rachel take a controlling stake in the business. But how else was she to be prised out of what she calls her perfectly good career with the council? And even that act of magnanimity could only be formalised after he'd won the tug of war over Oscar, whom Diane felt should have been given a chance with the firm, him being the eldest after all. 'Think about it,' Diane said. 'Isn't Oscar the one who needs a bit of direction just now? Isn't that what you keep saying?'

It was the night of the fireworks and fancy dress here at the Willows, two years ago, returning home in the taxi, Diane in an angel costume, her hair gloriously unleashed and glittering with silver, he remembers, for the occasion. Stuart had gone as Guy Fawkes in a tall hat and carrying a

73

bomb with a fuse. 'I have thought about it,' he said. 'It won't work.' Diane clammed up for the rest of the journey, offering no more than an impatient look even when, on arrival at their old house in Malting Street, the taxi had almost driven off with his full-length conspirator's cloak trapped in the door. What had happened to the old Diane, he wondered, who always insisted that Oscar needed the space to find himself, and other such hippy nonsense? Oscar had made his bed. You reap what you sow.

He imagines a better-ordered life in which Luke would have been the eldest, go-getting son, Rachel would have given him a grandchild and if necessary sorted herself out with a jobshare at the council, and Oscar could have continued to enjoy himself on the outskirts of the planet. Nothing is so simple. With his doubts over Rachel, Stuart feels a disintegration of things. What is it with families that for a while seems so uncomplicated, when children are young and happy to be led by the hand, all that innocence captured in memories of picnics or seaside outings and everyone singing in the car, but then is gradually lost until it's as much as you can do to get everyone round the supper table once a year? Even Diane is floating off doing her own thing after years of knowing she was there needing him, and vice versa. He feels the pull of her now, tugging at him in a vague, barely perceptible way, like a drifting thought you can't bring to mind.

He runs his hand through his unstoppably thinning hair, frowns, then digs out the business card given to him by the rep from this so-called Rael Eastern outfit. He hands it to Tony. 'You ever come across these guys on your travels?' Tony shrugs and passes it to the others, who inspect it dumbly.

'Importers. Rachel has started moving in exotic circles.' Stuart puts the card away again. 'They're not listed with any of the trade associations, and when I rang the number, the woman was foreign. Asked if she could take my number for someone to ring back. Spanish I'd say she was.'

'Doesn't mean anything. Everything's global now,' Tony says. 'I wouldn't worry about Spanish accents. Business is business these days. You've got to take your opportunities wherever they come from. Even Barcelona.'

Gordon laughs. 'As long as it don't get delivered by donkey,' he says. 'Did I tell you about that trip we did in Crete last year, me and Ange? This village in the hills where they had us treading grapes? Those two goats and the donkey? Did I show you the pictures?'

'I believe you did,' Tony says.

'My shout, I think,' Pete says, getting to his feet. He makes a circle with his finger. 'Same again, boys? Gordon?'

'Ask Chris to give it a splash of soda this time,' Gordon says, rubbing his hands. 'I've got to drive all the way to Angela's mother's. There's a lot of nutters on the road in this weather.'

It's gone seven when Stuart arrives home. Diane shouts from the kitchen, before he's through the door, to say he left his birdwatching book out on the balcony in the rain. He follows her voice, thinking she must be preparing dinner, but no, she's washing paintbrushes in the sink. 'Strictly speaking,' he says, hanging his zipper jacket on the back of a chair, 'I didn't *leave* it out in the rain, because it wasn't raining when I was up there.'

'Well it's still wet,' she says, too busy to look at him, too busy splashing the window as she works, sending pink streams wriggling down the glass.

'Where is everyone?' he asks.

She glances at him quickly, turning the taps off, squeezing the brushes, in a rush as usual. She has paint in her hair. 'Upstairs. Luke's teaching Oscar how to use the computer if you please, when he should be revising his German. And of course neither of them has eaten. Actually . . .' She points at the fridge. 'Would you mind cooking? I got some of those ready-meals from Marks's and I think there's still a Viennetta in the freezer.' She ducks past him, as though avoiding an embrace, though he knows better than to offer one. 'Sorry, I must get organised,' she says, 'I've got a colour seminar first thing in the morning and I haven't even sorted my emulsion palette out yet.'

'That sounds urgent,' Stuart says, though Diane is now out of the room and halfway up the stairs.

He's just found the ready-meals when Luke comes in and hunts in the cupboard for crisps. 'Don't eat those,' Stuart says. 'I'm just about to cook.'

'But I'm hungry now,' Luke says, already ripping the packet apart as he turns and hesitates, his jaw hanging open in that look of sullen complaint teenagers have. He seems taller by a foot than Stuart, standing here in his socks, his white school shirt hanging out at the front, ink on one of the cuffs, a boy with everything in him to be a man.

Stuart relents. 'OK, I'll call you when it's ready.'

Rock music thrums through the ceiling as he sets the microwave and stands with a fork in his hand, sees himself in the darkening window, his widening bulk, the spotlight bringing out the best of his scalp. Three days after Stuart's own sixteenth birthday, he remembers his father driving him to Cambridge early one morning in the Bedford and putting him on the train to Pressman Mills Limited of Birmingham to see how a carpet was woven. His father gave him instructions not to mumble if someone addressed him, but to speak up and indeed, if invited, to ask questions himself. A lady of his mother's age from the office had been sent to meet him at the station, and from there they took a

76

bus out to the factory on the outskirts. Sitting next to him, she asked his name and pointed out the city's main streets and buildings as they passed by, and offered him a sweet of some kind which he was too nervous to accept, feeling only later the shame of his ingratitude – or stupidity, or both – in refusing it. What stays in his memory is her heavy secretarial glasses, and then – suddenly looming – the statue of a Victorian gent, seated high above the cobbled courtyard, and on top of that, later, the chattering of the Axminster looms in the great weaving hall, the jagging movements of the needles and spring of the coloured yarns, the smell of the dyehouse and, later still, the gleam and smoothness of the wood in the director's office where tongue sandwiches were served in the afternoon by a maid with a trolley. There was a cake on a stand and cups and saucers for the tea. The director – a Mr Threwell with a high, pink bald head – took a genial interest in the boy sitting before him in his itchy Sunday jacket, and related the history of the company under a portrait of its founder Sir Titus Pressman, not seeming to mind that Stuart could barely bring himself to utter his own name in return.

He remembers being driven back to the station in one of the company's flatbed trucks, but not much more of that journey back in the dark, via Cambridge and the low-lying spread of East Anglia. He didn't have the understanding then to think of his visit as a rite of passage, or to wonder how difficult it had been to arrange or what insights he was expected to gain from it. It was only the next evening, after work at the lock-up on Woodhampton Road, when his father marched him into the tap room of the Ring of Angels and set before him a half-pint of Adnams best bitter, that he began to sense what hopes he had for him. He held the glass as he had seen the older boys do, with his little finger stretching to support the base, and sipped cautiously at the creamy head, now and then taking a potato crisp from the waxy bag with blue writing as he watched the labourers from Winstons throwing darts at the board while his father stood at the bar exchanging the day's woes with other men of the town. It must have been in the seventies that the Ring of Angels got knocked down when they widened the road, a whole beery history of urinals and nicotine buried there, under three lanes of slow-moving traffic. All the men wore caps in those days. No one questioned it. You just did. Learning was looking and listening, not making it up as you went along. That's how the knowledge was passed on, not just the fact but the thrill of it. You became a part of something bigger, the rhythm of its machinery pulsing in your ears, its regular movement with you for ever. It drums in him still today like a second heartbeat.

So, he thinks, what if it is true? What if he *is* too set in his ways, as Diane believes? What if Rachel *does* have the brains and stamina and an eye for new things? The fabric of a business is like a carpet itself, if that's not too fanciful, and only experience can reveal its shades of meaning, its many ins and outs, the implications of its repeat patternings, the character and content of its fibre – see, for instance, how it can look darker depending on the angle of the pile, depending on whether you're staring into the lay or away from it, depending on how much you're seeing of the yarn, which (as Stuart's father once explained to him, crouching and pointing with a length of gripper) will always reflect more light than the cut ends of the tufts. Anyone can admire a carpet, but few know – or, actually, care to know, and that's fair enough – the mysteries of its durability, its capacity to absorb the whispers and echoes around itself, to hold the electricity of human movement in the fine and wiry sculptures of its natural or manmade extrusions. A business has hidden depths in the same way, doesn't it?

There's the gloss of it – your advertising, your shop window, your ambience and cunning. But there's also the works – your systems, your stock-keeping, your clerical, your facts and figures. It's an art but it's a science too. You have to master the whole shebang.

Chapter 6

When Oscar arrives at ten-thirty to pick Diggsy up at his 'flat' – it's no more than a room he lives in, rent-free, above the Green House – Bonner and Ralphie have suddenly sprung from somewhere. The curtains are closed to the morning and Bonner is on the edge of the sofa rolling a cigarette under the light of the one bulb when Diggsy opens the door and lets Oscar in. 'My *God*, look at you,' Bonner says when he sees him. Reaching out with his foot, he nudges Ralphie, the mound of him covered by a blanket on the floor, still as a dead horse and giving off the smell of one. Ralphie grunts then turns quickly, like someone caught asleep on watch, and blinks up at Oscar. 'Jesus . . .'

Oscar has had a haircut and a shave, and is wearing new clothes – combats, suede trainers and an inoffensive sweat-shirt he bought off a stall in the market. 'Dude,' he says with dryness to Bonner, nodding. 'Ralphie.'

'I hear you've joined the global capitalist classes,' Bonner says, looking at him, weasel-faced, running his tongue along the cigarette paper, manipulating the roll-up between his thin fingers, spitting a strand of tobacco. Ralphie turns his bulk to the wall. 'That's treason, man,' he murmurs in a cracked voice over the hill of his own shoulder.

Diggsy pulls on a T-shirt and shakes his hair at the mirror, where Oscar is staring pointedly back at him. 'I only mentioned it in passing,' he says. Diggsy's defensive face is redder and blotchier than usual, the telltale battle-field of an acned youth. He looks terrible, glowing with it.

'I haven't decided anything,' Oscar says. He sits down on one of the two chairs at the table, sticky with spilt sugar and takeaway detritus and last night's teabags. 'So what brings you two to our lovely town?'

'Meet a few people,' Bonner says, 'about local issues. See Diggsy here. Then we're off to Norfolk, meet a few more people. Got any spliff?'

'Diggsy's your man,' Oscar says.

'He tells us his stash is bare,' Bonner says, glancing at Diggsy. 'I'd love to believe him but somehow I don't.'

Though Bonner speaks in the manner of someone accustomed to being listened to, there is a sneer about everything he says. He is older than the others here – mid to late thirties – a child of the miners' strike, or so Oscar has gathered from Bonner's tales, which evoke vivid images of a sixth-form gesturer in boy bandanna and boy sunglasses, then a student digger, a damager of property and upholder of common rights, a soldier of the ragged army that stalked Thatcher's Britain and saw no reason to stop when she did – saw, rather, his triumph in her fall, legitimacy for more fight. He still wears the badge of anarchy on his clothes. This is what he knows. To latecomers to the game – inquisitive drifters like Oscar – the Bonners of this world within a world have their threat to recommend them. The basic unit of struggle, he believes, is the mad cunt willing to cast the first stone. How else do you get on the news? In the protests and marches Oscar has attended he has only once seen anyone throw a petrol bomb and that was Bonner – an animal-rights standoff at a lab outside Cambridge, the arc of the bottle terminating abruptly (with a surprisingly deep breaking sound, he remembers, not the tinkling shatter you expect) right in front of a police horse, the carpet of fire setting the beast rearing and swivelling in one movement like a billowing flame itself, all but unseating its rider, a woman officer, her face illuminated with panic. Bonner made his escape in the uproar and they all met up afterwards. Oscar joined in the laughter but the episode scared him to death. If you're going to shoot a prisoner, Bonner said, his eyes shining with vanity, make sure the others are watching. It's an old Japanese proverb.

That was in '98 and the moment Oscar felt himself slowly retreating from the fray. It had been a rugged sort of fun. He had lived in trees to save wildlife from the brutal aftershock of transport policies. He had been dragged unresisting by police out of the path of oncoming earth-moving equipment, been up in court for obstruction and spent five days in jail (without the knowledge of his parents) for non-payment of the resulting fine. He had watched Bonner rifle a cash register in broad daylight. If he had once flattered himself into thinking he was front-line material, Cambridge was the day he changed his mind. It wasn't his revulsion at the carnival air of violence and casual destruction that marred these supposedly peaceable protests – he had stomached this without complaint in the past – so much as Bonner (and his acolytes) refusing to countenance the irony of animal rights activists throwing bombs at horses.

'I'm waiting for supplies,' says Diggsy, the lie all over his face.

Bonner turns to Oscar. 'Oscar, you're a man of substance,' he says, exhaling smoke. 'You could stand half an ounce for your old mates – for old times' sake.'

Oscar is keen to take Diggsy and leave. 'I'll see what I can do,' he says, feeling an unfamiliar empowerment in having favours to bestow.

'Good man. We promise not to leave town.'

He nods. 'Diggsy, are you ready? That traffic's going to be a nightmare.'

'Actually . . .' Diggsy says, 'the thing is, it's a bit tricky. I said I'd do the lunchtime shift for Ray. He's a bit stuck without Sheila this week.'

'But I thought you said he'd got Sophie coming in?'

'Yeah, she called in sick. She's got her period.'

'When?'

'What, her—'

'No, no, when did she call?'

'Last night,' he says, staring hard into Oscar's eyes. 'After you'd gone.'

Oscar reads the stare. 'OK. I suppose I can manage. I'd better go. I'll catch you later, Diggs. You guys too.'

Oscar leaves the flat and goes back down to the van. Troy is at the driver's side, jumping up and down and clawing the window excitedly. Oscar is set to open the van door when Diggsy comes springing after him in his stockinged feet, his face even redder out here in the daylight.

'Well?' Oscar says.

'Sorry, mate,' says Diggsy, 'I can't leave them up there on their own.'

'What, they might find your drugs?'

'No, no, not that – well, not only that. I need to be

83

around. Ray's already pissed off with me for being out of my face at Sophie's on Tuesday when I was supposed to be working, and he'll go spare if he finds out I've got lodgers. I mean, he wouldn't mind if it was a girl I'd got up there, but these two? And with the club right below us and Ray still massively paranoid after last year with that northern bloke, what was his name, drinking the bar dry every night and fucking off without notice . . .'

'So Sophie's what?'

'Oh, she's fine. Well in fact she *has* got her period but—'

'Stop right there,' Oscar says. He digs in his pocket and counts out two tens and a five. 'Here, let them have some of that grass you've got.'

Diggsy looks at the money. 'Are you sure?'

'No problem. And if there's any change, maybe you could get Ralphie some deodorant. My treat.'

Miriam rang twice while Oscar was out at the club. The second time she left a message with Mum to say there was a tenant lined up for the unit at Crown House, and though obviously there was no rush – if it was too difficult or inconvenient – officially the lease was up at the end of the month, so if Oscar could give her or Ken a ring just to let them know.

'What is this *about*, Oscar? Who is this girl ringing up every five minutes?' Mum demanded to know, shaking her newly unruly hair at him.

'Nobody. She works at Michael's studio. I told you, there's some stuff to pick up. Ken's one of his old friends and Miriam is his daughter. He said you might remember him – Ken Downey?'

Mum clattered dishes in the sink. 'No, I don't. I don't remember any Ken, or anyone else from those days. My advice is just to collect these things and come straight home.'

Oscar laughed. 'Mum, listen to yourself. What's happening to you?'

'It's not funny, Oscar. There's more to life than coming and going as you please, and upsetting everyone. Think of how others might feel.'

He ducked the argument and went up to his room to read. He could have pursued that point. It's not true that he doesn't think of how others feel. Didn't he spare Mum's feelings when he shrugged and said it was cool that Rachel was coming into the business with Dad? Didn't he relieve Dad's awkwardness (he could tell they'd discussed this carve-up a hundred times before announcing it) by showing enthusiasm for the proposed changeover? Didn't he poke fun at Rachel about it so she wouldn't mistake him for someone who had changed his spots and craved the trappings of ownership and power? Of course he had no interest in carpet retailing. But then neither did Rachel. It wasn't as if *she* didn't have to be talked into it.

Increasingly he has become aware of playing the role of himself – a person of no great appetite, someone who bends with the wind, with no feelings either way. It is a hard habit to kick, sustained as it is by others with a stake in it too. Without complaint he accepts the small burdens of his mother's need to mother him, his father's to disapprove, his sister's to look down on his aimlessness. He is in no position to confound expectations. In return for his family's indulgence, he forfeits the right to change. And yet all around him change is in the air. He is learning to breathe it.

When Oscar hits London's eastern suburbs, he has the idea of calling Emma at her office. She often says he should

ring if he's in town, and here he is, with the City's financial citadels in clear sight. He has no particular plan as he
pulls over to the side of the road and calls up the number
she gave him. He hardly expects her to drop everything
with a view to meeting him miles away on the other side of
London and helping him fill an old van with old rubbish;
in fact he barely expects her to be free to come to the
phone. He is surprised, then, when she not only answers it
herself, but says it would be great to see him and maybe
she can buy him lunch.

She can't get out of the office for forty minutes at least,
but that's OK because it takes that long to lose himself in
the canyons of narrow streets that lead him more than once
at walking pace around St Paul's, pursued by a convoy of
blaring black cabs, and then, having pinpointed his position,
to find somewhere to park near enough to Blackfriars
Bridge.

He waits with Troy on the appointed corner and eventually sees her hurrying along, dressed in banker's black
apart from the white blouse, the corner of her mac flapping
in the wind. He gives her an awkward hug and she fusses
over Troy and ruffles Oscar's new hair ('very stylish') and
tells him she's found just the place to eat – a gastro pub
that just opened near the river. 'By the way,' she says in his
ear as she takes his arm to walk, 'I'd arranged to see
Vaughan, so he'll be coming too – I hope you don't mind.
He said he'd meet us there.'

'No that's cool,' Oscar says, not missing a step, but feeling the threat of this new prospect. He has nothing
personally against Vaughan – he seemed pleasant enough on
the one occasion they met, just before Christmas, when
Emma stopped off with him to deliver an armful of presents
on their way to Penny and Tony's – it's just that he would
have rather had her to himself. To start with, there's the

vague social awkwardness he often feels around people with jobs and mortgages. For all that he is happy with who he is, he is nevertheless an habitual avoider of situations in which he might come under pressure to be more like everyone else. But he feels the hurt of disappointment, too. He is disoriented by the way that this new lunch development – the way he is being dropped awkwardly into the middle of a prior engagement between Emma and her boyfriend – seems to put into a less flattering perspective her enthusiasm for seeing him today, somehow casting a shadow on his assumed intimacy with her. The closeness between them that since their childhood days effortlessly transcended family connections is belied here by the ease with which she has now slotted him into her other plans. There are few enough people in your life you can talk to. For him, Emma is one of them. But, of course – and, stupidly, he realises this only now, here on alien territory – she's not really like him at all. It is different for her. She has this whole other life here, whole other sets of people to talk to.

He tethers Troy to the fence outside. His mind hasn't registered the name of the pub, and inside, at the table, where Vaughan greets Emma with a kiss, and Oscar with a powerful handshake, he stares for some time at the print on the menu before ordering at random, while doing his best to appear animated and friendly. The food, when it arrives, seems to daze him further. He drops his fork and waits for another to arrive under the onslaught of Vaughan's conversation. Vaughan is bigger than Oscar remembers, the heft of his rugby player's physique moving beneath the cladding of a chalk-stripe suit as he attacks his lunch, asking urgent questions in the manner of someone schooled in business and finance, eager to waste no time. It's a rapid, interrogative style which, despite Emma's attempts to nudge things on to neutral territory, seems designed to funnel Oscar's life into a single course. Vaughan's small eyes flick quickly from his food to his subject and back again as he eats and hears Oscar explain himself, and his exact relation to Emma. 'It's complicated,' Oscar says.

'It would be easier to say we're cousins,' Emma says.

'Though we're not,' Oscar says.

'That's clear then,' Vaughan says, on his final lap. 'So what do you do?'

'Do? Well, I work a couple of nights in a club,' he says. 'Just local, in town.' Oscar takes only his second or third forkful of couscous.

Vaughan nods. He has finished eating and pushed his plate to one side. He wipes his mouth. 'OK,' he says, nodding. He pauses. 'Is that it?'

Oscar shrugs but feels the heat of what Vaughan is saying. 'Pretty much. I write the menu boards too. I get extra for that.'

'Oscar does a lot of travelling,' Emma says pleasantly.

'OK,' Vaughan says, nodding.

Oscar finds he dislikes the way Vaughan nods and says 'OK' as though he's agreeing to some unexpected request, where other people might just say 'right' or 'really?' or 'that's interesting'.

'Ever find yourself in the Far East?' Vaughan asks. 'Emma and I had a great couple of weeks over in Bali back in February, didn't we, hon?' He reaches over easily and covers Emma's hand with his own.

She gives a quick smile. 'Well, remember, we did manage to get those amazingly cheap flights.' She extricates her hand but holds on to Vaughan's mansize thumb.

'I don't think I ever got there,' Oscar says.

Vaughan turns in his chair and catches the waitress's eye. 'Can we have some coffee here?' The waitress comes, gathers up plates.

88

Oscar is still eating. 'Don't mind me,' he says.

'Would you like dessert?' she asks.

'Just coffee, I think, yes?' Vaughan says, glancing round. He exchanges thin-lipped smiles with the waitress and she disappears.

'So what now?' he demands. 'What are you doing in London?'

Oscar finds himself telling what he wanted to tell Emma on her own – that he is thinking of setting up in the heraldic shield business with the money he's been left in the will, and that he's been looking into the whole area of genealogical research, and that Michael – his biological father – had clients in Canada and Australia.

'Well that sounds interesting,' Emma says.

Oscar nods and eats. 'Might be.'

'And what's Rachel up to?' Emma asks now.

'Probably changing all the locks at the warehouse. Dad hasn't quite—'

'So, hang on,' Vaughan interjects. 'What sort of clients?'

Oscar turns to him. 'I'm not sure yet.'

Vaughan draws his eyebrows together. 'Not sure?'

'Well no, that's why I have to get the computer home. It's all in there, but the phone was cut off and there might be more information.'

'OK . . .' Vaughan says. 'But back to this shield thing – how does that work?' He glances at Emma now, as if something is amusing.

'I'm not entirely sure, but . . .'

The waitress arrives with coffee.

'Aha, you're not *entirely* sure.' Vaughan smiles.

Oscar looks at him calmly. 'Well, basically, you just look up people's surnames in a big book and match the name to the family crest. Then you paint the crest on the shield. Do you really want to know this?'

'Then you send it to Canada or Australia?'

'No, I don't think so. To be honest, I don't know. I'm still at an early stage, but, you know, I've got this four thousand pounds.'

Vaughan gives a low whistle. 'Sorry,' he says, and laughs. 'But it's not a fortune, is it?'

'*Vaughan* . . .' Emma says, punching him on the arm.

'What?'

'It's OK,' Oscar says, sipping his coffee. 'I've got to work out the sums yet,' he adds, 'but if I can get a stall at the market back home, there's no reason why I shouldn't make a go of it. My outgoings aren't what you'd call extravagant.'

'No, I imagine not,' says Vaughan. He gives Emma another quick grin, as if they have a private joke. Emma offers Oscar a disappointed smile, as though she knows that whatever she says now will be the wrong thing. They sit for a moment until Vaughan exhales loudly and drums on the table with his thick fingers. 'Well, I guess I'd better be heading back.'

'Actually, I have to go myself,' Oscar says, getting up. 'I've got a ton of stuff to do. You guys stay and finish your coffee.'

'Oh, Oscar . . .' says Emma.

'No, really. Thanks for lunch. It was great.' He leans over to kiss her on the cheek. 'Keep in touch. And nice to meet you again, Vaughan,' he says, shaking his hand.

'Yeah, best of luck, old chum,' Vaughan says.

There's a speck of sauce on Vaughan's chin.

Emma will wipe it off once Oscar is out of the way. *Hold still* . . . he imagines her saying, dabbing with the serviette, annoyed with herself, wishing things hadn't turned so awkward towards the end.

Outside he unhitches Troy from the fence. 'Come on, boy.'

He feels the weight of this failure. But how else could Emma have expected it to go? Maybe she's wondering now whether she knows him at all. Maybe she realises that it's only in the dark of his own cave that Oscar can seem to shine. Out here in Emma's world his substance is revealed – out here, where there will always be someone like Vaughan to hold up the papery thinness of his life and show how the light comes through.

Since Diggsy let him down this morning, Oscar has been assuming that Miriam will be around to lend a hand, but when he gets to Crown House her unit is locked. He waits a few minutes, thinking she might have just gone out for something to eat, then sets to work alone, ferrying the manageable items – the books, the boxes of shields, the brushes and the tins of paint and varnish, the contents of the stationery shelf, a chrome desk fan, the phone, cups, kettle – to the camper, parked in the yard at the back. The computer and accessories he packs into the trunk under the long seat, cushioning them with blankets and pillows. He pushes the small table to the back of the van, with the filing cabinet fitting snugly beneath it, then comes back up the stairs to start dismantling the drum kit and to match the various tom-toms and cymbals with the black cases piled around like hat boxes. He works off the humiliation of lunch.

It all takes time, but by three o'clock there's only the chair and the desk left, and the little fridge. Apart from this, there's just a bag of rubbish that he has left outside the door for the cleaners. He sits and rests now, and rolls himself a cigarette, flicking the ash on to the floor as he smokes. He figures that once he takes the legs and shelving and drawer units off the desk (he has found a screwdriver – along with an Allen key and a working torch – in the spoon

91

drawer under the sink) he ought to be able to get everything in, even the fridge at a push.

It takes a while to figure out how to dismantle it, and even then, progress is slow. But, once started, he falls into a rough method, sitting on the floor with the desk on its side, taking out the various types of screws and bolts, putting aside the sets in envelopes and taking care to mark the underside of the desk in pencil – 'A', 'B' and so on – to remind him how everything fits together again. This is not work he's used to. The more screws he accumulates, the more there still seems to go, and he stops more than once to stretch his back muscles and rest his wrist and suck on the blister that has risen across his palm. An hour goes by, and he's just about done when the door opens and Miriam is standing there. Her wild hair is all over the place and today she's wearing little round wire glasses.

'Need any help?' she asks.

'Good timing,' he says. 'There's just the heavy stuff left.'

'This is one of my market days,' she says. 'Is that your van down there with all the writing on it?'

'How did you guess?'

'Your dog told me. Or maybe he was just telling me to fuck off.' She smiles.

'Ah, sorry about him. He's a bit territorial.'

'Let me just sort my things out and I'll give you a hand,' she says.

Together they take the desk top and the fridge down the iron stairs, making more trips for the chair and other pieces. Then Miriam goes to her unit to put the kettle on while Oscar finishes in the studio. This is how life ends, he thinks, relatives tidying the last crumbs of us away. Michael's empty shell. There's something sad about it. He sweeps the floor and washes his hands at the sink, working up a lather with the hardened oval of pink soap he finds there, its grain darkened with the dirt of the previous owner. He thinks about the DNA you carry in the flakes of your skin and marvels at the idea of leaving these traces of himself mingling here with those of his dead father. Meeting, in a way, after all these years.

In Miriam's unit they drink tea while she shows him her work.

'Do you always do cats?' he asks.

'No, but I've just got the hang of them. I've made sheep too. I used to do more abstract pieces but they weren't too great. I was just making it up as I went along. Which at first I thought was really, like, *creative*, if you see what I mean. But needless to say, it wasn't. I decided not to keep anything from that period.' Oscar smiles, happy to listen to her talk. She offers him a biscuit from her tin. 'I realised that to get better I needed the discipline of trying to do fig-urative things, because that's harder. Or at least it's harder to get it right. Sometimes it's just a trick, which I really hate because it gives us all a bad name. You see those little hedgehogs sometimes, at craft fairs and so on, and it's obvious you could teach any idiot to make one in five min-utes. These, you see, are all different, even though they look similar. I think you have to start each one as though you've never made one before. If you look at this . . .'

He is led by this sureness about her. He watches the bird-like flicker of her eyelashes as she talks, her delicate fingers on the pale sculptures as she adjusts their positions on the table. It's as though what she says is stretched and rolled in her mind for so long that she knows exactly what shape it will be when it comes out, in the same way a cat or hedge-hog can emerge from the clay just by her hands knowing it's in there. The two things are linked, and in this she is like Bonner, and others he has met, who fascinate by talking and

93

whose words lead to action without that breath for doubt. He wishes he had it, even in this small way, like Miriam.

'So I've been working at that now,' she is saying. 'I've realised that to express yourself, you have to be master of your medium. Otherwise it looks like you're not choosing what you do. It's like Picasso – you know, when he started painting women with both eyes on the same side of their face? That was an amazing thing to do in those days. But at least, by then, he'd already established himself as a genius for painting in the normal way. I mean, I suppose everybody knew he could do it properly if he wanted to, so they had to take him seriously. Not that they did, of course, as it turned out.'

She laughs, showing the gap between her teeth. His own gappy smile he reveals less readily, an anti-reflex from his teenhood, when someone made an insensitive joke, as kids do. The detail of those days is gone but the meaning of it stays. It's one of those uncomfortable things we inherit from the life we've had so far, he understands, one of the faults that lie below the bigger surface of what we allow to be seen of ourselves.

'I haven't always done cats with long necks,' Miriam says. 'That came after. I'm developing. Eventually I'll get where I want to go. Plus, to tell you the truth, people love cats. I've sold two today.'

He ought to get back, he thinks, unload the camper, give Luke a couple of quid to get the computer hooked up. But they hang out some more, talking about Miriam's stuff and how she got into it after helping her dad out for years with his various enterprises when she left college. 'I did business studies,' she says, 'which was a mistake.' She started the ceramics gig at evening class and still fires her pieces at the adult learning centre. 'That's my big ambition – to get my own big studio with its own kiln.'

Miriam puts some music on she wants him to hear and Oscar rolls cigarettes for them both, and the time drifts by. They hear the loud clang of the shutters in the corridor outside and the voices of people locking up for the night and Miriam suggests they eat somewhere. Although lunch was a while ago now, Oscar is not really hungry, but there's a pub Miriam says she knows that does very good chips.

Oscar checks Troy is OK and gives him water and some dog food out of a tin, then he walks with Miriam down Camden High Street. They stop at a high-ceilinged trad-itional Victorian boozer, painted red, with big windows and tables outside on the street and a board advertising live music on Fridays. It's already filling up and Oscar has to wait to get served. 'The chips are on me,' he says. Miriam drinks Guinness by the pint. Oscar takes it easy with a half and tells her about his deejaying at the Green House, and Diggsy, and what he has been doing with his life outside of that in the West Country. 'That sounds pretty cool,' she says, dipping her finger in the mayonnaise.

'Yeah,' he says, 'I suppose it does.'

He doesn't mention his mother, or his decision to carry on with Michael's heraldic shield business, but is happy to explain how cheese is made. He talks about Edie, whom Miriam reminds him of slightly, with her corkscrew hair and fondness for Guinness, though Edie is taller and talks less.

'Were you, like, together?'

'On and off,' he says. 'She's a freer spirit than me. In that way.'

Oscar is thinking about coming down from Glastonbury last summer and finding Bonner with his feet under her table. He won't go back. He knows that now. The thought insinuates itself somehow into his feelings about tonight, here in the corner of this pub, its warm, companionable

95

ambience creating this pocket of intimacy for him and Miriam. He senses an inevitability, in the way she sits leaning towards him, winding a tendril of hair round her finger as she talks, that he will stay at her place. It becomes too easy not to leave. The drive home is too long. It is Miriam who buys him the drink that will take him over the limit and keep him here in London.

Out on the street, among the after-pub crowd, when they walk together – closer now than before – she barely comes up to his shoulder. And in bed, in his arms, her body feels light enough to carry, like a small animal, her hips narrow above his when she climbs on top of him, her heart beating in its wiry cage, her breasts sitting up there asking to be kissed. Now clean-shaven and pink, his cheeks feel the smoothness of a girl's skin for the first time in years. She keeps condoms in a drawer under the bedside lamp. At one point, Troy's breathy scuffling outside the door sets the two of them laughing. He is in the kitchen listening, whimpering to be let in, wanting to share the fun.

Chapter 7

Rachel is a woman in a hurry as she steps through this new life of hers in a dark Italian suit bought in a flurry of purpose from an end-of-line designer 'retail village' in Essex and crowned with blonde highlights and edgy styling by Toni & Guy. Robert hardly recognised her when she walked in the house, which struck her as a favourable omen. These past weeks (as she has begun to tell anyone who has crossed the path of her urgent rovings), life at Duttings has never been more frantic. Initial approaches to two large potential clients have been rewarded with firm indications of interest, along with a strong enquiry from a start-up converter of waterside holiday properties in Norfolk. She is courting a company with *such* a major project brewing down the line that her dreams are full of unreadable shadows and outcomes before the invitations to pitch for contracts have been written. Credit arrangements have been agreed with three brand-new suppliers, including

Rael Eastern. Staff 'downtime' at Duttings has been spent filling a skip with rubbish – unsaleable lines, mouldering offcuts, hideous vinyls, various tubular carousels buckling under the weight of their mud-coloured samples in the spidery dark of the disused office under the mezzanine, along with whole shelves of catalogues down there, outdated stationery, hole-punched sales literature featuring vacuuming housewives of the 1970s, furred mugs, thick-paged girlie calendars, damp boxes of white dockets recording the details of carpets long heaved on to November bonfires. Such is Rachel's zeal that she is able to smile deafly at the mutinous mutterings of Barbara and Brian, who have been here the longest and are accustomed to being consulted about unpleasant changes to their working patterns.

But changes there must be. The agent from Mallicks came up trumps with the broad-fronted showroom on the corner of Market Street that used to house the small Skoda dealership that went under two summers ago. 'It's the best of both worlds because you get both kinds of passing trade,' he said, meaning high-street shoppers and people stuck at the traffic lights on the Great East Road. Rachel had not given two thoughts to this place with the windows covered with chipboard and the flaking white frontage and litter-blown forecourt, but now it seems to make inspired sense, with its bonus upper-floor space for real, *in situ* displays designed by interiors consultants and loading yard at the rear with ample customer parking, and at a rent barely higher than some of the single-fronted premises on Market Street itself. There were scares with finance, Rachel having failed to sidestep the petty obstacles thrown up by the small-business manager at Lloyds who, though struck by her ambition and enthusiasm – and notwithstanding the excellent relationship the bank had enjoyed with Duttings down the years under the stewardship of Mr Dutting himself – felt, in the final analysis, that the project lacked sufficient detail in view of existing charges against the business. Rachel was nonplussed. And though, prompted by her injured silence, this impossible man had hastily added that of course the door was always open to a revised submission, or indeed for any advice they could offer on any number of small business solutions, she had left his office coldly, the spirit of endeavour seeping from her like a lovely fruit burst by a careless touch.

But then, like fate itself, hadn't Gareth Newnam dropped by to find her poring over the quarterly sales breakdowns Barbara had churned out of the firm's old Amstrad, listened to her woes over coffee then talked her into a sundown cocktail at the Belvedere? In the time it took the barman to mix, pour and deliver two Cava Fenlanders to their table on a silver tray, Gareth had insisted on giving Rachel the number of an absolute *prince* of a finance house, which harboured a passion for wooing and nurturing fledgling niche entrepreneurs like herself in a way that left the bigger traditional banks looking like Bill Sikes. And no obligation whatsoever, Gareth said. He would follow up with a call himself, if it helped. Just say the word. Herring, they were called. An introductory letter arrived, stamped with a curving sword in the corner and a little star. Think the Unthinkable, it said. There were papers to hunt down and contracts to send back, but twelve working days later the money was there, burning a hole in the firm's No. 2 account – a stout line of credit to pull on and a loan secured against the warehouse, which was safely paid for right down to its concrete floors, barred windows and doors so stiff with age that customers needed to be helped out in the winter months. The warehouse was a company asset to use as she saw fit and one signature was enough. They'd agreed to that. She and her mother had agreed. You couldn't run to your parents every time you needed to make an executive decision. She sent Gareth a card, a bottle of champagne and an order for six hand-knotted ethnic rugs.

'Never underestimate the value of cultivating new contacts,' Rachel said gaily to Robert as they tucked into dragon prawns in a piquant sauce, a celebratory supper she had cooked herself, or at least brought home from M&S and blasted in the microwave.

'And these people, their rates are . . .'

'*Very* comparable. On the whole.'

'What does your dad say about all this?'

'Please don't spoil things, Robert,' she said, issuing a mischievous high-pitched laugh that surprised even herself.

The new premises are nearly ready. It is almost against Rachel's own expectations that what she planned – and during the months she spent working at her father's elbow, 'soaking up' his experience, as he called it, this often seemed like wishful thinking – has actually come to pass. But yes, the painters and shopfitters are working towards completion. The inspectors have been in and out. The window cleaners have done a fine job. Display stock is being delivered and signed for in Rachel's frequent absences by Mum's college tutor Marj, who has been hired to advise on layout. Even Oscar has been down to snoop around with his dog and to whistle at the new signs, one vertical, and the other above the main window.

The old Duttings warehouse, newly stripped and manned by the ridiculous Brian and his two fitters, will be used to store bulk orders of carpet for the commercial jobs Rachel expects to come their way soon. Barbara, whom Rachel would ideally like to fire (along with everyone else she'd like to fire), has been retained as a sop to Dad on condition that she takes over accounting duties from old Walter (old Walter *has* been fired), starting by transferring the last two years' accounts from handwritten ledgers to computer files (a new PC fitted with twenty-first-century software has been purchased) and cross-referencing weekly sales to inventory and running costs, thus removing the need to do everything six times, which has hitherto been the practice, and giving Rachel a running snapshot of profit and loss. The trainee, Josh, who though an early school-leaver seems at least as bright as Rachel's younger brother Luke, can put his Year Seven IT skills to good use by helping key in the numbers. By the time he has finished, he will be begging for a low-paid job alongside Paul in front of showroom customers.

It's Wednesday, just after midday, when Rachel parks the blue Avensis opposite the offices of County FM Radio on the London road. She is half an hour early, and rather than go inside she remains seated and unnaturally still in the car, the warmth of the May sun becalming her stirring nerves as she watches the day's quiet movement out here beyond the west peripheral, where the town's whiskered merchants and aldermen once lived long ago, their tall, solid houses reapportioned now into smaller habitations for students and the families of foreign labourers you see coming for the seasonal agricultural work, though many stay on the farms, out of sight. The advent in recent years of these distinctively swarthy and unshaven Balkan and East European peoples, with their overpatterned sweaters and headscarves for the women, who look old and hardened at thirty, wandering up and down Market Street on Saturdays with gangs of tangled-haired children in their charge, has become a symbol of all that is wrong in England for a vocal minority in the town, especially, it seems, readers of the *Gazette*, whose almost comic prejudices are clumsily aired in the letters page, citing the rise in petty thievery and vandalism wherever these economic migrants and so-called 'asylum seekers' show their grubby faces. One correspondent wrote warning of Albanian criminals bringing forced prostitution of white girls to the area, as has been the problem in London and elsewhere. Another spoke of donkeys reportedly being stolen for food in some parts of the country.

In recent months, the *Gazette* has introduced a crime hotline by which readers may demonstrate their good citizenship anonymously. It is true that Rachel once found herself defending the importance to local concerns of the *Gazette* against the metropolitan irony of Emma, who said it was the job of local newspapers to make their towns and villages seem more dangerous, and therefore more interesting, than they really were. But at any other time, whether among her former colleagues in the cafeteria at the council offices, or at home in easy range of Robert's more acute sense of social outrage, Rachel has winced as earnestly as anyone at the casual xenophobia and inadvertent sexism and sly gay-baiting arising from the columns of the *Gazette* in its role as a community forum. The council has always worked hard to promote its policy initiatives regarding equal opportunities (Rachel herself sat on the Disability Committee for a year and spoke from the heart about the woeful lack of wheelchair ramps in the town), and its members themselves will write to the paper, often in the guise of ordinary good neighbours, in an attempt to shame those who would deny a second chance to the unfortunates who have chosen this unspoilt county to improve themselves and earn a modest living.

It is probably not to Rachel's credit that, in the twenty months since giving up the council in favour of the family firm, it has slowly become her habit to see such concerns only in so far as they colour the fringes of commercial life, or at least the housing market, where most of the Dutting bread is buttered. In this way at least – though she pushes the thought from her mind whenever it arises to accuse her – Rachel has been drawn closer to her father's side. Like all pillars of the town's trading community, Dad offers a cheerfully unquestioning defence of self-interest that can silence even Robert, who though customarily willing to die on the barricades for all underdogs – who though now safely *married* – maintains the nodding deference of the prospective son-in-law, especially at the Sunday dinners they have attended at the Dutting home. Here her father presides unironically over the carving of the roast, sharpening the knife against a foot of matching Sabatier steel and distributing with indecent relish the slices of steaming meat, like some rouge-cheeked grotesque out of Dickens. 'Minding your own business is not a sin but a virtue,' he said one Christmas, as if happily quoting from the Book of Psalms.

This week's edition of the *Gazette* is open on the seat beside her. Rachel has taken out a three-page 'advertorial' spread to publicise the opening of the new showroom, with a portrait of herself standing under one of the new signs that she knows her father has secretly visited and seen with his own disbelieving eyes, and other photographs of Marj and herself – Marj putting the finishing touches to the first of four fully mocked-up 'unique display living areas' on the upper floor, furnished in association with other local retailers 'to reflect a range of contemporary styles'.

In her life, Rachel has followed a steady and dutiful course. She prospered at school; she succeeded at university; she married her student sweetheart; she laboured in a public service department of her home town. For most of her adult years she has lived within a mile of the house she was born in, as if on call for further personal sacrifice. What a contrast with Oscar's charmed adolescence, his comings and goings without redress or expectation, his subsidised wanderings! Everyone remembers the cool American baseball and glove Dad brought him back from his trip to Germany and the blatantly educational astronomy construction kit she herself received. She is Dad's safe pair of hands, just as he was his own father's, a child of his own stamp. She looks at the photograph of herself in the paper, at the slightly overfleshy nose passed down from her grandfather and the Dutting cleft of anxiety between her eyebrows that gets deeper with age. Who knows? Perhaps all she needed was the chance to see things differently and seize her moment. Perhaps she never really was that child who did all the right things in the right order, the one who could be relied upon to build a working universe just by following the instructions on the box. In the end, everyone wants to do their own thing, to make their own stamp, to turn the world upside down, to subvert their destiny and step forward when life calls their name. *Carpe diem*. Or carpet *diem*, as Gareth said.

He's *so* quick. Thinking about him fills her with hope. She gets out of the car and locks it, and walks briskly up the two steps and into the purpose-built low-rise eighties block, with its pale toytown brickwork and tinted windows. She has never set foot in a radio station before but she has subdued some of the fluttery nervousness she had in the car with thoughts of the money Duttings has put into County FM's coffers for a series of commercials scheduled over the next three weeks. It is this harder business face, and not that of the breathless virgin, that Rachel presents to the girl at the desk (Kayti, her badge says), explaining that she is here as a guest on *Gillian Reed's Afternoon Break*. Kayti smiles and takes her name and calls through to the office to

104

say Rachel Dutting has arrived. 'Craig will be out in a sec,' she says. 'He's the producer, OK?'

Rachel waits, leafing through a magazine, until Craig comes out and leads the way through a surprisingly heavy swing door, showing her to a seat in a small waiting area with a table scattered with magazines and a view of the control room and studio where a woman who must be Gillian Reed herself sits with giant headphones on, the bottom half of her face obscured by a crossing of microphone booms and other technical equipment. The show – Rachel often catches it when she is out in the car – follows the usual format of music and harmless chat, interspersed with traffic, weather and news reports. In addition to Rachel, as Craig explains before hurrying off to organise coffee, there'll be someone else in the same slot whose name she doesn't quite catch, along with Simon, who does the sports and film round-up, plus the regular phone-ins and listeners' emails. 'Don't worry – it's all very informal and lively,' Craig says. Rachel is amazed that Craig – who barely looks old enough to buy fireworks – is not only telling her not to worry but seems to be in charge of everything, like a sixth-former being allowed to run the railways for a day. Just as amazing is a girl, equally young-looking and wearing baggy black trousers and trainers, who stands joking with one of the sound engineers for a minute before calmly entering the studio with seconds to spare and reading a news bulletin in an entirely different voice. Everyone here is a high-flyer, Rachel decides, her panic starting to rise again.

But Gillian Reed herself is reassuringly in her forties, with an explosion of unfashionable eighties curls and rimless glasses perched on the end of her nose. She reaches across the desk to shake Rachel's hand while an ad plays over the monitors. 'Carpets?' she asks.

'Afraid so!' Rachel hears herself trill, auditioning for the part of a lively guest.

'Don't worry,' Gillian says, rearranging the papers in front of her. 'We've got a Hernam Peters coming in. He's doing greenhouse gases. Or the other one, the ozone layer. I always get them mixed up, don't you? Environment anyway. I thought we'd pop the two of you in together. About five minutes?'

'Fine!'

'Fabu-lous,' Gillian says, but she is already listening to someone else.

What a terrifying profession, Rachel thinks, so much to keep your eye on and having to sound interested in every-body at the same time. She adjusts her headphones inexpertly while Gillian takes a call from someone in Colenden who is complaining about the new level crossing, which is *ridiculously* slow and now lets at least three trains through before it opens to road traffic again, by which time there's a tailback right up the hill to Morthorp. 'And you're there right now?' Gillian is asking, laughing, though her eyes are already on the next item. 'You'd better get off the phone before a policeman sees you.'

'No, no. I'm not even moving. That's the point, you see . . .'

'Well, best of luck there, Jonathan of *Col*-enden,' she says, shaking her head at the sound man through the window.

Craig is ushering someone else into the studio, a man of Oscar's stripe by the look of him, someone who equates saving the environment with not buying new clothes. Gillian leans across to shake his hand. Behind him the girl in the black trousers whom Rachel saw earlier arrives out of nowhere and slips into a seat to her right as the station jingle rings out. 'It's twelve forty-five and time for a quick travel update with me, Angie Andrews,' she purrs.

And then they're on. Gillian introduces them as her guests, then tosses Rachel a friendly, open question that allows her to tell them about the firm and its history and the importance of family enterprises to the local economy and sense of pride. It's like an ad in itself, except better. Rachel makes much about her father learning the trade at the feet of Grandad Dutting in the old days and the growth of the business, though in truth Duttings has been stagnant and living on past glories, if that's the word, for God knows how long. 'Which is why we are spreading our wings, so to speak,' Rachel hears herself saying, keeping her voice animated, as if trying to coax a child out of a sulk, as Gareth suggested that last time she saw him. Or imagine yourself speaking to the hard of hearing. Radio loves emphasis, he said.

'And I gather you're striking out under a slightly different banner, Rachel,' says Gillian.

'Absolutely,' Rachel says. 'Dutting *Modern*. We'll have the wealth of tradition and experience behind us, but in a newer, more contemporary *idiom* and setting. Hence Dutting *Modern*. Old customers who drop in to our new showroom are in for a few surprises. And, of course, new customers are welcome too, especially those who are looking for something just that little bit different in the way of . . . shall we say *edge*.'

'Perhaps the *Dutting* edge,' says Gillian, raising her eyebrows over the microphone.

'Absolutely,' Rachel says with a blank smile at this sudden brilliance, an alarm ringing in her heart for an instant as she wonders whether 'The Dutting Edge' wouldn't in fact have made a good straight slogan for the commercial, rather than the musical option she was sold by the ad agency – 'If I Was a *Carpeter*', a jingle based on the old Four Tops number which on reflection she feels lacks gravitas. Carpeter! And for all their promised top-dollar production, it still sounds like karaoke. She looks for an opportunity to say 'Dutting Modern' again but Gillian has turned to the other guest, and is gaily linking business matters to the problem of environmental pollution. This Hernam Peters – hard-faced with a pale-eyed, goatlike look about him – is in no humour for County FM's lightness of touch, however, and begins delivering a credo on the need for sacrifice and a greater sense of common purpose in terms of energy-saving and living less frantic, consumer-driven lives. The market towns are gradually turning into cities, he believes. England's green is disappearing under a tide of housing developments and attendant infrastructure – roads, airports, hypermarkets, telecommunications masts. And what about the planet? CO_2 emissions from the manufacture of cement *alone* are greater than those created by the worldwide aviation industry. He has the statistics in his head and reels numbers off in the manner of an obsessive hobbyist. He's here today, Rachel now realises, because of the Five Ponds Lane proposal that Robert frets about with increasing frequency.

'But, practically speaking, how do you see your idea of community differing from, say, that of Rachel here, who is investing in the town and creating jobs?' Gillian blinks at him pleasantly.

The bowel of Rachel's mind, still processing the amazing question of cement manufacture, instantly empties as she sees the discussion coming her way. She takes a deep breath, as Gareth has advised before speaking on the radio. Emphasis. Focus. But also lightness of expression. *Woo* your audience.

Hernam stares at her. 'Luxury carpets? Peddling lifestyles that are intrinsically unaffordable to the majority of the population doesn't sound like a solution to me,' he says. 'More like adding to the problem.'

Gillian looks at her over her glasses. 'Rachel,' she suggests brightly, 'you're adding to the problem.'

Rachel finds it in herself to offer a light chuckle before she speaks, as though called upon to deal with a provocative teenager. 'You can't halt progress,' she says. 'As the government keep telling us, people have to live somewhere. Mr Peters talks about sacrifice,' she says, deepening her voice slightly now. 'Perhaps those of us lucky enough to live here in our leafy communities should do our bit too.' She thinks about those immigrant workers for a second, and wonders whether herding them on to her side of the equation is likely to win the listeners over or antagonise them.

'*What?*' Hernam almost squeals. 'With acres of executive housing?' He looks at Gillian Reed wide-eyed as though appealing for a ruling of some kind.

Rachel appraises him calmly. 'Well, of course, I'm not the one building them. Even so, if it frees up the property market in general and people aspire to move up, then housing at the bottom of the ladder becomes available to the rental sector or first-time buyers, and more houses in the market keeps prices stable for young couples. Isn't that a good thing?'

'It's good for estate agents and lawyers and companies selling carpets.'

She laughs with exaggerated force. 'And very good carpets they are too,' she cries gaily, deciding that the best form of defence is to treat Hernam as an irrelevance.

'I am sure they are,' Hernam says, momentarily losing the tune of things in Rachel's unexpected key change. 'But . . . but at what *price?*'

She sees Craig at the control room window half smiling, his arms folded, his lip tucked under his front teeth. He says something to the sound man, then winks at Gillian. Rachel smiles herself. Being watched like this – even in the act, as it were, of standing up for greenfield executive developments – quickens her blood, and though she hopes Robert has kept his promise and is too busy with meetings to listen to this, her media debut, she knows she has it in her to keep this up all afternoon if necessary. 'Price?' she says. 'Oh, I couldn't say off the top of my head, but why not pop down to the showroom and have a look round – I'm sure one of our friendly sales staff can sort you something out. We've got some very good offers this week. Dutting Modern, a cut above the rest,' she adds, rosy now with inspiration.

Hernam is stranded, mutely furious, watching the question of the green belt and its cargo of valuable social issues drifting out of range, hauled to open water by Rachel's plucky tug. Hurrah!

Safe now, her mind turns with relish to her enquiries into the project in question, to her discreet, informal lunch at the Orange Tree with Bill Kepp, a high-up buyer at the Mosely-Baker consortium who – once they got the green light – would, he could confirm, be tempting prospective housebuyers with the usual inducements (free kitchen appliances, curtains, blinds and, yes, carpets), and would, of course, be happy to consider a quotation from Dutting Modern in the fullness of time, though she really must understand that everything was provisional and that he couldn't talk precise numbers. Absolutely understood, she agreed, as she listened to him describe the long and tortuous road from Whitehall's initial directive on new housing in the south-eastern counties, through to the county and district councils' consultation drafts regarding the relaxation of rules governing land usage, to the innumerable subsequent hearings, to the revised plans and pre-inquiry proposals, to the inquiry itself, with its literally dozens of representations by community and pressure groups and other interested parties for and against. 'For the council, understandably,' said Bill Kepp, over dessert, 'it's always been a question of how much land could be safely removed from the green belt without compromising the integrity and character of the affected towns and villages. For us it was, and still is, a question of numbers of dwellings per hectare. Obviously that's crucial for an upscale development such as the one we ourselves envisage. As you know, we're not the only developer in the frame, nor indeed the biggest.'

Yes, yes, but what was it Robert had said – *fifteen hundred new homes on the Windhill site alone*? A girl could dream.

Chapter 8

Stuart hears the phone ringing on the lower floor, but as he lays down his binoculars and turns to the door, something hits the window with a thud that makes the pane tremble. He just catches a glimpse as it bounces off and down, out of sight, a rolled-up damp glove of a thing. He's noticed this before, the wing marks on the glass where small birds fly straight into it unawares, and this is another one. Hurrying down the stairs, he makes a mental note to stick something on the window so they won't mistake it for a fresh horizon.

'It's Barbara,' says the voice on the line.

'How's it going, Barbara? How's Dutting *Modern*?'

'I'm sure I've no idea,' she sniffs. 'Rachel won't let me near the new place. I'm still at the warehouse sorting out the accounts. She refuses to read them unless they're on a computer. Josh is out with Brian somewhere. Anyway, I was just ringing to say that your Oscar has turned up here

112

with that strange friend of his with the bad skin. He said you told him he could use the downstairs office for his . . . well, whatever it is he's doing.'

Stuart sighs. 'Sorry, Barbara, I didn't know he was thinking of coming today. To tell you the truth, he's turning the house into such a pigsty with his rubbish and books that I thought, why not? You must be rattling about down there now in all that space.'

'Does Rachel know?'

'She won't like it, but that's just bad luck. I'll give her a bell,' he says. 'Or maybe I'll just let her find out.' He laughs uneasily. 'Any other business?'

'Not really, Stuart. You know what I know.'

'I might pop down later, OK?'

He puts the phone down and goes out back, down to the garden to find the bird. It's not one he has spotted before. A fat little creature with its eyes closed. Bullfinch, is it? The Duttings have never had windows that birds fly into before, one of the hazards, he guesses, of having a bigger house and living in a nicer area. With all their superior navigation and general obstacle-avoidance skills, you'd think they'd at least see themselves coming. He flips the bird over with his foot. He'll tick it off in his book, so its life won't have been entirely wasted. Like one of those posthumous medals you get for just turning up at the war.

Back in the house, he finds his reading glasses and checks his *British Garden Birds* while the kettle boils. Bullfinch, yes. He claps the book shut and hunts in the cupboard. Biscuits. No, jam tart. He bites into it hungrily and takes a second one. He feels a curious new fellowship of equals with Barbara, alone and robbed of purpose down there on the windswept peripheral while he's up here with the house to himself until Luke gets home wanting his tea and Diane not back these days till gone six. How long was

113

it Barbara said she'd been with the firm? He and she have history. Just that one occasion when he got into something inadvisable with her, one of the first Christmases, both of them drunk in the back of a taxi after a works outing to the bierkeller on the Great East Road. Bauhaus? No, Brauhaus. Diane at home pregnant, her sleeping body rising and falling under the covers when he crept in, like a fairground inflatable. Sixteen years, then, it must be. He feels the shame of it even now, though of course there is little of real substance to regret, not when you think of what some people get up to. At first Barbara wouldn't let him touch her, just kiss in that mad, uncontrollable way, but things went further until just when they were both on the brink of the inevitable, *he* had been the one to pull out, so to speak, mumbling about how he'd hate himself in the morning, which he would have, for sure. He loves Diane. Thinking about it now, his heart thumps. As if now, with the imbalance of things, it might tip him into some long-earned punishment, as DNA can do with murders committed years ago. It was a stupid moment. Barbara agreed too, though he is certain that, in her heart, she wonders what would have happened if it had gone further. Sometimes she looks at him as though it happened only last night; as if they're both still thinking about it but not saying anything. She would have been about thirty-five. It seems somehow to make it worse that she has never married, that she has aged in that time, as though it's all to do with him and what happened that night. Strange, this thing between them that means nothing and yet is always there, like a scent only the two of them can smell. For sixteen years she has fussed mutely around him at the office, so resolutely *his* – at least in this sphere – watchful as a nurse as she has gauged his requirements, as if by knowing when tea was in order or sensing when to close his office door she was his partner in some

114

tacit conspiracy, his trusted agent in his cold war against complacency or absenteeism or shoddy workmanship.

Now Barbara is the double agent, lately giving Stuart the lowdown on Rachel, who has yet to measure the implications of Barbara opening the morning post that still arrives at the warehouse, regardless of whom it is addressed to or how sensitive its disclosures. It is through her that Stuart has knowledge of Rachel's crisp new financing arrangements with a firm called Herring Associates ('It even sounds fishy,' he murmured to Barbara as he scribbled it down), and is privy to the contents of a short informal note from Rael Eastern's Gareth Newnam congratulating her, thanking her for the order and champagne (!) and suggesting a date for lunch. Stuart hears, too, of astonishing bulk quotations provided by a half-dozen manufacturers – including one in America – for the supply of enough good 42-ounce plain twist to carpet the county from here to the North Sea.

He tries to read Rachel's thinking here. He feels an urge to reiterate his warnings about the false god of piling too high on the back of tempting supplier discounts, but how to raise it without alerting her to the spy in her midst? There has been a rapprochement. He has capitulated on the name-change and admitted in public that the showroom looks just the ticket. He has heard, second-hand from gay Ricky at the barber's, that she was on County FM and went down a storm. And talking to her on the phone – Rachel much prefers this to the risk of him visiting unannounced and makes a point of being available when he rings – she is confident and even upbeat (at times it has crossed his mind that she might be taking those herbal mood-enhancers he has read about but can't remember the name of), hinting at exciting things 'in the pipeline' and telling him that the 'once-only special launch offers' at the new place have been generating much coming and going.

'So how are sales?'

'Oh, very buoyant.'

'Buoyant?'

'There's a lot of positive traffic,' she says, whatever that means. 'We think we can take this all the way. We've got so much interest out there.'

'We?'

'We, the company of course.' She says this with a snap of impatience that brings something slamming down between them, as if she has been angling to take offence, making it easier to replace the unwelcome intimacy of business talk with the empty chitchat of hearth and home.

'And you – are you OK?' she asks after this tricky moment of changing gear. 'How's the garden?'

'Little growth,' is his reply to this. 'I've been doing some birdwatching,' he adds, in a tone that he hopes carries the right note of pathos.

'Excellent!' she says.

'And playing a bit of golf.'

'That's the spirit.'

Rachel continues in the same vein, asking after her mother's health, discussing the weather, rejoicing in being so near to the heart and soul of the town, not least for the shops. 'Not that I have time for shopping,' she laughs, in a way that makes him feel like wringing her neck.

He waits to be consulted, for his experience to be made use of, for his status to be acknowledged, but in vain.

In the meantime, Stuart has been finding things out. His roofing and golfing acquaintance Pete Tree, on a business trip to the old country (Sweden? Denmark?), said he saw that name, what was it – yes, Rael Eastern – pop up on a TV documentary in his hotel room while he was getting ready for dinner. 'I thought of you straight away,' he said. 'I remembered you asking about them. Tony – you

116

remember this outfit,' he said, turning to Tony Ennick, who was sitting legs apart casually digging into the bowl of peanuts at the Willows bar. 'Spanish, you said, didn't you?'

'No, it was *me* who said Spanish,' Stuart said. It annoys him that Tony must constantly be deferred to, even when it's not his story.

'This is Rachel's supplier, right?' said Tony, not missing a trick. 'I hear she was on the radio.'

'Yes,' Pete said, 'but it happens that they're not Spanish, but Bulgarian.'

'Oh,' Stuart said.

'Cut to the chase, old chum,' Gordon said.

Pete's story, as he told it, was about bad employment practices in the carpet factories of the Far East, where in the worst cases you got kids as young as six being signed over by their cash-strapped parents into debt-bonded contracts in exchange for loans. According to this TV investigation, the kids slaved away in the factory chained to their looms sixteen hours a day, breathing in the wool dust and contracting spinal deformities and so on until the debt got paid off, which was often never because if they made the slightest mistake or didn't work quick enough, the debt went up again, or they got beaten with a stick.

'Sounds feasible,' Tony said. 'You can believe that happens.'

Gordon made a sour face. 'It's a problem of education, isn't it? No wonder they come over here. I mean, say what you like about your Pakistani community, but they're bloody hard workers and hardly any trouble, most of them, apart from the odd nutter in the inner cities, but you'll always get that, especially with the current situation. Extreme elements, rabble-rousers. One of our William's bosses is coloured. Genius on the technology side, by all accounts. It used to be corner shops and takeaways, then

117

doctors, and now it's computers. You can't fault them for enterprise.' The others nodded their agreement as Gordon got up to go to the toilet.

'Don't say I didn't warn you,' Tony said.

'But you were the one who said not to worry. You said everything was global these days.'

'Stuart, mate. We were discussing *Spain*. Bulgarians are an entirely different kettle of villains. Since the wall came down you're talking about a bandit economy.' He scooped up a handful of nuts. 'You can't expect best practice from people like that.'

With what information Pete scribbled down, and some grudging help from Luke at home, Stuart turned up a website run by the Swedish (or Danish) human rights activists who made the film and who had the sense to publish their findings in English. They had all kinds of cases like this from Pakistan and others from Thailand and Afghanistan. And, sure enough, Rael Eastern was right up there, one of the firms cited as sourcing stock from these manufacturers.

'It's not illegal, but it's not nice,' Stuart told Diane in bed that night.

'You might try not to sound so triumphant,' she said.

'Don't you think Rachel should know?'

'Only if you're abso*lutely* determined to rain on her parade. Forget it, Stuart, for goodness' sake. Half the products in the southern hemisphere are probably made under those conditions. I read just the other day about footballs – probably the very one Luke kicks against the garage door – it's the same story. And football boots made out of kangaroo leather! If we looked into everything we bought, we wouldn't buy anything, would we?'

Diane was right, but that didn't make her *right*. Still, he retreated into silence. Diane's voice had reached that pitch

118

where her ears shut down, that peak of impatience she reaches almost instantly these days, like a broken thermostat. She doesn't want the hassle of him muddying the water right now. There's enough water being muddied at the other end of the family is her real problem, the one that doesn't get discussed, Oscar's trip to London to see some girl, Miriam, is it? And when did Stuart suddenly start worrying about international child slavery, is what Diane was saying. It was all about Rachel, wasn't it? Rachel taking over. Just thinking about it makes him want to pee.

So Stuart hasn't mentioned it to Rachel. Maybe he should back off and hope for the best, worried though he is that things are moving too fast and costing too much money, anxious that baling out was the wrong thing to do in the light of going for the new house as he did without – it had to be admitted (though this was not the moment to admit anything) – fully transparent discussions with Diane, still tormented, too, by Tony Ennick's tactless remark a while back that retirement was the short cut to an early death. He gets his jacket, locks up and drives to the warehouse. He will take Barbara to the Beehive for old times' sake, treat her to a ploughman's or one of their steak-and-ales. He sees her up in the office when he arrives, and waves. He tries to nod approvingly as he surveys the old place. Sure, it looks clean and bigger but, divested of its rubbish, something of the Dutting character has been swept away. The old smell has gone. Someone has been round the iron pillars and girders slapping on a navy industrial gloss. He frowns, recalling the old joke about the Queen thinking that the world smells of fresh paint – because isn't that how it is for carpet fitters too when they turn up at customers' houses? Oscar's whip of a dog Troy is wagging around the aisles, and there's a light on in the newly empty storeroom under the office. With the accumulated years of filth cleaned off the windows he can see the backs of younger heads at the bench and the glow of a computer screen.

'Hope you're not using too much of my electricity,' he shouts.

Oscar turns, surprised, and comes out wiping his hands. 'Dad, hi.'

'How's it going?' Stuart says, moving towards the storeroom. He reaches the door and looks in. Oscar's friend Diggsy glances up shyly. There's someone else in there. '*Luke?*'

Luke turns and presents what he hopes will be an endearing look. He's holding an artist's brush and has one of Oscar's wooden shields in front of him on the bench. 'Hello, Dad.'

'Shouldn't you be at school?'

'It's all right, I've got a study period this morning.'

'Well you're not going to learn anything here. Except how to . . .' He stops himself. 'Just make sure you're there this afternoon, young man.'

'Cool,' Luke says, glancing at Oscar.

Stuart looks at Oscar too.

'He asked if he could help,' Oscar says.

'For money, presumably.'

Oscar shrugs and then grins. 'Anyway, guess what? I've got one of those little walk-in kiosks to rent in the arcade just off Market Street. I'm in business. They said we can have it this weekend, which is why we need to do these shields – you know, for display purposes, for the wall. And I'm going to have a big one made as a sign for out front. We thought of calling ourselves "Roots".'

It sounds like a hairdresser's, Stuart thinks, but he nods approvingly. 'So who's this *we*?'

'Me and Diggsy. Well, Diggsy's just helping with the painting, part-time. I'll be manning the kiosk and doing the

120

surnames and offering consultations on how to trace your family tree.'

'Waiting to be consulted can be a lonely business,' says Stuart.

'What?' Oscar gives him his puzzled look, a thing he does with his bottom lip coming up to cover the top one. He must have got that from Diane's deceased ex, this Michael, along with those teeth. Diane even has him thinking about the guy now.

'Nothing,' Stuart says, looking at his watch. 'I'd love to stand here talking all day but I just popped in to see Barbara.'

They turn with matching concern at the sound of a car pulling to a halt outside. A door bangs and Rachel appears at the entrance. She is walking towards the office steps when she spots Troy sniffing up and down the aisles. She stops in her tracks, gives her head a little shake, and then sees them all standing there. She comes clicking in their direction now, her new blonde hair bobbing as she walks, her face a picture of annoyance.

'Ah . . .' Stuart murmurs.

'You didn't tell her?' Oscar says.

'Don't worry, I'll smooth things over,' he says, patting Oscar's shoulder. 'I do still have some say around here.'

He believes this but, even as Rachel opens her mouth to speak, Stuart can't help wondering what has happened to make Oscar suddenly almost reasonable and his sister now the difficult one, as though a sprite or fairy has swapped labels and they have ended up in the wrong bodies, like characters in the Shakespeare play he and Diane saw at Luke's school. It reminds him of the moment when you realise that the scenery has changed, all the colours are different, and what you think is real suddenly isn't. Suddenly you're wearing the donkey's ears yourself.

Chapter 9

It is June and the cherry trees that hem the loop of road serving the little cul de sacs and the Duttings' own quiet crescent up here seem almost overnight to have erupted in that frothy blossom, the scent of it swimming in the morning air, the petals heaping drifts of feathery snow against gate posts and shallow walls. Oscar deeply inhales, as if harbouring some small private satisfaction, as he begins the descent from High Firs to catch the first off-peak to London, a slow train that stops at every station. So steep is this topmost section of the hill (driving up the first time in his VW camper, he was surprised to find himself hurriedly having to change into first gear) that he is obliged to adopt the sideways lope of a tall man coming down stairs. From this elevation the town centre is deceptively lifeless with its facing slate rooftops that obscure the shopping area beneath, though you can see the traffic thickening into chains around the car parks. Higher, across town, beyond the station, above the cartoon choppy sea of gabled streets, cars zip like paper messages in a tube along the brief stretches of the peripheral not hidden by trees.

Thursday is market day, which with regard to business at the kiosk has proved in the past weeks almost as good as a Saturday. He is leaving Diggsy in charge, accompanied by Troy, to whom sleeping under the counter has become a familiar pleasure. Though he has been left alone before, Diggsy is nervous at the prospect, not merely because of the responsibility, Oscar realises, but also on account of his pitted, blotchy face, which is why he has always stuck with bar work. 'I look better in a darker light,' he once told him. 'It's a fact.'

The main thing, Oscar said, is to be positive and pleasant, to explain to customers the principle of the family crest, remembering to ask about their particular origins. A Hertfordshire Thompson is not the same as a Lancashire one, though Hertfordshire Thompsons, Tomsons, Tomsens and even Tomassens are likely to be the same stock, or near enough. At this level, it's not a precise science. If someone has an unusual or interesting name, it's a useful sales tactic to remark upon it. People like to be thought interesting, Oscar has found. And when handling the big book of names, he advised Diggsy, remember to show a bit of reverence. He blew imaginary dust off its leather casings as he opened it. 'Like this,' he said, turning the pages with care, smoothing them with his hand, running his finger lightly down the entries. It's a nice touch, too, he suggested, to frown a little and to say 'hmm', and consult the other book with its alternative spellings and cross-references. You might too take time to peruse the atlas of England and Wales or the separate maps of Scotland and Ireland with their fancy line drawings of forts and bridges and rivers with leaping fish.

123

Despite his early misgivings, Oscar is warming to all this, to this unexpected beginning of a different life here in his home town. Not a dream, not California, a place of endless imagined skies. In the past, travelling through a remote city in Europe or elsewhere, he has tried to think what it would be like to live there, to *be* the person sitting on a bench in a bus station reading a foreign-language newspaper or eating a sandwich, perhaps wearing an item of dress signalling some unknowable religious or cultural observance. Who are they? What do they go home to? He has imagined himself stranded there without resources or friends. Just to think of it made him shudder with apprehension and he took comfort in the confines of the throbbing bus, belching its fumes, his forehead on the cold window that separated him from that threat, that brink of the unknown.

'The truth is, people are all the same,' Diggsy said some days ago, sitting in his room above the club after the evening shift, sharing a spliff. 'Genetically speaking,' he said. In fact, he added, humans were almost identical to mice or fruit flies. Oscar laughed at the impossibility of that. Talk of genes seems to be everywhere since his 'blood father' walked back into his life. Genes jump out of the headlines. And now here was Diggsy talking about it too. 'It's just the minutely different ordering of the code,' he said. 'Like a spelling gone wrong. The same string of letters with just one out of place. In a way it's the same with places. To a Martian landing here in this town, he wouldn't see anything different from California.' He fell quiet for a minute, smoking and thinking, lying on the bed while Oscar sat in the chair. This was Diggsy's ideal of philosophy, hanging out, making spliff wisdom out of these connections, far from the baffling metaphysics and epistemological puzzles of those seminars at North Essex before the two of them dropped out and ran for their lives. 'So this

124

would be Aliforniac,' Diggsy said at last. 'You could be anywhere. People are the same, see. It's people who make places what they are. Unless you live in a cave or whatever.' Diggsy said the word again, Aliforniac. It sounded less like a place, more like someone with a disorder, like an insomniac or amnesiac. A dreamer, a seeker of utopias, a wisher of things to be different.

And things are different. Oscar is coming to like the people who come and go at the arcade, the rhythm of retail, the gentle drawing and retreating of customers, like a tide lapping at his window. The kiosk looks grand now, with its display shields and large vellum wall chart Oscar ordered from a website that lays out a whole family tree illustrated with faded photographs and printed in gothic script to show how it can be done. The more he thinks about it, the more possibilities spring to mind. With the summer coming up, Diggsy could run the kiosk here on Saturdays and Sundays, freeing Oscar up to travel out to the various weekend country craft fairs dotted across East Anglia. It would be like having two outlets. To keep costs down, he has a local carpenter making the shields now, and in two sizes, not just one, and has started to offer a 'His-and-Hers' double shield designed to look a bit like two hearts with the names of both partners joined in the middle. Parchment scrolls, too, are an idea Oscar has stolen from other businesses he has seen on the net, tied with a ribbon or set in a glass frame – the perfect birthday gift, as it says in the little display ad he has placed in the *Gazette*. To this end Oscar is learning calligraphy from a book he bought from the little art materials shop in Beefer's Yard. He has always liked art, in his amateur way. As a kid he used to spend school breaks copying out frames from American action comics, and has often supplemented his pub and club work writing out the menu blackboards, jazzing them up like a pro with pictures of steaming meat pies, fresh-roast chickens or bunches of grapes. Diggsy too has a careful hand and a half-decent eye, enough to paint the shield backgrounds – a chevron, a 'fess', a 'bend sinister', a 'saltire' – leaving Oscar to do the details – a sword, a dragon or an eagle – with a finer brush or rotoring pen. There is still much to get the hang of. Oscar has a little book called an 'Ordinary of Arms' to copy from and has been studying the different sorts of crowns and crosses, mythic beasts, wreaths and crescents and other heraldic symbols that brought honour to your family way back then. One is a Saracen's head dripping blood. He hasn't had to do that one yet. But he is learning every day. He trawls the internet to steal ideas from genealogy websites. He sits leafing through his 'Ordinary' at home in front of the TV, soaking it up, this weird stuff from Norman times. '*Bezantee*,' he said out loud.

'What's that?' Dad asked, half interested, half asleep.

'Strewn with bezants.'

Oscar is impassioned with the hidden specifics of it, its system of arcane rules and hybrid vocabulary. It's like something out of nowhere, an undiscovered language and science in one. *Reguardant*. Looking backwards, that means. He loves this stuff.

'Roots', it says, the sign outside the kiosk, and it hangs free like those you see outside pubs, the word cut into a shield like the ones inside, though bigger and painted gold with black lettering. Trade is promising. The first customer through the door on the opening Saturday was a Mr Laing. The name was Scottish, he said, but then Oscar discovered that the first Laings – or Layngs as it turned out – lived in Northumberland in AD 872. The coat of arms was a knight's helmet wound up with some sort of twining plant life. When Mr Laing had placed his order and gone, Oscar ran almost whooping out to Oddbins to buy a bottle of champagne. Diggsy came down later and they drank it, like the homeless with their cans of Special Brew, on the steps of the Town Hall. Oscar sold six shields that first day and another fourteen in the week, including market day. The second week was even better, with a total of twenty-six shields. The tourist season has yet to start. The town is a hub for those who come from far and wide, amazingly, it seems to Oscar, to inspect the peculiar flat beauty of the Fens, the pebbly Suffolk coast, the mazy waterways of flinty Norfolk. McDougals from Canada, Smiths and Joneses from New Zealand and other remote dominions of the old Empire. At this rate, after paying for materials and rent on the kiosk and Diggsy's piecework, Oscar will be rich! Or at least self-sufficient. Or at least not as much of a bloodsucking parasite on Mum and Dad as Rachel says he is.

There have been no 'consultations' yet, though the genealogy kits and the books are selling. And when not busy painting shields at the warehouse, Oscar has been sifting through Michael's correspondence. He is in contact with two small voluntary organisations who wrote regretting hearing about the sudden death of his father but begging Oscar, it seems, to carry on the work of tracing the families of their members.

'Members of what?' his mother practically snapped, when he told her.

He has learnt to take care with his answers these days, she is getting so weird about everything. Is it his imagination that her eyes follow him round the house? Before he finally moved the stuff out to the warehouse, Mum seemed unable to resist huffing aggressively in his presence, as though he had been keeping Michael's dead body in the garage. He can understand her unease, but not the intensity of it – not the way, for example, she went berserk when she came home to find Luke crashing away at the drum kit Oscar brought back from London; not the silences that have greeted Oscar after the three or four times he has been to see Miriam and not got back till the next day. 'It's not that big a deal,' he said.

Mum said nothing, but filled the dishwasher more noisily than usual. Dad sat behind his newspaper, shaking his head. At times like this Oscar carries on as if things are looking up, which to all appearances they are – Dad has the retirement he wants, Mum has her decorating course to keep her busy, Rachel is flying, Luke is happy, and he himself has found something interesting to do. But, still, the unsaid is unsettling, and when Mum eventually barks – when she forgets not to ask the questions that eat her up from the inside – it comes as a relief.

'These people were child migrants back in the forties and fifties,' he told her. 'They were kids sent to orphanages here – sometimes just illegitimate kids with young mothers who weren't allowed to keep them – who eventually ended up being sent out to Canada and Australia to start new lives on farms in the middle of nowhere, or skivvying as maids. They had no idea who they really were. Some were told their parents were dead when they weren't – that sort of thing. Now a lot of them – or their own kids – are trying to trace relatives out here. Some of them remember having an aunt or a cousin. Others have kept letters that trickled through from their first days there. Some have nothing but the orphanage records they arrived with. Some aren't even sure of their own real names. There were thousands of them over the years. They have these support groups helping them find their roots. It's a bit like black people in America did in the seventies.'

Mum blinked. 'It's not the same at all,' she said, then looked away. 'It's not as if they were *actually* slaves.'

'Even so,' Oscar said, 'they're all pretty sad stories.'

He buys breakfast to eat on the train and works on his orphan project. He has two families to find, both in London, which is part of the reason he's going into town today – the reason he has given Mum. Mr Hawkins was good enough to put him in touch with a contact of his – a Mr Barry – a man he knows who traces people for wills and the like. Mr Barry turned out to be the helpful sort, keeping Oscar on the phone for almost an hour telling him about the numerous kinds of registers you can look at, websites to bookmark and the address of an archive in west London full of old microfiched newspapers. For local papers, go to the local library. 'Births, marriages and deaths,' Mr Barry said. 'Just think of everything that way and you won't go far wrong. School sports days too, village fêtes, bonfire nights, amateur dramatics, Christmas carols. You'd be amazed. When you think about it, we're followed every step of the way.' Oscar got the feeling Mr Barry didn't have the chance to discuss his work very often with anyone who was interested. 'Start at the very beginning – as the *Mary Poppins* song goes,' he chuckled, and started singing it down the phone. Oscar laughed too, though obviously Mr Barry meant *The Sound of Music*.

Oscar has drawn a blank on the Hackney Dawsons, whom Michael, he discovered, had gone some way to investigating, armed with the birth certificate of one William Dawson, who is now in his eighties and lives in retirement in Winnipeg. He followed up an address for two cousins he found in the files – a brother and sister who lived together in Bethnal Green – but neither is still alive. He knew it couldn't be the house when he arrived; you could tell by the decor, seen through the big sash window at the front. A woman in her early twenties in charge of two children came to the door and shook her head, said sorry in a foreign accent and explained she was just the nanny. Oscar, his pen hovering over a small pad, then spoke to an elderly woman two doors down who remembered a daughter who used to visit but that was two years ago or more. 'Another gentleman came looking for them,' she said. 'A while back now. I told him the same thing. I can't remember the daughter's name now.'

Oscar presented her with his business card. 'Another gentleman?'

She lost herself for a moment as she studied the print on the card. 'Very polite he was,' she said at last.

'Was it a Mr Edwards?' It alarmed him for a moment to think he was literally following in his own dead father's footsteps. 'Did he wear cufflinks?' he heard himself ask.

She worried with the question for a few moments, impatient with herself, as though it was the kind of thing perhaps a younger person would have been sure to remember, then shook her head. Most of the other neighbours had sold up and moved out, she told Oscar, as though any information was better than an empty hand. 'It's all young people down here now.'

Oscar emailed Greville Wood in Canada and actually wrote the words 'the trail has gone temporarily cold', and though he has done nothing but waste time so far he can't help being hooked by this. He imagines it's like being a private eye, but without the guns and girls and the bad diet. Greville Wood says the organisation has funds and offers Oscar eighty pounds a day plus expenses for foraging in London and elsewhere, with a lump sum payable on results. This seems good enough – even generous. They trusted Michael, so they trust him, thinking he knows what he's doing – maybe even thinking that, as Michael's son, he already knows the ropes. And you can probably get a lot

130

done in a day, Oscar thinks, though most of it so far has been spent eliminating possibilities.

The family he now needs to trace is called Daykin. Amy Daykin was brought up in a Barnardo's home and sent to Canada when she was eight. She has no documents but believes she was born in Islington, London, in 1919 or 1920. Her mother was May Daykin, unmarried; Amy's father is a mystery. She remembers a baby brother, Tom, but that was before she went to the Barnardo's home. Perhaps she was about five or six then. They lived in a house together. Amy remembers the baby crying. She remembers an 'uncle', as they called them at Barnardo's, telling her she was going to start a new life in Australia, but she ended up in Canada.

This early life is laid out on four neatly handwritten sheets of lined notepaper in Amy's own words, enclosed with a couple of photographs, one old, one more recent. It's not much to go on, but Oscar is touched by the story. And how powerful this urge to go back – this woman who is now in her eighties, a widow with a grown-up family of her own, craving to know where in the world she came from before she departs it for good.

Amy and May, anagrams of each other.

When Amy's details came through last week, he followed Mr Barry's advice and started at the very beginning, calling the Family Records Centre in London to enquire how he might go about obtaining copies of birth certificates and the like. The woman advised him to come in and search in person. That's what he's doing today. The train pulls in on time, and at eleven-thirty Oscar finds the place, a new-built facility with an angular redbrick and concrete façade, wheelchair ramp and revolving doors and security area where they check your bags for bombs. The interior – an arrangement of interlinking galleries with bordered study

131

areas – is church-quiet with people seated at tables and computers. There's just the steady sound of books being removed and put back. Oscar is stiff with the awkwardness he feels on the threshold of social gatherings, but someone directs him to a stand of leaflets that explain the layout and facilities and how to use them in bewildering detail. He wanders on until he stumbles upon the row of aisles signed 'Births', then stands for a moment transfixed, watching what everyone else is doing, some taking or replacing books, others reading, the rows of heads – many of them grey-haired at this time of day with everyone else at work – retirees they look like, their restless eyes flitting behind spectacles, their pale fingers running down the entries, tiers of print that from a distance could be hieroglyphs or grid references to maps of the past, clues to burial sites.

Gently, Oscar slides one of the great books from its place, takes its weight and lays it on the lectern. He leafs through the pages, wonders at these hundreds of newborns, most of them now deaths of course, recorded elsewhere under this roof – marriages too, whole, lived-long lives marked by three lines of type separated by time and circumstance, just sitting there in the dark waiting to be discovered and reunited, lost parts of a story.

Oscar sets to his task. The time passes as he works along one side of the back-to-back rows of lecterns, selecting one after another of the tall, leatherbound registers ranked on the metal shelves behind him, ordered quarterly by year, and within by surname. He works like everyone else, hits a rhythm of hauling a book from its space, opening the page at the DAs, checking the Amys, closing, replacing, swinging the next one down. After a time, when he finds his mind sliding over the words, he stops and has a cup of tea in the basement before resurfacing, wandering among the browsers and researchers, orienting himself as he must to do this job. The red books are for births. Other aisles contain green books for marriage, yellow for adoptions, black for death.

There are records of nine Amy Daykins born in different boroughs of London between 1919 and 1920: Lambeth, Westminster, Southwark, Stoke Newington, Pimlico, Hackney – none of them Islington. Disappointingly, the listings give no information on parentage, just a numbered reference to the birth certificate itself, which can be ordered at £7 a copy. After some deliberation Oscar decides to order three certificates at random, filling out green forms and paying at the cashier's window using his new cheque-book. The certificates will take a few days to arrive, the man says.

He wonders now about May Daykin, Amy's mother. Unless she was especially promiscuous, it seems safe to assume she must have been born at least fourteen years before her daughter, though he has no idea where. Going backwards from 1906 he jots down details from thirty entries before stopping, exhausted, at 1898. Lincoln? Bloomsbury? Stoke-on-Trent? Margate? It could be any of them, or none. He carries on, sticking to southern England, but even now he ends up with too many to handle. The woman on the information desk suggests he try the online census for 1901. 'That would give you the girl's age,' she says. 'If you're sure that's her maiden name. And if you know the rough area she came from.'

'I don't know anything,' Oscar says. 'I don't even know if she'd even been born by 1901. What about a later census?'

'The next one would be 1911, but that's not available. They're only made public after a hundred years has gone by.'

Seeing Oscar's face drop, she takes a look at his notes

again. 'Daykin doesn't sound so common a name. It's worth a try.'

Oscar nods. 'So, if she was alive in 1901, she'll be in the census?'

'Unless she was Irish,' the woman says, smiling. 'Or Scottish. We don't have those records here.'

Oscar buys a £5 voucher and sits at the computer seeking Amy's mother, May. He imagines May as an infant, in the bosom of a family, still dreaming life is safe. He now confines his search to London, and the computer comes up with nineteen listings but only a handful are children. He goes through these, hitting 'view' each time to access a facsimile of the original page from 1901, showing the area, the street, the house, the head of the household and his dependants or lodgers. Nothing leaps out at him. While he waits for printouts, the woman from the information desk wanders by. 'Any luck?'

'Not really.' He peers at the information on the screen.

'It occurred to me that May was often a shortened form of Mary,' she says. 'That might help.'

'Mary?'

'Or it could even be Margaret.'

'Margaret. Great.' Oscar goes off to buy another voucher.

'You might need ten pounds,' the woman calls after him. 'Mary was a very popular name.'

Mary is Mum's middle name and also, now he thinks of it, the name of *her* mother, whom no one in the family has ever met. They were never close. Her parents had problems and at some point split up. Mum had no siblings. She was sent to boarding school and – as amazing as it seems now – was almost expelled in 1968 for smoking pot, a rebel sixth-former who came to London to art college and ended up hardly seeing her parents. But running away from home didn't make her bad at bringing up a family of her own – quite the opposite. 'You're all I need,' she once told Oscar. He wouldn't have been older than six or seven. He had been helping her in the kitchen and had slipped off the chair and hurt his knee. She'd patched him up and kissed him better. 'You and your sister.'

'What about Dad?'

'Dad too.'

She would never have met or married Dad if she'd had a normal childhood. There are unravellings all over the place if you just look, and new beginnings. The more of a mess things are, the more interesting.

It's two-thirty by the time Oscar emerges from the records centre and buys a sandwich at a nearby café which he eats walking to the tube at Farringdon. He has to be at Finsbury Park by four but plans to drop in on Miriam first and maybe arrange to meet up later. It's odd, this thing he has with her that seems purely to hinge on him turning up out of the blue, as he has on three occasions now since that first evening in the pub. Miriam has never called him – not since ringing the house about the lease expiring – and he doesn't call her. How can you have a sexual relationship with someone but not presume the liberty of a phone call? It is strange, and yet he feels to ring her would be to violate this protocol they seem to have established, as if phoning is an intimacy too delicate, or at least too close to official dating, which neither of them has sought to encourage.

Were it not for these lingering thoughts as he arrives at Crown House, it is unlikely Oscar would sense a premonition in the absence of Miriam's car from the yard, or find himself climbing the iron stairs more quickly than usual to the first floor, where he finds her studio shuttered and

135

bolted. A yellow printed card is fixed to the metal roller encasing the door – a forwarding address, in France – Lyons. He stares at it for a moment, like someone contemplating a result of their own forgetfulness – a roomful of steam from a boiling kettle or a window left open to burglars. He goes to the next unit along and taps on the window. The Asian girl – Darshan, is it? – who makes the turquoise jewellery. She looks up at him and gives a blink of recognition. 'Ah, Miriam's gone,' she says, 'but hang on.' She runs to the other side of her workbench wiping her hands and reaches for a white envelope sitting on the shelf. It has his name on it. 'She said to give you this if you asked.'

'Oh, right, thanks,' he says, taking the envelope. He waits till he's in the street before he reads it – a hurried note written with the nearest fat red pen, Miriam's handwriting, which he has never seen before, a looping style telling giddily of a two-year ceramics course with the chance of working part-time with a well-known ceramics firm, a supplier of department stores. 'God knows if I'll last that long,' she writes, 'but Dad's paying. Who knows – I might learn something!' Oscar's mouth dries up as he looks at the words, the high excitement of those exclamation marks. Is it sorrow he feels at her taking off like this, or envy? 'Call me up if you ever come this way,' it ends, which is goodbye however you say it.

A fatigue hits him, like the one he remembers feeling when he first came to Crown House to claim his inheritance, a burden that descends when the happy course of routine is altered by events not of his own making. He walks to Camden Lock and drifts with the market crowds, eventually settling near the canal bridge, sitting with his back to the sun-warmed wall. He rolls a cigarette and leafs through his printouts again, scanning for details he may have missed when he scrolled through the pages on screen at the records centre. The inclusion of the many Marys and Margarets has increased the total number of pages to eighteen, and deciphering the faded, curlicued handwriting of the original recorders has tired his eyes. On his first run-through he sought out the poorer-sounding areas that he seemed to know from the pages of Victorian novels – the East End, Southwark, Greenwich – but now he is reduced to feed on any crumb of promise, however far west of the smoke and squalor his mind is obliged to travel. But it is out here, in one of London's more affluent quarters – 12 Peel Walk, Notting Hill – that the first, early fruit of Oscar's efforts falls with an unexpected thud. Fuck . . . He controls his breathing as he reads it, as though the words are written in dust and might get blown away.

Margaret, granddaughter, aged two. Her parents are here – William and Victoria – but it is on the entry for the head of the house, and his wife, that Oscar's eyes are fixed: Thomas and Amy. Three generations at one address. Margaret – or May (was she always called May or did that come later?) – named both her children after her grandparents. It has to be her.

Oscar gets to his feet and starts walking, faster now, spurred by this find, working out the dates in his head, refining the story as he imagines it. He heads for the underground, takes the escalator down, calculating, conjecturing. Thomas the elder was an importer of teas; his son William – only twenty-two at the time of the census – is described simply as a 'manager'. What happened to their little girl? Rattling along on the tube, looking into the shuddering glass of the train window, he sees the infant May blossom into a beautiful but daring young lady of seventeen or eighteen, only to be then seduced by her raffishly handsome but ruthless piano teacher, who makes her pregnant

137

and abandons her to her fate. Thrown on the streets by her father (yes, now a paterfamilial forty, presumably living in his own house, or perhaps he has inherited the one at Peel Walk, Notting Hill) and condemned never to darken the Daykin door again, she falls among kindly prostitutes (yes, *this* is when she gets to be called May . . .). Barely weeks later, a daughter is born – Amy, named not after her cold, estranged mother but her dear grandmama, by then of course long dead. Or, no, perhaps still alive – perhaps May names the child in the hope of reconciliation with her family and a tearful reunion. Or maybe there are no prostitutes – maybe May has been secretly kept in modest comfort by her sympathetic grandparents until the fateful day she falls pregnant again, the result of some second cad promising to marry her. Doubly disgraced and disinherited – perhaps *now* May falls in with kindly prostitutes – or destitute and sent mad with despair, she is incarcerated by the mental health authorities and her children seized, Amy being dispatched to Barnardo's, thence to the wilds of Canada, and poor baby Tom to who knows where. Oscar's heart and mind are racing each other and he almost misses his stop, gathering his papers and darting for the train doors before they slam shut. At the top of the escalator the machine swallows his ticket and offers it out at the other side like something new. Finsbury Park.

He emerges from the underground as if from a dream. Now he must turn his thoughts to his own grandmother, who lives and breathes nearby. Mr Hawkins said he was glad he'd decided to see her, when Oscar rang to arrange this meeting. 'I know it's not really any of my business,' he said, 'but solicitors have feelings too. We wonder what clients get up to when they leave our offices. We wonder how the story ends. And I'm sure Mrs Edwards would like to see you. After all, you're the only family she has left.'

It's this thought that makes Oscar nervous as he surfaces on Seven Sisters Road and looks up the page in the index of his *A to Z*. It amuses him, too, to marvel that after a lifetime of avoiding responsibility he should be so quickly acquiring a taste for it. But, of course, it's not just a desire to do the decent thing that brings him here. The affairs of exiled orphans and coats of arms have made him curious to inspect this withered lopped branch of his own family, perhaps to see a reflection of himself in his grandmother's eyes, to do this against his mother's unaccountably fervent wishes, to work out for himself what she won't tell him.

Mrs Edwards lives in sheltered housing, a neat, purpose-built, single-storey development that looks on to the park itself, a sunny expanse of green, wherever you look, dotted with joggers, walkers and mothers out pushing buggies. Oscar rings the buzzer and is admitted to the lobby by a woman wearing a quilted housecoat and tinted glasses. 'Come in, love,' she says, yanking a vacuum cleaner behind her like an unwilling dog. 'I'll let her know you're here.'

The woman comes back after a few minutes and has him follow her down a carpeted corridor that opens out into a sunny communal room with one or two old people sitting around watching TV, then halfway down another corridor. She stops and taps on the door before opening it a few inches. 'Your young man is here, Mrs Edwards,' she warbles kindly. She turns to Oscar. 'In you go, love.'

And there she is, a tiny sparrow of a woman locked in the embrace of a large wing chair, a chequered blanket covering her legs, an oxygen bottle set at the side like one of those old-fashioned long-stemmed ashtrays Oscar remembers seeing in his childhood when smoking was sociable and even glamorous. A TV with the sound turned down offers a sideways blur of horseracing. 'Hello,' says Oscar, smiling, stepping further into the room.

139

She gives him a painful stare. 'I can see your mother,' she says at last, in a sharp, breathy voice. 'Sit down, help yourself.' She lifts an arm, soft and pastry-white, and gestures at the small table in front of her arranged with tea things and a plate of fig rolls. 'I can't get up. Mrs Raines says I ought to rest my knee.'

Oscar has no ready response to this, but pours the tea, trying not to rattle the saucers. 'It's a lovely day out there,' he says, edging a cup towards her. 'And this is nice,' he says, taking a biscuit.

Her worried eyes are on him as he eats, appraising him. She has to take a long breath before she speaks. 'Baby Oscar,' she croaks, 'all grown up.'

'I guess so,' he says, grinning through a mouthful of fig roll. They are pressed in by furniture: on one side a drop-leaf oak table holding a bowl of fruit and two anglepoise lamps; at the other, an old-fashioned ghetto-blaster sits on a mahogany sideboard, with three or four birthday cards. Although the room can barely accommodate her armchair, there's a second chair along with a two-seater leather sofa pushed into a corner, its cushions obscured by piles of junk – photograph albums, shoe boxes, books. Shadowed behind Mrs Edwards, the fixtures of a yellowish kitchenette are visible through a curtained opening, and two other doors lead off behind the scenes, to a bedroom, a bathroom.

'Some of these things were Michael's,' she says with a small cough. 'Most of the furniture went with his flat. I just have a few bits and pieces left. I've put some things in a box for you too. One or two photos you should have. And his work papers. He was always working. The solicitor has been ever so kind. He said you're carrying on with Michael's business.'

'I am, sort of. There's a lot to learn.'

Mrs Edwards puts her cup and saucer down and fiddles with the control on her oxygen tank. She turns it on and clamps the mask to her face for a few moments. 'Sorry,' she says.

'I could do with one of those,' Oscar says.

She gives a pained expression, missing his joke. 'No, love,' she says. 'You wouldn't want that.'

'Did you know his friend Ken?' he asks. 'He has a daughter called Miriam.'

She closes her eyes. 'He talked to me at the funeral. I remembered him, though I hadn't seen him for years, of course, not since he got married. I wouldn't have recognised him. I don't get out often now. Into the park every now and then with Mrs Raines, that's all. I have a walking frame. The doctor says to exercise my knee but Mrs Raines says I ought to rest it.' She laughs unexpectedly.

Oscar laughs too. 'I could take you out if you want.'

She shakes her head. 'Too out of puff. Next time,' she says.

They sit in silence for a moment, drinking tea.

'Ken told me what happened. Where Michael worked, I mean. When he died.'

She nods. From nowhere, it seems, a cat – black trimmed with white – strolls lazily into view, then springs into her lap, where it settles, looking at Oscar through half-closed eyes.

'This is Tippy,' she says, smiling. 'He's not mine but he likes to come in. We're not allowed pets here. Some do, but here they don't. For safety reasons. It's because of the electricity, I think.'

'I have a dog,' Oscar says. 'Troy. Dad doesn't like him too much.'

She nods. 'Your dad,' she murmurs.

Oscar looks around. 'Is it your birthday?'

141

'I was eighty-one on Sunday.'

'That's brilliant. Can I see your cards?' He gets up and reads the messages.

'They're from some of the other residents,' she says. 'The ladies are very nice. Maureen and Mrs Dobson and the others. I usually have my pictures up there, but Tippy knocks everything over. Can you see them there?'

Oscar picks up an oblong hinged frame lying on its face. It's the kind that holds three photographs. He brings it to the table, looking at the pictures: one black-and-white of a man taken ages ago, another in colour of another man about the same age, and the third of a boy in his teens, long-haired and pouting slightly for the camera.

'This is Michael,' she says, indicating the older man in the middle picture.

Oscar stares at the face, pale-eyed, bearded and earringed like his friend Ken, fattening up for middle age, arms crossed, collarless shirt and, yes, one chunky cufflink showing.

'And this . . .' she says, pointing at the black-and-white picture, 'this would have been your grandfather, if he'd lived. He died when the boys were young. It was very hard on them. He had a weak heart.'

'The boys? But is this not Michael too?' Oscar asks, pointing at the third picture.

'No, no, love, that's Sean.'

'Sean?'

'My youngest.'

'And he's . . .' Oscar can't say this.

'He was seventeen. He had a weak heart too.'

Oscar doesn't know what to say. He expects her to start crying but she just looks ahead at the soundless TV, at sleek racehorses being led round a paddock. 'It was a long time ago, love. He was mad about music, Sean was, like his brother. I'd bought him some drums, and Michael helped him set them up in his room. He was playing them when he died that same day. That's how they found him – Michael and your mother came in and found him – slumped at the side of his drums. It was a Saturday and I'd gone out shopping. They came in and found him dead. Didn't she ever tell you about it?'

Oscar shakes his head.

Mrs Edwards moves sideways in her chair, and the cat drops, resistingly, to the floor, waits, then pads away. 'Your mother was carrying you at the time, though nobody knew it. She and Michael broke up not long after you were born. I only saw you once, when you were a few weeks old. Before she took you away. They were going to get married, you know. It was Diane who changed her mind. Not Michael. He loved her. He wouldn't have abandoned her.' She says this fiercely.

'Sorry . . . did you say they *weren't* married?'

Mrs Edwards composes herself. 'No. Michael was upset by it, especially this coming after Sean. I don't know what happened. I think losing our Sean must have given Diane a shake too. I always thought afterwards she was running away from Michael, from the sickness, what she thought might happen to him one day. The doctor at the hospital said you couldn't predict something like that, but she saw something in it. And she was right. Michael's father and his brother were a sign of it, and Michael dying was proof itself.'

She reaches for her mask and gives herself a blast of oxygen.

Oscar waits. 'Do you think he knew he was going to die?'

She nods. 'He had tests. More than one. And then he made that will, didn't he? He thought about you, carrying on after him. Let me show you something. Pass me the box on top there . . .'

Oscar hands her a blue box – an office file – and she

143

clicks open the button clasp, her lumpy old fingers searching through the papers inside. 'This is it,' she says, giving the box back to Oscar and hurrying to unfold a large document, a chart. 'I found this among his things. He'd probably want you to have it, I think. He was tracing his family on his dad's side – the Edwards family. He's put you on it too. Look, there you are.'

Oscar crouches beside her chair, and gives a start as he sees his name here with all the others. The chart is handscripted in ink with scrolls and ornate headings and a key of symbols at the top with little graphic babies and bells representing births and marriages and a whole field of black crosses for deaths, some circled in red.

'So many of them died young,' she says. 'He guessed it and found it out for certain. You can see it from the dates. He showed me.'

Her eyes are watery now as she turns to look at Oscar, shaking her head, then looks back at the chart, not saying more. Oscar wonders about Michael in his studio trying to keep death away with the beating of those drums, like sacred relics cased in chrome and red glitter. And then he turns suddenly cold with fear. This is what Mrs Edwards is telling him. This is about *him* too, *his* fate written here in this chart. He thinks of his mother protecting him down the years from life's stormier trials, standing against the force of the history now laid out in this great puzzle of lives, his own crooked piece looking to be slotted in, like one of those family vaults waiting for everyone to arrive so they can close the lid for good. He imagines now the workings of his own heart, pulsing away, just as Michael's did, heading for a stumble of some sort, a breathlessness perhaps as a prelude to that final spastic jerk of muscle and valve, that last gasp of life and movement.

They sit for a few moments more, silently poring over

the chart. Long ago, before things soured between them, he and Rachel would sometimes share a comic like this, elbow to elbow on the new carpet while it rained outside. They always had a springy new carpet. It never occurred to them how lucky they were. It never occurred to them that what they'd always had could end.

The cat is at the door now, miaowing to get out, as if like him it is being invaded by a great and growing fear.

'Send your mother my best,' Mrs Edwards says at last. 'I won't get up.'

Chapter 10

'I can't get over how *well* you look,' Mum says. 'Doesn't she, Stuart?' Dad raises his eyes from the plate in front of him and takes time to frame his thoughts as he chews, holding a loose fist in front of his mouth for politeness' sake. Mum can't wait for his reply, and turns back to Rachel. 'Have you been on a diet, my love?'

'She's been to her fitness centre,' beams Robert, his attention busy with the last scrapings of his own food, his prudently saved measure of meat, his veg, mash and slick of gravy squashed to an even flatness and pushed the old-fashioned way on to the back of his fork to form a small, satisfying heap. 'Putting us all to shame,' he says, spitting a fleck of something – a fragment of pea – as he speaks. 'Not to say I won't be having pudding, though, Diane,' he adds, grinning lopsidedly. 'I wouldn't miss one of your puddings.'

'You've no weight on you, Robert,' Mum twitters,

moving quickly to take his plate though he's barely done putting his knife and fork to rest. She never quite sits up to the table; she's like a waitress taking a guarded break, ready to look busy at a moment's warning. 'Stuart could stand to lose a few pounds, though.' She gives a ridiculous wink all round.

Rachel responds blankly to the wink. She sees in Mum's chirpiness the attempt to keep the peace between father and daughter, to keep the conversation away from flashpoints. Have they been talking about her, about the direction she's taking the business?

'Nothing wrong with me,' Dad says, duly following her script as she disappears off to the kitchen, looking pretty good herself for her age. Oscar's dog – Troy he calls it, no doubt after some rap singer – pokes its head round the door, takes in Dad's glower and declines to enter.

'No Oscar tonight?' asks Rachel.

Dad looks now in the direction of the kitchen, where Mum is stooping to feed plates into the dishwasher. 'Who knows,' he says. 'He'll be out at that club with that mate of his, I imagine. Not that I've had much to complain about. You wouldn't believe how busy he's been, down to London and back every five minutes, or sitting in that hut of his in the market, or painting those shields, or up in his room reading. We hardly see him. He's got Luke scouring the internet for him, too, evenings and weekends, looking up God knows what, but . . .' Dad looks unusually wistful for an instant. 'To tell you the truth, I think Oscar's turned a corner at last, and that can't be a bad thing.'

'No sign of him moving out, then?' she says.

'I'm working on it.'

'And how are you, Dad? How's the gardening?'

Mum returns carrying a tray. 'The *gardening* is how it was when we moved in,' she says. 'I'm taking that spade and fork back to the shop, sitting out in the garage brand new and wrapped in their polythene still. We've had bird-watching since then and now it's astrology if you can believe it.'

'Astronomy,' Dad says.

'With a bloody great telescope costing I don't know how much up in the turret, if you'll excuse my French.' She sets the tray down. 'It's only ice cream, I'm afraid. I thought I had some apple crumble left. I've hardly time to cook these days. Maybe your father will take up cordon bleu cooking next. That would be nice.' She scoops Neapolitan balls from the tub, two into each glass dish. Pink, grey and yellow, they remind Rachel of lumps of wet clay.

'I won't, thanks,' she says.

'You look after your figure, Rachel,' Mum says, licking her fingertips. 'Keep yourself fresh. Isn't it your anniversary coming up?'

Is that what she thinks? Rachel, reddening as she smiles, hates herself for this, and suddenly feels as you do in a dream, walking unclothed down Market Street or sitting on a toilet in public view, except here it's her head that's transparent as glass, showing her thoughts – revealing a scene from Wednesday evening or the Wednesday evening before: a scene not from the air-conditioned, cool and efficient whirr of the fitness centre, as Robert might have expected to see if he could look into the window of her mind, but from an unfamiliar place that would have left him shaking his head, as puzzled as he often finds himself when he records a TV programme only to find an entirely unexpected one when he runs the tape, not quite willing to blame himself for getting it wrong. 'How did *that* happen?' Rachel imagines he might say, peering not at treadmills and step machines and weights, but at a furnished room with prints on the wall, a burning lamp (though there is still plenty of light out there beyond the swagged curtains), a reproduction walnut bureau, a bedside ashtray with two cigarettes lazily releasing twirls of smoke, a good inch of ash on each, slowly consuming themselves while their owners, just coming animatedly into shot, are otherwise engaged, a flash of their white skin reflected in the mirror, a private smudge of pubic hair.

How *did* it happen? Rachel doesn't quite know. She only knows she can't bring herself to be sorry that it did; she only knows, when she thinks of it, that she hugs herself like a breathless girl, marvelling at it, crouching in the darkness of this tight secret, suppressing the scream of excitement that would otherwise bring the world running, wanting to know the news.

It was by chance she'd been at the warehouse. The showroom was quiet, and she'd left early and gone there to look at the new stock, sign off some invoices for Barbara, walk the aisles, inspect Oscar's untidy den under the stairs, which she'd finally agreed he could use two days a week. When she came out half an hour later, it was Gareth Newnam's Audi there on the forecourt; his face at the open window grinning at her. 'Quick drink?'

She remembers her foolish hand going up to touch her hair and then putting on her best smile, as if it were a photographer that had suddenly pulled up and asked her for a picture. 'How did you know I was here?'

'I rang the other place and you weren't there.'

'I was on my way to the gym,' she said. 'My bag's in the boot.' But still she stood there.

'I wondered how things were going. We could have a chat.'

She looked at her car for a long moment, as if she hadn't already decided. The truth is she has become addicted to Gareth, to his voice, the soothing way he uses it to describe

149

those personal qualities she has that will guarantee her success, the way he echoes and builds on her enthusiasm like the best sort of soulmate. Just listening to him makes her soar.

And so they drove to the Belvedere. 'Don't let me have too much to drink,' she said.

'Did I tell you I was staying here?' he said, glancing at her, as they pulled into the pebbled yard at the side.

'Really?' She blushed, felt the blood booming in her ears. 'I hear the rooms are very good.'

'Come up and see me some time,' he quipped.

'I might just do that,' she heard herself say, her heart racing.

They were both smiling as they egged each other on, as if they knew that everything they said after that was part of a winning number, heading for something big. It was as simple as that.

Robert reaches over and takes Rachel's hand in what he intends to be an amusingly sentimental way. 'Six years on the fourteenth, if memory serves. And let's hope it does,' he adds, a mock nervousness in his glance. He kisses the ring on her hand.

What can she say? Except that, at the end of those six years, though they still have their moments, though she still loves him in a vague, half-forgotten way, Robert no longer makes her soar. Lost for a response, she simply raises her eyebrows at him, his hand squeezing hers, until reluctantly – because he needs to return to his ice cream – he releases her, awkward in his puppy happiness.

'Is it really six years?' Dad asks, shaking his head, working his tongue into a dental cavity. He turns to Robert. 'So how do you feel about Rachel not being Mrs Parsons any more?'

'Well, it's a professional thing, Stuart,' Robert says

easily. 'It's the modern way. She's still Mrs Parsons at home. Well, at the newsagent's, for instance.'

'That's the modern way, is it?'

Rachel can see where this is headed. 'You have to keep up, Dad, if you want to be taken seriously.'

Luke comes yawning into the room and grunts an unsmiling greeting at Robert and herself. 'Is there any Coke?' His hair has grown six inches. They watch him open the fridge, pour a glass from the bottle and gulp it down.

'Put the cap back on,' Mum says. 'And close the fridge door.' She shakes her head as he slopes out again.

Robert gets up, grinning for no good reason. 'Nature calls,' he says.

The three of them are silent now, as if with Robert's absence from the table a discreet switch has been thrown. Rachel's mind turns to Gareth, that effortless grace and strength he seems to have about him, an honesty of movement, you might say, an immaculate control. The way – for example – he so casually draws her right up to his body when they make love, with one arm underneath lifting her towards him while he eases in and out, and the way he's not afraid to look her right in the eye when he does it (unlike Robert, who when not approaching from his favoured rear reminds her these days of a man doing press-ups, concentrating, as he does, on a spot above the pine headboard, as if actually seeing how many he can get up to) amount to a synergy, you'd call it, a single, focused purpose that seems effortlessly to drive all of life in the same direction with one powerful, unstoppable sweep, a ride so thrilling that he makes her want to (thinking about the words of a song in her mother's collection of cassettes from the seventies) *strap her arms across his engines*, or something very much along those lines. It sounds corny but, no, he has that runaway quality, that magnetism and vision thing that makes a woman open her eyes to possibility and say yes to everything, even more so now, with his thing inside her and his whispering her name just before he comes. He has such big, sure hands.

'Stuart's worried about his prostate,' Mum says as Robert returns.

'*Diane*,' Dad complains, his spoon hovering, 'do you mind?'

'I've told him he shouldn't drink too much before bed.' Mum pours more wine. She is tipsy, unused to having more than one, pushing the boat out for the odd occasion like this. She and Dad hardly ever go out together now. When Rachel and Oscar were young, Mum and Dad would get a sitter sometimes on a Saturday and go see a film at the Odeon. Once in a while they even made a foursome with Tony and Penny, usually for a golf dinner or something else in town you had to dress up for. They're not real friends with the Ennicks, of course, but they make a show of it for Emma's sake, and have done since Emma was little, at least before she was sent off to boarding school and came to tea on alternate Sundays, the only day of the week Dad wasn't at work.

Rachel and Emma have never hit it off. It seemed unfair to her that Emma got to share Dad even though she had one of her own. It seemed unfair, too, that Emma, three years older than Rachel, preferred Oscar's company and would persuade him to take her to his den on the waste ground near the park, leaving Rachel alone with her dolls or a book until Mum took pity. 'Come on,' she would say, 'you can help me make the sandwiches.'

Is this where the resentment comes from? If they'd been real sisters it might have been different, but of course that was impossible with two sets of parents. The tangle comes from Dad splitting up with Penny, Mum arriving on the scene with Oscar. What twists lay behind those faraway transactions that are consummated in the way they see each other now? For some reason she has found herself imagining it these past weeks – Tony pursuing Penny, stealing her away behind Dad's back, even with a young child to think about. It could have happened that way. No one talks about it, of course. She has imagined, with a knowing shiver, Tony and Penny at the Belvedere, having to do it with Emma asleep in her buggy by the bed. Or, a worse scenario, with Dad at home looking after her and Penny making some excuse about needing to go into London. Penny was probably high maintenance even then. What did Tony have that Dad didn't? Money in the bank, better prospects than Dad, plus that something extra, that touch of glamour and flash that Dad lacked; whatever it is that keeps Tony leaner and more youthful-looking and of course a head taller, with suspiciously reddish hair – a bit creepily vain in that way, not giving up on himself with age, on that slightly roguish image he has of himself. Rachel can't imagine Dad with Penny. She's so quick and fashion-conscious, in that thin, brittle way, always at the hairdresser's or reclining at Hollywood Beauty having her nails done or a facial. Perhaps Dad was an idea that ran its course. An opportunity that fizzled out when a better one came along. But what Penny rejected, Mum went for. Stability. There was Oscar to consider. A girl from London, *complete* opposite of Penny – complete opposite of *Dad*. Didn't Mum once live in a squat? She still has the floaty dress sense and mad hair.

Mum never talked about what happened with her first marriage. She had no support, Rachel knows. A rebel public schoolgirl, fallen out with her parents. They were divorced, and destructive drinkers the pair of them, Dad once told her. Neither came to their wedding. Mum didn't attend her father's funeral, though she still makes the trip to the south coast to see her mother a couple of times a year. That's why Mum was always so protective of Oscar, Rachel figures, transferring her vulnerability to him. But she and Dad needed each other, she looking for someone like Dad at a time just when he needed to pick himself up after Penny. And amazingly it worked. Look at them now. Chalk and cheese but it worked. Afterwards, of course, Rachel herself came along, and much later Luke. But, for Tony, nothing. No children. None of his own. Penny had some sort of ovarian growth, not fantastically serious but scary enough to send her screaming into the operating theatre to have the whole lot whipped out, Mum said. After that it was just little Emma. No wonder they had her hot-housed. Precious.

'Enlarged prostate is pretty common anyway,' Robert is saying, adopting his serious voice. 'It's a gradual thing. It doesn't have to mean anything. I can pick you a leaflet up if you like – there's a Well Man right opposite our offices. It's no trouble. I could pop in at lunchtime.'

'I've said he should go to the doctor's if he's worried, but of course he won't,' Mum says, sighing. 'Typical male.'

Dad says nothing, just digs into his ice cream until it's gone. He licks the spoon. Rachel watches him. She has been bracing herself for an inquisition about the business, but apart from a few opening sallies about display and the new flip carousels Heldin's provide there has been nothing. Perhaps he senses how well she is doing. Though little is certain, she is buoyed by a conviction that this year will be hers. There's a small risk, ordering stock ahead in numbers, but prices won't stand still, as Gareth has said, and margins are especially crucial on a large project where the client makes it a buyer's market and suppliers are left clamouring to get in. And neutral colours are the key for show houses, Gareth said. A good twist. Calico or similar in colour. Or perhaps something with a small motif. You literally cannot lose. She has six of Gareth's rugs fanned out in the window. Just looking at them makes her tingle, right *there*.

Mum starts telling them all about her course, and about her tutor Marj, whose brother has come to stay. 'He hasn't got a job, doesn't want one and thinks everything's a global corporate conspiracy, Marj says. There's a gathering of the unwashed somewhere he has to go to, one of those demos they have when it gets warm enough and they throw dustbins through the windows of McDonald's. He was supposed to stay for the weekend and that was last Thursday.'

'Now who does that remind me of?' Rachel says.

As if on cue, a key turns in the lock and a moment later Oscar pops his head round the door. 'Oh,' he says, surprised. 'Hi.' He looks tired. The dog rushes in from the kitchen in a frenzy and starts licking his hand.

'You're back early,' Dad says, turning with some effort in his chair. He *has* put on weight, Rachel now notices, and yet somehow he seems diminished by it.

'I've been down to London,' Oscar says. 'I had to see somebody. I just got back on the train.'

Is he drunk? Rachel wonders. No, perhaps not.

'I thought I'd have an early night,' he says.

He looks at Mum and she at him, her face slightly flushed with drink herself, a hint of worry in her eyes. 'Aren't you going to eat?' she asks, getting up. 'Are you all right?'

'No, I'm fine,' he says.

Why she still fusses about Oscar, Rachel can't think, but her mind is so brimming with Gareth, the delirious pleasure and consuming guilt of him, that this is a mellower feeling than irritation, more like the sentimental impulse she has when she gives money to beggars on Christmas Eve, or other days when favourable omens come together to bring a glow to her spirit.

'Is there any more of that ice cream?' Dad says, tipping the tub towards him and peering in, the tip of his tongue touching his upper lip.

He has aged too, she thinks, and she feels a wave of pity, regret even, for the way she has had to stave him off lately. Although Dad responds to all displays of affection like a man of wood, she has a strong urge to take him in her arms, sitting there as he is in the middle of the week wearing one of his easy Sunday rugby-style sweatshirts, available in a palette of soft-washed colours from one of those mail-order catalogues. There's a happiness and sadness to it, but in the end isn't it natural, she reflects, the power commuting from parent to child, the instinct to protect passing from the one to the other like this? Gareth's parents are both dead. It wasn't so much like taking on the mantle of duty and responsibility, he told Rachel, lying there, the two of them, smoking his cigarettes and looking at the ceiling. You had to imagine the old and young moving towards each other down a long street, barely pausing to speak, before moving on. We're so busy after that – after the long, slow childhood that seems a lifetime in itself – you forget to look over your shoulder. And when you do, of course, they're gone. That was so beautiful, she thought. So very Gareth.

'There's still that Viennetta,' Mum says. 'Robert, will you have some?'

Chapter 11

What adds to his ailment (imagined or otherwise he will soon find out – but getting up in the night to urinate, sometimes two or three times, only to stand there in the light from the landing waiting for something to happen is hardly a figment, is it?) is the dull ache of Rael Eastern. Over lunch at the Beehive, Barbara said that the rep – the one with the blond highlights – had arrived one day at the warehouse for absolutely no reason and sat outside in his car just looking at the place. The man didn't see her because of course there aren't any windows to speak of at that side, just the one she was watching him out of in the toilet on the mezzanine. 'He sat there talking to himself,' she said, carefully lifting the roof of her pie with the edge of her knife, releasing the steam. 'I could see his lips moving.'

'Maybe he was singing,' Stuart said. 'He could have had the radio on.'

'Well, he *looked* like he was talking.'

'He could have been using one of those hands-free phones. Or speaking into a dictaphone. That's not too unusual.'

It wasn't unusual, but Rael Eastern is eating away at Stuart. It troubles him further to realise that it's the same corrosive discomfort he used to feel when Rachel started bringing boys home from college, though he knows that was different – that's what fathers are supposed to feel about their daughters. And he won't complain about how things turned out in that respect. Robert has solid qualities, though his voice can be grating. But this man, this Gareth Newnam, gets right under Stuart's skin and he has only met him once. He'd be hard pressed to pick him out of an identity parade. But it's what Newnam stands for that Stuart can't work out. Yes, he deals in those hand-woven Berbers and kilims and Turkish prayer mats – which Rachel will never shift at that price, not round here – but what else is he, this guy, creeping about like that? It doesn't compute, as Luke would say. It's not as if Newnam's got anywhere with the smaller retailers; this much Stuart is sure of. Carpet Land and SuperRug aren't stocking Rael and neither are First Flooring, who fancy themselves as upmarket and trendy, targeting those riverside conversions and the like. According to Barbara, Duttings have an exclusivity deal with Rael, but how does it benefit an importer to have all his rugs in one basket, so to speak?

'Brian seems a bit depressed,' Barbara said. 'He doesn't think he has Rachel's confidence.'

Stuart looked at the open pie on his plate as though the answer was in there, deep down in the dark gravy and button mushrooms. 'No one does.'

Today, he is heading for the doctor's – not Dr Bingley's surgery, which always seems to be full of people they know – but the anonymous new walk-in clinic across town near the football ground. He is hoping to get in and out by ten but has hit a standstill. It's especially galling, this grid-lock at the basin of the town, even after the rush hour, where the one-way system designed to handle the traffic traversing the central area is stymied by the recently added slip road. You can see the exact problem from the turret balcony back home. Perhaps he will write to the council. He'll ask Robert. Robert will know the precise department, the name of the man who heads it, the size of his budget, the name of his cat, how many sugars he likes in his tea.

He sighs. The ache returns. Of course, it's not just the fact of Rael. It's the sick, jittery feeling you get when you know you've acted in haste, done something to regret and in the process let yourself down irreversibly badly. The ache recalls that creeping taint of dishonour he felt after the fiasco with Barbara in the taxi years ago after the Christmas party at the bierkeller, the aftermath of that, awaking with a hangover next to Diane, innocently pregnant with Luke, Diane indulging him with a cooked breakfast and giving him more affection than he deserved. *That* is still with him, has become a part of him, like a lewd, hidden tattoo.

Is it a character flaw, this tendency towards regret? There was also, now he thinks about it, an occasion years ago, uneasily driving out to a job in Aldensey when his father was still alive. Though Stuart had nominally taken over the day-to-day running of the business, his father continued to control the finances and make the major deci-sions until he became ill and eventually died, aged only sixty-eight. The job was some way beyond the limits of Duttings' usual sales territory but the client was an acquaintance – masonic, probably – of his father's, a medium-sized hotelier calling in some favour. 'Look after him, Stu,' his father told him. 'It's cash,' he added. Stuart took this to mean that the money shouldn't go through the books but was to be salted away, undeclared, and the stock used written off at the year-end as damaged or otherwise unsaleable. It was no doubt a practice that went on in every small business. His father, he knew, had skimmed profits off certain jobs to pay staff bonuses at Christmas, but he also used it to sweeten larger clients, which generally meant a big lunch with brandies at the George Hotel in town. There was a certain pride in this and he took to carrying banknotes in his pockets like wads of used tissues. Did this cash change hands too on these occasions? Certainly, the commercial side of the business thrived while his father was still in charge and dwindled when Stuart himself took over, though domestic business became Duttings' meat and drink in any case as the town flowered on the back of the out-lying housing and infrastructure projects of the seventies.

Stuart was himself nervous of the way his father had nurtured this culture of casual dishonesty – not least for the risks of throwing temptation in the way of staff – and after his father passed away installed a proper billing, accounting and stocktaking system through old Walter, now replaced by Rachel's computers. He had never liked dealing in cash without the raising of duly authorised invoices and receipts, signed and if necessary rubber-stamped with the mark of Duttings. Collecting from jobs like the one at Aldensey made him nervous, as though eyes were upon him and judging. 'Take some pictures for the sales folder, Stuart,' his father said. 'It's a lovely chintz. Pure wool. Low static. Ideal for those long corridors. Take the big Kodak. Don't forget the flash.'

The place wasn't quite a hotel – barely more than a large pub or inn, a three-storey stone building situated in its own sheltered grounds a few minutes' walk from a shingle beach that ran down to the sea at a raking angle. The fitters were

160

almost done when Stuart arrived, and after taking his photographs of the completed sections of corridor there was little for him to do but hang around, ostensibly to oversee the work, but in essence to wait – to stand in the shadows like the sweating 'bag man' from the pages of the American detective comics he read as a teenager – for the proprietor to make an appearance and pass him a bulky envelope, perhaps under cover of a put-on embrace or enthusiastic handshake. In the end he sat out in the car until he saw the fitters emerge and pack their gear into the yellow Duttings van.

The proprietor was now waiting for *him* and beckoned peremptorily as he came back into the hotel, as though summoning one of his own waiters.

'Mr Callington?' Stuart began. 'Duttings, sir—'

'Yes, I realise that,' he replied. His curt manner took Stuart aback. The man – improbably smooth for someone his father might know, tall, clean-jowled and crisply tailored in a Prince of Wales check – had him come quickly into the bar where he laid the money in five- and one-pound notes on the counter with the bearing of a croupier snapping down cards. He told Stuart to be sure to give Mr Dutting his regards and strode off again without ceremony, clicking at a lurking member of staff to follow. That was it. The fitters had left, and Stuart should now have made a rapid exit himself. But something stopped him. Perhaps he was ashamed of his anxious performance with Mr Callington – felt the need to retrieve some dignity by doing something other than allowing himself to be dismissed like the courier he was assumed to be. Perhaps he would stay for lunch. It had gone twelve-thirty and the handful of guests he had noticed in the lobby – a man reading a newspaper, an elderly tweedy couple – had moved into the bar. A girl in uniform was busy checking the optics.

161

Undecided, Stuart stepped outside, the envelope in his pocket distending the line of his new brown suit from the John Collier next to the Corn Exchange. The grounds were small but offered leafy areas for residents to relax – to the left a honeysuckled pergola and a pathway leading to rustic benches and a pond of some sort; to the right a children's swing, more seating and a pair of hutches with rabbits visible behind the wire. It was early in the season but the sun was out, and Stuart stood on the apron of the gravel drive and lit a cigarette. It was now that he saw Tony. For a second his eyes refused to place him, as often happens when someone you know appears without warning in an unfamiliar context. But yes, Tony it surely was, waiting at the corner of the hotel, presumably having just emerged from the car park at the side of the building.

Stuart hesitated. Time enough had passed – two or three years since Tony had taken up with Penny, a year since Stuart had married Diane – for relations between the two men to have thawed, as they inevitably must between small-town business people with common interests and shared social connections, not to mention the question of Emma, now a toddler whom Stuart was allowed to see once a week. If this had been the builders' merchants, or the Lloyds in town where they both banked their takings at the end of each day, they might simply have exchanged a nod, each having the easy excuse of being too busy to stand around chatting – not to say that such encounters around town were too common to demand uncommon niceties, in much the same way that you wouldn't kiss your wife every time you saw her round the house. But here was different. Here they couldn't just nod. And there was still time to have *not* seen Tony – time *not* to call out and attract his attention and be obliged to exchange awkward greetings, to marvel at each other's presence so remote from their

162

respective patches, a prospect aggravated by Stuart's misgivings about what he himself was doing here exactly, with the evidence of unclean money still weighing heavy in his pocket. And yet it was something else entirely that stopped him. It had been his initial assumption that Tony was here on a job, perhaps via the same loose network of affiliations that brought Stuart himself to this genteel Suffolk resort in the middle of the week. But in the moment between recognising Tony and the impulse to catch his eye, he registered two things. The first was that Tony seemed not dressed for work, wearing neither his white tiling overalls nor the dark suit he favoured when out drumming up business, but instead sporting a then-fashionable wide-check sports jacket, beige flared trousers and maroon leather boots. The second (and it was at this point that Stuart found himself quickly backtracking into the hotel) was that Tony was not alone.

From the phone booth in the lobby, Stuart watched as they entered the bar and found a table; he watched, hardly daring to blink, as Tony helped her choose from the tall, ribboned menu. And when it was safe to move, he ducked outside and followed the arc of the bar to a half-curtained window. Here, at a short distance, he stood and watched until eventually Tony signed the bill and the two of them rose from their table, walked arm in arm to the lobby, paused for keys at the little desk and disappeared up the narrow staircase.

Stuart didn't know the young woman. She could have been anyone. A mousy shopgirl from the market, a typist from his office, a barmaid. But his curiosity was overshadowed by a sense of the offence committed. How could Tony *do* this to Penny? Penny – who everyone knew had recently suffered a second or third miscarriage?

But then, conversely, Stuart found it hard – even in the

days that followed – to examine his own motives for what happened next, to read his own confused emotions. After all, he owed Penny nothing, certainly not his sympathy. Indeed, one of the first thoughts that assailed him as he hurried back to the car was whether Tony had ever brought Penny here when they were doing the dirty on him. This hideaway so far from home. Of course he had never proved – not beyond doubt – that Tony and Penny had been carrying on behind his back, though it was clear something had been brewing. Their problems had started after Emma was born, which had left Penny depressed to the point of hysteria. 'Trapped and empty' was how she put it. She cried for hours when things went wrong. She said she was lonely. When the doctor prescribed Valium, Stuart suggested instead that she take herself off dancing once a week with her old friends from the office at Tattersall's while he looked after the baby. On more than one occasion Penny greedily hijacked the Wednesday afternoon Stuart took off every second week, pleading that she needed to go shopping in London or Cambridge. None of this helped. The light in their marriage faded, and soon afterwards a sobbing Penny suggested a trial separation – her keeping the little garden flat they rented near the college, him moving back to his parents' place out at Rhyton. That way he could see Emma as often as he liked. Though Penny seemed relaxed with this arrangement, Stuart was distraught. More so when legal separation ensued, and later divorce proceedings – more so again when Tony Ennick materialised with indecent if not outright suspicious haste to offer Penny a second shot at happiness, her own small car and one of the new double-glazed maisonettes on the fringes of the desirable Woodhampton estate within easy reach of shops and services.

So what, then, did Stuart care that Penny had been

cheated on in Aldensey, as she herself had cheated on him two years previously? He who, after all, was contentedly remarried himself by then with the unborn Rachel on the way. What was it to him, this act of treachery? Why the anger? Was it that Tony – in now dishonouring the woman he had stolen from Stuart – seemed to be adding insult to injury and deserved to be unmasked? Or did Stuart's indignation spring so defiantly from a sense of duty to his three-year-old daughter Emma, who had already had her short life ripped in half and deserved more serious consideration. In the end (he acknowledged this now), it was simple spite as much as moral agitation that compelled him to position his car across the road from the hotel and wait for the monstrous couple to emerge; to raise the big Kodak, his hands trembling, to take the picture. It took over a week in those days to get the film developed. ALDENSEY, MAY 14th, he wrote on the back of the photograph in pencil, before dropping it in the box outside the post office in town. Of course he didn't know – because how could he? – of the trouble stirring up inside Penny at that time. In fact, thinking about those two or three miscarried pregnancies – in the light of Penny's old problems handling the responsibilities of motherhood – he had caught himself wondering whether Penny was somehow *willing* it to go wrong, if not something worse. He couldn't know for sure the timing of things – when it was she found out about the tumour growing there. But the thought returns to trouble him at times like this. The tumour was benign, but when the doctors offered the option, as they did in those days, of a quick hysterectomy, what was it that made her say yes?

In retrospect, he might simply have mailed the photograph to Tony – a warning shot. He could have just done that. It would probably have worked. A chance to do the right thing without being found out doing the wrong thing. The shame was sending it to Penny and rubbing her nose in it; the satisfaction from saying, *this is what you get*.

And now this. The ache. There's the ache of what he has done, then the ache of a physical, pelvic kind. Two aches in one – three including the house, out there on the outlying margins of his anxiety – indistinguishable sometimes, lying in bed, the ache and the black thoughts about Rael and Rachel, and the weighty loan he took out to pay for their new home at High Firs pressing down on everything, crushing the hope out of him. He eases the wide Lexus down the narrow road lined with parked cars, many jutting out. So near to the clinic now, he is in a fret about his prostate. The Willows these days brims with experts on the subject. It is a source, though, of laughter not wisdom. Jos it was, the clubhouse manager, who had mentioned a type of umbrella-like probe he'd heard had to be inserted in the penile canal.

'I know some blokes who'd pay for that,' cackled Gordon.

'Not funny though,' Tony said gravely, and then started chuckling. They all did, even Stuart himself. No one knows about his worry, except Diane, and now of course Rachel and Robert. It's probably nothing, he says to her blackly. It's probably just cancer. But if it is? If it IS? A little time bomb to go with the others. The one at the warehouse, the one under the house.

He halts the car in the middle of the road, scans the line outside the clinic for a parking space and to his surprise sees Oscar's VW camper sitting there in its glowing force field of green. He pauses, sees properly for the first time its absurd slogans, seemingly speaking directly to him. Take No Prisoners. Free The Land. For reasons he cannot explain, he is filled with panic. He forgets he is in gear and

166

stalls the engine, turns the key again and drives off at speed. He is sweating.

If God takes the ache away, he vows to tell Diane everything – about the house, about Barbara and the taxi, about the photograph he sent to Penny thirty years ago. And now something else – an email dispatched in a moment of pique or blighted faculty (Tony is right – everything starts to go) to the most rabid-sounding human rights nutters he could find on the internet, alerting whomever it concerned to the activities of Rael Eastern, to their role as child-exploiters in Pakistan and elsewhere, to the presence of their vile merchandise in the high street of one of Britain's foremost market towns in terms of quality of life, low crime and traditional values. On this frightening precipice, he clings to his love for her. He will tell her everything.

Chapter 12

In the weeks following the day with his grandmother at Finsbury Park, Oscar has seen the doctor, and had his blood pressure and heartbeat and cholesterol levels looked at and pronounced normal. He told the doctor about the history of problems on his father's side and, when asked, searched his childhood memories for instances of respiratory weakness or trouble with his circulation. The doctor nodded as Oscar told him how in primary school he once suffered a dizzy spell after being made to stand motionless in a corner for misbehaving in class. He remembered his mother coming in next day to complain to the head teacher. He remembers, too, how he never lacked for a note excusing him from PE for reasons of a cold or other common ailment, especially during the long afternoon periods of winter games, which he spent in the relative warmth of the gym, quietly reading and earning the resentment of the other boys, who rehearsed football tactics in a lashing rain.

The doctor nodded more and stuck out his bottom lip, but Oscar saw in his eyes that there was nothing unusual in this.

But the more he looks at it now, the more significance he finds in the agglomeration of small things, a patterning in the details of his mother's gentle cushioning of the everyday trials a boy has, an unusual caution in the face of exertion or excitement. Where adventure beckoned – a summer's afternoon swimming with friends where the river bends near the bridge, tree-climbing for conkers in the autumn, sledging in the winter – he felt her presence at the margins, a figure among the trees appearing unexpectedly with sweets or drinks for everyone. Without expressly forbidding anything – that would never have been her way – she would subvert his wants with promises of something with rarer attractions: a drive into Cambridge to buy American comics (a taste for which he inherited from Dad, who back then still kept boxes of ancient 1960s *Sinister Tales* and *Twilight Zones* in the attic) or money to take a couple of friends to see a film at the Odeon. At other times she would call him in from play to take him to the barber's. And then there were the barriers she seemed instinctively to raise against academic expectation or criticism about his taste in music or clothes. Mum was relaxed about everything – the happy languor of her sixties youth set against Dad's market town conservatism. But now Oscar sees this, too, less as a general corrective to his stepfather's wish to mould a son with the character and application to match his own than an attempt to ward off any susceptibility to sudden shock she suspected ran deep in his blood but was afraid to know more about. He avoids her eyes now in the same way she has been avoiding his.

Once or twice he found himself, trance-like, in his room, sifting as if for clues through Michael's papers, looking at the three or four photographs here – there's only one of Michael with Mum, posing arm in arm in front of a shoe shop on Carnaby Street – but always returning to the two ECG readouts dated a few months before he died, one produced by a hospital in London, the other by a private healthcare facility. Normal, they both concluded. And yet how could it be normal? Oscar told his doctor about his father's tests and the story about the boy who, had he lived, would have been his uncle. The doctor listened and, to put Oscar's mind at rest, referred him for tests of his own, in another part of the clinic, with the result that, a week later, Oscar had his own 'normal' ECG readout to compare with Michael's.

But Oscar's mind cannot rest. One night, after leaving Diggsy at the Green House, he walked most of the circumference of the peripheral before surprising the dozing attendant of an outlying minicab office in the early hours. When he got home he pulled out the chart of his family tree and laid it out on his bedroom floor, studying the branches and foreshortened spurs spreading from his grandfather's entry in 1921, taking down the names of blood relatives probably unknown even to Michael and his mother. He spent the next days trawling the Records Centre and other archives and repositories of personal and business information in London, separating the living and the dead, ordering certificates, looking at wills and directories, tracing possible career paths and places of work. He has scoured the internet for school reunion sites and genealogy groups, firing off speculative emails. Taking out subscriptions to online 'people finding' services that can pinpoint individuals through cross-referencing electoral rolls and commercial databases and records of divorces and title deeds and God knows what else, he has the numbers and addresses for a dozen or so Edwardses more or less likely to be related to himself and he has written to them too – the desperate raving letters of a madman that only a madman will reply to.

But he waits. He wonders whether Michael tortured himself with thoughts of mortality, or whether in time the knowledge assimilated itself, like an acquired habit or slowly failing eyesight. Oscar is throwing himself into his work, spurred partly by a letter from a Dora Whately (Mrs) who was writing with details of a Mrs Brenda Cole (née Dawson), neither of whose names he recognised at first, but finally connected to his visit to Bethnal Green in search of the Hackney Dawsons. Mrs Whately was the elderly neighbour he had spoken to, and Mrs Cole, Oscar worked out – looking back at the file and his notebook – was the daughter of one of the deceased, formerly co-habiting siblings (presumably the brother, since Mrs Cole carried his name until she herself married), both, then, cousins of the 'orphan' emigrant William Dawson out in Winnipeg. Oscar emailed the results of his enquiries to Greville Wood, who replied with an excited message of thanks, and said an official approach was in the pipeline.

There is progress too with the Amy Daykin job. To his surprise, Oscar found her great-grandfather Thomas's company – Thos. Daykin (Tea Importers) – still extant and listed at Companies House under Daykin Group (UK & O/seas). He has phoned for an annual report and history. He has applied to see the will of Thomas (died 1923) and that of his son William (died 1950) – father of Amy's mother, poor Margaret or May, outcast in disgrace to an unknown fate. He has written, too, to Barnardo's asking to see Amy's records and for any details they might have regarding her baby brother Tom, and has received an acknowledgement giving the reference and name of the department looking into it. It all costs money, but the more he uses these up-to-the-minute research tools, the quicker he gets at guessing where to go next. He has rung Mr Hawkins for advice and a chat. 'Don't worry,' Mr Hawkins laughed, 'it's all tax-deductible.'

These affairs and the work at Roots keep Oscar occupied. It's late Sunday afternoon and he is alone painting shields at the warehouse when Emma arrives unexpectedly, calls him 'stranger' and ribs him for not being in touch, especially when by all accounts things are beginning to take off for him. He has never been more glad to see her, but his smile gives less away, as it always does. Even this – this controlled response to the small pleasures life throws up – seems a reflex from his childhood, his mother's pacific influence, though there is something else too, held over from his last meeting with Emma in London, a residual injury that adds a layer of awkwardness between them. Yes, he tells her, the kiosk is doing pretty well. He wipes his hands, and makes tea for them both.

'Dad said you were here. He dropped me outside just now. I hope you don't mind me turning up like this.'

'Course not. I was just doing some catching up really. Diggsy's had to put some hours in down the club.'

They stand nodding at each other for a moment. 'Things are looking busy round here too,' she says, glancing round at the new stock of carpet, which takes up all the aisle space and stands in vertical ranks where it can, shoulder to shoulder in plastic wrappings.

'Rachel's big project,' he says. 'Come on, we can sit over here.' He shows her to a corner of the warehouse that the fitters have turned into a den, with a couple of old office armchairs and an upturned box for a table. 'Hang on a minute,' he says. An offcut forms a soft pathway behind the last aisle, and Emma holds the mugs of tea while he plugs in a hoover and vacuums it quickly up and down.

'This is my hideaway,' he says. 'I take a break here with my books sometimes.' They settle down with their backs leaning against the last roll of carpet. 'Rachel doesn't get up here much now. Even when she does, there's so much stock that she can't see this end of the warehouse from the office.' He starts to roll a cigarette. 'She doesn't mind having me in the workshop, but she'd kill me if she caught me down here smoking. Or at least make me give the key back. You can imagine the place going up in flames. Have to be extra careful.'

'No grass then?'

He frowns. 'Tell you the truth, I've been laying off it recently. I need to keep a clear head.'

'That doesn't sound like you.' She smiles at him quickly. 'Well, you know what I mean.'

He forces a smile in return and hands her the cigarette, and rolls one for himself. 'I do know what you mean. But . . .' He licks the paper.

'What?' she asks, looking at him now, as if she knows something's not all right.

He lights the cigarette and takes time to peel a fibre of tobacco from the tip of his tongue. He tells her about the meeting with his grandmother, the family tree with its black crosses, his visit to the clinic.

'But your heart *is* OK, right?' She touches his wrist. 'That's what they said, isn't it?'

'Well yes, but that's what they said about *his*. My father's.' He stares down the aisle and fixes his eyes on the brick wall. It feels strange saying 'father' and not meaning Dad.

Emma looks at the carpet. 'Have you told your mum?'

'I can't speak to her. She got so weird when I brought that drum kit into the house. Even weirder when she came home and found Luke bashing away on it. The death drum

173

kit!' He laughs but then catches his breath. 'The thing is, they were never married, Mum and Michael, so I thought that must be it – why she didn't want it all dragging back up again. But talking to this old woman – my grandmother – she seemed to think Mum was running away from it all. She must have thought about it a lot when I was little and growing up, but Michael dying has brought it all back. It's not that she seems worried about *me* any more – but I don't know, maybe she does. I get the sense, though, knowing what I do know, that she's feeling the shame of it again, what she did to him. That's why it's hard for me to say anything to her, or her to me. And I feel – and I know it's wrong – but I feel really pissed off with him. The way that he left me the money and his shield business – which I'm really getting into, and that's great – but now it's like I've also inherited this fucking . . . *thing*. It's as though he knew that, and that's why he left me the money. I'm thinking maybe it's just guilt, you know, something to soften the blow when I found out.'

Emma puts her arm round him. 'Hey, you don't know that. Not everyone inherits what their parents have, do they? It's not inevitable.' She gives him a hug, as if not believing that herself. 'Come on,' she says. 'Let's get a drink somewhere.'

He stifles a sigh. 'The Bull might be open, but it's a bit grim.'

'Why don't you drive us up to the Two Fields? That way I could walk back to my mum's, and you . . . well, you could take the van and get pulled up by the police for drink-driving,' she says.

'Sounds like a good deal,' he says. They lock up and walk to the camper. He tells her about his late-night hike around the peripheral. 'It's so bizarre. I've been trying to shake it off but I can't. I feel cursed. Sorry,' he says. 'I'll

174

try and cheer up. Believe it or not, I am glad to see you.'

'And I'm glad to see you too.'

The Two Fields is open all day, but these are the doldrums between the last of the long Sunday lunchers and the first dribblings of the evening session – three men at the bar rocking on their heels, sharing a joke, a couple not talking in a corner, as if engrossed by the CD of easy-listening standards whispering like air-conditioning in the background. Oscar remembers Dad bringing him to this place years ago, a few days before he went off to college, a man-to-man thing, he presumed – Dad showing him what he might be if he ever grew up. It was about this same time of day too, the bar gradually filling with moderate, older drinkers in slacks and golf sweaters or jackets and ties while younger people, lively but respectable, with good jobs – their sons and daughters, perhaps – filtered in to occupy the surrounding tables. It's that sort of pub, upholstered in magenta plush with gleaming brasses and framed photographs of brewery drays, proud of being one of the nicer pubs in one of the nicer parts of town. The landlord and his wife dress as though for a night out themselves, and their scrubbed, acned bar staff – recruited from the upper sixth at the private boys' high – wear bowties and paisley waistcoats. On that night, Oscar remembers, Emma's stepfather Tony was there. He came over and shook his hand and wished him the best of luck. Emma had already left for Cambridge by then, without saying goodbye. It was a time when she and Oscar saw little of each other and spoke less, those last two or three years of boarding school when Emma's visits to the Dutting house were infrequent and fleeting, and the awkwardness of teenhood stood like a foreign language between them.

Oscar carries their drinks to a table and they sit down.

'Don't you have to get back to London tonight?'

'I'm taking the week off,' Emma says. 'I've got some thinking to do.'

'What do you need to think about?'

She gulps down a mouthful of beer and licks the rime of froth from her upper lip. 'I'm leaving the bank.'

'What, you've got another job?'

'No. I've just had enough. I've handed in my notice.'

'Wow.' Oscar nods. 'Isn't that a bit dangerous?'

'I suppose so. It feels good though.'

Oscar has to laugh. 'I can't believe you're giving it up just like that.'

She gives a dismissive wave of her hand. 'To tell you the truth, it doesn't do it for me any more. It's become just about money.'

'But isn't it supposed to be about money – isn't that what banks do?'

'Earning it, silly. I mean, obviously I like the money, but what satisfaction I used to get from the doing end of things, that's all gone. You work to get these companies cranked up and watch them take off – or, occasionally, not take off – and then you start all over again with the next. It's a bit like being a midwife, or a foster parent or something. I don't know.' She sips at her beer. 'There's something sort of sad about it.'

'The world needs its midwives and foster parents,' Oscar says.

'Well, I've done my bit. I've got money put away. I want to do something different. I don't know what. Something a bit more . . .'

'Worthwhile?'

'Ha-ha! I wouldn't go that far. Maybe though.'

'What does Tony say?'

'I haven't had a chance to mention it yet.'

'And Dad?'

176

She shakes her head. 'There's no rush.'

The pub is getting busier. Emma takes her cardigan off. She has a sleeveless pink top on and her blonde hairs show against the brown of her arms. Oscar starts to tell the story of Amy Daykin, but by now he's on his second Guinness, and without his notes to hand realises that he has confused the three, or is it four, generations, imagining the grandfather as the tea merchant and the older Amy as the poor girl's mother and the poor girl, Margaret, as Amy herself. When he gets to the question of wills, Emma remembers someone at the office who used a brilliant online registry of unclaimed assets. 'I'll send you it,' she says, 'if I can remember who had it. Can't have been Jeremy. No. Maybe it was Miles . . .'

This talk of Emma's office sucks the air out of the conversation. They sit for half a minute not speaking, watching one of the staff mopping up a spilt drink at the far side of the room.

'So, how's Vaughan?' Oscar asks, as he knows he must.

Emma sighs. 'I know what you must think. I'm sorry about that lunch. Vaughan can be an arsehole. In fact, OK, Vaughan *is* an arsehole. And I know I should have said so, instead of trying to keep the peace. I meant to call you, but it seemed difficult apologising for him being an arsehole while I was still going out with him.' She pauses. 'Which, I can tell you, since you expressed an interest, I'm now not.'

'Not what?'

'It's over. He's over. We are, that is.'

'Wow. I'm sorry to hear that.'

'Are you?'

'No.' He grins. 'But I'm sorry if you're not happy about it.'

'Well it's been a while coming. Vaughan was fun to start

177

with, especially around other people, when we went out with friends, at parties and so on. And he could be sweet. But, thinking about it, we didn't really have too much to say to each other. And then going on holiday together this last time was a bit of a damp squib. We should have finished it then but neither of us could be bothered. I think that, unless you fight all the time – which we didn't – you just fall into the habit of being together. It occurred to me the only reason I was still with him was that Tony and Mum liked him. Anyway, we're done. Fresh starts all round.' She raises her glass.

They stay at the Two Fields, drinking slowly and picking at the plate of chilled snacks one of the barmen has brought to their table – cubes of sausage and roast potato left over from the carvery buffet they have here every Sunday – until the landlord calls time. Outside, the evening is mild, and they stand in the car park for a moment looking at the camper. 'I'd better leave it here, I suppose,' says Oscar.

Emma smiles. 'It'll give the landlord a nice shock in the morning.'

'Come on,' Oscar says. 'I'll walk you back.'

'Stay for coffee,' she says. 'And then you can ring a cab if you can't face the haul back home. Especially that hill at the other end.'

'Isn't it a bit late? I wouldn't want to disturb Tony and your mum.'

'Now *that*,' she says, 'would be unlikely. They're in Tenerife for the week. Which is why I'm here – looking after the house. Didn't I mention it?'

'I don't believe you did.'

'Mum wants to top up her tan with a real one.'

'Lead the way,' he says.

The sky is full of stars, and they walk slowly, savouring

178

the air, as though there's no hurry to get to the house. Emma is swaying nicely, her cardigan draped over her shoulders. She swats Oscar with a sleeve as he jokes about lifestyle statements here in this neighbourhood – the perfect geometry of hedges and lawns, the way the MPVs and four-by-fours squat on drives like guard dogs, the competition going quietly on for illuminated statuary. It's no more than an easy ten minutes to the Ennicks' place, an executive-style bungalow built on a big plot set back from one of the quiet roads on the Ivesy estate. Oscar hasn't been here for years – not since Emma's birthday parties, when they were both little and were encouraged to think of themselves as cousins, the days before Emma had to go away to school. One thing he remembers is the house always being neat and tidy – he was amazed to find that the Ennicks employed a woman to clean – and so spacious and modern and centrally heated compared to their own end terrace with its two square downstairs rooms and dark hallway and living-flame electric fires. On the occasion of these parties, Dad would only stay a few minutes, enough time to give Emma her present. Oscar always sensed a prickliness between Dad and Tony, though of course he didn't understand it until he was older. He remembers Mum once telling him how, years before, when the Ennicks moved out here from their flat in the Woodhamptons, Tony pointedly went to an out-of-town firm to buy their carpets. Dad feigned indifference, she said, but felt the snub. Back then, the Ennicks were always felt to be one or two social notches above the Duttings. It's only recently, since the move to High Firs, that Dad has caught up with Tony, maybe even gained the edge, as he would see it. Mum, Oscar knows, would have been happy to stay put at the semi in Malting Street they all liked well enough, which was nearer to Luke's school and where at least they could cope with the gardening and all their friends were right on the doorstep. The move out to High Firs, impressive as the new house is, was a sop to Dad's pride, his last throw in the game that he still had going with Tony. It looked like a new start, but when you thought about it, it was the beginning of the end of everything for Dad.

Emma unlocks the door. 'Shh,' she whispers. 'Better not wake the neighbours.' The kitchen is yellow and spotless, almost as he remembers it, though the units look new and they have one of those big American fridges. He goes through to the split-level sitting room while Emma puts the kettle on. Here too are the same fringed sofas, occasional tables, the long sideboard arranged with glass animals and family photographs, the dining area up the two carpeted steps. 'Not much has changed,' he shouts to her. Even the TV is in the same corner, though it is the latest giant flatscreen model. Perched on the big sofa, he points the remote and the TV comes to life with a small explosive pop. A weathergirl is gesturing at a chart busy with arrows. After a minute or two, Emma arrives with mugs of coffee and a bottle of wine and glasses. 'I thought a nightcap might be in order.' She steadies the tray on the coffee table. 'Whoops,' she says. 'Red wine, good for the heart.' She unearths a box of Black Magic from a cupboard under the sideboard, then sits next to Oscar on the sofa. '*Voilà*,' she says. 'Mum's secret stash. Mum's one of those people who just pretends to be thin.' She tucks her feet under her body. 'Here, let me,' she says, snatching the remote and finding a film channel showing an old black-and-white movie. 'Perfect,' she says. They sip coffee and wine and eat the chocolates.

The film is a Hitchcock, with the action taking place in one room because James Stewart has a broken leg and spends his day looking through binoculars at the people in

180

the apartment building opposite. 'It's like Dad and his telescope,' Oscar says.

'Except he hasn't got Grace Kelly in and out making him cups of tea. Don't you just love Grace Kelly? I could watch her in anything.'

It's happening. He knows it. He on the brink, conscious of his heart beating, like someone about to make a leap. 'I could watch you,' he murmurs. He can't believe he's gone and said it – *made* the leap – but he's out there now, suspended in the silence, waiting for the fall and the crash and the noise. Emma pours more wine. Maybe she didn't hear him. She's looking at the screen again, at James Stewart, helpless and frantic about Grace Kelly, who is now on the ground below, snooping around in the garden of the apartment building, about to be discovered by the murderer. But then he feels the cushion dip as Emma shifts her position, and he's aware of her nearness, the tips of her fingers lightly brushing the back of his neck. He turns, and she's looking at him curiously – he thinks he knows all her expressions but he's never seen this one before, and he knows what's going to happen now though he can hardly believe it, the way lips come softly together and find each other like the contoured halves of the same fruit, and all else is miraculously locked out – Vaughan, the life of Amy Daykin, the code-spirals of his chromosome nightmares, the chocolate box sliding from her lap, the music from the film, all torn to a floating storm of fragments now – in the pitch and yaw of a wanted kiss.

181

Chapter 13

Flemings has gone under. Rachel has been half expecting this, and now Barbara has rung from the warehouse twenty minutes before closing. 'How much do they owe?' she asks, turning to the wall in her new office, where her framed university degree from UEA hangs, fixed there by her mother.

'Including VAT, just over three thousand.'

Barbara says it in a curt, accusing way, as though this is something Dad would never have fallen for, giving credit to a start-up wine bar at the wrong end of Dock Street. Rachel knew that three months ago when she stood out there on the sales floor telling the guy it was no problem, and with her new no-nonsense glare chased the doubt off Brian's watching face.

'Well, it can't be helped,' she says to Barbara.

'Robert phoned too. He's been trying to get you all day

182

at the showroom, he says, so could you switch your mobile on, please.'

'Thank you, Barbara.'

She has heard Robert's two messages to call this afternoon, and calls him back, hoping his evening meeting hasn't been cancelled. But now his phone is switched off, which is a good sign. 'I'm going into a client's now,' she tells his voicemail, 'and then I'm going to the gym, so don't ring again. Oh, and don't wait for me to eat. I'll get something while I'm out and see you about nine.' She blushes as she speaks, talking about eating, and all the time thinking about Gareth waiting at his hotel with champagne and his great thing springing out at her like a jack-in-the-box the minute she walks in the room, hardly waiting to be in her mouth in a way that seems almost natural. She's only ever done that once with Robert, in a hotel room, drunk in Dieppe on their first trip abroad together, both faintly aware the morning after of a lapse in taste, though relieved to have tried it, like the snails they'd ordered in a fit of foolish giggles at the restaurant on the seafront.

She picks up her keys and bag and crosses the ground floor, raising a hand towards Paul, who is busy helping Josh with the last customer of the day. Someone is sitting on the forecourt wall, three men looking in, one of them sucking in his cheeks as he stares at the window display. He sees Rachel notice him and says something to the others, and they go sidling off, a trio of scruffs. But she knows this one man – the thin, hard face with its pale eyes that reminds her, as it did before, of the skull of a goat or sheep. His weird name. Not Herman but Her*nam* – Hernam Peters, who sat across the table in the studio at County FM and wittered about the green belt and the role of businesses like Dutting Modern in its despoliation. She waits and watches him and the other two turn down Market Street before she gets in the car and starts it up. Of course it's not unusual he should cross her path again. It's not a big town. They're on the main road. But coming on top of bad news, seeing this Hernam standing out there has unnerved her, like the appearance of a crow on the eve of one of those ancient battles in Shakespeare.

Later, in the orangey shadows of the room at the Belvedere, she seeks reassurance in this wonderful entanglement she has with Gareth, her body clinging to his as if for life itself, the warm skin of his shoulders matted with soft bristly hair beneath her fingers. It is beautiful the way he has of intuiting her rhythm and positioning, like a horse reads its rider's mind in the language of small adjustments. The horse thought excites her more, and though he is on top he makes her feel she's the one in the saddle. She needs to do it like this today, flying with the wind. The more robust the sex, it seems, the more pure and lasting its tender aftermath. 'People like that have never allowed themselves to mature,' he is saying as she lies in his arms. 'They spend their lives looking for reasons the world is wrong just because it's wrong for them. They haven't learnt to look inside themselves for answers. They're acting out their fears.' Gareth is not short of answers. He is strong in all the ways that count. In her disappointment and anger about Flemings, he fathoms deeper anxieties about the stock at the warehouse, bought early at good prices for the proposed Mosely-Baker project at Windhill. 'What's the worst can happen? That it all falls through and you have a huge sale next spring and still turn a profit? Just relax, everything's going to be fine.'

And everything is fine until, driving home with the feeling of Gareth still tumbling through her mind and veins, a police car looms abruptly in her mirror, its lights flashing. She pulls to the side and rolls the window down, and prepares a submissive pout for the approaching officer. 'Sorry,' she says, though she is not yet sure what for, being so abruptly dragged from her own world like this, with no time to think.

'Is this your vehicle, madam?'

'Yes – well, company vehicle. Strictly speaking. In fact it's my company, so I suppose, well, yes, it is my vehicle.' She smiles.

'And are you aware of the speed limit here, on this road?'

She turns her head and looks beyond the patrol car parked some way behind with its second officer positioned in the passenger seat. 'Fifty, is it? Or, no, sixty, being a dual carriageway.'

'This particular stretch is fifty. We clocked you at sixty-six.'

She gives him her open-eyed look. 'You're kidding.'

'I'm afraid not. And you do realise it's an offence to drive without a seatbelt?'

She looks down and then back. 'Oh my good God, what am I thinking of?'

'Do you have your licence?'

'Sorry, I don't. It's at home with . . . with all my other documents. If you needed to see those too, I mean.' She flicks her hair back, as this new style encourages, and smiles pleasantly.

The policeman nods. 'May I ask when you last had an alcoholic drink?'

'Drink? Well, quite recently actually, but not much. I mean just one.' She looks at him now in rising panic. She had a glass of champagne, topped up with half at the most. How many units could that be?

'Would you mind getting out of the car for a moment, madam, and coming with me?' He steps back to let her open the door. Vehicles on the road slow visibly as they pass, people peering out at her as she stands in the lay-by in her jogging bottoms and sweatshirt. He leads her back to the police car and opens the back door for her to get in. The policeman in the passenger seat glances round at her but says nothing. The other climbs in the front.

Her heart stops as he produces his breathalyser, a sort of black leather case like a radio, and frees a little plastic tube from its crimped wrapper, like a supersize drinking straw. 'If you could just blow into this, madam.'

She takes a breath, blows hard and hands it back. If she has to go to the police station, they will ask where she's been and the lie will be in her eyes and body language for all to see. She thinks of American cop shows, where incidental male witnesses – it's always men – are caught in compromising situations. *Does my wife have to know?*

'Thirty-four,' the officer says, looking at the reading. 'That's just bubbling under the limit. Fortunately for you. Another occasion, another half-glass of wine, it's a different story. You need to be careful what you drink if you're thinking of driving afterwards. Especially after strenuous exercise, where you're losing fluid.'

'I *will* be careful,' she says. 'Thank you.'

He produces a pad of forms now, and a pen. 'What I'm going to do now – I'm going to issue you with fixed-penalty tickets for the seatbelt and speeding offences,' he says. 'You're on a bus route here. There's plenty enough signs and, to be fair, madam, there's no excuse.'

'Absolutely not,' she says, waiting for him to get out again and open her door. 'You're right. I wasn't thinking. I was going with the flow.'

He hands her the paperwork. 'Going with the flow is an extremely common error,' he says, 'but not, as yet, a defence in law.' He pauses for a moment for his message to

186

sink in, then accompanies her back to her car. 'You'll need to present your documents at your nearest police station,' he adds, then returns without haste to the lazily blinking patrol unit, its rotating light a warning to others. He takes off his hat, and gets in at the driver's side. In her mirror, she sees him speak to his colleague. She waits for them to drive off first, but no, they're waiting for her. She indicates, waits for a respectable gap and then pulls out into the stream. They follow and sit behind her for a half-mile or so before overtaking and losing themselves in the traffic ahead. She is trembling.

Robert is watching TV when she gets back. He leaps out of his armchair to kiss her. There are flowers on the table in a vase.

'Flowers?' she squeals, her thoughts racing. Has she missed something?

'For you. How was the gym?'

She lifts her hand to her forehead. Sweat is pouring off her. 'Fine. How was the meeting?'

Robert is harbouring some unexploded enthusiasm. 'Let me tell you.'

'Hang on. Can I have my bath first?'

'Sure. Massage?'

'No. Thanks. Bit knackered. Just need to . . .'

'I've got a surprise . . .'

'I won't be long.' She closes the door on him.

Upstairs she turns on the taps, adds bath oil, brushes her teeth, undresses, then lowers herself into the slow-burgeoning froth. After a minute she hears him come up. He's outside on the landing. 'Hey, you should have seen Harrison tonight,' he shouts. 'He was seething. Jonathan too. But you'll never guess who pulled out . . .'

She can't listen. She submerges her ears in the quiet heat of the water and closes her eyes. His voice comes from

187

miles away, eventually tailing off. She drops off to sleep. It's only a few moments, but her arms have gone cold.

'Rachel?'

She surfaces and calls to him. 'Robert, could we do the local politics some other time? Why don't you go down and make me a coffee?'

Pause. 'No problem, my love.' She hears him retreat, humming a tune.

He's in the chair watching sport on TV when she enters the sitting room wrapped in her robe, her hair in a turban. 'Coffee's on the tray in the kitchen,' he says. He bites into an apple.

'Thanks.' She looks at the back of his head, his jaw moving up and down as he eats, like a child in some ways still, his feet up on the table, socks threadbare at the heel, slightly different shades of grey. Eventually she will make a mistake and he will know. Dates not adding up, her contraceptive cap absent from the medicine cabinet, underwear in her bag, an erotic appeal to Gareth in her sleep, a final demand for a speeding and seatbelt fine left carelessly on the mantelpiece ('Hey, what's this, Rache?'), eight-fifty-five p.m. on this day at Furnwell, five miles from her gym. Robert doesn't deserve this. And yet, right now, it's all she can give him. She will do this thing to him, bring it all crashing down. Wedding vows. It has a ring of antic novelty about it, like the Ten Commandments. As if you couldn't *ever*, really, under any circumstances. Promises are ornaments on a shelf just waiting for someone to walk in and slam the door hard enough. But does it matter? Worse things happen in life. They are both of them still under thirty. Nothing is too late.

On the tray in the kitchen he has set out biscuits on a plate, and mail to open. She sits at the table in the quiet, sipping coffee, flipping through a catalogue of garden furniture. There's a mortgage flyer from the bank, an offer of a maintenance contract for their gas central heating, a postcard reminder of her dental check. Then, there, at the bottom of the heap, a glossy paper wallet marked 'Travel Documents'. She opens it. Inside are air tickets to Venice, Orient Express to Prague and Paris, hotel reservations. Open-mouthed she turns to the door, where Robert gives a small cough and awaits praise, wearing a wide grin, misreading her dismay for amazement as only he can. 'Our four-day anniversary weekend,' he announces. 'Your dad watches the shop while we swan about on gondolas. Am I a romantic fool or just a genius?'

Chapter 14

It's just Stuart and Pete Tree at the Willows. Outside an unseasonal wind is blowing hard across the course, rippling the grass like water on a lake. They played nine holes – the only party out there – but they haven't come for the golf. It was far too last-minute for it to be just that, Pete's message waiting on the answerphone when Stuart got back from the doctor's, inviting him out here on a Monday morning of all days. 'Only if you're at a loose end,' was the way he put it. 'Give me a bell!'

Loose end – is there any other kind? These days, even at his busiest Stuart is more preoccupied than occupied, vaguely waiting. The more he fills his day with birds and astronomy the emptier it gets. Duttings is off-limits. The new house, without Diane bustling around, makes a dwarf of him. Only the Willows holds firm against change, a mini-Brigadoon where what he means and stands for is the same as it ever was, a place of business chatter where his opinion is still sought and heard.

Young Chris, hair combed up into a blond grassy divot, brings the beers and sets them down with his barman's flourish, each with one of those floury paper discs that at first glance look like something you might eat. It's getting on for one and the club has a few lunchtime regulars dotted around in their suits. Some bring clients here for lunch. Imperceptibly, he hopes, Stuart shifts his buttocks on the seat, troubled by the rectal sensation of having had Dr Bingley's finger up there. Not discomfort exactly, something more tingly. 'What have you got by way of sandwiches?' he asks.

Chris recites the bar menu and waits there, black-trousered, holding the tray like a discus.

'What do you think, Pete?' Stuart turns to ask.

'I would like, I think . . .' he says slowly, 'the smoked salmon on brown.'

Scandinavian option. 'And I'll go for ham and cheese farmhouse wedge,' Stuart says. 'With pickle if you have it, but don't bother with the garnish. Hate to see waste.'

'No problem,' says Chris, with a chuckle. 'Anything more?'

'Bowl of chips on the side? Mayo?'

'One bowl of chips, mayo.' Off he goes.

'So,' Stuart says. '*Skol.*'

Pete lifts his glass, his eyes full of secrets wanting to be told. He has something to say about Rael Eastern. It could be nothing else. There shines in Pete a desire to please that you sometimes find in people who don't quite fit in. Strange after all these years, growing up here too, Pete's slight differences, despite that Englisher-than-thou way of talking, that two- or three-second time lapse at seeing the joke when the group of them are all here together. Discreet of him, in the light of that, to engineer this meet in the absence of Tony and Gordon. Stuart appreciates it, and to show goodwill has already extended the hand of greater intimacy out there on the course, opening up about prostates, his in particular. Not easy, but made smoother by the honest broadloom of Pete's concern, bordered with plain tact. No prurience, Pete proving a decent man of sympathetic clucks ('I see . . .') as they walked up the fourteenth green, Stuart talking all the more freely for not being asked embarrassing questions. Dr Bingley's probing was enough, coldly forensic in his enquiries about urine flow, delays, stops and starts, trickles, staining, bladder discomfort, tiredness, that sandy-grey hair of his spouting from his ears and nostrils – he maybe has some problem down there himself if, as he claims, half the men over fifty do – and then, without so much as a pause to change the subject, snapping on latex gloves and spread-eagling Stuart against the back of a chair for a 'digital' search of the anal canal, as he called it, fearing suspect nodules. 'I think I'll take a blood sample at this stage,' he said, dropping the gloves in a white fliptop bin. 'It can't rule you in, as it were, but it can rule you out, more or less.'

'But that sounds like a positive thing,' Pete said, offering the second opinion Stuart wanted to hear, the two exchanging grave nods. Someone like Tony would have just carried on and taken the putt.

'Most people who die of prostate cancer don't even know they've had it,' Stuart said, eventually sinking his for a five. 'But that's men in their eighties who are dying of something else. It's probably nothing, but sometimes you can't tell without whipping it out and having a look, and it's not as if you can put it back, is it?' He found himself speechless when it came to asking old Bingley what happened if you did have it whipped out. Was that the end of sex?

192

Could you have sex without your seminal fluid? And the thought Stuart has been pushing to the back of his mind – has he already had sex for the last time and not known that that was it? He can't even remember the last time. Months ago. Now it may be too late. He has begun to see in Diane's absences from the home a matching pattern to this lull in their intimate relations. She has become unreachable, and not just in the way she seems always to take the contrary view or lapse into a remote silence – but physically too, always somehow managing to leave the room as he enters it, impatient to get to her work, this new wild-haired life at the college with its allure of brainy strangers – her tutor Marj and who knows what others, laughing together about art and whatever. In his darkest moments – in the small hours, stumbling back from the bathroom – he fears losing her as he lost Penny years ago. Anything can happen. Nothing is sacred.

Pete takes a sip of his drink. Stuart lifts a buttock to contract his still-quivering sphincter and lays his arm across the back of the seat and waits. Confiding is the start of a game – your turn, my turn. Confidence breeds confidences.

'This company, Rael Eastern,' Pete begins. 'I've got good reasons to think they might be stalking you.'

'Stalking?'

'To take over Duttings.'

'Won't happen,' Stuart says. 'We're not for sale.' His mouth dries up as he says these words. He takes a drink of beer and sits back, his mind whirring. 'What makes you think that?'

Pete Tree leans towards him, his hands in a praying position, unaccustomed to being the centre of attention in this place, even with an audience of one. 'Have you heard of Aladdin Carpets?'

Stuart nods. 'Just about. They turned up at the

193

Birmingham show last year. They're a small northern chain. Yorkshire or thereabouts.'

'Northern and spreading bit by bit. And, actually, not just northern here. Northern Europe too. Germany and France, spreading gradually, grabbing at minnows. No offence . . .'

Stuart shakes his head. 'No worries. So . . .'

'Anyway, Rael Eastern is who owns them. They're registered in Germany.'

'I thought you said they were Bulgarian.'

'Originally, yes. They're quite legitimate. You can view their holdings on this German business website for all to see.' Pete has written it down for him. He winks. 'At any rate, know thine enemy, as they say.'

'Well, I suppose you can never be too careful,' Stuart says. 'Thanks, Pete.' He folds the paper and slides it into his wallet, thinking now about Diane sitting at home at High Firs with her paints and papers and the timebomb under the house. He will tell her. He just needs to pick his moment.

Pete's smile hovers, as though he expects more for his efforts.

Chris arrives with the sandwiches. 'Let me get these,' Stuart says.

Diane is out when he returns. The afternoon is warm. Stuart, in short sleeves, has brought a folding garden chair and a cushion up to the turret roof, a tiny space where his telescope stands on its tripod, his beginner's map of the stars lying open on the cement floor where he left it the night before. He goes back down to the kitchen and returns with a tray of coffee and lemon cake. He picks up the book and starts to read. The beers at lunch have made him sleepy. He takes off his reading glasses and lays the book in his lap for a moment, feels his eyes droop and the sun on his face. He finds a last crumb with his tongue at the corner of his mouth. Reclining still, like this, just the faint pulse of his rectum where Dr Bingley has been, there's the near chittering of birds, the far mild chaos of traffic.

He awakes suddenly, as though he has bitten his tongue or dreamed he did. He hasn't been asleep long, but his lips feel tacky and his coffee mug is cold. He raises himself carefully out of the chair. 'Bloody arse . . .' he murmurs to himself. Standing chest-high at the crenellated wall of the turret, he looks out over the town below. Though Market Street itself is obscured from here, he can see the beginnings of the arcade that curves away off it, the first two or three shop windows. He removes the big lens cap from the telescope and puts his eye to the black rubber surround, trying to find his bearings amid the shifting rooftops, the strange glimpses of gutters and sloping lead flashings. He takes his eye away, looks up to locate its position – a downward angle from the Town Hall clock, slightly to the right – and back again. He adjusts the wheel and the entrance to the arcade sharpens out of the blur into a patch of sunlight, worn Victorian tiling, then Oscar's little place, Roots, and the florist next door. He holds it there. If he moves half an inch this way or that, the picture is lost again. No sign of Oscar. There's someone at the window, though, peering in. A girl – tapping, is she, on the glass? A man passing behind the girl turns, disappearing into Market Street. Stuart pauses for a second, then follows, imagining the man's progress – past Superdrug, the phone shop, Barratt's, the Chinese medicine place, The Coffee Kitchen – counting the seconds before he reappears outside Wilson's on the corner. Tall bloke in a suit. The man pauses, goes into the shop and a minute later comes back out carrying one of their little striped boxes tied up with ribbon. So close it seems that Stuart can almost hear the mellow tinkle of the bell on Wilson's door, almost reach out and touch the worn metal latch. Wilson's do a very nice fresh cream tart with glazed berries and kiwi fruit. He loses the man again – he could either have turned right at the barber's or gone straight on. But why would he turn right, unless he planned to walk round in a circle? Stuart waits a few seconds. There he is, just coming up the bend towards the showroom.

Stuart frowns. Now that he sees where the man is going, he knows in an instant who it is. He tries to get the face, tries to match it to the recollection he has of the man, sitting in his chair that day at the warehouse. And now he follows him as he steps with some awkwardness over the low white wall, then across the forecourt and into the showroom. He can't see him now. He raises the telescope to the upper floor, where the displays are partially visible, edges sideways to the little office there. Rachel, standing at the window, is struggling to lower the blind. She turns and moves away. What's happening? He waits a moment. There is movement, just discernible, but he has to imagine now, which is the worst thing. He is holding his breath, not daring to blink. Is there anyone else up there on the display floor – Paul, Josh? Nothing moves. Christ.

He stands for a moment, looking with his naked eye at the white building with the vertical strip of sign you can't quite read from here but he knows says Dutting Modern. He limps quickly downstairs. Luke is slumped in front of the computer.

'I've got a study period before you ask,' Luke says, not looking up, his hair curtaining his eyes at an angle. There's a page on screen pulsing with effects and hostile-looking graphics, a game of some sort and that confusion of links they have on the internet that takes your eye everywhere but where it needs to be. Global Anarchy, it reads. Destroy. Free the Earth.

'Well can you do something else for a minute? I need the computer.'

Luke sighs, closes the window and logs off. 'All yours.'

'There's some cake in the kitchen,' Stuart says.

He sits down and keys in the address given him by Pete Tree. Is this Newnam cunt trying to get Duttings through Rachel? Is that what's happening? There's no way it *can* happen. How could it? But there's something going on between them for sure. There's probing of one sort or another going on, creamy sweeteners in the striped box from Wilson's. *Bastard*. If they're not at it already, it can't be far off. He feels a moment's irrational impatience with Robert, the bloody fool, who has even asked Stuart to mind the shop while he takes Rachel off on some surprise anniversary trip. And this happening. Jesus Christ.

Diane will know what to do.

The name of Rael GmbH is on the screen. Stuart clicks on the Union Jack option, and follows the prompts until a panel appears showing a menu of companies. Aladdin he immediately sees, and – via the sub-menu that flips open like a smile when he hovers with the cursor – the territories they cover; and, here, Rael Eastern's export business; ware-housing interests; two or three foreign-sounding outfits dealing in textiles. His eye falls on Herring Associates. He stares at the name and the crescent sword and little star of the logo he recognises from the photocopied documents Barbara gave him, and feels the hairs on his bare arms standing on end. Oh fuck. Holding his breath, he clicks on the name and watches the screen change. Herring, it says. 'First for Finance.' He closes his eyes against the blinding light of what it means.

Asset-Based Loans.

Lending Solutions.
Need to Grow Your Business?
Think the Unthinkable.

Stuart *is* thinking the unthinkable. He's thinking that this loan on the showroom and Rachel's new stock is secured against assets already straining to prop up the loan he took out on the house. But what's propping *that* up now? What's paying for it all? What's to stop the whole lot from tumbling down? Rachel knows something he doesn't. She must.

Chapter 15

This is the eighth day. It's only in the past week that Oscar has allowed himself to realise how long Emma has been quietly inhabiting his thoughts – how long, while refusing to have those thoughts stirred by the breath of his imagination, he has sought this outcome of being more than the brother everyone expects him to be. And yet have not Oscar and Emma always been each other's natural half? She is Dad's daughter, but not Mum's. He is Mum's son but not Dad's. They are twinned in their detachment from this new-fashioned family tree twisting laterally from Michael to Diane to Stuart to Penny to Tony. They each have half-siblings in Rachel and Luke. They each were raised in a stepfather's house. In blood they are nothing to each other and yet, in their pounding hearts now, every-thing. The symmetry, it seems to Oscar, endows their love with heavenly meaning, as though some great prefigured thing now come to pass. With everything else, all his life's drama has come at once, his battle of fortunes between love and death. Emma laughed at that. 'You take everything so personally.' But she held him close.

'When did you first know?' she asked. That was on the first day.

'It's hard to say – Christmas, for sure. When you came round with the presents, with you-know-who. You were wearing a fluffy jumper and that kilt thing. But before that, I first had a thing for you that first half-term you came home as a student, and everyone was making a fuss of you. I know we didn't see each other much back then, but when we did it always gave me a . . . you know, a feeling. What about you?'

'Me? I *always* fancied you. Even when we were little. It's just that I'd never managed to get you on Mum's sofa before.'

But what he had felt at Christmas was more envy than love, a yearning for what he couldn't have. Not only her – he could only imagine Vaughan here, nuzzling her hair, or other versions of Vaughan – but her accomplishments, too, the things that had made her what she was now, the confident and successful part of her that set limits on what he could hope for, that stopped him contemplating the outcome he most desired. This he cannot tell her. Michael dying, and all that followed, gave him the reason he needed to stay. It was nothing stronger than a vague hope for change. But when he thought, vaguely, of change, he thought of her. He thought of her seeing the change in him and the possibilities – as impossible as they were – that might ensue. It's too delicate to talk about. While he was edging forward, did she take a step back – away from the bank – to be nearer him? To ask seems to ask for trouble. Amid the passion, he fears the provisionality that all newness carries.

Emma doesn't mention love. Instead she talks about wanting him in a way that makes her seem more serious, less frivolous, truer. She watches him sometimes as if from a distance, as if seeing things unfold. 'What?' he says. This Emma is new to him. He is new to her.

No one knows about them. He has been conscientious in parking the camper at a safe distance from Tony and Penny's, stealing out in the early hours to drive back to High Firs, Emma's beguiling smell still on him. And when Tony and Penny returned from their break on Saturday afternoon, he and Emma relocated their love-in to the magic carpet at the windowless warehouse, naked under the dusty striplights, their clothes in garish heaps, the sound of Troy shuffling back and forth in the workshop beneath the mezzanine. And when on Sunday they drove to London, to Emma's flat with its eastern-style furniture and views of the Thames and glass domes of the City, he made certain – though neither of them wanted it – to come home the same night. 'They're bound to be just weird about it,' Emma said, meaning Tony and Penny and Dad and Mum. 'It's best not to tell them just yet.' She kissed him at her door and waved from the window as he stood on the deserted street below. It was gone three and she had clients in six hours.

Nothing matters. She has kept his anxieties at bay with her tender whisperings. Nothing can happen while she is wrapped up with him. If he is to die suddenly, let it be here, he thinks, in this great glory on earth. She laughed at that too when he told her. They both did.

But in her absence now, the fear comes back. Death looks cruel and magnified from this new vantage point of having so much more to lose. He awoke with it this morning, as if the fear moved while he was sleeping into the warm space in his mind vacated by Emma. And then, opening his mail over breakfast coffee, copies of wills he has ordered, other certificates, a letter tumbles forth – it chills him to think that this has been lurking at the edge of the postal system, waiting for the moment he is alone again – bringing the news he has dreaded, though he has summoned it himself, from an address in Luton.

Dear Mr Dutton

Without wishing to cast alarm, what you may have is something called 'Long QT Symdrone', which is a heart irregularaty. I lost a younger brother before it was diagnosed. It is rare and often goes unoticed, even by hospital doctors. But it does run in family's. On the other hand you might not have it, or have it but never show the symptons. I have an elder brother who is fit and well, as I myself am. However, we are advised to take 'beta-blockers' for the condition, just in case it comes out. You may have heard of it as 'Sudden Death Symdrone'. What you described about fainting is quiet correct. Sometimes that is the first sign of it – and sometimes the last. Your father was not a cousin in fact but from your explaination my mother's grandmother was an Edwards, his grandfather's sister.

I hope this helps you.
Yours sincerley,
Mrs A. Thorpe (née Horne)

At the kiosk, he re-reads the letter, typed on a single sheet of lined notepaper, and puts it back in its envelope, which is large and white, the sort intended for a greetings card. Mondays are quiet. He rings Emma but she's unavailable. He refuses to panic. In itself, the letter means nothing. Nothing has changed. He leaves Diggsy in charge of things, picks up the Daykin file, heavier with this morning's documents, and walks to the public library. This is how he will deal with it. Work.

At the library, he sits and thinks. According to the copies of the wills he has received, Thomas Daykin left his estate to his only son, William. This was the heartless William, whose estate on his own death passed to his wife Victoria, there being no heir except the poor ousted Margaret/May, long vanished or perhaps even dead by 1950, by which time Amy had been in Canada – what? More than twenty years. Oscar doesn't know when Victoria died . . . or does he? He looks through the scribbled notes in his file. Yes, 1952, two years after the husband.

There are vacant terminals, so he pulls up a seat and logs on. It doesn't take long to find the website Emma told him about, an archive of unclaimed assets, but it's mainly insurance policies and occupational pensions. Following the links, though, he discovers an 'heir search' site, offering probate records from 1858 and electronic sweeps of data from electoral rolls and Land Registry archives. He keys in Victoria Daykin's details but nothing shows up. But there must have been a will. If she's got no kids, who does she leave her money to? Does she have second thoughts about her poor, long-lost daughter? With the husband now out of the way, maybe she 'reaches out', as they say in the American cop shows, for the girl, hires a team of private detectives to search the bawdy houses and low hostels of 1950s England for a woman – now in her early fifties – answering to the name of Margaret Daykin. And how old is Amy by then? Thirty-something? And what of little Tom? Barnado's have yet to reply.

He spends another hour reading through the annual report and potted history of the Daykin Group. There's a picture here of old whiskered Thomas surrounded by tea chests, one of William too, dated 1924, the cruel father, now the new boss in a stiff collar and hat. He looks gaunt and pale, undernourished for a man of substance. Maybe he suffered for his decision to cast his child to the cold winds of chance. Maybe he was treated to a lifetime of silence and neglect from his wife for doing it. Oscar turns the pages. Who is on the board now? There are no Daykins listed and the narrative doesn't dwell greatly on family detail. He emails the human resources manager, explaining what he's doing and asking for information on what happened to the original family interest in the business.

Oscar sits for a while. This is the new library but it still has the big old clock he remembers as a kid, sitting in the warm next to the radiator in winter, its fins bumpy with the layers of paint. You could watch the minute hand until it suddenly jumped the space between the leaded markings.

He fights the urge to unearth more about this Long QT Syndrome, afraid of what he will discover – afraid of the knowledge of it, a knot of cancer eating away at his new happiness. But he loses the fight. He sits here and reads the case studies he finds online, the statistics, the science of this fault in the electrics of a heart. He follows the links to other sites that tell him the same thing about this eccentric, singing rhythm that tries to disguise its giddiness on the waves of a cardiogram, that takes longer than normal to get its breath back between two peaks called Q and T before coming swinging back in on the beat, or in certain tragic circumstances not swinging back in at all. As anyone would expect, physical exertion can set it off, but so can a thunderstorm. One American mother writes about her twenty-one-year-old daughter who dropped dead after seeing her better than predicted exam results posted on the college noticeboard. Another woman's son couldn't watch a football game without fainting. An act of kindness can do it. A fire alarm going off. A stroke of luck. Anything that makes the heart jump for joy or catches it napping. A champagne moment for Michael's fiftieth birthday. That was his warning. But then what?

He takes the long route back to the kiosk, walking slowly. He will ring Emma. Reaching Dutting Modern, he stands at the window looking in. Rachel is sitting at the far end behind the sales desk. 'Rael Eastern', a sign reads. 'Authentic Oriental Craftsmanship from the Cradle of Carpet Making.' He needs a drink of water. He could go in, speak to his sister. She knows nothing of his heart. Illness brings families together, yet he is not ill. Not yet. Maybe he won't be.

Beta-blockers regulate heartbeat. If that doesn't work, an automatic defibrillator may have to be implanted. Nerves in the neck may have to be severed. Vigorous or competitive sport is discouraged. *It is a timebomb.* 'Most doctors are unaware of the condition.' Cardiologists miss vital clues. *An ECG must be specifically evaluated for QT prolongation.* Faulty wiring equals fast heart rhythm equals sudden loss of consciousness equals death. *The sudden loss of consciousness is called 'syncope'.*

Oscar has the knowledge in his head, rudimentary but already working on him. He has a fifty-fifty chance of having inherited the thing that killed his genetic father. This is what he is hanging on to now. One in two. The rest of your life – do you walk through this door or that one? Guess.

Four figures are crowded into the kiosk when he returns, Troy yapping excitedly. Bonner and Ralphie have turned up, but Luke is here too. Hope is in his eyes as he looks at Oscar. He is wearing his school tie as a bandanna.

'So,' says Bonner, 'this is where the entrepreneurial classes hang out.'

Oscar ignores him. 'Shouldn't you be at school?' he says to Luke.

'Study period. Then these friends of yours knocked for you so I brought them down here. We've been putting posters up down the hill.' He grins. Dad'll go apeshit when he sees them.'

Bonner puts his hand on Oscar's shoulder. 'Sorry, mate, I couldn't stop him. Obviously it runs in the family, this commitment to righteous causes.'

Ralphie has taken one of the display shields down. 'Righteous? It's like the Domesday Book round here, all that robbing the peasants and grabbing the land.'

Luke turns to Ralphie, uncertain of his tone.

Oscar takes the shield out of Ralphie's hands and hooks it back on the wall. 'Just a bit of harmless recreation, if that's not contrary to natural justice. Was there something you wanted?' he says. 'Handbook of Cornish surnames? A video about Highland clans?' He has no time for this.

Bonner chuckles, reaches into his bag and unrolls a poster dramatically. 'Think of it as election week, where your local anti-global anarcho-environmentalist candidate comes round asking if he can rely on your vote next Saturday.'

'I heard there was a march. Is that it?'

'Finger on the pulse, dude.'

'And you're just here in support, this not really being your patch.'

'More of a delegate. It started as a local push about the green belt, but the organisers were persuaded to hook up with other groups campaigning on wider, more global issues, Third World debt, workers' rights, exploitation, GM, eco, animals. Hence, I've got a crew coming, so have others. That way we pool our strength, and instead of having chickenshit turnouts of five people and their dog you get proper organised demos in different towns over successive weekends, the last one coinciding with the EU summit in Berlin.' He waits for Oscar to look impressed. 'Assemble at the Five Ponds site at ten, speeches, march at eleven through town, finishes at the Town Hall for a rally and more speeches. Very peaceful. All official.'

'Sounds like a lot of fun,' says Oscar.

Bonner isn't sure if he's joking. 'So we can count on your support?'

The phone breaks the silence. They all look at it. Diggsy picks it up and is talking. Oscar looks at him, distracted. It's the way everyone stopped when it rang. The phone call could have done it, he is thinking. A sudden ring in the quiet of a ghostly building. That could have been enough. He sees this blood father of his working alone in the unit the night he died. He can remember precisely the words of that last email to him from Greville Wood in Canada. *I'm so excited about this, I tried to call earlier, but will try again.* So maybe he did try again. A hard, metallic, sudden ring echoing out in the dead of night. Maybe that was it.

'So?' Bonner waits for his answer, holding the poster.

Troy, beneath the counter, looks up enquiringly.

'I can't make it Saturday,' Oscar says. 'I have to be here.'

Bonner turns, nodding to Ralphie with a leer. 'Ever the lightweight.'

A shadow of disappointment crosses Luke's face, followed by the scowl that disfigures it so easily these days. 'You're selling out, man.'

Oscar sighs. 'Grow up, Luke. Go back to school.'

Bonner puts his hand on Luke's shoulder and turns to Diggsy. 'Diggsy?'

Diggsy looks at Oscar.

Oscar shrugs. 'It's up to you.'

'No, I can't,' Diggsy tells Bonner. 'I said I'd help. Saturday's busy.'

'And about to get busier, dude,' Bonner says, smiling. 'Come on.'

The three start to move.

'Luke,' Oscar says, 'what are you doing?'

'What's it to you? You're not in charge of me. I can do what I want.'

They leave. They don't look back. Oscar can hear their footsteps on the tiled surface of the arcade, their voices carrying, a backdraught of staged laughter. 'He's only my *half*-brother,' he hears Luke say.

Oscar closes the door. Of course it is natural that Luke should want to engage himself with wider things, with globalisation, with environmental issues and whatever else. It's not Luke he should be telling to grow up. His real target – he knew this even as he said it – was Bonner, the eternal radical, cursed to roam the earth, his heart in his hands, feeding on negative energies, shaking his rags and bones at everything, stirring disharmony. Bonner is in it for himself. Where does that come from? What impulses drive him, what needs? What's in *his* blood? Oscar has moved from one world to another. He is free of those old spells. He knows that now. And though it troubles him to awaken so easily Bonner's talent for finding moral weakness in others, and though it is true that he was always a light-weight, and though he feels the tug of shame in so readily abandoning the mask of angry protest for something more congenial, he is hot with resentment. What do they know? Fuck them. Taking a book down from the shelf, he starts to turn the pages, Troy yawning now at his feet, Diggsy quieted by the exchange of animosity.

Oscar looks at the pages but does not read. In the silence is a distant threat, intensifying. He can feel it. Soon he will hear it. Something is coming.

Chapter 16

On the upper floor of Dutting Modern, Rachel is look-ing at numbers through eyes half closed to the screen glare. She has a headache. She needs to lower the blind, but for the moment she will sit here. Robert tells her she is run down, that the job is taking its toll, that what she needs is a proper break. He lies in wait for her with his good cheer when she gets home, assails her over supper with the glit-tering details of their trip this coming weekend – the opulence of the hotels and train, the gourmet dinners that await. But for his sake – because he doesn't deserve *this*, what she is doing to him – she musters the will to stare at photographs of Prague and Venice in the travel guides he shows her and affects to share his enthusiasm.

She is tired. Gareth is away on business. In his absence the numbers speak to her in an urgent voice. The ware-house is full to the rafters. Nothing seems to move except the money, trickling in at one end, cascading out at the other, a deafening Niagara of credit. What is to be read here in these rows and columns of figures, what state of play? The episode with the police, farcical though it was, has invested Rachel's sleep with an unspeaking fear that lasts into the day. She cannot shake the feeling that, having escaped one danger, she is in the market for another. It reminds her of a dream she has sometimes, of finding herself behind the wheel of a slowly moving car, unable to reach the brake pedal, or, having reached it, lacking the strength to push it.

She rolls her chair away from the screen and stands up. Below, Dad's car pulls into the forecourt. She watches him get out, lock the door and button his jacket and walk towards the building with an effortful gait that makes him look older than he used to. Rachel lowers the blind. A moment later the phone buzzes and Josh's voice tells her he is here.

'I'll come down,' she says.

'He's on his way up.'

'OK.'

She puts on a smile as his face appears round the door. 'Dad, an unexpected pleasure. Still keeping an eye on us?'

He comes in sheepishly, looks around the office. 'How are things, Rachel?'

'Excellent. How could they be otherwise?'

Dad sits down heavily in the chair and looks at her for a moment before speaking. 'These Rael Eastern people.'

Rachel's smile vanishes as she swallows hard. Can he know? 'Yes – nice rugs, authentic, hand-made,' she hears herself say, pleasantly. 'If you're interested, you know we always do a deal for friends and chosen relatives.'

That line used to be Dad's, but he doesn't acknowledge it. 'They're up to something. I think you ought to watch out. I think . . .' He pauses. 'I think you need to watch out for that rep of theirs. I gather he's been sniffing around.'

Though she feels her stomach tighten at this talk of her father's, Rachel folds her arms and fixes him with a cool stare, half indulgent, half impatient, as though he is a subordinate come to waste her time. 'What are you saying, Dad? Yes, he visits here, if that's what you mean by sniffing around. Isn't that his job?'

'Right, his job. But what I'm here to tell you, Rachel, is that Rael Eastern aren't just importers – they're rivals. They're major retailers in Europe. And they're here in England too. They've got outlets up north. And right now, as we speak, they're growing like crazy and smothering little firms out of existence. Family firms like ours,' he adds. He seems breathless, trying to get this news out. 'They're predators.'

Rachel's mind is whirring, taking it in. Calm. It isn't about *that* after all, it's about business. The usual. This she can handle. For the sake of goodwill, she sits on her anger. But the irony of it – Dad having the nerve to say this about Gareth, who has been right behind her from the start, while he, Dad, has done nothing but stand in her way! If anything, there's something about this account that makes her heart beat even faster for Gareth. Doesn't this prove his feelings for her – the fact that he will help and advise her and stand by her even when it's against the strict interests of his own employer?

She forces a smile. 'I appreciate the warning, but I do think you're barking up the wrong tree. Gareth Newnam has never come out and said Rael didn't have *any* retail interests. In fact, why should he even mention it? It's hardly an issue if their shops are in the north and he's based in the south-east, just as we are. I imagine it never crossed his mind.'

'But he's not based in the south. *National* representative, it says here on his card.' Somehow, Dad has Gareth's card right there in his hand and is waving it, like some absurd Inspector Poirot confronting her with the evidence, as if he expected that answer. 'Look,' he continues, 'if he's on the importing side and offering exclusive distribution to a few chosen outlets, surely he'd have to cover the whole country? Otherwise, what would he do with the rest of his week?'

Rachel shrugs. 'But most of the population lives in the south,' she says. 'So there are more territories for him to cover.'

'Right. So why would it be worth their while having a specific northern representative – especially if their own chain would presumably already qualify as exclusive distributors?'

'But what about Scotland? For goodness' sake, Dad, what are you trying to prove? Get a grip. We have half a dozen rugs in the window and you act as if . . . as if Gareth has his foot in the door. He hasn't, Dad. I know you mean well, but – why not just let me handle it? Everything is fine.'

'Have you tried ringing these people? Because I have—'

'But why, Dad? Why have you tried ringing them?'

'*Because*. Because I care what happens here.'

Rachel throws up her hands. 'And I don't? Haven't I given up a perfectly good career to make a go of this? I'm trying to grow the business, Dad, and all I get from you is abuse and distrust. Does Mum know you're here?'

He pauses. 'OK, let's calm down,' he says, though he is the one sweating. 'How about financially? Where do we stand on that?'

She gives him a stare. What is he getting at now? 'Where do we *stand*?'

'There's an awful lot of money tied up in stock,' he says.

'Yes I know. It's under control. I am, actually, a qualified accountant.'

'Public finance is different,' he says.

She gives an exaggerated puzzled look. 'Dad, what is this *about*?'

'I'm just saying . . .' He pauses, as if there's something he's not saying. 'Is the warehouse involved – in the finance?'

'Well of *course* the warehouse is involved. Otherwise it's not working as an asset, is it? Which it wasn't before. I mean you might as well just rent if you don't have it working. You have to make your money work hard in this environment. Everyone knows that. And anyway, haven't you raised loans on the business?'

He stares in panic at her. 'Things seem precarious,' he says at last.

'Dad, if you really wanted to help, you might have thought about that Lexus you're still driving around in – which the firm is paying the lease on.'

He blinks. 'What?'

'The car. I mean, why do you even need it? Apart from keeping up with Tony and your other golfing cronies.'

'Of course I need it. Our agreement was I'd be retained for consultation.'

'Well, consider yourself consulted. I'm sorry, Dad, but I'm running things now. I have the thirty-four per cent. I'm sorry if I'm not the easy touch you thought I'd be, but it's my job now, for better or worse. Give yourself a break and for God's sake give me one.'

In spite of herself, she has raised her voice. People will hear, customers. Dad looks drained. 'Fine,' he says. 'Just do me one favour.' He hands her a piece of notepaper. 'This is their website. Humour me. Just take a look at their holdings, and tell me nothing's going on.'

She takes the slip of paper off him. 'If you're trying to frighten me with what major players they are, perhaps you ought to stop for a moment and ask yourself a question. Why did they come to us, rather than Carpet Land or SuperRug? And why now? I'll tell you. Because *I* am ambitious. Because *I* am attempting to put this firm on the map after years of neglect. Companies with the calibre of Rael Eastern are always—'

'*Neglect?* Now that *is* out of order, Rachel. Duttings has always been a healthy business – and always paid its way without bloody great injections of cash. That's asking for trouble.'

'What are you saying?'

'I'm saying nothing. I'm just registering my misgivings. That's *my* job, for better or for worse.'

He leaves without saying goodbye, injured and indignant. From the window she watches him walk stiffly to his beloved Lexus, this symbol not only of waste but of his lost empire. He will hang on to it, she knows, like a child with a toy. She shakes her head. She doesn't want this any more than him, this bad feeling, especially with this weekend coming up. Not that she has any real fears about leaving the showroom in his charge. What damage can he do? It's only for the Friday and Saturday. He'll only be helping Paul out on the sales side. He can't stick his nose into anything else. And so what if he gets to stride around in his best suit again, carpet king for a day? Maybe it will be good for him to see what she has achieved with the new premises, the sort of customers they get coming in now. Maybe it will keep him off her back, encourage him to retire properly, dig the bloody garden.

She sits at her desk. What is needed, though, is the stamp of an unequivocal triumph, a coup so transforming as to redeem all acts of seeming treachery in the healing light of prosperity, to justify in the eyes of family and the world at large the dishonouring of a father's wishes. To this end Rachel waits for confirmation of the Five Ponds development, which seeps darkly back into her consciousness in the temporary absence of Gareth, her rock, her barrier against the cares of office. Impulsively, she rings his mobile and leaves a tender message. *Love you*, she whispers, a fortifier for herself as much as an endearment for him. And if this, too, snags in her thoughts – this new image of herself as a woman who communes with her lover before hurrying home to help her husband pack bags for an anniversary trip to Venice, city of romance – it all seems part of the struggle for change, which if you look at the world or nature always brings hardship for those least willing to move. Standing still has never been an option. It's the law of evolution.

Chapter 17

Diane stands at the kitchen sink with her back to Stuart, filling the kettle. 'But if you knew about these people, this Heron—'

'Herring.'

'If you knew about these Herring people, why not say so?'

'Because then she'd have asked *how* I knew, and I didn't want to get into that. We'd have ended up arguing about *how* I knew instead of the thing itself. You know Rachel. She has a knack of twisting everything so it turns out to be my fault.'

Diane takes down two mugs from the cupboard and spoons coffee into them. 'So how *do* you know?'

'See? Now you're doing it. It's irrelevant. I know, that's all. I found out. What matters is that the firm currently bankrolling the business is the same one with its rugs on display in the window . . .'

'Ah yes. Child labour.' She stands at the sink, rinsing the few dishes in there, while the water comes to the boil.

Stuart waits too, quietly eating a biscuit, as if taking cover in everyday activity makes what he has to say seem everyday too. 'And now,' he says, 'this same company is spreading like a virus, buying up smaller firms all over the north. This guy of theirs, this smarmy, bottle-blond sales rep, practically lives at the showroom by all accounts. Something's going on, I'm certain. Between the two of them.'

'With Rachel?' Diane hovers with the milk jug. 'You think something's going on with Rachel?'

'I don't know.'

Diane shakes her head. 'For goodness' sake, Stuart,' she says. She sets the mugs on the kitchen table and they sit down. There's a pause as she looks at the table and then at him. 'How's the problem?' she says softly.

'Not bad. Bit sore.' He stirs sugar into his coffee. They sip together, Diane watching his face, expectant. 'The house is tied to the warehouse,' he says at last. 'And the warehouse is tied to the loan with Herring. The business is being stretched by two loans now.'

'Our house? This house?'

Stuart shakes his head. 'Half the house is owned by the business. If the business gets into trouble, the bank could call in the loan.'

'For God's sake, Stuart, why don't I know about this?'

'Because . . .' He sighs, speaks softly. 'Because you were against buying the house to start with. Because you would have said we couldn't afford it.'

'Bloody hell, Stuart, obviously we *couldn't* afford it. What on earth were you *thinking* of?'

'It would have been fine. It might still be fine. Maybe there's more business going through the books than I know about.'

218

There's no way this is true. The stock just sits there mounting up. He stops short of telling Diane about Barbara being on the inside smuggling out the evidence.

'Is Rachel aware of this? About our house?'

He makes an impatient gesture.

Unblinking, Diane looks at him. 'Stuart, *answer* me.'

'She must. She knows there's a loan. Christ, how could I know what she was going to do, ploughing the business into so much debt?'

Diane shakes her head again, says nothing more, listens to him return to the vexed issue of Rachel's decision not to sell factory offcuts or room-size remnants, thus sacrificing half of Duttings' customer base in one ingenious swoop. 'And that office of hers,' he says. 'Do you know, there isn't a single bit of carpet in there. Not on the floor, no samples, nothing. It was the first thing I noticed. It seemed so sterile. Pictures on the wall, designer lamps and high-tech this and that, but no sales paraphernalia, no trade calendars, none of the real fabric of the business. How can you work like that?'

Diane is defeated. 'It's irrelevant, Stuart. Times change. To her it's a business, not a love affair. God, what am I saying?' She presses her hand on his, and inhales sharply. 'What's the worst that can happen?'

It sounds like a rhetorical question, but it's a real one – one he can't answer without hard figures and prospects. They turn their heads as they hear the front door open then slam shut, announcing Luke's homecoming. It's after six. He's probably been hanging around in town. His bag hits the floor in the hall and they wait for him to emerge. 'Hello, parents,' he says in his monotone, slouching past to get to the fridge.

'How was school?' Stuart asks.

'Not great,' he says. He rips open a can of Fanta and takes a long slug.

Sensing an audience, he hoists himself up on to the work surface. 'I know something you don't,' he says.

'What's that?'

'About Oscar.'

'What about him?' Diane asks, turning in her chair.

Luke smiles, then jumps back down. 'No, better not. Ask him yourself. I just saw him at the station. He'll be back soon.'

'What were you doing at the station?'

'I was on the bridge with James doing posters for Saturday. I saw his van in the car park and he was down there in the station, seeing someone off. Snogging her on the platform next to the snack bar. Practically eating her he was. I've never seen him having so much fun.'

Stuart can see Diane is getting wound up. Is it this girl Oscar was seeing in London? It must be – the one he said he wasn't seeing any more, this girl whose father used to know Diane's ex. This is all they need in Diane's mood.

Luke starts to escape but she pulls him back by his arm. 'Who *was* it, for God's sake. Just stop buggering about for once.'

Luke's smirk momentarily falls as he shakes himself free of his mother's grip. 'OK, OK already.' A pause to lick his top lip. 'It was Emma.'

Stuart opens his mouth. 'Our Emma?' He turns to Diane in disbelief.

'Yes, *our* Emma,' Luke is saying. 'How many Emmas do we know?'

'Brilliant,' Stuart hears himself say. 'Fucking brilliant.'

Chapter 18

Oscar watches the London train disappear then goes to the van. He sits behind the wheel, the keys in his hand. What to do about this. What to say.

Who was he, that old Oscar, back then in the West Country, the Oscar who thought there were no tomorrows, just a succession of todays? That's what he told himself, as they all did in that floating community of souls he saw as his spiritual family, his fellow sharers of spoils, his peers in heedlessness. It was a philosophy for those with no one to please but themselves, though the community that has only *that* to bind them – unless the avoidance of steadiness or the distrust of convention counts as shared values – melts away like soap in water. Luke was right. Oscar has sold out, though only in the way that Luke one day will. What amazes him is how, in changing so little, he has changed so much, now seeing Bonner or Ralphie as others see them, seeing the glaring twist in the mission to seek out allies with whom to share the enemy for a day – even allies (tweedy village women, defending forests against roads) who on other days might *be* the enemy. It seems a simple step to relieve himself of this life of being against things.

He opens the Daykin file beside him on the seat and looks at the creased photograph of Amy as a bewildered English child in Canada, a weatherbeaten farm girl squinting out among other workers. Then her face as a woman in her eighties, still out there, married and now widowed, a grown-up child of her own, grandchildren, and yet leaning to what she belongs to, severed from her native tradition, still hearing it speak to her like a phantom limb. He turns the ignition and revs the engine once, but still doesn't move.

This morning seems like a long time ago. He spent a good part of it at the offices of Thomas Daykin, tea importers, near London Bridge. It began with an email from the human resources manager yesterday, asking him to call for an appointment. He rang the number. The assistant there said that Ben Winter, the company's managing director, would be happy to answer his questions and show him round. He didn't know what to expect – perhaps a short history of the firm; a peep through their archives; a scrapbook of faded pictures taken at staff outings.

He turned up at ten-thirty wearing a suit Diggsy had had to buy for a family wedding, and a tie from Dad's wardrobe. Ben Winter was late thirties, likeable and not at all like a man of business. There was a youthful enthusiasm about his movements, and though well dressed he didn't strike Oscar as someone who wasted too much time shaving or combing his hair. He ordered coffee for them both (explaining with a friendly chuckle that he only drank tea when protocol demanded it) and asked Oscar to sit down and tell him what was on his mind. He seemed eager.

Perhaps it wasn't every day that an outsider took an interest in an old Southwark tea company. He looked politely at the information and photographs Oscar had brought and listened intently to the story of Amy Daykin, to Oscar's various hypotheses, which seemed whimsical even to himself now, here among the hard-won badges of trade, the Queen's Award for Export, the pedigree wood panelling. 'This is our original building,' Ben said, 'though remodelled for modern comfort and business practice. The whole wharf area has been redeveloped as you can see. Most of the firms round here are high-tech or financial. They like the view. But our history is tied up here on this stretch of the river, and has been since 1834.'

'I suppose what I wanted to know,' Oscar asked, 'was what happened to the Daykins' interest in the company. I mean it still has the name, but I noticed there were none listed among the main shareholders.'

'No,' Ben said. 'That's true. The company kept the name on because . . . well, that's what it's always been known as. There have been three Thomases including the founder,' he added brightly. 'Come on, let me show you our little museum.'

He took Oscar downstairs to a large room one level below the street but one level above the wharf, its warehouse doors rolled back to reveal a balcony overlooking the river. They made their way through a party of uniformed schoolgirls, mostly black or Asian, Oscar noticed, wandering among the exhibits, some making sketches of a scale model of a tea clipper that stood as a centrepiece, its sails a permanent stiff billow, while others directed their wavering attention to 'The Story of Tea' mounted on the wood and hessian room dividers patterned with engravings and photographs of plantation workers and London bargemen and mustachioed auctioneers, along with facsimiles of production records, tariffs, bills of lading. On the walls hung boathooks and field tools, posters advertising tea and illustrations demonstrating the processes of picking and blending and packing. Glass cabinets displayed the pages of yellowed manuals, antique spoons, silver tongs, caddies and decorated ceramics. 'This is our community access project,' Ben said, with a sweep of his hand. 'We like to give something back. A bit of education, presenting the story of tea as the story of globalisation. Our own wealth, needless to say, was built on opium, cheap native labour and every other sort of unpleasant colonial exploitation. Slavery too, originally, of course. It was abolished by the time the first Daykins came into the business, but without it there'd be no teapots on English tables today. We can't do anything but acknowledge it. It's part of our history. Part of my own, to some extent.'

Oscar turned to him. 'Yours? Why's that?'

He smiled. 'Well, because I take a profit from it, I suppose. Though I hasten to add that these days our employment policy is second to none.'

Ben excused himself to take a call on his mobile, leaving Oscar looking at leaf-grading and flavour charts. Darjeeling was a delicate flowery tea that grew during the springtime in the Himalayas. Assam was 'robust and full-bodied'. There were photographs of the old Daykins he had already seen, along with others of more recent directors and staff from the fifties and sixties, plus a series of pictures taken during redevelopment of the wharf.

Interesting though this was, Oscar wondered why he was still here. But when Ben came back it was to usher him outside into the sunshine. 'I must have a quick fag before we carry on,' he said. 'Do you smoke?'

They stood for a while making admiring noises about the river and the bridges. A family of ducks swam in busy circles below them, diving to find food, popping up like corks. 'Daykin is an extremely successful company,' Ben said, turning to Oscar. 'We floated in the eighties, though the majority of the shareholding is still in private hands. I imagine you know this.'

Oscar laughed. 'Me? I wasn't *that* interested in the company. I was just looking for names. I saw it as maybe a way of tracing this family.'

Ben nodded. 'Good. I want you to meet someone. He's up in the library now.'

'That sounds mysterious.'

'It is in a way,' he said.

The library was a private upstairs room, no more than a large study with a solid desk, bookshelves, comfy chairs and two windows looking out across the street. There was a man standing at the windows, elderly – taller than Oscar, with only the slightest stoop of age – a teacup raised in one hand, a saucer in the other, casually dressed in a brown corduroy jacket and a shirt open at the neck, his face tanned, healthy-looking. He turned to meet them as they entered, his lips pursed in an expectant smile.

'Allow me to introduce you to my father,' Ben said. 'Thomas Winter. He used to run this place.' Even before Ben had finished the preliminaries, Oscar knew who this was, the mystery Ben had been holding back. Tom, now in his seventies. Here was Amy's baby brother.

'Oh my God,' Oscar said, smiling. 'I didn't expect this.'

'I gather you have news for me,' Thomas said.

After pleasantries, Ben left them to it. Oscar showed Thomas what he had – Amy's handwritten childhood, the two photographs. The old man's face creased with a smile as he read, and studied the photographs, then he broke down with breathy sobs, laughing as he tried to hold back the tears. Oscar couldn't trust himself to say the right thing but touched his arm. Tom produced a handkerchief and wiped his eyes, apologised, and told his story, staring ahead sometimes, as if reading from a distance. He was fostered, he said, by the Winters in 1934. He was eight. Their natural son had died of TB and they brought him up as their own and gave him their name. Tom knew he had a sister, Amy. He was bright and was working in an architect's office in the fifties when he found out he had come into an inheritance. Daykin's lawyers had him traced after the death of his remaining grandparent – Victoria, wife of William and mother of the disgraced May.

'I did a search on that,' Oscar said. 'I thought Victoria didn't make a will.'

'Which is why the administrators started the search for the next of kin,' Tom said. 'My mother, Margaret, had died by then – she'd been in an asylum for indigent women in London, a charity-run sort of home. The local authorities knew her and knew she'd had two children, one of whom had been put in care. They tried to trace Amy but couldn't. According to Barnardo's, she was sent to Australia in 1928. They found me though. I was luckier than Amy, far luckier.'

'So how did they find you?' Oscar asked.

'Pretty straightforward detective work. My mother had found refuge at a hostel for homeless women, where she was able to stay, doing menial work, helping out. But she had drink and growing mental health problems, and the hostel couldn't keep two children – not indefinitely. I never discovered the precise circumstances behind it all. Obviously there was a man involved – my father. But they never married. He came and went it seemed, but took off for good when my mother became pregnant with me. Eventually the authorities took Amy into care, but I was never officially adopted. The Winters were steady,

226

respectable people. Very kind. Mrs Winter had become involved in voluntary work after the death of her own son – women's welfare in particular – and knew the people at the hostel. My mother was frightened that I would have to go into Barnado's too and it was agreed that the Winters would take me on. I think they may have pretended to be relatives. I don't know. I was too young to know what was happening. The Winters told me everything when I was older. They told me I'd had another mother, someone who had loved me but was unable to take care of me, and that I had a sister who had had to go away into an orphanage. I accepted it, as you do as a child, but I thought many times about that sister. When the question of the inheritance arose, I started thinking about Amy again. I had agencies searching Australia for her, but we had to give up.' Mr Winter shook his head, then smiled. 'And now this. I don't know what to say.' He looked at Oscar and then back at the photographs in wonder. 'But what's the procedure now? How can I see her?'

Oscar realised that he had no idea what the procedure was. 'Leave it with me. I'll get in touch with the charity and they'll make the arrangements, I imagine. To be honest, you're only my second find. I haven't been doing this very long.'

The old man laughed. 'Well, congratulations.'

He asked Oscar how he got paid for his work. 'The charity pay me a day rate. It's not too bad. Maybe I'll get a bonus at Christmas.'

Oscar put the documents back in the file, but handed him the photographs and his sister's handwritten notes. 'You should have these.'

Thomas picked them up and held them. He seemed at a loss for something more to say. 'My wife died the year I retired. My son has his own share in the business. He's been quite brilliant – for someone who doesn't care very much for tea. I wasn't sure how he'd take to it. He'd only been with the firm two or three years when he took over. Up until then he was one of these eternal students, you know. Marine biology. One tiny research grant after another, polar expeditions, saving the whale, having to share a flat, clothes from Oxfam – that kind of thing.'

Oscar nodded. 'Sounds vaguely familiar.'

'Half of what I have is hers,' he said. 'Amy, I mean. Amy.' Mr Winter said the name as though getting used to the taste of it.

Oscar left him to savour his news and slipped away. The encounter left him feeling good and he followed an impulse and travelled on a bus north to Finsbury Park to see his own rediscovered relative, Mrs Edwards. Her breathing was improved with the warmer weather, and they sat out in the garden. He didn't mention his own health. He let her do most of the talking, reminiscing about Michael. She had a school photograph of him from 1960, his hair greased down and parted in an old-fashioned style, those pale eyes. Oscar promised to send her a photograph of himself.

'Call me Gran,' she said when it was time for him to go.

There was a message from Emma on his mobile. He listened to it as he walked to the tube. She was calling from her mum's place. 'I came to surprise you at the kiosk, but – surprise – Diggsy said you were in London. Just my luck. Give me a call?' He walked faster, though it would be an hour before his train left Liverpool Street. He would call her when he got back.

He couldn't say what he needed to say on the phone. He hadn't seen her since Saturday, when she'd cooked dinner in her flat and they'd talked about Long QT Syndrome. 'The question is,' he'd said, 'do I want to know if I'm

228

carrying the gene? Because even if I have it, I might never show symptoms.'

She had her back to him, slicing mushrooms. 'But you might.'

'But anyone *might* have anything, right? In some ways, isn't it better not to know? Then you can just get on with your life without the threat hanging over you.'

She turned to him with a puzzled look. 'Well maybe. Except that you already know you might have it – that there's a fifty-fifty chance of having it. You could have the test and be completely cleared. Or you could find that you do have it, and control it with beta-blockers – isn't that what you said? Don't they work?'

'Usually. Not always. What if they didn't work?' Emma shook her head and set about emptying a bag of salad into a bowl, leaving him to drive the argument. 'I mean, can't we just be allowed to live the life we're given?' he continued. She didn't answer. 'Emma?'

She gave him the salad, and knives and forks for the table. 'You're talking about fatalism. But what you have is fear.'

It stopped him short. 'Is it?'

They sat down at the table. 'And, actually,' she said, heat rising in her voice for the first time, 'we *can* do what we like with the life we're given. We can change things. Look at you. Look at me. Us.'

'I know, I know, but . . . I don't know. I can't think about it.'

They tossed the subject back and forth until at last she shrugged and let it drop. She looked sympathetic, but there was frustration in the way she squeezed his hand across the table, and when he left there was a feeling of things left unsaid. Sunday went by without a phone call. Monday too. Her phone was switched off.

He knew now what it was about. She was right about the fear. But the fear wasn't in the knowing – it was in the not knowing how Emma would take it, what was really in her heart. She said she loved him, but how could she devote herself to a man who could die at the sound of his alarm clock going off? How could he expect her to? It was one thing for long-married couples facing the frailties of their later years, becoming each other's natural carers, anchored as they were by the weight of their time together; but what sort of prospect was it for people taking their first faltering steps in a relationship, people with the smile still on their faces – people still at the stage of not believing their luck? True, they had known each other all their lives but not in this way.

On the train out of London he turned the pages of a book, holding back from calling her until they were pulling under the bridge and into the station. 'Emma?'

'Where have you been?' she said. 'I came to see you.'

'Well . . . I would have been there if I'd known you were coming.'

He heard her sigh. 'The trouble is I now need to get back to London by six. There's a dinner I have to go to this evening. Where are you?'

Ten minutes later Emma's mother dropped her at the station and she came hurrying to meet him at the café-cum-bar nearby. They sat at one of the two tables outside. He ordered a beer and she a mint tea. He told her about his extraordinary day. 'That's excellent, well done,' she said, but her eyes were fixed on the table in front of her. She declined his offer of a cigarette.

'What we were talking about on Saturday,' she said. 'Whether you should find out about this thing. You have to, I think. We need to know. I need to know.'

'I know, I see that now,' he said, hurriedly. 'I can't

expect you to . . . I mean, I don't expect you to stick by me just for this. Sorry, I know that sounds pathetic. What I suppose I mean is—'

'What are you talking about?' She seized his hands. 'That's not in doubt, you idiot. For God's sake, Oscar. What kind of a woman do you take me for?'

He shook his head. 'I don't know. What kind of a woman are you?'

She hesitated, then took a sip of her mint tea. 'At the moment? A pregnant one,' she said.

He drives home now, up the hill to High Firs, feeling the clutch slip on the last bend, and pulls haltingly into the drive behind Dad's Lexus. He gets out and takes a deep breath beneath the high canopy of the monkey puzzle. He finds himself smiling. He smiles though there is danger afoot, though he has set a tiny new heart in motion that even now may be drumming the rhythms of his own precarious fate. He smiles for the uniqueness of this moment's joy. He is still smiling as he opens the door and watches Mum and Dad turn their heads towards him. Neither speaks.

'What?' he says, bemused by their stares. 'What?'

Chapter 19

'**I** ought to be there,' Robert says, his eyes suddenly blazing at the thought. 'Not that I wouldn't rather be here, obviously,' he quickly adds, realising his faux pas. He gives her his zany grin. 'Happy anniversary, Muffin.' Not for the first time in their thirteen hours on foreign soil he raises a glass to their marriage, obliging Rachel to swallow her dread and find in her repertoire an attitude of resignation that will pass for serenity. The whistlestop romance of Venice – with its citadels of culture, its lapping green waters, its encouragement at every turn to envisage their own blissful harmony reflected in its realised, sculpted beauty – has been endured. Prague and Paris are to come. The truth is that Robert's almost sexual delirium at speeding through the darkening southern provinces of Austria aboard the Orient Express is heightened by what is going on back home – tomorrow's rally and march in town – and the late thrilling news that Monday's knife-edge vote is poised to turn down planning permission for a village of executive homes at Five Ponds. There is talk now of rebuying the land for a youth, sports and multi-faith community facility. The march will seal it – a good show of local opposition can't be argued with, Robert says. There is no doubt he will be right. His information is always on the button. She registers defeat with a cold, ignored silence. If, in his excitement, Robert is blind to the irony of sitting here in evening dress amid the polished oak and chandeliered splendour of the dining car while talking about the triumph of the little man over the interests of fat-cat developers, it is as nothing to the greater fault of imagining that his wife's feelings in this matter are indissolubly wedded to his own. She sits and watches him and listens to the details of this impending victory that will ruin her. To some extent she is to blame for not coming clean with Robert when it became evident that their respective hopes were beginning to diverge, though this thought is not in itself enough to quiet the nagging compulsion Rachel has to lunge across the table, with its snowy tablecloth and stupid silk-tasselled lamp, and bring an end to his wittering with a teak-handled steak knife engraved with the company logo.

She, herself, is as good as dead. Outside the world is passing her by, quick as lightning. She smiles weakly, leaves the table and locks herself in an Edwardian WC for fifteen minutes. She tries to vomit but nothing comes. In the mirror she looks into her own vacant eyes.

Later, in the rumble and sway of the cabin, the shapes of nameless sleeping towns and villages throwing their foreign shadows and splashes of light on the polished walls as they clatter through, she lies awake while he snores. She is thankful for the five-course dinner, and the drinks that kept them chatting in the piano bar till gone two with an elderly American garden equipment millionaire and his

233

hard-of-hearing wife, all of which combined to sabotage Robert's attempts at sex, an impossible feat in any case on these narrow bunks that fold out into brocaded day furniture under the practised hand of Jurgen their uniformed steward, resplendent in powder blue, whom Robert was panicked into tipping lavishly before the poor man had even done anything. 'Best wait, Prague,' he slurred. 'Nice hotel.'

But the hotel in Prague reminds her of Gareth. He is in London but she has received a brief, delicious text from him (*cant talk rt now. confce. G*) that arrived while Robert was in the lobby asking the concierge for tips on places to eat. Fortified by a couple of vodka miniatures from the minibar, she stabbed out two frantic messages in return. *Stuck here n Prag. Cantwait to see u!* and *I WANT Uxxxx*. Gareth is the strength she needs to follow Robert round the crowded tourist areas, to respond in kind to his avid pronouncements from the guidebook on paintings by Klimt and Egon Schiele, Pilsner beer and cemetery architecture, to wait at his elbow while he gets his bearings and tries out Czech phrases on shopkeepers who at their worst speak better English than Josh. They eat sausage with gravy and cabbage at a subterranean Tyrolean restaurant with heavily varnished chalet-style pine furniture and cheerful waitresses wearing gingham skirts and white knee socks.

In their room that night, after an evening of goulash and apple strudel in the same Tyrolean restaurant – the price of the evening meal includes a medley of Mozart favourites performed by a string quartet, and a glass of Slivovitz ('Here's to us . . .') – they consummate their anniversary in the time-honoured way. 'My parents were asking again when we're going to give them some grandchildren,' whispers Robert, nuzzling Rachel's ear as he kneads her breast with his left hand, bringing to her the recollection of a man at the council who would sit in finance meetings manipulating a stress reliever.

'Maybe next year,' she says, abandoning herself to thoughts of Gareth.

'That's what I call playing for time,' Robert chuckles.

There is another quartet at the railway station in Prague the next evening. Here, Rachel and Robert, along with their fellow passengers for Paris, sip tea and admire the art nouveau domed ceiling while their suitcases are wheeled and loaded by liveried porters trained to simulate old-world standards of courtesy. Rachel holds two fingertips to her throbbing right temple. The musicians, dressed in medieval garb, launch unexpectedly into the *William Tell* overture to the delight of the crowd, some of whom start to clap along or beat their straw hats on the table. She is moments from detonation when at last they are called to the special desk on the platform to have their documents inspected, and then to the train itself, its gilded indigo *voitures lits* stretching in a gleaming arc down the track like limousines freshly waxed and valeted. Jurgen, wearing gloves and a pillbox hat, is on hand to welcome them aboard and usher them into their compartment. Robert fumbles in his pocket and produces a wad of euros. 'Is that OK?' he asks. 'I just changed all our money.'

'Absolutely fine, sir, thank you, sir! And dinner?'

'Second sitting, don't you think, Rachel? I wouldn't mind a nap.'

It is fifteen minutes before departure. Robert settles near the window and unfolds a map of the route the train will take. 'Isn't this the life?' he sighs.

Rachel gazes at him, this man she married six years ago, his thick finger on the map, studying the names of the

235

towns. She looks at his grey shoes he bought at Clarks – his travelling shoes, he calls them. Whatever your heart says, it's not as simple as just undoing love, she knows that. Undisturbed, love becomes a settled thing, like the once defined layers of something crushed by time to a single, blunt conclusion – like time itself, you might say, meting out its distinct moments until all you've got is aeons, the carbon imprint of its distinct pterodactyls and fern life buried deep and forgotten. The particulars of why she fell in love with Robert are lost to her. Whatever she feels for him has this other quality, this residual tenderness for a life that was. To call it fossilised seems cruel, but aren't romantic trips like this designed to remind people how much they used to love each other? Don't we associate romantic gestures with a sentimental desire to freshen love, to halt the hardening process?

She sits down for a few minutes and leafs uninterestedly through a copy of *International Herald Tribune*. 'I'm just going down to the bar for a cigarette,' she says. 'I might take this to read.'

'OK, petal.'

She picks up her handbag and makes her way down the corridor. The sun is falling now and the antique glass and walnut marquetry and even the brass fittings are warmed in its salmon blush. She steps aside to let a young couple pass, whispering and giggling like children. Rachel noticed them on the first leg of the journey from Venice. Perhaps they are newlyweds. The prospect of so much old romance and luxury must have seemed to them an ideal honeymoon, but they are conspicuous here, surrounded by ageing couples socialising in the piano bar, calling out requests for old show tunes; even so, they make a happy conspiracy of two, unafraid of their own company, unneedy of outsiders.

She walks through the empty bar, past the steward, who

236

looks up from his preparations and nods graciously as she passes. 'Good *evening*, madam.'

Nothing is good. There is no way out of this.

At the end of the train, she pauses. Two latecomers just boarding. A steward behind them with their hand luggage. Rachel waits, then proceeds, hears them talking in the compartment as she slips past. She seems to scent the city from the open window. Prague is out there, not yet left behind, not yet a hard dab of memory to be recalled in years to come but still fluid and real. How strange it would be to go back right now, beyond the station wall, and find it again. To see it with her own eyes, to surprise it with her return, to stop it hardening simply by refusing to leave. It seems so simple.

The door is open wide, awaiting the hand of a steward. She pauses and then decides. Two deep metal steps, and it's done. She is walking along the platform. No one seems to notice her. A group of uniformed staff wait in line on the platform to perform a leave-taking ritual; locals are gathered here, too, to marvel at the Orient Express, which visits only on appointed days of the year, bringing its old-world glamour. She walks quickly. The train windows are high. There is movement in the corridor but Robert will have dozed off by now. It has been a tiring day, a second haul up to the Castle to see the mosaics and frescos of St Vitus, shopping for souvenirs. Jurgen will be doing his rounds, tapping discreetly on doors, ensuring the comfort of his passengers, taking orders for tomorrow's breakfast, answering timetabling queries. The hour of departure is nigh, a moment of relief when the wheels slowly start to turn and the smiling guests are properly able to congratulate themselves on their good fortune. At some point, with the train well beyond the suburbs and thundering through wooded valleys and remote peasant communities, Robert will wake

237

up, notice the change in the light, wonder where he is and then, after a moment, wonder where she is.

She is free. Outside she finds a taxi and instructs the driver to take her into the city centre, back to the hotel. The windows of the cab are wide open, and the wind blows through her hair like a gale. The young driver, eager to impress with his language skills, is expansive in English about the beauty of the city at this time of the year. At the Cosmos he opens the door for her and bows graciously when she tells him to keep the change. But once inside the lobby she reconsiders. No. Not this hotel. She needs to choose one Gareth would choose. Surprise him. Money first. The cashpoint in the lobby accepts her Duttings debit card and deals out a heap of purple banknotes. She picks up a city guide and sits in the bar with a large gin and tonic, a chic, cosmopolitan woman at large in one of Europe's most beautiful ancient capitals. She checks the hotel listings. The Palace? The Diplomat? The President is nearby, but there is no rush. The bar here, its big old windows facing out on to the square, is lively without being full – tourists mainly, dropping in for an aperitif or a post-sightseeing sundowner. As she reads, she picks from the bowl of salted nuts the waitress puts in front of her. She smokes a cigarette. If only Gareth could join her here. Of course! Together they would sort out the mess back home, the chief one being the warehouse full of stock. What did he say – she could hold a clearance sale. But haven't they just had one? And this proposed youth and sports and ethnic facility is not promising. Even if it needed carpets – and right now Rachel cannot envisage a public complex of this description requiring anything more than doormats – the timescale would be up the wall. A private developer can knock together an estate of timber-frame executive brick and flint-fronted homes in months, but experience tells her that any project with the word 'community' in its title will eat up whole years while committees sit around deciding who to name it after and setting up studies into the impact of the landscaping on the regional ecosystem. She orders another drink.

A threesome in business outfits arrive, two men and a woman chatting animatedly. They sit at the next table and briefly consult the cocktail menu before summoning the waiter and ordering Manhattans all round. The woman opens a briefcase on her knee and hands round glossy brochures of some kind. Rachel can hear them talking in American accents. 'Who translates this stuff?' one of the men is saying. "*Tastively decorative.*" Did you see this, Bob?' Bob shakes his head and smiles.

'We may laugh,' the woman says, 'but just take a look at this place on Moravska . . .'

The two men move forward to the edge of their seats. 'And this is where?'

'Doesn't matter. Two blocks from here. Double storey, each with parking, a private *roof garden* . . .' She looks up at them, an emphatic eyebrow raised. 'This is a former shoe factory remodelled in the art nouveau style, with a choice of floors from marble or hardwoods. And the pièce de résistance – a pool in the basement. *Voilà.*'

'*Mozaik.* What is that?' the first man says, squinting at the page.

She looks impatient. 'Mosaic.'

'And remodelled art nouveau?' says the second man. 'Does that mean not original, but just made to look that way?'

'Does it matter? You're talking eight mill, local – that's what in dollars? Less than three hundred thou.' She shows them the palms of her hands, like a magician. 'The actual building is seventeenth century. That's practically Pilgrim

Fathers.' The two men mime a low whistle at this information. She smiles, revealing perfect teeth.

Rachel *loves* this woman.

'Anyway,' the woman says. She snaps the case shut and puts it at the side of her chair, then smoothes her skirt with her hands.

The waiter arrives and the three make a fuss of clinking their glasses as though they have something to celebrate. Rachel smiles pleasantly in their general direction, as if sharing their happiness. She catches the eye of the man called Bob, who smiles back. Rachel crosses her legs and goes back to her guidebook. Her three neighbours are now discussing the prospect of dinner.

Rachel smiles and leans sideways towards their table. 'Whatever you do, don't ask the concierge here – he's terrible.'

The woman turns to her, amiably. 'Excuse me?'

'He sent me and my husband to just the worst place last night.'

'You're English?' Bob is leaning forward now.

'Yes, I am. And you guys – you're American, I guess.'

'Delaware,' says the woman, smiling. 'Dover.'

Dover? Rachel wonders if the woman just introduced herself. It's possible.

'Rachel Dutting,' she says, offering a handshake. She's noticed before how formal the Americans can be, introducing themselves like delegates, with their names and where they live.

'Pleased to meet you. I'm Helen Miller – and this is Dean and Bob Rich.'

'Hi,' they say, both at once.

'So what's the name of this place again we have to avoid?' says Helen.

'Let me think – Kolosso, that was it. With a K.'

240

'Greek?'

'German actually. If anything a little *too* German for my taste.'

'Actually, I'm German myself,' Helen says. 'Or at least my family were.'

'Oh my God, I'm sorry,' says Rachel, clapping her hand to her mouth. 'I just meant . . .'

Helen laughs. 'Don't worry. I know *exactly* what you mean. Bratwurst and dumplings and sauerkraut, right?'

'That's the place.' Rachel thinks it best not to mention that she and Robert ate at Kolosso twice.

'Are you waiting for him now?'

'Who?'

'Your husband.'

'My husband? No.' Rachel drains her glass. 'Sadly, he had to fly back to London unexpectedly. Business crisis of some kind. Something has fallen through. He's in property.'

'Ah, isn't everyone?'

'You too?'

Bob speaks up. 'Perhaps he was looking for business opportunities here in Prague? I hope not. We don't want *too* many competitors.'

Rachel laughs. 'No, we were just taking a break. But thanks for the tip.'

The drinks have mellowed her mood. Her headache is gone. She likes this Helen and this Bob and this Dean, the way they just swan into Europe on the scent of business deals and drink Manhattans in the cocktail hour. They're so at ease.

One of the girls from reception is approaching rapidly, her shoes clacking on the wooden floor. 'Excuse me,' she says, 'Mrs Parsons?' She's looking at Rachel. Rachel guesses now that Robert has rung, unable to contact her mobile, frantic no doubt by now, hoping she has come back here to the Cosmos. She can see him now, the panic in his face as the train hurtles through the Black Forest or wherever, wondering if she's somehow fallen off, explaining to Jurgen that his wife merely wandered down to the bar. She imagines the consternation of the chief steward and the *herr direktor* of customer relations, dashing around trying to reassure Robert that they will do their utmost to . . .

'Sorry,' Rachel says. 'You must be mistaken.'

The girl is confused. 'You're not Mrs Parsons?'

'I think I'd know,' Rachel laughs, glancing round at her new acquaintances.

The girl hovers for a second, then smiles. 'Sorry to disturb,' she says, and clacks off again back to the desk, shaking her head at someone.

But it is not over. There are discussions being held by the reception staff, and glances are cast in Rachel's direction. 'Excuse me,' she says to the others, rising to her feet. 'I just need the bathroom.' She heads purposefully towards the far side of the bar and follows its curve until she is out of sight. The toilets are straight ahead, but an exit calls her from the left, its ornate wooden doors open to the mild darkening evening out there, the lights of the lively cafés and shops and the advertising billboards winking above illuminated baroque façades, like coloured chalk some of them, and grand spires and arches and stained glass and promenading crowds. The breeze is on her face as she glides along now, inhaling deeply, feeding on this new night as if in some wonderful narcotic reverie. Her pace slows and she wanders at random until she finds herself at the river. Here she buys a hotdog and sits for a few minutes on a bench while she eats. Then she turns back towards the old town. Hotel, yes. She searches her bag for her city guide, but remembers now leaving it on the table at the Cosmos. But Prague is full of hotels. A bar presents itself on the corner of a square. She ventures in. The music is loud in here and alive with younger people – goths you would call them in England, hanging about outside the Town Hall on Saturdays with their boots and pierced eyebrows and white faces and black hair. But otherwise the place seems no worse than the pubs back home, and the staff are friendly. Rachel sits on a stool at the bar and asks the girl for a Manhattan. The girl isn't sure what one is, and has to ask the barman, who doesn't know either. 'Perhaps I can fix you Jack Daniel's with club soda?' he suggests.

'OK,' says Rachel. 'And cigarettes, please. Marlboro.' She lays a note on the counter. 'I was looking for a nice hotel. Can you recommend somewhere?'

The barman looks at her clothes – her Orient Express daywear of smart linen jacket, casual black top and trousers. Perhaps to him she looks well-off. 'There is the Nicholas nearby.' He draws a map on the back of a discarded bar tab. 'Small and beautiful. Though expensive,' he says, rubbing his thumb and forefinger together. He goes off to serve someone else.

She lights a cigarette and takes time to finish her drink. More people have arrived, pushing around the bar area. At home she would feel uncomfortable with this, but here it seems just fine. A recollection of something tries to surface in her mind but it gets lost in the lazy pounding of the music and the hum of foreign chatter. She goes to the Ladies to pee and apply fresh lipstick and eye make-up. Her face in the mirror is strange. For a moment it looks like someone else staring back – a sultry, after-dark Rachel with strong appetites. She half closes her eyes and smiles at herself. The folded bar tab with its drawn map is in her hand. She comes out and edges through the press of customers now thronging the gangway.

Outside, it is cooler now. She switches on her phone, skips through the increasingly alarmed messages from Robert ('OK, Rachel, I know you're around here somewhere . . .'; 'Rachel, where the hell are you?'; 'For God's sake, just please *ring me* . . .'), looking for signs of Gareth. No calls. She dials his number now as she walks along. No one answers, but his voice is there, loud and clear, telling her to speak after the beep. Her breath quickens with the excitement of just hearing him, having him here with her. 'Gareth. Guess what! I'm just about to check into a hotel. It's so beautiful, and right in the old town near the astronomical clock, which has these brilliant little mechanical figures of the Apostles and Death who come marching out when it strikes the hour. You *must* meet me here. Call me and tell me you're on your way. Miss you,' she purrs. 'Love you.'

She turns the corner into the square and the Hotel Nicholas is right there, with its tall, narrow frontage of yellow-and-green stained glass and old wood, lit up inside like a huge wartime radio. The lobby is much smaller and more intimate than the one at the Cosmos, with club chairs and green plants and a bookcase. It's perfect.

She strides up to the front desk. 'Do you have a room?'

'For tonight?'

'If that's possible. A double.'

The receptionist looks doubtful as she consults the register. 'Ah. Normally is not possible, but luckily we have a room. A cancellation.'

'I'll take it.'

She gives Rachel a form to fill in. 'You have luggage?'

'My husband has it. He'll be here soon.'

'I understand. Could I have your passport, please?'

'Yes, hang on.' She opens her bag, then freezes. Jurgen has her passport. He took both passports when they got on the train. 'Ah,' she says. 'My husband has that too.'

The woman looks at her more closely now. 'Your husband will be here soon? Perhaps you would like to wait. I cannot proceed with check-in. It is the regulation. There is a coffee shop if you care to wait.'

Behind her, a group of guests have appeared and are waiting to be dealt with. Rachel lifts her jacket sleeve to look at her watch but it's gone too. Did she leave it on the train? 'Don't worry,' she says. 'I'll come back later.'

It's not a disaster. Back in the street, she tosses her hair and holds her head high as she walks. A Eurythmics song is on her mind, the one about the rain. *Walk with me*. On the corner she stops and tries Gareth's number again. Amazingly he speaks. 'Rachel?'

She is aware of causing a hold-up on the narrow pavement, but daren't move in case she somehow loses him. 'Gareth, I can't believe it's you! I can't believe it. Can you come? Can you?'

'For Christ's sake, Rachel,' he says quietly. 'I can't talk right now.'

'Did you get my messages?'

'Well, yes, I did.' He pauses. 'Are you all right?'

'Of course.' Just hearing his faraway voice makes her giddy out here in the fresh city air. She hears laughter nearby and the sound of car horns, though the traffic is light.

'Look, I'm sorry,' Gareth is saying. 'I'll have to see you later. I have to go.'

'Yes, of course you do,' she whispers. 'I'll see you though, yes?'

Pause. 'I think maybe we ought to cool it for a while.'

'But I will see you . . .'

245

'I'll call you, OK?'

The line is dead. She stands uncertainly now at the intersection of narrow streets. The Koki Lounge sheds blue light across the pavement and the warm slap of music from within. She approaches and hovers at the doorway. Inside, the crowd, moneyed singles in their thirties, dressed for Saturday night, are laughing and drinking, the women Slavic-looking blondes in revealing outfits, the men extravagant in their gestures and wearing vivid designer shirts, Italian shoes. She could easily be meeting someone here. She steps in. She likes this expensive monochrome decor and cool violet floor-lights like a runway, and illuminated bar stacked to the ceiling with every imaginable colour of drink. She sees herself pass by in the long mirror, finds a table and lights a cigarette. A waiter comes. 'A Manhattan,' she says. The waiter is young and good-looking, and flatters her with a gaze when he comes back and sets the glass carefully before her. A jazz-funk track throbs and blows in the background. The tables, she sees now, are mostly taken by foursomes or bigger groups. Further back, on a higher level, the pastel lights of a dance floor – still empty at this hour of the evening – pulse gently. A man old enough to be her father raises his glass in her direction. She ignores him. She strikes a match from the book in the ashtray and holds it till it burns out. She lights a second and a third, watching the flame devour the curling paper layers. The next time she turns to look, two girls have joined the man and they are all drinking champagne.

Her own glass is empty now. The waiter comes to take it away. She orders another Manhattan and smokes another cigarette. Hollywood films from the forties and fifties are playing out silently on small screens dotted around the place. It's comfortable just to sit here watching, with the music playing and the clamour of talk. The evening slips by. There is general movement to the dance floor. At one point a man leans towards her and whispers something she doesn't understand. 'English?' he asks. She shrugs and laughs, and he goes away. The bar is full now. It seems hours since she left the train. The train is in a different country now. She has the idea of staying here, hiding in the dark and the smoke, insulated against the outside and the back home.

'Hey, look who it is . . .' She glances up and sees the two American men from the Cosmos. They each have a hand raised in greeting. 'Remember us?'

'Of course,' she says, surprised at the sound of her own voice. 'Now let me see. It's Bob and . . .'

'Dean,' says Dean. Yes. Dean is the shorter of the two.

'Dean, that's right. Bob and Dean. But you've lost someone. Dover from Delaware . . .'

'Helen? She got tired and headed back to the hotel. Do you mind if we join you?'

'Sure, why not,' she says, the American way.

Bob beckons to the waiter and orders drinks. 'You'll have to excuse us,' says Dean. 'We closed two deals this morning, so we're celebrating.'

She finds, during the conversation, that Bob and Dean are brothers. Bob and Dean Rich. She notices now a family resemblance, a softness around the chin. Dean is the shorter one, she reminds herself. Rich Realty is the name of their firm, based in Dover, Delaware. 'So are the three of you partners?' asks Rachel.

'Yes, though Helen is also Dean's ex-wife . . .' Bob lights a cigar, puffing hard to get it going, the tip glowing beneath the flake of ash.

'Which sounds kind of weird,' Dean says, 'but it works out.'

The two explain how it works out, but the music is louder

247

now that the dancing has started and it's harder to follow what they're saying, and they seem to take so long, the way they finish each other's sentences. Her head nodding to the rhythm, Rachel finds herself counting the number of women wearing white and the number of men in black.

'It's a kind of chemistry, I guess you'd call it,' Bob is saying.

'Have you ever tried it?'

'Sorry?' Rachel says.

'Absinthe. You should. It's quite something.'

'Absinthe. Isn't that supposed to be . . .' She can't quite get the word on her tongue. '. . . hallucinogenetic?'

'It sure has some kick,' Bob says. 'The way the French fix it, they take a shot of the stuff in a wine glass, lay a flat spoon with slots across the rim, place a couple of sugar cubes on the spoon, drip cold water on . . . is that right? . . . releasing the oil, which then makes it kind of milky.'

'Pretty much, bro,' Dean says. 'Or *soak* the sugar and put a flame to it.'

Rachel squints at him. She sees herself looking through slits. 'Why does this sound like what you have to do with, what is it – the drug?'

Bob laughs. 'Don't worry,' he says. 'It's not crack. But the reason we come to this place – they do great absinthe cocktails.'

'And there's no way we can get this back home. Allow us to recommend the B-52 number four – that's a quarter absinthe, and a third each of Baileys Irish Cream, Tia Maria – you know Baileys, Rachel?'

She finds herself needing time to answer. 'It's my favourite.'

'Attagirl,' says Bob, slapping the table.

The waiter brings three shot glasses, and with a flourish puts a burning taper to the liquid. '*Voilà*,' he says.

'You have to slap out the flame and drink it in one. OK? Here we go . . .'

They are in the back of a taxi. There has been dancing. It seems a long time ago, but Rachel remembers falling over but was caught in time by Bob. The bar was closing and they had to leave, but Dean and Bob know a casino that stays open late. The taxi dips and veers on hills and corners and they bump against each other as they gather speed, the orange lights from the street hitting the laughing faces of the two men in the dark. Across town they stop at a hotel, lit up like a birthday cake with a burly man out front in a bowtie. Bob speaks and winks and touches the man's arm in a friendly way. He presses something into his hand, and in they go. 'Do you have a coat?' Dean asks. Dean is the shorter of the two. There's some delay. They have to show ID to the woman at the desk. No one asks Rachel for hers. 'No problem,' she hears one of the brothers say, 'she's with us.'

Inside is bright and swaying and they each buy bundles of chips from the man behind the grille. Everyone knows how to play the wheel – you just pick red or black, or put your chips on the squares with the numbers. Dean takes a vacant chair at the blackjack table but Bob sticks with Rachel. They lay down their stakes. Rachel is distracted by the wide, beautiful ceilings, the statues set in niches in the walls, the attendants who stand on watch. 'Look,' she says, looking around. With the people wandering around in evening dress with drinks, it's like a party held in a museum.

'Hey, you won!' Bob says. They try another couple of times, then move away. Dean has won too. He is already at a table and ordering champagne. They drink, and Dean starts to tell Rachel a story about a man who came into the office by mistake, thinking it was a travel shop.

'It was when we were just starting out,' Bob says, interrupting. 'The doors were adjacent, you see – the travel shop here and our office here.' Bob lays his forefingers side by side on the tablecloth to show her.

Dean picks up the story. It turns out that, coincidentally, the man had been thinking about moving house. Dean sent him away with details on a number of loft properties and that same afternoon—

'Yes, didn't he come back with his wife?' Bob interjects.

Dean shakes his head, and removes an olive stone from his mouth. 'Girlfriend. Do you remember, they were looking to buy a home together, and planning to get married?'

'That's *right*. That was the trip – the honeymoon.'

Rachel excuses herself and goes to the ladies' room. She stops at the roulette wheel on the way back, buys more chips and pulls up a seat. 'What are the blue ones?' she hears herself wonder aloud. No one answers. She watches the wheel spin and the silver ball, how fast and amazingly smoothly it travels until it snags and tumbles and jumps and then lodges with perfect stillness in the space on the wheel. 'Fourteen,' says someone in English. She stares at it and waits.

That's not one of Rachel's. She has a number of numbers . . . but not that one. The man scoops chips this way and that with his wooden rake. More chips? She loves the feel of these, the plasticky milled edges, the shape and thickness of them in her hand, the clacking sound they make like shoes on a floor as she allows them to drop one by one from her fingers on to the pile. Then the man's gloved hand sets the wheel in motion again, drawing everyone into its orbit, the pull of its gravity. It's the thrill of hope that she feels suspended in that spinning when time stands still. But the wheel slows and halts and the number is called and she finds that time has moved on more quickly

250

than she imagined. Bob is behind her with his hands on her shoulders. 'Jesus, Rachel, are these your chips? There must be two thousand dollars here.'

'Really? Is that enough?' she asks.

'For what?'

Rachel is confused for a moment, as if she has forgotten something. Bob vanishes. What has she arranged with Gareth? She meant to call him and make him come here. Did she call, or was that a dream? Flights are so inexpensive now, and he will come to her rescue. And yes, Duttings must be rescued too – re-engineered, as they say, as a corporation. In her mind she sees the Prague offices of Dutting & Newnam Real Estate Consultants, occupying the top floor of a converted eighteenth-century rococo palace with views of the Charles Bridge and the astronomical clock, if that's possible. She takes a deep breath and pushes two great columns of chips forward and waits for the wheel to spin again.

She opens her eyes to the sun knifing through a chink in the curtain. Her throat tries to swallow, but there is nothing to swallow but itself. She imagines a glass of water. In her surfacing thoughts comes the sound of running water mocking her need. She blinks. Adjusting the angle of her vision, she sees the outline of a table, the laminated wigwam of a sideways menu bearing the hotel logo. She is back in the Cosmos. For a moment, then, it is Robert whose body she feels lying behind her. Nothing has happened. But it comes to her now, in its own order – first, the recollection of her faux pas with the American woman about German cooking, and only then the escape from the train that makes everything else real. She turns quickly in the bed and sees the man sleeping at her side. The thoughts come tumbling now, in a panic. She is naked under the sheet. But is this Bob, or the other one . . . Why here? This is his hotel.

The phone is ringing, she realises. The water stops running and a door opens abruptly. A second man wearing a towel emerges, his hair dripping as he picks it up. She closes her eyes. Jesus Christ. 'Hello?' he says, into the mouthpiece, keeping his voice down. Seeing Rachel staring at him, he gives a sheepish smile. 'Just a moment.' He holds out the phone to her.

'Gareth . . .' she murmurs, reaching for it, the bedsheet clutched to her throat. But she knows it is not Gareth. How could it be?

'Rachel? Is that you?'

'Mum? Oh God.' She starts to cry. 'Mum . . .'

'Rachel, for heaven's sake, what are you *doing* with yourself?'

'I don't know. I . . .'

'We've got the bloody Czech police out looking for you. Robert says you haven't even got your passport. He's in Vienna now, waiting for a flight back to Prague.'

'I don't want to see him,' Rachel sobs.

'I don't care what you want. I want you back here. There's been an accident.'

'Oh my God, what? Who is it – Dad?'

'No, it's not Dad, it's Oscar. Your *brother*.'

Chapter 20

This was a stupid idea. He sees that now. Green Street, which would provide a fast and reliable cut-through most Sunday mornings, is today jammed, the two cars ahead of Stuart stuck behind a team from the council cleaning up the debris and litter from yesterday's march: four dustmen – one of them a girl, in fact – with yellow tunics and gloves and boots, working behind the barely moving truck, one of them using a broom, one a shovel and the others pushing garbage into bags. For God's sake, MOVE. He mouths these words. In the back of the car he has a change of clothes for Diane – jeans, fresh underclothes, her blue sweater – and an ill-constructed cheese-and-tomato sandwich wrapped in foil. 'I *knew* we shouldn't have tried this,' he says, hammering the steering wheel with the heel of his hand. 'The peripheral would have been completely clear on a Sunday. We should have gone straight on at the lights. For the love of *Christ* . . .' He gives the horn a blast.

He is sweating. These days he can sweat at the drop of a hat.

'Calm down, Dad,' Luke says, leaning back, shading his eyes. 'We won't get there any quicker.'

One of the refuse team gives Stuart a long stare, and with a studied lack of urgency tosses a black bag into the open-sided truck.

'That's what they do when you try to hurry them. They go even slower.'

'Ring your mother and tell her we're held up.'

'You can't use a mobile in the hospital. She won't have it switched on.'

'Just try. Or leave a message.'

'We'll be there by then – what's the point?' Luke says, but he starts keying in the number with his thumb, as the young do.

In the complexity of recent things, yesterday's march had slipped Stuart's mind entirely, though there were enough notices up all over town, and police signs warning of road closures, diversions and severe delays. He had been immersed in preparations for the day ahead, having Josh give the main displays a tour with the vacuum, making sure the pathways were clear. He'd gone out early into the fresh morning air with a bucket of hot water and soapsuds and washed the front windows himself. Friday had gone by smoothly, with two jobs completed and another three to quote for. But for any retailer Saturday was your chief trading day. You couldn't let the complexity of things interfere with that. As a salesman you learnt to avoid communicating anxiety to a customer. You didn't raise your voice on the sales floor, you avoided sudden movements and you left your domestic concerns at home. Customers flourished in an environment free from the grubbier sort of human contamination. Customers could sense jangling nerves just standing there on the threshold, like birds on a fence, looking this way and that, deciding whether it was safe to come into the garden. The trick was not to frighten them away.

'While you're here, you *are* the face of Duttings,' Stuart told Josh, as he had told others before him. 'You have to be clean-cut and ready to roll, like a good Axminster or Wilton. You're looking to provide an oasis of calm. No distractions.' He looked at the boy to make sure he was listening. 'You know how hard it is to concentrate with something blaring in the background?' Josh nodded. 'Exactly. That's what customers are trying to do here. They want to make things add up for themselves, in their own heads. At the end of the day, they *want* to say yes. We provide the conditions, they get to say yes. That's the positive mode.'

'But what about sales technique? Rachel says—'

He shook his head. 'Judgement. Body language. Nothing else. Some customers will fly the minute you take a step towards them. Others will eat out of your hand. That's experience.'

Did Rachel offer this sort of leadership? Stuart doubted it somehow. He shuddered to imagine what kind of distractions were daily offering themselves to Rachel with this Newnam in tow, what kind of a mess she was getting into. He hoped she and Robert would be able to sort *that* side of it out on this anniversary trip of theirs – if there was something to sort out, and it was hard not to think the worst, even though thinking the worst was the worst kind of distraction for Stuart now that he was here running the show. And it wasn't even just Rachel. There was Oscar too.

He had expected Diane to say something to Oscar about Emma, but she'd just sat back and watched Stuart's own stammering attempts to interrogate him when he'd arrived home for supper on Wednesday unaccountably wearing a suit and one of Stuart's ties, as though everything was just fine and dandy.

'Luke told you what?' Oscar said.

'You're not denying it.'

'Actually, no, I'm not denying it. Why should I?'

'Why? What are you thinking of? You're practically *related*.'

'Dad, we're not even distantly related. Not by blood. It's not even as if we're step-siblings. In the whole time we've known each other, we've never spent so much as a night under the same roof. Well, not until recently.'

Stuart winced. 'Please. I do *not* wish to know.'

'Well, don't ask then. Look, I'm sorry, but it just happened, and I realise it might make you feel a bit weird, but—'

'Weird? What do you expect, carrying on like, like . . .'

'Like what? What are we? For *fuck's* sake . . .'

'Diane, you say something.'

Oscar turned to her. 'Yes, Mum, *you* say something.'

There was a challenge in his eyes that Diane visibly shrank from. 'Don't bring me into it,' was all she said.

Later, Diane told Stuart he was overreacting, that it would probably blow over anyway, that doubtless Oscar and Emma were enjoying the novelty of this, enjoying the effect their little fling was having on their parents.

'Rebellion? Aren't they a bit old for that? Well, OK, we might have expected it from Oscar . . .'

'Ah, I *see*. So this is about Oscar.'

'Of course it's not,' he said, but held his tongue. He saw the way this was starting to go – saw Diane glimpsing in his sense of indignation the profanity of *her* idle son fucking *his* brilliant daughter. Was that his problem? Was that the disappointment he was trying to hide even from himself?

But then, next morning, he had been wrongfooted again – in effect been goaded into defending the indefensible – when Penny rang up in a panic to tell him that Emma had casually mentioned in *passing*, if you please, that she was 'seeing' Oscar, and that understandably Tony was livid even at the thought of it. 'He was all ready to call you himself, but I stopped him,' Penny said. 'He was just too upset.'

'Hang on,' Stuart said. 'First thing – she's my daughter, remember, not his. Second – come on, it's not as if Emma and Oscar are related, is it, so why the drama? Maybe Tony would like Oscar better if he happened to be a merchant banker, but hasn't it occurred to him that Emma might want a change from this fat-cat, quick-buck lifestyle most of her boyfriends have?'

'You always said Vaughan was a real catch. You were happy when they seemed to be getting serious.'

'Vaughan was fine. I don't know. Maybe they weren't suited. All I'm saying is maybe we ought to give the poor girl some credit for seeing through to Oscar's inner qualities.'

Tony was not one for open confrontation, but he did call Stuart himself later in the day, ostensibly to enlist his help for the Willows charity summer barbecue but also, eventually, to wonder aloud what Oscar's inner qualities might be. 'I can't believe you're happy about this, Stuart. You probably don't know this but Emma's talking about leaving her job too. Who's put that idea in her head?'

Tony was right, though on a scale of personal disasters, it came a poor third to Stuart's prostate and the problems at Duttings. 'What do you expect me to do? It'll probably blow over anyway, Diane says. Give it a couple of weeks.'

By Friday, striding out to the car in a business suit he had all but given up hope of wearing again – certainly by

257

Saturday, out early washing the showroom windows in his shirt sleeves – Stuart had pushed these torments to the outer limits of his mind. And with his radar locked in positive mode, the scheduled march from Five Ponds, too, barely registered. Even when it had impinged on his consciousness, it brought with it only a half-formed image of locals who stood to be most inconvenienced by whatever they finally decided to build out at Five Ponds; the usual flag wavers handing out leaflets to shoppers. There had been nonsense in the *Gazette*, and on the radio, about anti-globalism, but this was hardly the place to campaign against Disney and McDonald's and EU economic policies, was it?

It was the faraway drums he heard first, then a burst of what he thought was a brass band but later turned out to be klaxons and horns – the sort of horns used by hunt saboteurs to confuse hounds. Beneath these sporadic, sharper exclamations the sound increased gradually, a long rising wave, the sound of an ordinary day that was being slowly turned up. Business had been lively on both floors of the showroom. But then Stuart raised his eyes from Rachel's enquiries log to find the place almost empty. A minute later, Josh hurried back from Wilson's with doughnuts to report that Market Street was practically deserted. 'No customers – what do we do?' he asked, breathless, almost gleeful at the eerie novelty – at least in this town – of excitement, the idea of people shifting like nervous animals catching the scent of a distant fire.

They stood at the door listening to the swelling cacophony, the beginnings of chanting, the rasping call of a loud-hailer. 'Well, we're not closing,' Stuart said. 'If that's what you were hoping.'

Paul came down from the upper floor to stand with them. 'It'll be over in a couple of hours. There was one of these in Cambridge last summer.'

'And how long did that last?'

'Well, most of the afternoon. But this isn't Cambridge, is it?'

'Sounds like a lot of people, though.'

Paul said nothing.

Stuart went quiet too. He could only think of menace. There was something about it that reminded him of *Zulu*, this gathering out there of dark and inscrutable forces.

'I'll make some tea,' Josh said.

The refuse truck moves forward a few feet, followed by the two cars in front, then stops again. They are almost at the junction.

'I can't believe this,' says Stuart. He needs to pee. This of all moments.

The truck moves forward again. 'About effing time,' Stuart mutters, putting the car in gear. And now the phone is ringing. 'Tell her we're running late,' he says to Luke.

'I'm not stupid, Dad.' Luke puts the phone to his ear. 'Hello? No, it's Luke. He can't, he's driving.'

'Tell her we've been held up,' Stuart says.

'*Shh*. What? Oh. Right. I don't know. We're on our way now. Yeah. Uh? No. I've got no idea.'

'What is she saying?'

'It's not Mum, it's Robert. He says he's had a call about the alarm going all night again at the warehouse.'

'Great. Just what we needed. Well, tell him it'll have to wait.'

'And he wants to know when Rachel gets in.'

'How should I know? First flight she can get on, that's all she said. We've heard nothing since.' He shakes his head. 'Jesus, what a bloody mess.'

'First flight,' Luke is saying. 'I dunno. Nobody knows.'

Chapter 21

He is fourteen. He sees himself as if in a mirror, though the precise image – his expression, the shadow masking half his face, the oversized black CND T-shirt, the grubby suggestion of facial hair – is lifted from a photograph taken by his mother on the garden step of their old house at 22 Walsh Street. It's the year of Chernobyl. He moves without effort, across the upstairs landing, and stops at Rachel's room. The door is ajar. Rachel is sitting on the carpet with her back to him, surrounded by paper and bits of string. She turns and sees him, Mum's big sewing scissors in one hand. Her face is sullen and tear-stained. He remembers. She has been sent to her room for arguing with Mum. It's not like Rachel to argue with Mum.

'What?' she says. But when she says it, she's not eleven but the grown-up Rachel of today.

'Nothing,' he says. He sits on the top stair. Something is wrong. He sees it in her face as she gets up from the floor and moves quickly towards him, holding her stomach. As she sweeps past him, before she gets to the bathroom at the end of the landing, he sees the dark blood. It's a trickle running slowly down her leg. It shocks him to see it.

Now he himself is sitting on the carpet in her room. He knows he's not supposed to be in here but he can hear his sister's voice downstairs now, and Mum's. They're not arguing, though Rachel's voice, full of tears, carries up the stairwell. Everything is out of the box in front of him. He looks at the diagram and watches himself arrange the polystyrene spheres in order of size on a sheet of news-paper. He has the paintbrush in his hand, feels the satisfaction of the loaded bristles pliant against the skin of each sphere as he works his way along, turning. Each planet has its colour. Earth is blue. Mars is red. Jupiter is yellow. Saturn needs to be fitted with rings pressed out of a sheet of thin card. The spheres, pitted and light as hol-lowed eggshells, sit like alien pods on the radiator drying while he constructs the frame from which must eventually be hung a revolving grapefruit-sized sun, the surfaces of its plastic hemispheres already brilliant with the spiralling flames and gaseous explosions snipped from the adhesive pages of the accompanying craft book, and carefully patched into place by Rachel. He is anxious for a moment, seeing her hand at work here. But he casts it from his mind. Rising in his imagination now are these planets as he will later remember them, hanging from Rachel's ceil-ing, travelling their nine elliptical paths in soundless motion, finger-spun orbs threaded on wires like spokes on a buckled wheel that disappear into the narrow slot girdling the sun and locate a spindle and cog run by a small churning motor.

The illustration on the box shows the planets against an inky sky with comets and distant stars, words in German and English. Fully operational! ERZIHUNGS. Scientifically correct! Battery not included.

Oscar . . .

Someone is calling. Fast-approaching footsteps pound on the carpeted stair, and Rachel rushes angrily into the room, followed not by Mum but Dad. They stop short, seeing what he is doing. Rachel shouts at him and Dad cuffs the back of his head. His ear pounds, and he raises an arm against a second blow and feels himself redden with shame, caught like this. But he can see regret in Dad's eyes along with disappointment. Mum, alerted by the commotion, is on the stairs now. 'I didn't know,' he hears himself say.

Didn't know what? What he meant to say was 'I didn't think', or 'I didn't think she'd mind'.

Oscar . . .

Now the CND sign is incorporated into the circled 'A' of the anarchy logo, worn on T-shirts and canvas bags and on the pockets of combat wear. It floats in front of his eyes as he watches himself standing again at the end of the arcade as the procession shuffles by, shepherded by good-natured policemen along the tapering confines of the old market area, its deafening horns and drums, its banners pronouncing against corporatism, global wrongs, child poverty, the ravaging of land, US imperialism, its chants one after the other demanding satisfaction for an impossible coalition of desires. Oscar hears again the familiar language of denunciation echoing fiercely in the loudspeakers as the rally gathers density at the steps of the Town Hall. Later, he remembers the smell of smoke and cooking drifting into the kiosk, aromas of ethnic cuisines, frying onions, barbecued *merguez*, baked potatoes, the work of enterprising stallholders flocking into town to feed the crowd, making business from anti-business, making new customers of those who have driven out the old. The pubs have thrown open their doors. The early afternoon air grows warm. Chanting persists. There are scuffles, voices raised above the general din. Breaking glass echoes a warning. A siren sounds. The crowd is dividing up, its clans floating past the neck of the arcade like a shipwreck. A trio of eco-warriors, loud with drink, come to urinate in the doorway of Joan the florist, who has locked up for the day. In Oscar's mind's eye, Diggsy is answering the phone. 'It's for you. Sounds like your dad's having trouble.' His ear still pounds, in time now with nearby drums.

Is he remembering this?

Somehow he is with them, hot with the thrill of action, missiles gathered from the roadside debris. He is masked like the others, amid the noise and horns and burning rubbish bins. In the distance, police charge the crowd. A flag goes up in flames. Black smoke is pouring from a kerbside skip. It's not the high street here in town he sees, but a city centre, London or Manchester. He is staring into the heart of a sports shop, its logos dangling from the gutted interior, the blazing rags of Nike and Adidas. 'FOR JAKARTA', someone has sprayed on the outer wall. Boots crunch on the carpet of glass. Bonner's mad eyes above the mask. They have lost Ralphie and Diggsy. Bonner pulls him along by the sleeve.

Oscar . . .

No, he says. He feels the stones still in his hands. Another street – an alley of smaller shops selling old books, maps, posters – and the sound of himself running, his own breath, blood pumping, pounding in his ears. Bonner halts. Wait, he says, panting. He vanishes into the shop, window full of prints. Oscar waits. The sound of drumming and horns and crowds and sirens is nearby, over the buildings. He hears it as though he is standing outside a seething stadium, cowering in the shadow of its mass and noise. Bonner comes out. Come on, he says. A man, glasses perched on his head, appears in the doorway but does not follow or even shout. Thrilling with fear, Oscar throws his stones at random as they run, doesn't stop to watch the glass break. No rules. Anarchy. That's what it means.

He hears the dog bark. He is walking back from the village with tea, sugar, two uncut loaves. In the earlier days, they had tried making their own bread, but the discipline was too demanding. It had to be made early in the morning, and it was enough for most of them to be out of their bedrolls for the milking roster. He himself enjoyed that dawn air, crossing the damp field, the warmth of the animal bodies in the cow shed, the heavy stamping movement in there, the sour-smelling juice of the straw, the swish of tails and deep lowing in the crisp silence. They made cheese, butter too.

Edie was born in the village and owned the place outright. After her mother died, she had sold off most of the fields to other farmers and kept what she could manage. She had local help, hired the services of a cowman. The people in the village shook their heads when she packed a bag and took off in early summer. She made a point of hitchhiking – though she had money – down the coast, where she would meet up with Oscar and, later, the others. Then at summer's end they would all sooner or later turn up at the farm. They smoked dope, dug the vegetable patch, rode the horse, threw sticks for Helen, the farm dog. Oscar slept with Edie. So did Bonner – and maybe others too – once Oscar had left Taunton and driven back east for Christmas with his folks. Oscar was her favourite. *Why do you always go back to your parents?* he remembers her asking.

He wonders what her own parents, both dead, would have thought, seeing most of the farm sold off and the house crowded with these friends of Edie's – some she barely knew – helping themselves to the cider in the family cellar, some waking up in Edie's bed. He wonders what, if any, allegiance Edie feels to her parents' wishes, what hard-laboured fortune is dwindling with her profligacy, what guilt fermented there.

'She's just playing at it,' Bonner said once, meaning the cheese-making – meaning cheese-making as a going concern, which seemed a harsh criticism from someone who so disapproved of profit in all its forms. But the cheese was pretty good. Edie supervised the process, and they took turns at the double boiler, stirring the curds for forty-five minutes at a constant temperature, or helped with draining the whey or used the press. An outbuilding housed the equipment and the line of refrigerators in which the wheels of cheddar sat hardening in their wax coats. It produced a nice crumbly cheese – it was the acid that did that, Edie said. It concerned the pH levels, which Oscar seemed to know about from chemistry lessons at school. She sold the cheese at the weekly farmers' market in Taunton, along with churned butter packed in greaseproof wrappings. They ate cheese for lunch every day, with bread from the village shop.

Oscar . . .

He hears a dog bark and looks up towards the barn as he walks. Two of the younger girls come down the track to meet him, baggy-jumpered, their hair knotted into ribbons. 'Helen's just had her pups,' one says.

Troy is there at his side as he hurries from the arcade, zigzagging through the people. Outside the showroom, a swaying, chanting crowd has massed. Dad, beneath the vertical sign bearing his name, stands in his suit shouting

265

back at them, his words lost in the uproar. Oscar feels the hard fury of this crowd – dreadlocked, mohicanned, some ethnically frocked and bearded, others in Countryside Alliance quilted gilets and Barbours, despite the heat – as he tries to elbow his way through the swarm of bodies and printed yellow placards that read, 'Say No to Five Ponds!' and 'Free the Land', and handmade ones that say 'Corporatist Parasites' and 'Insult to God'. A stone is thrown. It's just a forecourt pebble that hits the front window with a crack and bounces off, but it is enough to spur his father, who now lurches forward, red-faced, into the heaving mêlée, one arm outstretched towards the thrower. Oscar hears himself shout now – a bellow with no meaning other than the noise it is intended to make – and makes a path towards them, pulling people out of his way at either side like a swimmer struggling through an impossible current. Something large is heaved into the air – a black wheelie bin, its contents spilling as it crashes through the window. Nothing can be settled now without violence. He has seen it before, like a lever is pulled undamming a crowd's hostility. More stones are thrown. Dad is grappling with the man. Oscar, roaring, reaches forward and grabs the man's shoulder. He sees Ralphie's surprised face, hears Troy barking, and has time again to survey the message of a yellow Five Ponds placard before he is hit by an explosion of pain that sends the world tumbling from apprehension in a moment of beautiful but faintly worrying clarity. Boom, boom, boom is the feeling.

Oscar . . .

A light with the pinkness of mouthwash pulses against his eyelids, and he tries to lift his hand to his head. He cannot feel his ear. The sound comes muffled. Mum speaking his name. The way out of this. He follows the sound.

266

He opens his eyes and she is holding his hand. Seeing his eyes, she stands, panic in her own. What's *wrong* with her? Is she hurt? Someone behind, a nurse, coming into range. A dream it is he's been in. Once he woke on the carpet at home and didn't know where the hell he was. A flat sea of pattern. Objects under the sofa. You just had to wait. Come round. Familiarity. Shoes, a tea-cup placed there out of range, a dusty ping-pong ball.

'Shhh,' Mum says, though he has said nothing, her breathing close to his cheek. 'You've had an accident. Don't move. Everything's fine.'

'No, no, I know what it is,' he is saying, remembering the baby, needing to say this now while he still can. Not to waste time. 'It's not an accident . . .'

He blinks, looks for Emma, but she is not there. She knows. She can say. Tell Mum what Mum already knows. Some home truths.

'Shhh,' his mother says.

Chapter 22

Her body aches. During the flight she sits motionless, allowing the poison of what has happened to inhabit her, to invade and settle in her nerves and blood and fibre. At this moment, enduring the pain of it without complaint seems to be some kind of achievable aim. She cried her tears while her black coffee went slowly cold at the modestly appointed departure lounge at Prague airport, earning curious glances and the solicitude of the uniformed officers accompanying her – this silly, abandoned tourist without a passport, returned to her owners under the benevolent auspices of the Orient Express. Now, unless the plane goes down, she will face whatever hell awaits with calm. The wreck of her marriage, the wreck of her Dutting Modern dream, the wreck of her father's good name. There is a loan charged against the company for the house. This she knows and has ignored. She has seen it in the books and turned the page, scrolled it out of sight on her desktop computer.

Even this she feels only as a secondary numbness. Gareth has gone, as she knew he would, and with him everything she most came to want. Her tears were for the loss of him and nothing more. It gnaws like the worst grief, usurping with its cheap deceit all innate notions of honour and duty. Gareth it is, not Robert, whom she has betrayed in the arms of two American brothers; it is Gareth's face that now rises to push thoughts of Oscar from her mind. You learn that love is good, but it is dark and destructive. It lives in the imagination like a devil, dreaming up unforgivable, atrocious hypotheses she cannot close her ears to. What would she offer this devil in exchange for lifelong happiness on earth with Gareth? Last night – a night of both madness and purity – she would have sacrificed all her father had trusted her with. Today her devil demands Oscar's life. She has no real fight in her, but she is seized with regret at the charges she has made against Oscar over the years, the resentments she has harboured – fearful that to allow them to surface now will tip the balance in favour of her darker longings and snuff out his flame wherever he lies. She closes her eyes and remembers an angry day, long ago, when she took his baseball – a present from Dad – and threw it with all her strength into the field of weeds and nettles near to their house on Walsh Street, a forbidden place where the gypsies used sometimes to camp with their caravans and horses. The ball was white with a red stitched seam you could feel like a scar. Oscar never even missed it.

Robert is waiting for her when she emerges – the only passenger without luggage – at the arrivals gate at Stansted. He sees her at the same moment she sees him. He hasn't shaved and, like her, is still wearing yesterday's clothes. He doesn't smile, just starts to walk towards her, his mouth slightly open, his eyes full of injury and questions. She says nothing, but lowers her head and allows him to fall in step with her. She feels his resolve crumple. Whatever anger he put into his rehearsal has evaporated. The stage is his, but the speech won't come. He fears her craziness.

'You know Oscar's conscious,' he says at last.

She sniffs. 'Mum said he was under observation. Bloody morons.'

'Why did you get off the train?' he asks gently.

'I don't know,' she says, looking the other way, at the taxis beyond the doors, at passengers hauling luggage out of car boots.

'I think you owe me an explanation.'

'I know.'

'What do you want to do?'

She says nothing.

'The car's outside,' he says. 'Will you come?'

The inside zip pocket of her handbag, she remembers, is stuffed with foreign currency. ('My God, Rachel, you really *are* a winner.' Dean and the other one, Bob, their faces lit up like pumpkins in the garish light of the casino bar, come pulsing into her memory.) She frowns, disoriented by the echo of noise, the competing information. All the clocks read 15.13. 'I need a bureau de change,' she says.

Robert reaches into his jacket pocket. 'You'll need this first.' He has her passport.

'Thanks,' she murmurs.

He stands behind her as the cashier at Thomas Cook counts out fifties and twenties and slides them into a plastic wallet. She has over fifteen hundred pounds here. His eyes are on the money, then on her.

'Are you OK?' he asks.

'Actually, no.'

'I should tell you anyway. There's been a flood at the warehouse.'

She looks at him. He has been crying too. 'What do you mean, a flood?'

He sighs. 'A break-in. Marchers presumably. Someone broke in, set the taps going, smashed the mains pipe downstairs. Quite deliberate. It was running half the day yesterday and all last night. The place is under two feet of water. Stuart's been down there with Luke and that friend of Oscar's.'

Rachel ponders this for a moment. Something is happening to her, from deep inside, like a well itself, upwardly brimming. Then she starts laughing. She can't stop. The laughter has her in its grip, a hysterical, uncontrollable laughter that frightens animals and bemuses passers-by. She has never laughed like this before. Robert's face is etched with the profoundest alarm. People are turning to look. She can't stop laughing. Tears are rolling down her cheeks. She feels she will laugh till she faints. She is screaming and shaking with laughter. A stewardess is asking Robert if he needs help. But he has his arm around her in a strong grip and is guiding her towards the doors. She laughs so much she is weeping. Floods of everything now. She can't help it. Nothing can help it.

Chapter 23

Stuart summoned Luke and Diggsy to help at the ware-house once the plumber had been and shut down the mains supply. The three of them worked for an hour, carrying out what salvage operations they could until Pete Tree eventually arrived in a flatbed truck and set two pumps running off a big yellow diesel-powered generator he had hauled in from his yard. 'That ought to do the trick,' Pete said, removing his gloves. 'I'd stay and give you a hand, but it's Matt's thirteenth and Lindy's on her own with a big gang of his schoolfriends and the barbecue to look after.' He grimaced. 'The house could be on fire by the time I get back.'

'You've done enough, Pete,' Stuart said, relieved at the sound of the chugging pistons, at the faintly trembling iri-descent surface of the water. 'How long do you reckon it'll take to clear?'

Pete, wearing his builder's wellingtons, cast an eye over

the half-sunken debris in the dim light that fell from the small upper windows near the roof – the bloated rolls of carpet looking like the washed-up bodies of sea beasts, the upended sample stands and cardboard displays, the flotsam of sales brochures, a broom, a trade calendar, a number of bobbing shields from Oscar's workshop, stray playing cards from the fitters' corner. 'It's hard to say,' he said. 'It doesn't help being below road level. You're in a basin here – the water just stays put. That's why I had to run a pipe out to the main drain. A few hours, though – that should do it. I'll give you a bell. Have the police been round?'

Stuart nodded. He picked up one of the playing cards lying face down in the water. 'It's hard to point the finger, though. All these different extremist groups get together, see? You've got the environment lobby – and Christ knows Rachel did her best to rub them up the wrong way, coming out in public for the developers as she did, by all accounts. Then there's those Eastern rugs we talked about, Pete – your tip-off came back to haunt us. It's like those sportswear firms that get hit for employing kids all over again.'

Pete looked troubled at the thought of being sucked into the ring of blame. 'How could that happen? How could they know?'

Stuart stared blankly at the water and then at the card in his hand, the king of diamonds. 'Word spreads. The internet and so on. Whatever, the human rights mob were out in numbers. Muslims, too, up in arms, getting in a right old frenzy about those little prayer mats Rachel had in the window. Luke reckons they must have been pointing in the wrong direction, or had some sort of offensive message on them. Anyway, you wouldn't believe the abuse. And there's a bloody awful mess down there. Broken glass scattered everywhere, windows boarded up. Poor Oscar in hospital.'

'How is he?'

'Bit of concussion. It could have been worse if the police hadn't turned up when they did. Trouble was, the mob just headed up here instead – or at least some of them did. It's not a coincidence, is it? The Shell station got it too. They reckon it would have been torched but it was a little Bosnian woman manning the place. Shouted them down. I suppose she's seen worse.'

'Damage?'

Stuart shook his head. 'We can say goodbye to most of the stock. And you can see the amounts Rachel is laying in these days. Ten or twelve times the normal, I'd say. God knows what she's up to. What's the point of getting the bulk discounts if you're having to sit on stock for months? I should have done something about it. I should have put my foot down.'

'What about the polythene wrapping? Doesn't that offer any protection?'

'You can see for yourself. It's designed to keep the dust out, not two feet of water. And it's not as if we can hold a flood sale. You can't dry rolled carpet, and bacteria and fungi sets in after twelve hours. I've seen it before. The latex backing gets buggered by water and the manufacturers' warranties are voided anyway – no chance. This is an insurance job.'

Even as he said this, his skin turned cold with doubt.

Now he sits in the office up the wooden stairs, his hand on the torch on the desk, its beam randomly directed at a bundle of receipts on a spike. He is hit by a wave of tiredness. By degrees, this has become Barbara's office now. Here, idling for these moments in her swivel chair, he thinks about the foolish night he kissed her in the back of a taxi, an uncharacteristic act kindled by circumstance and fired by drink. Nothing like that had happened to him before – not in his then twelve-year marriage to Diane. But the impulse that surfaced that night hadn't come from nowhere, merely elsewhere. There had been another woman, earlier that year, in the autumn. The woman he hadn't kissed – a stranger. It was the time of the flooring show in Stuttgart, and the woman had been in the seat next to him on the plane on both outward and return flights. They had not spoken on the way out, but coming back they had laughed at the coincidence. She had been in Stuttgart for the toy fair. She was the English agent for a German manufacturer. Stuart told her how he had planned to buy souvenirs for his two children but had run out of time.

'Ages?'

'Fourteen and eleven. Boy and a girl.'

'I have just the thing,' she said.

She was unmarried and lived in Hastings, which was her childhood home. She had recently moved back there from London to be with her mother after the death of her father. Her name was Sheila, and when the refreshments trolley came round he bought her a G&T. She wasn't beautiful, but in the quickness of her smile and the tenderness in her eyes when she spoke – or listened while Stuart spoke – he felt a warmth between them, a gentle affinity that made his heart beat with the unexpected pleasure of it. He found it in himself to make her laugh, even with stories of minor emergencies at the firm – tricky fitting jobs that had gone wrong or youthful errors he had made as an apprentice to his father, who like Sheila's had died in recent years. They talked, then, about their fathers – Sheila's had been in the Navy, and on his discharge had bought a toy shop, special-ising in models and hobby kits. 'Train sets, Airfix, that sort of thing. I grew up with toys,' she said.

'And I grew up with carpets.'

'Did you never feel like breaking out and doing something else?'

'It's what I knew,' he said. 'Breaking out was never an option. People talk about the enterprise culture now, but back then you did what you were expected to do. And the trade has been good to me,' he added.

She smiled and said she understood.

At Heathrow, when their luggage was delayed, she produced a box of crystallised fruits, which they shared while they sat and waited. 'I don't normally do this sort of thing,' she said, licking the sugar from her fingertips. He wondered what she meant, but it seemed thrillingly intimate. The luggage took an hour to arrive. Before they parted, she gave him something for the children, as promised – a model of the solar system or some such thing, a sample she was carrying. 'That's great,' he said. But it seemed now that it was just *this* they had been waiting for all along – the reason they had waited together. It broke a spell, returned Stuart to earth. He felt a hollow panic as they made their way to the exits, Sheila's effortless conversation – as though nothing special had happened – somehow making their imminent goodbye worse. Absurdly he found himself wondering if she would turn to him in their final seconds together, her face upturned, passion in her eyes. She offered her hand instead. It was warm and he held it as long as he dared. 'Well, it was nice to meet you,' she said.

He stood watching as she walked away, towing her large suitcase, skirted a train of luggage trolleys and vanished down the escalator to another world.

He hardly remembers the dash to get to the London stores before they closed – the walk from Piccadilly Circus up to Hamleys, the big toy shop in Regent Street. The solar system kit was too toyish for Oscar, who had withdrawn into sullen teenhood. That would do for Rachel. His

276

eyes cast around and settled on a display of American base-balls that came packed with one of those big padded gloves in tan leather. Perfect. It filled something too, this action, brought him back into the orbit of his family and respon-sibility. At Liverpool Street station he bought flowers for Diane, and cast this Sheila from his thoughts, this woman he had known for less time than it takes to lay a square room.

But what was it about her? What was the precise feeling?

He wonders, when he thinks about it now, whether it wasn't simply a sort of gratitude, unused as he was to the friendly scrutiny of passing women. Though Diane has never given him cause for grievance in the thirty years he has loved and supported her, neither has she ever sought to convince him that his being at her side has been crucial to her spiritual happiness.

Hooking up with Diane was the result too of a meeting during a trade show – his debut, at Olympia in London's Earls Court. She was waitressing in a small pub near the venue where he ate his solitary lunches, a retreat from his self-conscious tour of exhibition stands, thirty years old and barely out of his father's shadow, his inheritance still dangling in front of him on a stick, his own short-lived marriage in tatters, Penny stolen away from him. There had been girlfriends before Penny but none serious or suited to a man with expectations – or the expectations of his mother, who disapproved of all the girls he brought home and didn't live to see him marry.

He was surprised when Diane agreed to meet him the next afternoon in Hyde Park. To him she was an exotic, urban creature, an art-school dropout who wore long dresses and hardly any make-up. She lived in a rented house with a dozen other people with their long-haired scruffy children and cats. That evening she took Stuart up to her room, where they had sex, watched by Jimi Hendrix and other, less familiar, rock stars who leered from posters sellotaped to the walls. Her very easiness made him uneasy. She was beautiful, exhilarating, socially confident, sexually liberated. She was twenty-two. Smoking a joint, she told him her parents – whom she had long disowned – were divorced, and lived in Surrey's stockbroker belt. Even amid this casual squalor, as he saw it, she was a class above him in every department. What she saw in him he couldn't begin to guess. Perhaps he didn't care to guess. He was smitten. He arranged to come back to London to see her that Sunday, and found himself counting the days. Again they met in the park. But this time she arrived pushing a buggy with a child in it. 'This is Oscar,' she said.

Whatever personal sacrifice she had made to commit herself to Stuart's life of convention and decorous values, it was without protest. If he'd had worries that Diane might scandalise the neighbours in some way in those early days, she surprised him with her willingness to adapt to steadiness, to keep house and cook, to remake her careless beauty for a less flamboyant locality, to use her artistic leanings for the arrangement of flowers and furniture, and in the fullness of time to bear him children of his own. Equally surprising was that she did this without losing any part of what Stuart came to think of as her 'inner refuge', a tranquil, more soulful place that she reserved for her private thoughts and her quiet murmurings with Oscar, who he saw was slowly filling with Diane's essence, keeping it alive, carrying it forward. The easiness that had made Stuart uneasy, Diane and Oscar now had between them. It was what they seemed to be made of. It kept him at bay. Stuart harboured a foolish, shameful envy of Oscar's nearness to Diane, the way they so naturally breathed the same air. And yet his own relations with Diane had settled into a fair

278

enough routine that would have been familiar to any other married couple in town, better than some. Their sex life, while never recapturing the energy of their first urgent grapplings, was not merely perfunctory either. She devoted herself to this comfort as she did his other needs – his washing, his ironing, the social demands of town and immediate neighbourhood – and to her role as second wife in respect of Emma, Penny and Tony. They had a decent life. A holiday every year, Norfolk at first, then Spain when the children were older. Diane asked for nothing more, rarely referred to her unhappy girlhood at boarding school or her later period of rebellion, or Michael, the first husband who didn't work out. She never wondered aloud what might have happened had she stayed and taken her chances in London. She just got on with it. She made a life with all that Stuart had to give. Hearth, home, garden, family, car, golf, carpets.

He too was inclined to count his blessings. He still does. But his brief encounter with Sheila startled him with its glimpse of intimacy. It freed his mind to dangerous possibilities. It made what happened with Barbara – who had always been an entirely more available proposition – possible.

He wonders whether Diane ever guessed about Barbara, or minded enough to guess. Though Diane has had her moments of grouchiness – never more so than during the commotion of recent months – things have only ever flared up about Oscar. They have never rowed about their performances as man and wife. In this way, in her serenity, Diane protects the truth of how she feels and safeguards what they have. Stuart knows he could never have possessed her, but he has the next best thing. Only when life falters does he frown upon the accommodations they have both made – what ideal they have each learned to live

279

without. But it's more than enough. Passion is chaos. He is thinking now, with a certain inertia, about Rachel, the one who most reminds him of himself. He is too fatigued to condemn. It is as though, following a single wild impulse to cut the knot holding everything together, her whole life has been swept away in a torrent of feeling. And it's not over yet.

Still holding the torch, he peers down into the gloom from the so-called mezzanine office that juts over the mayhem below like the crow's nest of a sinking ship. Luke and Diggsy have gone to the pub to wait for the flood-water to subside. There has been no word from Rachel. He has tried her mobile and her house without success. Open on the desk in front of him is the insurance file from the cabinet. There's not much to look through – a single manilla file containing the latest policy for building and insurance. Barbara keeps the records up to date. If there had been a new policy, updated in recent months to take account of these untold thousands spent on unnecessary stock, it would be right here. He can't do the sums without knowing how much the company is in hock to Rael's financing arm. But one glance out there into this darkness tells him it will add up to trouble. That much he is certain of. He gets to his feet and stands at the top of the stairs, listening to the throb of the pumps, breathing the sick smell of saturated fibres, black water and diesel fumes, and starts to cry.

Chapter 24

No one thought to call Emma till Sunday afternoon. She drove up from London and sat holding Oscar's hand all evening, gazing at him with such pity in her eyes he had to tell her to stop. 'It's just concussion. I'll be fine,' he said. 'At first I thought it was, you know, something worse.'

She nodded. 'Your mum said you were burbling on about fainting. She said you're entitled to faint when someone hits you with a baseball bat.'

'I know. But I'm going to have to talk to her. About the tests. And everything else. Are you OK?'

'We're both fine, if that's what you mean,' she said, leaning over to kiss his head.

He rested his hand on her stomach. 'Anybody home?'

She smiled. 'Early days yet. Has Rachel been to see you?'

'Not yet. She's not feeling up to it, apparently. She's up at the house.'

'Your house?'

He nodded. 'Don't ask. Problems.'

'With Robert?'

'I guess. He managed to leave her in Prague.'

'That's romantic.'

'It doesn't sound good actually. And that's before they have to start sweeping up at the showroom.'

The evening came and went without a visit from Rachel. He slept and dreamed about crowds. Emma was there. He lost her in the crowds. The dream went on all night.

It's mid-morning on Monday, and sunny outside. Oscar and his mother are sitting in the TV room drinking tea while they wait for the consultant to come and sign him off. 'They probably just want the bed,' he says.

'You're fine,' she says. 'That's what they said.'

'Yes, that's what they said.' He gives her a frown. 'I think we need to talk.'

'Talk? What about?' She takes a sip of tea.

There's no one else in the room at this time. The TV is off. Nurses and cleaning staff flit by outside like fish in an aquarium.

'Mum, we used to be pretty close, didn't we?' Oscar says.

'We *are* close.' She puts her cup down and squeezes his hand, and gives him the same smile Emma gave him yesterday – the one carers and relatives reserve for the sick and injured.

'But you've been so weird lately. Since we got the news about Michael.'

Her smile doesn't falter. She shakes her head. 'Water under the bridge. I was just upset. Old memories that I suppose I didn't want dragging back up.'

He gathers his thoughts and takes a breath. 'OK. This is what I want to tell you. I've been to the clinic. The walk-in near the football ground.'

'Why not Dr Bingley?' she says, anxiety in her eyes.

He shakes his head. 'I think I might have a heart problem.'

'Oh God.' Her hand goes to her mouth, then she takes his hand again. 'What did they say?'

'Well, they said I was fine, but—'

'They said you were fine? So you *are* fine—'

'I said *I* think I might have a heart problem.'

She waits for him to say more, so he starts by telling her about going to see Michael's mother in London; how she showed him the family tree of early deaths, told him about the younger brother, Sean, dying at his drum kit. Mum closes her eyes and catches her breath.

He waits. 'She said you found his body. And there was Michael's father too – did you know he died of a heart attack when he was still young?'

She nods. 'I knew that. Michael used to talk about it.'

'Right. I did some research on the family. I got a letter from one of his distant relatives – a Mrs Thorpe. It turns out *her* younger brother also died of this condition. It's genetic, she said, inherited. It was her that told me there's a chance of me having it. Fifty-fifty, according to all the websites.'

'But the clinic said you were fine, you said. You had tests?'

'Yes, I had tests.'

'And?'

'Well, this thing, apparently it's easy to miss unless you're specifically looking for it, and this was before I had the letter from Mrs Thorpe. The thing is, Michael had the tests too.' He pauses. 'I'm going to have to ask you something.'

283

'Ask me what?'

'I have to ask whether all this is really such a big surprise. Or whether it's what you always thought might happen one day.'

Her mouth falls open. 'What do you mean?'

'OK. First, Michael's mother told me how the two of you never married. Which, you know, who cares? But she said she thought you were probably running away from it all – all the upset after Sean died. She said you were probably really scared of what might happen to Michael, and couldn't cope. And me, of course. You were pregnant with me, she said. Is that what all this was about – the way you've been lately? Scared that I'd find out about this . . . I don't know, this condition?'

'Scared? It wasn't that. It was never that. I wouldn't have just run out on him. That's not true.' Tears are in her eyes now. She digs for a tissue in her bag.

'So why not stay with him?' he asks.

She shakes her head, blows her nose. 'We did live together, for a short while. We had been close. But we split up before your dad – Stuart – came along. You were only little and . . . well, Stuart just assumed I'd been married and was divorced. I suppose it seemed easier to let him think that.'

'This friend of his, this Ken, who I met. He said Michael had wanted to carry on seeing me after you'd gone, but you were against it.'

'Ken doesn't know anything. It's not true. I'd moved out of London. And once I was out here with your dad, it just seemed . . .'

'Easier?'

'It was all different back then. Divorced fathers didn't always want to keep in touch. It wouldn't have been so strange. And then there was Stuart. Your new dad, remember? I couldn't expect him to think it was a good idea.'

'Dad? But he was in the same boat. He saw Emma all the time.'

She seems confused. 'Of course, yes, he was. I don't know. Maybe that wasn't it. Perhaps I just thought it best if we had a clean break.'

'But why? I don't get it.'

She gazes away, out of the window, at the trees at the far side of the car park. She looks like someone trying to solve a puzzle.

But they are getting deflected by this. Mum is focusing on the wrong issue. 'Look,' he says, 'can we get back to this thing I have, or *might* have . . .'

Her eyes, a mixture of impatience and sympathy, turn from him to the door as a nurse arrives to tell them the doctor needs to see Oscar. 'Come on, love,' she says, relieved it seems by the interruption.

The doctor is smiling, holding Oscar's notes. He tells him to take it easy, that he'll be as good as new in a few days. 'No more riots,' he says. 'Your father said you were very brave, fighting for the family honour. Very old-fashioned.' The doctor is Asian, gently mocking this idea of an Englishman defending his father's castle.

In the car park Oscar is surprised to see the camper. Troy, watchful at the passenger side, throws himself against the window with a muffled bark as they approach.

'I thought I'd better bring him to see you,' Mum says, smiling. 'I'll drive.'

But instead of driving home, she takes him to the river, where they leave the van and follow Troy's meandering progress along the grassy bank. She talks about the mess at the warehouse. 'We're vastly underinsured,' she says. 'Stuart thinks we need to retrench. There are payments to keep up all over the place and no money coming in. Not for the foreseeable future. At least you're OK,' she continues. 'You gave us a scare.' Oscar says nothing. He cannot remember the last time he and Mum were together like this, just the two of them walking along. It's like a childhood scene. And in a strange way he feels he is being cared for. But it is as though she is soothing some childhood upset by talking about something else. His mind is choked up with one problem while hers is occupied with others. He hears her move on now to the question of Rachel, Rachel's difficulty with Robert, some elaborately woven story Oscar can't follow about a housing development, some business that has fallen through, something involving the town council, some highly coloured tale of one thing leading to another. He cannot bring himself to care about this. The sound of her talking builds up in his ears so much he just wants it to end. He stops and lifts his hand to his injured ear.

She looks at him. 'Are you all right?'

He sighs. 'Emma's pregnant,' he says.

Mum blinks at him and grips his arm. 'Oh my God. Are you sure?'

'Yes, of course I'm sure. Which is why I need to know about my heart, and have the proper tests. Because if I have this condition, there's a half-and-half chance the baby will have it too. OK? That's why I'm bringing all this up. I'm sorry if it's hard for you, but that's why.'

'My God . . .' Mum says. 'Does she plan to have it – the baby?'

'Yes. We want it. It's what we both want. That's why I need to know if I'm likely to drop down dead tomorrow. Do you see?'

She pauses. Her mouth tightens and she shakes her head. 'You won't drop dead tomorrow.'

'Well, thanks for the vote of confidence, but I need to hear it from someone who knows. I don't understand. Why are you being so weird again? Don't you care?'

'Oscar, Oscar . . .' She puts her hand up. 'You've just told me I'm going to be a grandmother. Let's take one step at a time. You're sure you're happy about it – you and Emma?'

'Yes, we are. I know how you and Dad feel about us and I know it's not great timing, but when is it ever? Don't you have to seize the day or whatever, take a shot when it seems the right thing to do? Isn't that what you did when you were a single mother and Dad came along? Wasn't he the right thing?'

She is silent. They stop at the bridge and sit on the wall as Troy trots down the path ahead of them, sniffing at the grass, turns and then comes back. She ruffles the dog's ears, then sends it off again, nosing along the wall. She looks at Oscar, about to speak, forming the words in her mind. 'Michael wasn't your father,' she says.

Oscar is too surprised to respond, numbed by what seems impossible news, but at the same time the best possible news. He takes a breath but Mum presses her hand into his and squeezes hard. 'And that's why I had to leave him,' she is saying softly. 'It wasn't to do with Sean dying. But it was because of Sean that I couldn't tell Michael that you weren't his. It would have been too cruel. It was bad and it was stupid, I know, but I just couldn't hurt him. But I couldn't stay with him either. I withdrew. I became distant, and in the end I told him I didn't love him enough. I was living with a group of friends, who helped me out. I thought he'd forget about me eventually – about you too.' She puts her face in her hands for what seems like a long time, then stares across the river. Oscar puts his arm around her.

'I just need you to understand why I didn't want him to keep in touch,' she says. 'It would have been wrong of me – it would have been worse, I think, to involve you in that deceit. To involve you in an emotional attachment that might one day . . . well, come to this.'

'I do understand, but . . .'

'I never thought I'd be telling you this. I'm sorry. You think you can get away with something, ride it out. But you can't. It comes back. These things are never over.'

Troy is back, licking and nuzzling her hands, needing to be fussed over.

Oscar looks at her. 'So who was it? If not Michael.'

She hesitates for a long moment, but shakes her head. 'It was just one of those stupid things. Someone at a party, someone who was there one day and gone the next. What can I say? I was nineteen. It was the sixties. It happened.'

She squeezes his hand again, and starts talking more quickly now, remembering lying awake with Michael at her side, sick with sleeplessness and the awful fear that he would eventually know – her panic when baby Oscar's liquid black eyes settled slowly into brown, giving a beautiful lie to at least one half of his supposed parentage. 'We both had blue eyes, Michael's quite strikingly so. That's when I knew for certain – or at least when I knew I had to get away. It was one of those carefree things that turns out to be a mistake,' she is saying.

Oscar closes his eyes, shaking his head. But despite the secrets that have come to surface here, despite his mother's tearful presence, he feels his face broaden into an unsuppressible smile, the joy of this lucky reprieve working within him, unalterable even amid these revelations, seeming to make seeing the bright side not only possible, but necessary.

He doesn't press her further. A stranger from Mum's hippy era.

It is only later, unable to sleep, that his mind turns to Ken. Not a stranger but a friend – Michael's friend, his wife pregnant. Oscar stares into the dark. Here would be a story. Here, a bigger reason for Mum to run. Here, in Miriam, a bigger reason to be fearful.

Chapter 25

The house at Burrosden needs work – plenty of work by the look of it, Stuart observes, his eye drawn to the mossy roof and flaking paintwork and redbrick gable where the pointing is cracked – but, as Emma said, that's the fun of it, fixing and mending. It has the original sash windows, a duckpond with ducks, and a seventeenth-century Norfolk vertical bread oven in the sitting room. All the villagers, or hamleteers – there are barely a handful of dwellings in Burrosden, cottages in the main – have been invited this late September afternoon and some are already here, standing with glasses of white wine in the big open kitchen when he and Diane arrive. 'Something smells nice,' he says.

'That would be Oscar's cheese huffkins,' Emma says without further explanation, coming to kiss them both, allowing Diane to fuss over how much bigger she is now. Pregnant women used to cover themselves up. Now you see them going practically naked, displaying their bumps out front like the latest craze. Emma introduces him and Diane to everyone, including a quartet of her friends who have driven up from London – presumably in the gleaming black BMW parked out there in the muddy courtyard looking like something out of an advert. Emma's own sporty number has been traded in for a secondhand Golf in the name of 'downsizing', as she calls it, which he understands to mean living in an old farmhouse two miles from the nearest shop, even though she must have a huge stash of money in the bank.

'Wine?' Emma stands with a bottle in each hand.

'Well, one of us ought to.' He looks at Diane. 'Are you driving?'

She rolls her eyes like a sitcom wife. 'Well, one of us ought to,' she parrots. Everyone laughs.

'*Dad* . . .' Emma coos reprovingly, pouring red wine into a glass for him. Diane helps herself to orange juice and soda.

Dad. So familiar, yet it rings in his ears. Surrounded by polite, well-meaning strangers, he feels the urge to leave the kitchen before Oscar walks in and calls him Dad too. He can't get used to this. He takes a skewered sausage from the tray on the table and dips the end into one of the sauces. 'Tony and Penny here yet?'

'Oscar's showing them the barn.'

'Sounds interesting. I'll go and find them,' he says.

Outside he hears voices, and sees the three of them some way ahead, walking a stepping-stone path that leads across a small paddock to some sort of animal pen, an old cast-iron bathtub and – beyond the wooden fence – the pond, the green of it winking in the sun. They have the dog with them, dashing about. Tony has his hand on Oscar's shoulder as though he's showing *him* round, while Penny trails behind, picking her way down the path on those heels. Stuart watches them. In Tony's customary way of claiming a fait accompli as a personal triumph, he has more than come round to the idea of Oscar and Emma. Pete Tree reports that, far from playing things down, as Stuart would have preferred, Tony seems to relish his stepdaughter's cheerful defiance of convention, toasting his forthcoming step-grandparenthood in champagne at the Willows (notably in Stuart's absence) and holding forth on Oscar's many surprising qualities, not least his success at tracing the lost relatives of the chairman of an old established tea company (it made an article in the weekend *FT*!) – in the process earning himself a substantial five-figure finder's fee, as it were. Accordingly, the next time Stuart stopped off at the Willows he found himself having to bury his own misgivings amid the knowing cheers of congratulations that came his way for fear of seeming churlish, lacking in Tony's spirit of generosity and open-mindedness. But of course it's fine for Tony. And Diane and Penny for that matter. It is he, not they, who is facing the prospect of a baby who will simultaneously be his grandchild and step-grandchild. And worse (when Stuart can get his head round this), what about the poor kid, in the bewildering position of having two grandfathers – maternal and paternal – embodied in one person? It's freakish. It makes Stuart go hot and cold just thinking about it. He lives in dread of the christening party. To top it all, Diane says they're talking about getting married next year. What kind of a speech will he have to make as father of the bride *and* groom?

From the pond, Tony notices him and raises his hand. Oscar and Penny turn to look and wave too. Stuart lifts his glass towards them and comes back into the house. On reflection, he doesn't much feel like talking to Tony on this occasion. To make things worse, Tony insists on playing big brother about the sorry state Duttings has recently got itself into, and is almost bound to raise with Diane, in his blunt, casual way – as though discussing the price of golf balls – the possibility of just selling up at High Firs, getting some serious downsizing done themselves. It might still come to that and Tony knows it. Perhaps he wants to buy the place himself.

Everyone seems to know their business. They have drawn in their horns. They are tightening their belts. Even Oscar came discreetly to him and awkwardly offered money, a gesture that brought a lump to Stuart's throat. In the end the warehouse had to go. It tore him apart to sell it, but it was their biggest asset and it had to be done quickly. Herring was paid off, and the bank; and looking on the bright side they still have the showroom – modern, airy and central – and with running costs under one roof the business can start to wipe its own nose again. He doesn't expect a huge increase in income stream, but he is actively considering beds as an option for the upper floor, which reduces space for stock but seems to make sense in terms of retail synergy and offers a pre-emptive riposte to accusations of being set in his ways. Things are lean. Stuart is once again wearing the Dutting family suit, at least until Rachel comes back, and even then, there is an understanding – necessarily as yet unspoken, given the delicacy of Rachel's feelings and demeanour – that change came too fast, that mistakes were made, that stability will be the new aim. The Lexus was the first sacrifice – at least pro tem, as Stuart found himself explaining to Sam and Nicola, the solicitors from number eight, who had unexpectedly asked them round for supper after reading about their bad luck in the *Gazette*. No point having two company cars when one will do, Stuart said, and the Avensis was always more practical.

He has mustered the will to believe in this himself but cannot contemplate losing the house too. Having the extra rooms, he has argued, now seems less a luxury than a necessity, not least because, although Oscar is now out of the picture at last (a blessing in this ill wind), Rachel seems to have moved in permanently, the one or two days becoming a week, and the week becoming weeks on end. He harbours no hopes of an early remedy there. She spends a lot of time in her dressing gown, and has put back all the weight and more besides that she lost at the gym. No one is complaining, but Diane has to change the ashtrays every five minutes. They hear the TV on in her room at night. It's not ideal, but Diane says Rachel must be allowed to come to terms with everything in her own time. Stuart would like to see a less open-ended plan but knows better than to press the issue with Diane, who has been stoical in her refusal to blame anyone for anything, has been calm in the face of disaster, beholding beyond the roar and darkness of the storm the rainbow of Oscar's new beginnings and the silver lining of Dr Bingley's decision to subject Stuart's prostate to nothing more rigorous than 'active monitoring'. In this she demonstrates that family is about caring and togetherness, not just having a presence in the high street, status in the town, your name in the annals. And yet Stuart cannot think of Duttings without mentally adding 'the carpet people'. He cannot confine his idea of family to the four walls of intimate relations – of Sunday roasts, outings, helping with children's homework, relaxing in front of the TV. Look at Oscar's customers – peering into the concerns of their forebears in the search for grander histories than their own, that small print of lives fully lived but now forgotten just waiting there to be spotted in old newspapers and archives, like looking down a telescope and seeing the afterglow, as astronomers call it, of extinguished stars. We each have our place, strung out down the track in time like athletes in an endless relay, handing on what we have to the next runner before we stop running ourselves. It's not just the here and now but destiny too.

He loves Rachel, of course, in the way he loves all his children, but fails on every occasion to gauge her mood, cannot trust himself to offer comfort. He defaults to supporting his family in the way he knows best, feeling once more the pull of that old responsibility. The business with Herring having been settled, he has waited for Rael Eastern to make some predatory move – precisely what, he can't quite imagine – but there have been no stirrings in that quarter. The troublesome rugs Rachel bought are in the storeroom, awaiting some future sale when the affair of the anarchists and lunatics has been forgotten. Had it not been for the violence and stone-throwing the idiots might have won the day. That's the general view at the Willows – that the council swung behind the developers in the end not because of pressure on housing, or obligations to toe the government line, though that's how they had to sell it, but because enough of them got heated up about refusing to surrender, as they saw it, to intimidation from the extremist element.

And now a letter has arrived from the Mosely-Baker builders' consortium out at Windhill, inviting Duttings to put in a quote for the carpets. He is puzzled. Even with Rachel's stockpiling, there was no way they could have gone up against the contract suppliers and still made a profit worth getting out of bed for. Seeing the informal slip attached – 'best regards, Bill' – he will get Barbara to send a note back, kindly declining to bid, but asking this Bill fellow to tip her the wink on who eventually gets the job. On the fitting side there's often subcontracting work to be picked up on a major development. Horses for courses.

That's good business practice. Experience tells you that. You can't run before you can walk.

An arm slips through his own as he stands here on the step. He thinks it's Diane, but it's Emma. 'What are you up to?' she says.

'It looks a bit muddy out there,' he says. At the pond, a puff of white smoke appears above Tony's head as he lights one of his cigars. Penny has already set off back down the path, stepping carefully. She has always had nice legs.

'Come in,' Emma says. 'Come and see what Oscar's done in the nursery.'

'Nursery? Gosh,' he says, his voice full of admiration, though he finds himself unable to imagine anything other than a regular eight-by-ten kiddy's room, as they ascend the uncarpeted stair. 'A nursery, eh?' He shakes his head at the very thought.

The proximity of Tony's cigar summons Oscar's craving for nicotine. It is three weeks since he stopped. He breaks off from Tony and tethers Troy to his kennel. Across the yard, Diggsy is arriving in the '96 Mondeo estate he recently bought at the auction, Luke beside him in the passenger seat. Diggsy kills the engine but it is Rachel who gets out first and slams the rear door behind her.

'Hey,' says Oscar, hurrying across. 'You made it. That's great. How are you?'

'I thought I'd make the effort.' She looks up at the house and nods. 'Well, look at this. I have to say, I never thought I'd see the day.'

He knows what she means. 'Neither did I. Let's go inside. Let me get you a drink. Let me take your coat.'

'Don't worry, I'll find my way in.' She glances at him quickly and then back at the house. 'Really. No fuss, OK?'

He is surprised to see her, and genuinely glad. She looks

296

puffy and terrible, and yet heroic in her attempt to be upbeat and sunny, putting on make-up and decent clothes. She half smiles. Luke raises his eyebrows at Oscar then follows her.

Diggsy hands Oscar a sealed Jiffy bag he recognises from the kiosk. 'Happy housewarming.' He gives him an awkward punch on the shoulder. 'It's not much,' he says, and starts to follow the others into the house. 'In fact,' he adds, stopping and turning with a grin, 'you might end up paying for it yourself.'

Oscar holds the package. The Jiffy bag reminds him of his visit to London this week to see Mrs Edwards. It was only his third time but the supervisor at her sheltered housing unit said how excited his grandmother had been about his forthcoming visit. Sure enough, she took his hand when he came into her room, looked into his eyes with a longing that hadn't been there before. On the sideboard he saw the framed photograph he had given her of himself outside the kiosk. He'd brought that in a Jiffy bag too. The photograph was standing alongside the pictures of her husband and two sons.

He took her out into the park in her wheelchair. She talked non-stop.

'It was Michael who gave you your name. Did I tell you that? He and your mother took you to the register office together. I remember it clearly.'

'Really? I didn't know that. Mum never said.'

'Oh yes. Oscar was his grandfather's name. He was half French. What's your middle name?'

'James.'

'That's right. That was your mother's choice.'

The purpose of his visit was to tell her he wasn't her son's child after all, that it was all a terrible misunderstanding. But he couldn't. His fingers tightened on the plastic grips of the wheelchair. It wasn't a warm day and her breathing was no better, but she was wrapped up against the autumn gusts as he pushed her up one of the long paths that cross Finsbury Park. She was wearing a blue knitted cap pulled over her ears. He strained to catch her words as she talked against the crosswind. 'We could get a cup of tea at the café,' he said. 'My treat. Would you like that?'

She looked up at him with lighted eyes and chuckled. 'Oh, yes, let's.'

She was animated with the pleasure of being out. But everything she said magnified the lie. It grew with every word, every wheezy endearment as they toiled up the hill, the two of them legacies of the lie, each bequeathed to the other by Michael − a grandson for her, a grandmother for him. She had warmed now to this gift of Oscar, as if he was just what she'd always wanted. How could he now say, *This isn't what it looks like*?

And so he decided. Michael had been given neither the truth nor the benefit of the lie. Now that he was dead it seemed his mother was owed at least one of these things.

'Call me Gran,' she said, breaking off a piece of Bakewell tart.

'Gran,' he said.

Afterwards, he travelled by tube to Kentish Town, where he had an appointment with Mr Hawkins. The solicitor ushered him into his office, the curiosity there in his eyes. 'So, Mr Dutting. What can I do for you?'

'This is difficult,' Oscar said. 'I'm not sure where to start. It concerns Mrs Edwards. She's your client, right?'

'Correct,' beamed Mr Hawkins.

'I've just been to see her.'

'Excellent. And how is the dear lady?'

'Not too healthy, but ... well, she's pretty chipper, I guess.'

Mr Hawkins was attentive. 'Excellent. But?'

Oscar hesitated. 'I have a problem. Concerning her will. When she dies, I mean. Eventually, that is.'

He smiled. 'You must know I can't discuss Mrs Edwards' will. It's a matter of confidentiality.'

'Yes, I realise that. But, the thing is, it seems there's at least a chance, I imagine, under the circumstances, that she might think of leaving me something, and under those circumstances—'

'No, seriously, I really can't talk about this.'

'Please, if you could just let me . . . you know, finish?'

He nodded then. 'Sorry. Go ahead.'

'The point I want to make is, if she *is* thinking of naming me in her will, I can't accept it. That is, I don't really want it. If it's coming my way, I mean. *If.*'

Mr Hawkins thought for a moment, resting his nose on his clasped hands. 'OK. Hypothetically speaking, *if* there were a will and *if* you were named in it, why couldn't you accept it?'

'Can I talk to you in confidence?'

'Well, I'm not your lawyer. I act for Mrs Edwards. So if you now tell me something that happens to be against the interests of Mrs Edwards . . .'

'It isn't, or at least . . .' He shook his head and sighed. 'Maybe it is. I don't know.'

Mr Hawkins unexpectedly stood up and took his coat from the peg. 'Come,' he said, 'let's take this somewhere else.'

He told his receptionist he'd be back in half an hour, and Oscar followed him down the stairs and into the street. They went to the pub on the corner. Mr Hawkins brought drinks to the table. 'OK, off the record. Pretend we're friends. I'll call you Oscar, and I'm George.'

'George. All right. The simple truth is that Michael

Edwards wasn't my father. Even though he's named on my birth certificate, it wasn't him. It was someone else. My mum kept it from him, to spare his feelings – she moved away, and kept him at arm's length, as you know. But because of . . . well, things that have happened recently, she told me. But you see where this leaves me now.'

'I think I do.'

'On the one hand, I don't feel entitled to any further money that might come my way – in fact I don't even feel entitled to what I've already had. On the other hand, I can't tell Mrs Edwards.'

'Are you asking me to tell her?'

Oscar took a drink, felt the need for a cigarette. 'No. I wasn't thinking that,' he said. 'It's not a matter of having the courage to tell her. I was thinking of the effect it might have on her. It seems unfair after everything that has happened to her and her family. It seems to make a mockery of Michael, somehow. And I mean not just the mockery of someone else making his girlfriend pregnant way back when – which was basically what my mum wanted to protect him from, of course – but also the fact that Michael thought of me all those years later, and then gave me something to make me think of him too. I think it would be too hard.'

'But if you don't tell her, then what?'

'Well, my plan is to just carry on visiting her. She's a nice old lady who probably doesn't get many visitors. And, though we're not related after all, well . . . I still feel some duty towards her. And isn't that what Michael wanted – wasn't it part of the deal? Didn't you encourage me to see her because he wanted that?'

Mr Hawkins blinked and slowly sipped his drink, let Oscar continue.

'So I live the lie. It makes me feel better, and her too.'

'Let me ask you something.'

'Sure.'

'How's the business? The shields and so on.'

'Pretty good. I like it.'

Mr Hawkins nodded, adjusted his big body in the chair and stared at the ceiling for a few moments. 'What do we want when we die?'

Oscar shrugged. 'You tell me.'

'We want to be remembered. We want some part of us to live on. In our kids, yes, but in our work too. Wasn't it a big Shakespearean theme about gaining an immortality of sorts through poetry?'

'I wouldn't know.'

'My belief is it's the same with any sort of work. You want to leave your mark. Start something that succeeds you. And you – regardless of biology, you're carrying on with what Michael started, right?'

'I suppose I am.'

'So it works out. It's not ideal but it's not a mess either. As for Mrs Edwards, you can't know her intentions. Perhaps she will leave all her money to the cats' home or to the woman who brings her meals on wheels. Perhaps she will leave everything to you purely because you bothered to visit her. Or maybe she will die intestate.' He sucked air in and shook his head. 'Lawyers hate it when that happens. But back to you – if you do turn out to be a beneficiary, it would be up to you what to do with the money. You could plough it into Michael's business – or give it to charity. Didn't you say you've been doing work for some charity?'

Oscar nodded. 'I profited from that too.'

'Don't hate yourself for it. I imagine you'll do the right thing. And who knows, it might never happen.'

When they shook hands, Oscar felt older. A year ago he would have backed away from this. He would have gone back to Edie, joined the old caravan.

301

Crown House was only a ten-minute walk. He thought about it for a moment, about going there and waiting outside the place, perhaps accidentally bumping into Ken – an oblivious father, perhaps, the deaf man of this absurd orchestra – and engaging him in conversation, searching his eyes for clues to himself. But he wondered – he had wondered since Mum raised that question of Oscar's brown eyes, those damning eyes – whether Ken had already seen himself in Oscar's gaze that day in Michael's studio. Perhaps that was why he had stepped in and organised an exciting job opportunity for Miriam, far away from this budding romance with her half-brother. Or perhaps nothing. Perhaps he was innocent. Or at least ignorant. In any event, Oscar resisted the urge. You could dig for ever. Wherever you looked there was another side of the story. But you had to stop somewhere. At some point you had to think of it as the end, whether it was or not.

He stands holding the Jiffy bag Diggsy has given him – it's one they use for sending off finished shields. He has been thinking that Diggsy should maybe take over running the kiosk, at least temporarily. He has come out of his shell, losing the reticence he suffered on account of his bad skin, becoming indeed quite the personality in terms of his interface with the public. Arriving at the kiosk recently, Oscar found him with his head in a directory talking to a girl customer in that deadpan way he has about dreams. 'The thing is to go to bed in your glasses in case you need to read anything while you're asleep,' he said. The girl was laughing. Diggsy can do it.

If it works out, he and Diggsy can be partners, maybe open a second branch of Roots next year in Cambridge or Ely. Before that, there are courses Oscar wants to take, run by the Society of Genealogists. It's not the Daykin money that has made him hungry for more of this work – he knows not to expect a windfall from every job. No, it's the unravelling he is hooked on. It's the amazing thrill he felt when he realised that he had Thomas Daykin standing right there in front of him – a character from a story brought to life – and the satisfaction, too, he got from seeing the photograph the old man sent with the cheque, a shot of him with his lost sister, a scenic view with mountains in the background. Oscar imagined Amy as elderly and frail, but she was as tall as her brother, and 'rawboned', as they probably say in those parts. She was looking at the camera as though squinting into a wind. With training, Oscar will build on his expertise. Wanting to bring people together is wildly idealistic – even sentimental – but no more so than trying to save the white rhino or trying to destroy global capitalism. You can change small worlds.

The cash has enabled him to buy into the house on equal terms with Emma, or pretty much, and pay off a small mortgage. They both loved the house when they saw it. Emma has been nestbuilding these past weeks in the downstairs rooms, with Mum pitching in too with her ideas from college. Though she has been around the house lately, she has said nothing more about Michael. No one knows except Emma. If he is honest with himself, Oscar doesn't really know how he feels about any of this, how it has affected him. He fathoms his deeper self and comes up with nothing but the facts themselves. It would have been easier not to have found out. It has raised unsolvable questions. And yet he has arrived somewhere as a result. These things have been given to him to make something of. One day, when he is old, he will tell his son or daughter this story. It may be the one interesting story in the family, the one that carries down the ages into the future, that is further embroidered with each telling.

He opens the package, is puzzled, then smiles as he

remembers. It's a wooden signboard for the house, made by their usual carpenter and hand-painted in black against the light stain by Diggsy. ALIFORNIAC, it reads. The place in your mind you always wanted to go, wherever it turns out to be – even if, as in this case, it turns out to be the place you started out from. It seems like the opposite of escape and adventure, but of course the thing you want can be right there in front of you, and not just Emma but the town itself that he grew up in, ran away from, and that now, despite its familiarity, holds out to him a surprising promise. It's as though the place itself is a kind of inheritance, something just waiting there for him to come back and claim.

Rachel enters the hubbub of the kitchen and allows herself to be kissed by Emma, while Mum busies herself at the drinks table. 'Try some of Emma's non-alcoholic fruit punch,' she cries, with a little too much gaiety and not much tact. (Why not just announce it? Rachel thinks – *Rachel's on the wagon, folks.*) Mum herself is already tipsy and pink-cheeked. She has never been a daytime drinker. Rachel accepts the glass from her meekly and turns to congratulate Emma on the house, and remarks on her bump. As Luke and Oscar's friend Diggsy appear, Emma takes her by the elbow and guides her into a corner. 'Needless to say, Dad's not taking it too brilliantly.'

'He'll get over it,' says Rachel. 'Mum says you're thinking of getting married.' She speaks quietly. The others are drifting out now.

'I think we probably will. Not for a while, though. Let things settle a bit.'

Rachel nods and sips her non-alcoholic fruit punch. They are not accustomed to conversations like this, half-siblings but never intimates. They have always had Oscar

304

between them, ruining what might have been a sisterhood. It was always Oscar whom Emma had the bond with, an understanding of shared whispers and unexplained sudden laughter. It always maddened Rachel to see Emma so studiously failing to acknowledge this – going out of her way, it seemed, to appear airily unaware of any such special relationship. But Rachel is now seized by a triumphant sense of having been vindicated by events – as though she knew all along that it would end like this. But from this end – from the hybrid relations that follow from her half-brother marrying her half-sister – a new understanding can perhaps emerge. Perhaps she and Emma will learn to relax, if not as sisters – it seems too late for that – then at least as equals. She feels, in so far as she feels anything these days, some relief that Emma has given up on her shiny career and effortless, almost comic accumulation of wealth. She finds a comforting vulnerability in Emma's new condition, a satisfying dearth of ambition about this crumbling house in the sticks, with its ducks and mud and wet leaves underfoot. Even the flash car is gone. It all makes Emma's happiness easier to bear.

'And how are you doing?' Emma asks.

'Fine. It's all been a mess. Obviously.' She gives a quick smile.

Outside the sun breaks through the clouds. Laughter from somewhere.

'Do you want to come through into the sitting room?' Emma asks. 'Mum and Tony are here.'

Rachel hesitates, feeling the urge to keep Emma from the call of her hostessing duties. 'I've decided I can't go back to Robert.'

Emma is listening. 'I wasn't sure if that was still on the cards.'

'Well, he's been patient, coming round to the house,

staying away, coming again. He wanted to do the counselling thing. He wanted to forgive and forget.' She allows herself a smile. 'The truth is, he probably would have too. He has enough forgiveness for everybody. We could have gone back to how we were.'

'You didn't want that?'

She shakes her head. 'Do you believe that some things were never meant to be, and that bad things happen to change things for the better?' She doesn't wait for Emma's answer. 'I'm beginning to think that. So, no, I won't go back to Robert. And I've decided, too, not to go back to Duttings. I haven't told Dad yet – or Mum. No one knows.'

'But you surely don't blame yourself for what happened?'

'Not entirely, but maybe it'll turn out to have been just the thing that will have made whatever I do next possible. If you see what I mean.'

'So, what will you do next?'

Rachel pauses. She is thinking about getting into property, like those pioneering Americans she met in Prague, heading off and conquering the world, starting small and growing big. She will use her share of whatever profits there are from the house when Robert sells it, staying with Mum and Dad while she lays the foundations for her own Dutting empire. But she can't say this to Emma. It seems too foolish.

Diggsy arrives breathless at the kitchen door holding a camera. 'Emma, I need to take a picture of you and Oscar by the apple tree.'

'You *need* to?' She looks at Rachel. 'Sorry . . .'

'You go ahead.'

Emma touches her arm and follows Diggsy outside, wrapping her cardigan around her shoulders as she goes. Rachel waits in the kitchen, standing at the window gazing out over the yard. Does she blame herself for what happened with the business? Everyone assumes so. They tiptoe around her, trying to cushion her from the guilt they think must be pressing in on her. The truth is she thinks of nothing but Gareth. Although she knows she will never see him again, although she knows him for what he is (though it was never what Dad was getting at – it was always about pleasure not business), still she would burn down her parents' house to have him whisk her away in the night, to turn back the clock, to be told that his rejection of her (one brief but firm message on her mobile many weeks ago now) was all a mistake. In the end he rejected her and stayed away because he rightly feared that the adventure was becoming too hazardous, that her need for him was drawing her towards the forbidden planet of his other life. That he too was married was never in doubt – like her own marriage it was an untold lie, hovering above them like a physical presence that both pretended not to see.

Luke arrives now. 'You're wanted in the sitting room,' he says.

She puts down her empty glass and follows him. Oscar, Mum and Dad are stationed by the domed brick-lined hearth. The other guests have moved back to form a semicircle, like people round a bonfire.

'Sorry, but your dad wants a group photograph,' Diggsy explains.

'Well, it's not too often we're all together,' Dad says.

It's like a wedding, Rachel thinks. Groom's family – minus Emma for diplomatic reasons. Oscar gives Rachel a helpless grin – an old boyhood gap-toothed grin she hasn't seen in a long while. She positions herself next to Luke, surprised at how much he has grown, towering above her. Dad takes off his glasses just as Diggsy puts his on, like partners in a double act. 'And smile . . .' Diggsy holds the camera towards them, composing the image.

'Apparently, it was originally an old bread oven,' someone is saying.

Outside the dog is barking at something, then is quiet.

Diggsy looks up and winks. 'Perfect.'